Howard & Debbie

Christina,
Strength
&
Kindness,

Howard & Debbie

a novel by

Max Mobley

A Vireo Book | Rare Bird Books
Los Angeles, Calif.

This is a Genuine Vireo Book

A Vireo Book | Rare Bird Books
453 South Spring Street, Suite 302
Los Angeles, CA 90013
rarebirdbooks.com

FIRST TRADE PAPERBACK ORIGINAL EDITION

Set in Minion
Printed in the United States

10 9 8 7 6 5 4 3 2 1

Author Photo by SLV Steve

Publisher's Cataloging-in-Publication Data
Names: Mobley, Max, author.
Title: Howard & Debbie / by Max Mobley.
Description: First Trade Paperback Original Edition |
A Genuine Vireo Book | New York, NY; Los Angeles, CA:
Rare Bird Books, 2019.
Identifiers: ISBN 9781947856837
Subjects: LCSH Man-woman relationships—Fiction. | Online
dating—Fiction. | Kidnapping—Fiction. | Psychological fiction. |
BISAC FICTION / General
Classification: LCC PS3613 .O23 H69 2019 | DDC 813.6—dc23

In memory of Pam Davey

Chapter 1

1

HOWARD FECK PASSED INTO carnal knowledge at the tender age of thirty-three. His coworker, drunk but willing, took up the cause on a dare issued at the end of a company Christmas party. She had told herself that climbing atop a man who had yet to experience such a thing and who sorely needed it was a noble endeavor. And it was. But during the course of schlub-making, the woman had a sudden change of heart. As Howard convulsed, gasped, and apologized his way toward climax, she realized she could not accept it. Poor Howard finished alone—flopping around the supply room floor like a freshly caught fish while his repulsed strumpet jumped back into her pants and ran out the door. Howard lay there, a spent, humiliated mess. Afterward he vowed never to have sex again unless completely alone, which, once again, he now was.

It was a time when many households could not surf the web and make a phone call at the same time, and cell phones were stupid and camera-less. The internet was still a promise not fully identified, and nowhere was this truer than in chat rooms dedicated to virtual romance and cybersex. Safely alone, with the curtains drawn and the lights dimmed, it was the one place Howard felt capable of participating in the age-old quest for hot sex and easy companionship. For Howard, taking his clothes off in front of a computer screen while another person across the dial-up connection allegedly did the same delivered the ideal sexual encounter. He could enjoy sex alone while another person appeared to be involved, if solely through dirty words appearing on screen. Howard's sex life quickly evolved into servicing himself while reading nasty sentence fragments full of interjections and encouraging words with letters repeated for emphasis. He had convinced himself that a hot and horny female had typed the devilishly naughty words on his screen, though he was often zero for three on that score.

Then he met *Lil_Debbie*, a.k.a., Deborah Fairchild.

Ms. Fairchild's undeniable vivaciousness toyed heartily with the pornographic. In between salacious replies to Howard's misspelled sexual requests and instructions, she also exuded a gentle sweetness. Unlike most alleged women Howard dated in private chat rooms, Ms. Fairchild did not go all the way on their first date (though Howard did and lied about it—naughty boy). On subsequent dates, their conversations swung rapidly between sweet, purring admissions of love to winking and wide-mouthed emoticons punctuating pornographic suggestions and reactions. Soon, *HappiHoward* and *Lil_Debbie* were a regular item. Thanks to a gross misunderstanding of how female erogenous zones should be stimulated, date night for Howard revolved around the one-handed typing of convoluted sexual instructions. As if to prove their sexual kismet, whenever Deborah typed Howard off, she climaxed at the exact same moment despite being hundreds of miles away. Or at least she claimed to.

Deborah Fairchild possessed the libido of a teenage boy, the dexterity of a prog-rock drummer, the flexibility of a Cirque du

Soleil acrobat, and the heart of a wallflower. No wonder Howard fell so hopelessly in love.

When *HappiHoward* and *Lil_Debbie* exchanged pictures early in their relationship, both sent low-res images not of themselves but of someone much better looking. Howard's picture was obviously a fake as he had emailed a headshot of seventies teen idol Robbie Benson taken during the peak of his career. (Howard was unfamiliar with Mr. Benson's body of work.) Consumed with securing female interest, it had never occurred to him that Deborah would reciprocate in the deception. Thanks to a picture of an anonymous beauty scraped from a craft fair website, *HappiHoward* believed *Lil_Debbie* was doe-eyed and sylphlike, with dark, voluptuous curls and skin the color of tea with milk.

Having divulged his real name, and, on a separate occasion, the name of his employer, it took very little time for Deborah to learn what Howard Feck really looked like. On the last page of an electronic newsletter archived on a corporate website, Deborah found a photo with a caption that read: *Burke Packaging receiving clerk Harold Feck finds surprise in shipment of MP3GoUltras.*

The picture showed a sickly thin man in drab, ill-fitting office wear. He sported a fungal-looking moustache and a splatter of dark, greasy hair, which appeared to have slid part way down the back of his misshapen skull. The man in the photo was staring bulgy-eyed at the camera while grimacing to the gums. He was holding a paper towel at arm's length. Resting in the center of the paper towel: a piece of dried-up finger, replete with dirty nail.

Deborah could care less about *HappiHoward's* grotesque discovery, but she did find it interesting that he had not used his real first name in their correspondences. In fact, he had. The name Harold in the caption was a typo, a reflection of his standing in the company.

Three dates into their relationship, during which Howard had reached climax a stunning eight times, *Lil_Debbie* typed that she loved Howard enough to tell him her real name—Deborah Fairchild—which, of course, wasn't her real name at all. Howard responded by crying and making himself orgasm a ninth time.

By their thirty-fifth date in half as many days, Howard Feck had steeped himself in a ribald fantasy in which Deborah Fairchild played both wench and maiden to his chivalrous and lustful well-endowed knight. He soaked in this fantasy, sautéed himself in it, bathed, boiled, and basked in it until it consumed his every waking moment. Like many saps before him, he had lost sight of the delicate pink line that separated fantasy from reality in the earthquake-prone dominion of love. Typing one-handed was no longer enough. He desperately needed to consummate this fantasy in person, making it real as skin. Deborah had made it clear, however, that despite her desire to hold Howard tightly in the deepest part of her, private circumstances prevented any flesh-to-flesh encounters. Things would soon change, she promised. Howard just needed to hold on a little longer. But Howard's fantasy had overshadowed his reality, virtual though it may be, and a surprise visit to his wench and maiden seemed to him a damn good idea. He did not view this as ambushing someone whose words and fake picture he had repeatedly stained with his lust. He viewed it as aiding the hand of fate by placing it gently in his car, belting it in, and then driving it hundreds of miles to where it could best serve his destiny. Not one to pick up hitchhikers, it was quite a bold move for the man.

Despite looking nothing like seventies teen idol Robbie Benson, Howard did not fret over disappointing Deborah when they met face to face. He had uncharacteristically formulated a plan—one he had seen played out on TV and in the movies many times before, but that did not stop him from believing it was his own original idea. He would wait for Deborah at the café she frequented every afternoon according to her chats—just a stranger in need of coffee and shelter. Safe in the anonymity of his true appearance, he would watch her log on for their daily afternoon chat—the casual one where they flirted and teased about their cyber-date later that evening. Peeking over a newspaper or magazine, he would quietly gauge her reaction upon learning she had been stood up by the very man clandestinely studying her. Then, at the peak of her disappointment, he would present himself. Only he would use the name Fletch Howard, or maybe Harry Peck—he wasn't quite sure which—and figured he could make up his mind on the thirteen-hour drive. Then, using all he had learned from their internet courtship, he would commence pitching woo.

Howard regarded his plan as a slam dunk, can't fail, *why didn't I think of this before?* kind of solution, but not because he was blinded by new love and all its inebriating promises. Nor was it from the newly gained confidence earned from a string of successful sexual encounters with himself while *Lil_Debbie* typed him off. Howard thought highly of his plan simply because whenever he was "with" Deborah, she thought highly of him. And never before, in all his years, had he experienced such a thing.

2

THE SMALL TOWN OF Wilburn had just one coffeehouse, making it easy for Howard to find the Webspresso Café Deborah had written about in one of her rare honest moments. That is, he only got lost once.

He pulled into one of the many empty slots on Main Street and parked. Looking into the rearview mirror, he shook his head over what he saw looking back. At least he had a plan. He ran one sweaty finger across his stain of a moustache, briefly attempted to reshape the greasy black splatter of hair sticking precariously to his skull, then exited his dented Geo with what he had to offer.

He walked into the café and ordered a double soy java mocha. The word java did not belong in the name of his drink, but he insisted on using it nonetheless. While the barista went to work screwing up his order, Howard looked around the empty café. Its walls were a failed attempt at terracotta and covered unevenly with a few old movie posters and bad local art. Through a doorway behind the counter, he spied a little alcove with two computers. One had a yellow sticky note on the screen; the other displayed the Flying Through Space screensaver, Howard's favorite. Both were unoccupied. *Perfect.* Howard figured he could kill time splashing around the internet until the delightful and naughty Deborah Fairchild showed up according to plan.

Upon getting his drink, Howard walked around the counter and into the alcove. This was where they had first met. (Technically, Howard was at a computer in another state.) More hallowed ground he could not imagine. Howard sighed wheezily then sat down in an office chair that had known the sweet ass of his Deborah. He wiggled his bottom in greeting to any essence she may have left lying dormant in the cushion. *I wonder what sitting at her home computer would be like—the place she said and did all those incredibly wonderful and naughty things?* He surfed the web on the impossibly slow, meager wave of a dial-up connection, hitting his usual stops—heavily spun news sites, completely un-scary cyber-haunted house sites, movie monster fan sites in neglect, and so on. Half an hour later, thinking he just might want to take his lover someplace special, he searched for nightlife in the Wilburn area. Outside of handholding, gazing into each other's eyes, and getting his brains fucked out, this marked the first time Howard thought about what he was going to do with Deborah once she had surrendered to his woo.

Ten minutes past the time Deborah should have arrived for their afternoon chat, Howard checked his email. His unread messages consisted of a stale joke sent by a pitying coworker and several offers to improve his credit, his penis, and his access to horny Asian teens. Nothing from Deborah.

As Howard contemplated oversexed Asian teens, the bells tied to the café door jingled, startling him half out of his chair. He quickly and repeatedly clicked the sign out button. The computer responded slowly. The sound of heels on the café's hardwood floor grew louder. It was not the light, brisk chatter of a woman in high heels, but rather a methodical dull bunk, like a rubber mallet bashing a stubborn wooden spike. Howard stared bug-eyed at his inbox as, byte-by-byte, the scrawny dial-up pipe transferred droplets of information telling the computer to draw something else on the screen. The steps grew closer. The browser stubbornly showed *Welcome, HappiHoward* in twenty-two-point Arial. Panic-stricken, Howard poked the computer monitor's power button and turned away just as a very large, stout thing in a blue-and-green polyester housedress entered the alcove. She appeared to look surprised—or was it angry? She stood close to six feet tall and weighed north of three hundred pounds, easy. She had scrunched her dirty, shoulder-length hair into a torturous-looking claw-like clip at the top of her head. It crowned her overbearing aspect and reflected her disposition. She had pulled her hair so tightly into the device it created bald spots behind her temples. Her small green eyes pierced Howard, causing him to flinch. He turned back to face the dead computer screen as if that looked normal.

Howard Feck, meet your wench, your maiden, your *Lil_ Debbie*, your libidinous Deborah Fairchild.

A.k.a. Debbie Coomb.

3

DEBBIE COOMB WALKED INTO Webspresso Internet Café as she always did, wearing her foul mood on her short, puffy sleeve. The afternoon barista knew her more than he cared to, for she treated all service personnel with fervid spite. Debbie was not a people person.

Upon seeing Wilburn's most impressive contribution to the legion of hellish customers, the barista, wearing a tie-dye shirt with the words "Save Me" silk-screened on it, immediately went to work making Debbie's usual—a tall latté with extra butterscotch syrup. He would deliver it to her in her usual spot at the computer. Debbie may have been Webspresso's most despicable customer, but she was also its best tipper by a mile.

Years ago, the building held a bike shop. Kids once lingered outside the large storefront window to stare at the gleaming promises of speed and freedom lined up on the other side of the glass. Now, the name of the café and a steaming coffee cup on a flying carpet had been hand-painted on the very same window. White café tables and chairs had long since replaced the row of banana seat and sissy bar-bedecked Schwinns.

Debbie was about to yell at the dolt sitting at the computer when she recognized Howard's nuclear holocaust-survivor look. She checked herself, sensing a wonderful opportunity.

"Do you mind if I sit there?" she asked as politely as she knew how.

"Um…I guess so," Howard sputtered. "I…I was using it, but—"

"Well, it doesn't look like you even have it turned on," Debbie said.

Howard did not know how to respond since he was, in fact, sitting at a computer with its monitor turned off. He looked at the large woman. Her wide, flat nose aimed at the floor. Her skin was blotchy in some places and pristine in others, like the face of a dirty, poorly-treated doll. It was a face that seemed designed for makeup. Later, Howard would learn makeup was something Debbie Coomb did not know the first thing about, and would not wear even if she had. He found her size intimidating. The disturbing hair claw added a menacing quality to her presence. But it was the eyes that really got to Howard. They looked dangerously sharp and much older than the face surrounding them. There was something else about those eyes, though he could not name it. He surmised that if this large woman wanted to, she could get him shaking in his cheap shoes. And that was the last thing he wanted his Deborah to see.

Howard mumbled an okay and moved away from the computer so this beastie of a woman could use it.

Debbie sat down, and with the hands of a battered nose tackle, offered Howard his cup. "Don't forget your coffee."

"Thank you," Howard replied, stretching across some invisible barrier to reach his drink. He did not want to close the gap he had just created between himself and the rhinoceros wearing a blue-and-green tent. Debbie pushed the computer monitor's power button. It responded with a mild "boing" as the screen came back to life. The words "You have successfully logged out" stood out on the screen. So did the reflection of her Disney-villain smile. *What a first-class dolt*, she thought.

Debbie had no reason to check her email. Instead, she just kept hitting the back button on the web browser until she figured out what to do with this unexpected gift. And to that end, Debbie Coomb's twisted brain schemed.

"I'm off the computer now," she said loud enough for Howard, now lingering near the front window, to hear.

He shook a fist in victory—*finally*. Returning to the alcove, he found the stranger sitting on an old nag of a couch across from the computers.

Debbie wasted no time. "Never seen you round here before." She sounded like she had marshmallows tucked in her cheeks.

"I'm Howard, from up north," Howard squeaked shyly. "I'm on my way to…" he twitched a little as he sought to complete his lie. "Meet my Gramma. She's in Florida."

"Now that sounds nice, Howard from up North. Florida's supposed to be nice, what with Disneyworld and the Epcot Center and all that. Hey, isn't Shamu in Florida?"

"Yep," Howard answered after a brief pause. He thought Shamu was dead, but he didn't want to extend the conversation.

"You know, I have a roommate from Florida. She comes here all time to use that computer you're sitting at," Debbie said.

Howard's eyes grew wide.

"She moved out here to get away from some creepy ex-boyfriend she had back home. He stalked her, or so she says. She's pretty, so I can see it happening. It happens, you know." Debbie nodded for emphasis.

Howard could not believe his luck. The girl this fat woman described sounded a lot like his Deborah. Go figure, since Debbie was regurgitating the fictitious past she had given her internet alter ego.

Sensing that behind Howard's wide, surprised eyes, he was struggling for a response, she continued. "She's my roommate. Her name is Deborah, Deborah Fairchild. I always thought that was such a pretty name."

"I don't believe it," Howard slipped.

"You don't believe what? You know her?"

Howard attempted to recover. "Um…nope. It's nothing." He looked down at his cheap shoes. "My mind wanders sometimes," he offered. "I know it's not supposed to. But it does, that's all." Doubt, Howard's oldest friend, entered his head and whispered words of failure and foolishness.

"Anyway," Debbie continued. "I just came in to get my roomie some jasmine tea. She loves jasmine tea and she is home sicker than a half-dead pig."

Worry flooded Howard's heart. "What's she got?" he asked, with obvious concern.

Debbie smiled and said, "Well, I can't tell you that. For all I know, you could be her stalker ex-boyfriend trying to pump me for information so you can kidnap her. But I will tell you that it's pretty serious."

Any color in Howard's complexion fled, leaving him almost translucent. "How serious?"

"Pretty serious. She took ill last night. Been in bed all day. She has some condition that makes it sort of dangerous."

Howard looked like he was about to pee himself. "Lady, can I tell you something and you keep it a secret?"

"Of course, what's on your mind?"

And with that, Howard Feck spilled his beans all over the wide and wily Debbie Coomb.

4

DEBBIE HAD TO RESTRAIN from smiling as she heard from Howard's own lips how absurdly bad he had it for Deborah Fairchild, her creation. She knew there was no way this broken stick of a man would get away. This knowledge caused her to shudder briefly, as if thinking about what hot dogs are made of while biting into one, and then eating the damn thing anyway.

"That's very brave of you to come all this way and blindside her like that," Debbie said, her tone lost on Howard. "I know Deborah pretty well, and I bet she would be touched that you went to such trouble. Let me ask you, how close of a match was the picture you sent?"

"The hair was different. He was a little huskier, I guess."

Debbie remained quiet, assuming he was just getting started.

"He didn't have a moustache," Howard added, mostly to fill the silence.

Oh, that's supposed to be a moustache, is what Debbie wanted to say. "Well, I know it's a risk, but I think you should come out to the house and meet her. It might just do her some good. Lord knows it'll do you some good."

Howard wanted to squeal. "I think that's a very good idea Miss...?"

"Coomb. What are you driving, Howard?"

"A blue Geo," he answered, a little too proudly.

"I'm parked right next to you. Why don't you follow me?"

Debbie rose and headed for the door with her bottom-shelf carnie prize following close behind. She found herself growing annoyed by the springiness in his step. At least he had no intention of ditching her. She backed her car out onto the street and waited while Howard appeared to go through a seventeen-point safety checklist from the driver's seat. Eventually he backed out and pulled behind Debbie's large, clean, white Cadillac and off they drove—one fat cat and one squeaky little mouse.

Chapter 2

1

WILBURN'S MAIN STREET WAS long and lonely, with shops spread far apart on its edges and only one block where storefronts sidled up next to each other. It was a town made up of outskirts that joined together on the one lone block that resembled bucolic downtown America struggling to stay in business.

Tailgating Miss Coomb for fear he might lose her, Howard looked around and began perceiving a connection with the town. Maybe it was Wilburn's anonymity. Maybe it was a kind of perceived loneliness from being forgotten and out of the way—something Howard personified to no small degree. What he missed, however, was that the people of Wilburn made their town this way on purpose. Folks here lived off the grid and still got cable—letting the world into their living rooms while keeping it off their streets. Wilburn didn't consider itself backward—the rest of the world had simply gone in the wrong direction and they had refused to follow. It was a dirt town, a farm town, a poor town, and no attempts were made to disguise it nor rise above it. Pigs, dairies, enough alfalfa to feed the livestock, and during the hot months, tomatoes that grew like weeds—these were all that kept Wilburn from descending into dust.

Debbie lived on the old highway, about a mile from where it crossed Main Street as announced by the appearance of sidewalks. Traffic was generally light year round, and the speeding pickups and crawling tractors managed to avoid each other most days. Like the streets, the sidewalks were mostly empty, even during Christmastime.

The townspeople were nice enough if they knew you. And if they didn't, they would ignore you if you let them and harass you if they felt you had it coming. People dressed down lest they be accused of being uppity. The men kept cans of beer in their pickups, just in case, and the women didn't bother to quit smoking when pregnant. Most of the kids finished high school, and the ones who didn't seemed no different than the ones who did.

As is the case with many established communities, a small faction of culturally aware independents caused the townspeople to soften some over the years. The opening of Waker's Espresso Café on Main Street, where the bike shop used to be, was an example of this. Waker's opened in the mid-eighties and divided the town between those who felt Wilburn was finally moving forward in the world and those who thought it was getting snotty, just like Merritin, or even worse, Shipley. But caffeine is a powerful drug. So the dust settled quickly on this rhubarb, allowing the café to stay afloat with a clientele you would not expect to frequent a coffee bar. By the time Howard had met Debbie there under the cover of love and the reality of desperation, frozen yogurt and free internet access had been added to the menu, and the name had been changed to Webspresso Internet Café.

Wilburn was down to two churches, Baptist and Catholic, after a handsome turn-of-the-century Methodist number—white clapboard with black trim and a classic steeple—burnt down one Fourth of July night a long time ago. Had it caught fire any other night, it probably would have been saved. But in honor of Independence Day, folks let it burn. People brought lawn chairs and beer and food and picnicked in the burning church's parking lot as if watching a fireworks show. By the time the fire had dwindled to embers, people had started arriving with truckloads of trash and things they'd rather not have around to throw into the pyre's remains. This kept the flames going until dawn the next day. The reverend (no one seems to recall his name) was properly insured and seemed not to mind. He left town shortly thereafter, was not heard from again, and was not missed.

Liberty Market was the only full-sized grocery store in town, and the tiny Wilburn Grocery stayed open late and sold mostly half pints of hard alcohol, cartons of cheap beer, and cigarettes—individual or by the pack. The dirt lot behind it had become a makeshift bar ever since Teddy's Tavern had burned to the ground across the street from the old bike shop. The tavern fire did not draw a crowd. In fact, quite the opposite. No one wanted to build on the vacant lot it left behind, and so it had permanently surrendered to weeds and rumors. To some it was a reminder that even wickedness has its boundaries, and a fiery retribution awaited those that crossed it.

Since Wilburn's multitude of criminal offenses occurred in places not freely open to scrutiny, crime came to light only under investigation and pursuit—two things the deputies and townspeople agreed were contrary to peace. So long as victims suffered quietly, Debbie's hometown considered itself peaceful.

This was the town where Howard pictured himself walking arm and arm with Deborah as passersby tipped their caps and winked—no, better yet—offered their congratulations and asked about the honeymoon. As he contemplated settling down in this paradise by the plow and the fist, the Cadillac's brake lights came on, startling him back to the present. He slammed on his brakes, causing his unbuckled fantasy to fly from his mind. Then he winced, as if kicked in the gut. Stopped on the highway in front of Debbie Coomb's house, Howard Feck rubbed his stomach and groaned sourly.

2

DEBBIE'S FARMHOUSE SAT A good forty yards back from the highway. She parked at the top of her driveway and Howard pulled in close behind. Making her way to the front door, she realized Howard was still in his car. Debbie stopped and turned around. Probably got himself stuck, she thought. Looking at him through the Geo's windshield, he appeared upset. Afraid any sudden movement might startle him into flight, Debbie approached the car window like a kid approaching a dead animal on the side of the road. She was not about to let him drive off and get away, though he would be easy to catch, no doubt.

"Howard," Debbie said loud enough to be heard through the car windows. "You all right?"

Howard looked down and shook his head gravely.

"What's the matter?"

He did not know how best to explain his sudden and possibly dire predicament. Truth was, Howard had been in his car for eleven hours straight, after which he had drank a large coffee that he now believed was made with real milk instead of soy milk. In his home town's medical community, Howard's lactose intolerance was the stuff of legend. He needed a bathroom, and badly. The timing could not be any worse. It was as if his body had decided to play a cruel joke on him during the single high point of an otherwise flat life.

He looked at Debbie, then looked down and quietly groaned.

"Howard," she repeated, this time with a hint of don't fuck with me. "Tell me what's the matter."

Without looking up, Howard spoke. "Miss Coomb, I am so sorry, I have to use the bathroom really bad and—"

"Aren't you housebroken?" Debbie replied. "I got a toilet inside. I mean, I know this is the sticks and all, but we do have indoor plumbing, for chrissakes."

"It's not that!" Howard cried. "It's just…I'm supposed to meet Deborah and now I'm getting sick. You know, the bad kind of sick. I am so sorry. Maybe I should just go and come back when I'm feeling better. I'd hate for Deborah to see me like this."

Debbie had gotten a man onto her property. No way in hell would she let him leave, for any reason whatsoever. At least not until she had finished with him. "Look," she said, unable to stop glaring at the sick little man in his shitty little car. "You can use the bathroom by the kitchen, and I'll leave you a book of matches. Deborah is upstairs. I'll wait in her room while you do your business. And don't you mess up my daddy's bathroom!"

Howard agreed but didn't understand what a book of matches had to do with any of it. He squeezed his eyes shut and rucked his brow. A moment later, he opened his car door, struggled with the seat belt, and stepped out. Debbie walked to the front door with Howard trailing shamefully behind. She marveled how, given all the pitiful schnooks on the worldwide web, their godhead had ended up in her front yard.

Debbie unlocked and opened the front door. It was dark and cool inside. Twilight seeped in from a row of double-hung windows. They entered a living room sparsely filled with well-preserved, grandmotherly furniture. An overstuffed couch with a large floral print sat opposite a big recliner showing considerable wear. An aged big-screen TV sat against a wall perpendicular to the front door and beneath the stairs. A dull, brass bowl containing a dusty plastic flower arrangement had been placed on top of the TV—a feeble gesture toward interior decorating. Howard found himself drawn to it.

"Bathroom is straight through there," Debbie said, pointing to a short, paneled hallway. "Go through the kitchen, past the fridge, and head right. There's a little metal sign that says 'Gents' on the door." Without detailed directions, Debbie feared Howard might end up befouling the laundry sink.

As Howard entered the kitchen, a red tea kettle triggered his memory. He turned and lamented, "Miss Coomb, you forgot the jasmine tea for Deborah."

Snap.

You could almost hear the sound of Debbie's thin nice streak breaking in two.

Alright, you twiggy fucker, she fumed silently. *So much for a nice time!*

Debbie's anger gave her wings. During moments of indifference, she embodied sloth and gluttony like some gouty, inbred king. But when angered, she became swift and agile like an orca on the hunt. Scowling, she glided down the hall toward her sickly guest. She crossed the kitchen without seeming to touch the floor, passed the refrigerator, then landed at the bathroom door just as Howard pulled it closed.

Had he entered the bathroom one second later, he may not have made it. But he did, oblivious to Debbie's anger and frustration. Debbie stood there straining her spring-loaded hair claw—her nose just a few inches from the 'Gents' sign. Her fists, shoulders, and face remained clenched. She listened as Howard attempted to successfully operate a simple bathroom door lock. She could have busted in easily enough, but this was her daddy's house, and he was in her daddy's bathroom. Debbie unclenched.

An audible little twang of relief issued from the hair claw's spring. She walked away, defeated.

On her way back through the kitchen, she opened the fridge, grabbed two cans of pop, walked to her dad's La-Z-Boy recliner in the living room, and plopped down.

3

THE TWO-STORY FARMHOUSE NEEDED a facelift. A thick coat of cream-colored paint covered the clapboard exterior. Its red trim had faded to pink long ago. In the back, a long, narrow, screened-in mudroom clung to the rear facade. The absence of a wraparound veranda made the house appear unfinished. At the front door, a small, A-shaped porch roof sheltered a square, red-concrete stoop.

Yellowish Bermuda grass surrounded the house on three sides; the fourth—the side closest to town—held the long driveway. A fence badly in need of repair separated the driveway from the box lot of the Lone Tree Trucking Company, the only neighbor for at least a quarter mile. The lawn faded into scrubby woods at the back and ran clear to the old highway in front. The occasional shrub or stunted tree dotted the lawn like buoys in a pale-green sea. Dead center in the vast yard lay a broken fountain. The top piece was once a dolphin or cherub or something but now looked like a cement iceberg sitting in a large, faded-white dish. A clump of lawn daisies grew near the edge of the fountain's basin. It provided the only bright color aside from a dotted line of grotty rose bushes running between the driveway and the gravel walkway leading to the front porch.

As Debbie reclined in her dad's La-Z-Boy, swigging her second can of pop, she came up with a wicked idea. She gulped down the last of her soda, got up, and headed toward the back of the house. She passed the bathroom door behind which Howard was doing his dirty business and continued on to the mudroom. Her eyes fell upon an old ladder-back chair. She knocked the dirty laundry off it and then carried it back to the bathroom door. She studied the situation ever so briefly, then hooked the top rung of the chair-back under the door handle. In doing so, the chair's back legs lodged themselves against the opposite wall. Debbie checked to make sure the chair was thoroughly wedged against the door, then casually walked back into the kitchen. She made no real attempt at being sneaky about it, she was just naturally quiet in her too-quiet home. Plus, locking Howard in the bathroom had diffused her anger, though it would no doubt return. She grabbed a half-eaten bowl of leftover noodle helper and another can of pop from the fridge and then went upstairs to her room.

4

DESPITE HIS TERRIBLE PREDICAMENT there in the bathroom, Howard told himself that he was ahead of the game since he had somehow won over Miss Coomb, Deborah's roommate. The thought helped until a chorus of loud, crow-like voices cawed and cawed inside Howard's head, reminding him how pathetic he and his plan were. He should have known better than to try and meet Deborah face-to-oily-face.

Then he revisited all the things Deborah had written—not just to anyone, but to him and him alone. How she adored him. How she quickly eased into naughtiness with him over chat and email. How supportive and forgiving she was whenever he found himself apologizing for saying the wrong thing (or, as was more often the case, saying the right thing wrongly). Deborah Fairchild believed in Howard, and how many times had she said after cyber-coitus, "If only we could do and say these things in person!" Such thoughts had a Pavlovian effect on the man. Recalling Deborah's electronic expressions of sex, love, and admiration raised Howard's extraordinarily low self-esteem above the din of those cawing voices. Voices that recited his most embarrassing and shameful memories—of which he now had one more to add to the pile. Voices that reminded him that the utter lack of love and companionship in his life was earned and awarded for being...for being...well, for being born Howard Feck. Just thinking about his time with Deborah, even when sitting on a stranger's commode with a roiling gut full of shit, put all those voices just beyond his cognition. Lucky guy.

Howard flushed, washed his hands, and splashed cool water on his face. In a moment that was remarkably brave, for he loved her so and wanted her so, Howard reached for the doorknob, steeling himself for the biggest moment in his life. He spent a little time unlocking it before turning the handle.

The door moved not one inch.

And the crow voices cawed with laughter.

He fiddled with the lock some more, turned and pushed again, and again the door moved not one inch.

Oh, no. No, no, no.

Howard took this as a sign that the voices in his head were right (*weren't they always?*), and if he had any sense at all, he would just quietly go home. With any luck, Deborah would let him resume his virtual relationship, and they could pretend this dumb idea of his had never been thought of, let alone acted upon.

He tried the door one last time before calling for help.

"Excuse me, Miss Coomb," he said in a voice not much above a whisper.

There was no reply.

"Excuse me, Miss Coomb? It's Howard. I locked myself in the bathroom on accident," he said with a little more air behind it.

Silence.

"Miss Cooo-ooomb."

Nothing.

Finally, he went for a full yell. "Miss Coomb! I've locked myself in the bathroom—help!"

Still nothing.

Howard wondered if maybe they just couldn't hear him from upstairs. He surveyed the small room. Light blue tiles covered the floor and the lower half of the walls, where they ended in a row of dark-blue tiles set to look like diamonds instead of squares. The walls above the tile were painted a dull white. A couple handmade shelves had been mounted there. Each held a few small dust collectors, including a picture of a little girl and a seashell. Howard stood in the middle of the bathroom studying these things before staring straight up, hoping for a sound that signaled his release.

Nothing.

He sat on the floor in a little space between the door and the sink. He didn't know it, but he was shaking his head. Feeling something soft behind him, he leaned back and fell through a curtain hanging in front of the towel closet. The back of his head clipped the lowest shelf before falling hard onto the cold tile floor. He was too consumed with his plight to feel much physical pain. He wanted to curl up and hide at the bottom of the closet but felt that would be impolite.

Howard was used to things going terribly wrong because of something he did or had failed to do. But it never mattered before today. His boss once told him that he would make a great beta tester for Murphy's Law. Once that observation had been explained to him, he agreed. Found comfort in it, even. The more often bad things happened to him, the less often they would happen to someone who deserved better. He pictured a whole community of people living perfect, sunshine-and-white-picket-fenced-lives while the god Murphy focused his wrath on him like iron shavings to a magnet.

Howard lay on the floor with his head just inside the towel closet. He was crushed. Maybe, just maybe, he could convince Miss Coomb to lie to Deborah for him. Maybe a family emergency came up, or maybe he and his blue Geo were carjacked. Better yet, maybe Miss Coomb hadn't even told Deborah that he was in town—*man, wouldn't that be great.* And then he thought, *But what if they can't hear me because she's so sick Miss Coomb is preoccupied with taking care of her? What if Deborah has something really bad? Shouldn't I see her? Can we still screw?*

Howard wrestled with what for him was a serious conundrum—he was embarrassed and had lost what little mojo he had due to what his mind would soon catalog as "that horrible pooping incident at Deborah's." (There were several similar incidences in his catalog, hence the need to include a location in the description). But he had also come all this way—was even inside Deborah's house—and she was in bed! Maybe he could just crawl in there with her and cuddle. That would be okay. Sex could wait until she was feeling better. Once he was let out of the bathroom, of course.

He could not make up his mind on what was the best course. The thought of what had just happened made him want to go home without Deborah ever knowing he was there. The thought of touching her body, holding her in his arms, and looking into her eyes made him want to run upstairs as soon as he was freed. In yet another bold move for the man, he chose a middle ground. He would leave as quickly as he could and drive to the closest motel where he could spend the night, and more importantly, shower and spruce himself up. Trapped in Miss Coomb's bathroom, even the smarmy voices in his head hadn't the slightest idea that his driving days were over.

Chapter 3

1

DEBBIE COOMB DID ALL right living off the investments her daddy Delwin made after selling his pig farm to the trucking company next door the year she was born. On a moonless night fifteen years later, Delwin had been clipped by a slowly accelerating eighteen-wheeler as he stumbled home from Teddy's Tavern. The truck nicked him hard enough to bust his shoulder and toss him into a weedy, shallow ditch alongside the old highway that was their street. There, he had a heart attack and died. Until this point in her life, Debbie had been an okay kid. A little spoiled, she was all her father ever really cared about.

She was in the midst of an awkward phase when one summer morning she walked into town to find her occasionally missing daddy, probably sleeping one off on the dusty and smelly chesterfield in front of Teddy's. On the way there, Debbie saw an ankle and shoe jutting out of the weedy, shallow ditch alongside the highway. Recognizing the shoe, she went over to investigate. She found Daddy crumpled and discarded-looking at the bottom of the ditch. Flies buzzed his face. It made no sense. She jumped into the shin-deep water and tried to help him up. He must have had too much to drink, that's all. She pulled him by his shoulders, but her footing was bad and Delwin's contorted position didn't help any. She slipped and sat down hard halfway down the rampart. Her feet splashed the muddy water, some of it landing on her cheek. She didn't wipe it off because she didn't want to let go of Daddy. He was half of the Coomb team, an important half, and she owed it to him to help him home.

Their love for each other ran deep and never wavered. Even when Debbie hit her teens, she preferred his company to that of her contemporaries. She cherished the comfort and security she felt being around him and being home—his home. Home was the very best part of Wilburn, not that there was much competition for the title. She loved being the recipient of his glee and his guidance. In turn, Delwin Coomb loved Debbie's blissful acceptance of the few immaterial things he had to offer. He enjoyed her company, too, and considered himself a family man.

As a new parent, Delwin surrendered gladly to the revelations of progeny. But there was sadness, too—courtesy of Debbie's mother, who had hung herself from the high beam in the nursery while little Debbie lay crying for her milkies. Debbie's mom performed this insane act early one morning after Delwin had gone out to farm the pigs. He didn't come home until late that evening, having stopped by Teddy's for a few free rounds offered in tribute to fatherhood. Grimy, beer-buzzed, and whistling a country tune, Delwin came home to a dark house and the sound of a baby screaming itself hoarse. He bounded up the stairs and into the nursery. Debbie's mother's dangling legs blocked his view of the bassinette. Without hesitation, he walked around the sick piñata, scooped the infant into his arms, and placed her against his chest. Baby Debbie immediately started bobbing her face against his sweat-stained shirt, rooting for a nipple. He sucked his pinky finger clean and then offered it to his daughter. She took it hungrily and immediately quieted down, but after a few sucks and no payoff, she started to howl again.

Holding her tightly, Delwin walked downstairs and into the kitchen where he heated some formula. She drank the first bottle without hardly coming up for air, then puked it all over his shirt and pants. Its sour smell blended with the reek of beer, sweat, and pigs. The second bottle went down and stayed down. She was now content, and exhausted from a day of crying for love and food. With her wee head settled in the nook between Daddy's chin and collarbone, little Debbie fell fast asleep. Delwin gently removed her diaper, which had soaked completely through, and tossed it away. Then he reclined his La-Z-Boy and fell fast asleep with his precious daughter's naked bottom cupped in his hand and her soft new hair tickling his chin. Delwin never shed a tear for his dead wife. He was too angry at her for abandoning poor Debbie.

Almost sixteen years later, Debbie sat in a ditch with her daddy's slackened face nuzzled between her chin and chest. She brushed away the bugs as they tried to land on his face. He was cold and damp and stiff, but his hair and the collar of his jacket smelled like he was just fine. It smelled like Daddy. She closed her eyes. The possibility that Daddy was dead entered her mind like a rat squeezing through a vent enters an attic. She hated the thought but could not banish it. Tears began to fall. She hadn't realized how much she loved him until faced with the possibility that he was gone forever. She breathed in his scent, felt his weight and size against her body, and rained buckets of tears onto his head while sobbing the words, *No, Daddy,* and *Please,* over and over. She had not cried this hard since her mother had died.

She tried to pull him a little closer to the road but stopped. She did not like the feel of it. It felt like she was pulling dead weight, and this was Daddy, for crying out loud, not some dead thing. Eventually, a passing trucker spotted them and used his radio to call state patrol. They arrived quickly. However, Debbie refused to budge from Delwin's side, so the troopers stood there not knowing what to say as they watched this crumpled little girl hold her dead father in the weeds along the highway. They called the county coroner, who showed up half an hour later driving a black station wagon. He had a daughter Debbie's age, and this helped him deal with Debbie's shock and heartbreak. He talked Debbie into helping him and the patrolmen put her dad on the stretcher and into the wagon—*just to get him out of that ditch.* Then he put one arm around her, walked her to the passenger-side door of the coroner's wagon, and helped her in. Later that day, he drove Debbie home from the county morgue with Delwin's wallet, keys, and jacket in her lap. He walked her into the house, opened curtains, and turned on the lights to try to give the place some life. Debbie curled up in Daddy's La-Z-Boy recliner clutching his things, smelling his jacket, and secretly hoping it was just a bad dream.

The coroner asked Debbie for permission to use the phone. He had debated with himself over what to do with this new orphan on the quiet drive back to Wilburn. He knew that putting her straight into the foster care program would be a cruel fate in these parts. But legally, that was his, or more accurately, the county's, obligation. If only Debbie had some next of kin or had named a family friend in answer to those questions on the form. Truth was, Debbie had no one. No mother and now no father. No aunt nor uncle nor grandparent. No best friend and no family friends other than Delwin's drinking buddies, who she only knew by name.

After a brief call to consult his wife, the coroner decided to call a Wilburn church. He asked Debbie if she belonged to one. She shook her head no. Not really happy with the two choices for religious comfort in Wilburn, he decided on the Baptist one. Catholic priests gave him the willies ever since he saw *The Exorcist* as a kid. A church secretary promised that the minister and a woman from the flock would arrive within the hour to spend the night and help Debbie settle her guardianship. The coroner took a quilt from the back of the couch and gently laid it over Debbie. He stroked the hair from her eyes, and spoke words of sympathy until the minister and church volunteer arrived. He met them in the driveway, where they exchanged information and documentation that, God willing, would save Debbie and keep her out of foster care.

The minister and volunteer entered Debbie's home bearing a thermos of coffee, a pink box of stale donuts, and a serious case of halitosis. They appeared to be in a rush. The minister expressed his condolences before filling Delwin's living room with Psalm after Psalm, each blown away by the storms of Debbie's sorrow. The passages were read like incantations, and when Debbie did not respond like an infected patient to antibiotics, the church-folk decided it was a Bible-resistant strain of godlessness. The volunteer, clearly moved by the words, sat next to Debbie and held her hands. She occasionally squeezed them, as if cueing Debbie on when to take solace. They urged Debbie to come with them, which she was loath to do. She was not about to leave her daddy's home—*just in case, just in case, please God*. She wanted these grownups who were foreign to her and who somehow made her feel worse to leave at once. Debbie finally told a lie the church-folk accepted with relief: that her uncle was due before bedtime. She had no idea why the coroner said she was all alone—he must have forgotten, what with being so busy. Once Debbie had verbally agreed that her father was in a better place, the minister and his volunteer left. And while the people of Wilburn may have thought twice about leaving Debbie all alone, hardly anyone thought about it a third time.

2

DEBBIE STAYED CURLED UP in the La-Z-Boy until the phone rang the next afternoon. She got up and hurried to the kitchen to answer it, hoping it was Daddy calling to tell her it was all a mistake. It was not Delwin, of course, who rang, it was his bartender, Teddy from Teddy's Tavern. He told her he had heard the bad news about Delwin and was *real sorry*. He also wanted to know who would pay his bar tab. He offered to come by and pick it up if it would help. It was eighty-three dollars and Delwin always paid every Friday, Teddy explained. *And he'd usually include a good tip—ya know how generous he was n' all.* Debbie hung up without saying a word. She went back to the La-Z-Boy, sat and looked around the lonely living room through wet, sore eyes. Nothing looked the same. Nothing felt the same. And nothing would be the same ever again.

Chapter 4

1

HOWARD FECK'S CHILDHOOD LACKED the tragedy that defined Debbie's. It also lacked the joy Debbie knew prior to her father's passing. Howard grew up in a Christian home in a small Christian town. He was raised by his devoutly Christian grandmother, Helen Feck, a capable old woman accustomed to living alone and insulated by the constant fear that something could go horribly wrong at any moment. When driving, all she could think about was getting into a terrible car accident. When grocery shopping, she worried about slipping and cracking open her head, or that a pyramid of canned meat would topple and crush her. On the rare occasion when she was out walking, she just knew a car was going to jump the curb and pin her against a tree, or a jagged hunk of ice would fall from an airplane and pierce her skull. (A neighbor had told her it had happened to a distant relative). She followed each of these and other terrible thoughts by one even more disturbing: And then who will look after my little Howard?

Helen had lost her husband in the Korean War, and her only child, Howard Sr., in Viet Nam. Both men had a habit of doing everything they were told and both did exactly that right up until the end.

Helen did not know she was a grandmother until an attractive hippie-girl approached her at Howard Sr.'s funeral. The hippie-girl told Helen that she had gotten together with her son before he went to Nam, and now here she was one year later at his funeral holding his baby. And she demanded to know what Helen was going to do about it. In what would become another family tradition, the hippie-girl went on to confess that she only slept with Howard Sr. out of pity. Her brother had died in Nam and he was drafted a virgin. She did not want another young man to die without *knowing what it's like to love someone instead of just killing 'em, ya know?* The hippie-girl, who never introduced herself and merely went to the most matronly looking attendee of the sparsely attended funeral said this and a lot more, but Helen didn't hear her. She was too busy staring at the perfectly sweet baby boy in her arms.

Helen took the baby home and never saw the mother again. It was the right decision for all involved, she reckoned. Who knows if it was, considering this beautiful baby she had named Howard Feck, just like the son she had buried, was currently locked inside Debbie Coomb's bathroom with no means of escape.

If Helen could have put little Howard into a big plastic bubble, she would have. Then she wouldn't have had to worry so much. But with that luxury out of reach, she opted to keep ahead of baby Howard by disinfecting every surface he might touch, spraying insecticide into any corner a spider might call home, and removing any object within his grasp if she thought it or a piece of it could end up lodged in his throat or poking out an eye.

For his first few years, nearly all baby Howard had to play with was a colorful plastic ball and a teddy bear with its whiskers and eyes scissored off. The ball was taken away after he fell over it. Howard fell over a lot, but he was still a perfectly sweet baby boy.

Worn down by the hard work of baby-proofing, disinfecting, and bug-spraying Howard's entire universe, Helen reluctantly agreed to let Howard have a few more things as he grew older. Comic books were one, but if she came across an image of a girl not looking "Christian," she would cut it out and paste in its place a little scrap of paper with a crucifix drawn on it. Little Howard also had the board game Sorry!—though Gramma Helen had removed the dangerous game pieces and replaced them with little paper squares colored with scent-free markers.

None of this gave Howard many opportunities to make friends. So Gramma Helen was his main companion throughout his childhood. And that was fine by Helen, who loved and smothered him dearly. But Helen's mothering skills and paranoia had turned Howard's environment into a toxic hot spot, thanks to all the cleansers, disinfectants, spot removers, and bug sprays she was compelled to break out at the first sign of a bug, germ, spot, or bit of grit. The combination was as toxic as an arsenic smoothie in an asbestos cup, and it had retarded Howard's immune system by suppressing his exposure to pathogens normally found in everyday life. When Howard was a sickly fifteen-year-old with meatball-sized clumps of hair falling out of his head, the doctor told him he had the immune system of a third-world toddler.

Young Howard had missed so much school due to illness (and innocuous sniffles and coughs) that Helen ended up homeschooling him from the age of eleven on. She didn't do a very good job of it, and Howard never earned his high school diploma, let alone his G.E.D. But on the day she decided to stop teaching him, Grandma Helen made a big fuss by throwing a Helen Feck High School graduation ceremony. It was just the two of them, of course. They had fruit punch and homemade cupcakes, both of which tasted a little like Windex. Helen made a high school diploma out of a sheet of typing paper, rolled it up into a scroll, and handed it to Howard. She even played "Pomp and Circumstance" off a scratchy vinyl record when he came up to the kitchen table to receive it. She gave him a twelve-karat gold crucifix and chain as a graduation present and issued severe warnings about its pokiness when she helped him into it. She would have given him a ten-karat one if she didn't think it would irritate his eczema.

After the cupcakes and procession, they played a rousing game of Sorry! and shared a pot of not-too-hot chocolate. The next day Helen drove Howard to the hiring offices of Burke Packaging where years later he became known as "that dork from receiving who found the finger."

Helen died long before Howard could share the news of this high point in his career. A few years after Howard graduated from HFHS, he went down for breakfast to a perfectly quiet and empty kitchen that should have been alive with the sight, sound, and smell of Gramma Helen making Cream of Wheat or French toast. Howard called for his grandmother, but there was no answer. After standing quietly in the kitchen for several minutes, he decided he would have to do something that was strictly forbidden: enter his grandmother's bedroom. It was dark and clean, with a crucifix on the wall above the headboard. Lying in the bed, perfectly sweet and still, was Helen Feck. She had gone quietly in the night.

Howard called to her again and then mustered the courage to shake her foot. Then he went back to the kitchen and called his boss, who drove to the Feck house and immediately began taking care of all the things you must when your grandmother passes away. Howard did not go to work that day. He cried a lot and got a little sick to his stomach. That night he called his boss on the phone and asked him for a ride to work the next day. His boss suggested that it was too soon to go back to the receiving dock, but Howard said he was ready. What else was there to do?

After a week of driving him to and from his job, Mr. Templin signed Howard up for driving school. And when Helen's old Dodge gave up the ghost much less gracefully than Helen herself, he helped Howard buy his blue Geo.

2

DEATH KILLS BEYOND THOSE it calls. For the survivors, it kills a piece of the whole, leaves behind an ache. And with that ache, one supposedly feels the deepness and richness of life. And that feeling is supposed to guide the aching back to living. Stoically, perhaps, but happily, too. There is a multi-billion-dollar industry based on this premise, and it seems to work because hundreds of thousands of people die each day leaving behind hundreds of thousands of others aching madly. And sooner or later, most of the aching ones get back to their lives. Regardless, the world moves on.

Regardless.

While Howard moved on slightly, Debbie moved on not at all. For Howard, living had a very narrow definition, and Gramma Helen filled much of it. After he figured out how to live on his own and do grownup things like pay bills and do laundry, there wasn't much missing from his life. In fact, there was more to his life, and he took to the basics of independence fairly quickly. Howard could obey rules just as well as his father and grandfather before him. And like his progenitors, he could do things as long as he had instructions he could follow. Still, he missed the things one probably cannot live without and that come without instructions whatsoever. Things like love, companionship, another face to look at up close, and the skin of another brushing against one's own. Debbie was deprived of these things as well, and for her, things never really got better. She lived on her dad's La-Z-Boy and ached madly day and night. She also felt something she was not accustomed to feeling: good old fear. Bogeymen flee when fathers are near. And when fathers are gone, they return and bring their friends. Ever since Debbie's father had died, she had found herself drenched in fear's cold, syrupy wetness. She hated it. She hated the whole damn thing. Hate, hate, hate!

3

TEDDY FROM THE TAVERN called once a day "just checkin' up" on Delwin's daughter *because he always had the nicest things to say about ya*, and—*I know he loved ya a whole lot.* Then he'd ask about the bar tab. All Debbie ever said was hello. Once Teddy started talking money, she'd hang up. Sometimes she wouldn't wait that long. The only reason she answered the phone in the first place was because of the irrational hope that Daddy would call saying he was okay and he was coming home.

Aside from the occasional ring of the phone and bouts of intense, sometimes angry sobbing, the Coomb house was a very quiet place. Then one afternoon a knock on the door pierced the silence, scaring Debbie right out of a deep, grieving, sleep. Curled up in her dad's chair, with his jacket as a blanket, she looked at the door. A second knock came and went. With the same cruel hope that caused Debbie to answer the phone, she got up and answered the door.

It was an average-looking black man in a cheap suit, black-rimmed glasses, and a Kennedy-era buzz cut. The coroner. He was holding a casserole dish with a kitchen towel over it. At his feet were two grocery bags of comfort food. Stuff that required little or no preparation. Debbie backed up and opened the door wider so he could enter. She tried to say thank you but instead just started crying again. She looked like hell. She was almost sixteen, but her eyes looked triple that. She was a grieving mess.

"My family and I thought maybe you could use a little something. My wife made you this, and I brought you some things you can prepare yourself," said the coroner. "You got to take care of yourself now. Your father would have wanted it that way."

Silence.

"Who is here with you?"

Silence.

"Debbie, are you here all alone?"

Silence. Then the nearly silent whine of a hard cry.

The coroner set the warm casserole dish on a small square table just inside the door and hugged Debbie. She let him. He held her close as if she were his own daughter and said quietly, "I am so sorry. I know it's hard. I know…I know." He tried to look at her face, but her hair was glued to her cheeks by a mixture of snot and tears.

"You got your whole life ahead of you now, Debbie," he continued. "Don't you let this stop you. Your daddy wouldn't want that. I know he dedicated his whole life to you. I know you are at your darkest hour right now. But life carries on. Things do get better. And this pain will become more tolerable. I promise, Debbie. I've seen it."

Debbie cried hard. He rubbed her back and realized she was wearing the same clothes she had on the day she discovered the body.

"Debbie, who is taking care of you?"

Debbie wanted to lie, but gripped by the brutal truth of the situation, an honest answer was all she could summon. "No one." She heaved the words so hard her knees buckled, and the coroner had to catch her. "No one," she sobbed.

The coroner got her to the couch and comforted her until she settled down. "I'll tell you what," he said once the tears had subsided. "I'll put this food away. Why don't you go upstairs and take a nice long shower? Put on some clean comfy clothes. When you come down, I'll have a hot plate waiting for you. Laurette, my wife, makes the best enchiladas in the state. You've got to eat something. I mean it now."

The coroner looked to the top of the stairs and saw they disappeared into a maw of darkness in spite of the sunshine outside. "Why don't I go upstairs, turn the lights on—light the way so to speak—and start the water. How does that sound?"

Debbie nodded.

And with that, the coroner made good on all his promises but one—the one about things getting better.

4

AFTER HE HAD RETURNED from lighting the upstairs and starting the shower (he also closed her father's door, hoping it was the right thing to do), the coroner called his wife. The conversation was short and uncomfortable.

Debbie came downstairs after her shower. She looked much better, as if she only had a bad case of the flu. The coroner guided her to the kitchen table where two plates of food and two glasses of milk sat opposite each other. He purposefully avoided what he assumed was Debbie's father's place at the table and again hoped it was the right thing to do. The coroner didn't sit down until Debbie did, and then he respectfully joined her. He didn't eat until she did.

The comforting sounds of forks on plates and chewing and swallowing were broken occasionally by very light conversation instigated by the coroner. He mostly stuck to discussing his wife's cooking, since that was safe. Debbie's responses were subtle, mostly monosyllabic acknowledgements.

She had eaten next to nothing in the two days since her father had died and she surprised both herself and the coroner by how quickly she devoured two helpings of good, hot food. After her hot shower and hot meal, she did feel a little bit better. Not in any meaningful way, but it was still better.

"Good job, Debbie. Your—" He stopped himself from saying how her daddy would have been proud. "There's dessert in the fridge—watermelon slices and a homemade lemon meringue pie. That's one of my wife's specialties, too."

This time Debbie managed to say thank you without crying.

"Debbie," the coroner said, "what happened to the folks from the church? Do you need me to call them?"

"No."

"Are they coming back? How long have they been gone?"

It took a long moment for her to answer, and the coroner had to force himself to not break the heavy silence. Debbie finally spoke more than a few words. "I couldn't take them and they couldn't help me, so I sent them away. It's not their fault. I'm just not religious and so they didn't know what to do with me. They didn't know how to help. They just prayed at me, and it made me feel worse. It just reminded me of...it reminded me of..." Debbie started crying again and somewhere in the cries the coroner heard the word *Daddy*.

He reached across the table and took both her hands. "Debbie, I'm so sorry," was all he could think to say. He rubbed the back of her hands with his thumbs until she stopped crying. And then he resumed the conversation. Knowing she would probably cry no matter what, he dove straight in.

"I need to ask you a few things. At—" He paused. He wanted to be as gentle as possible to keep Debbie from crying again. But he thought if he substituted the word "office" for "morgue" he would sound like an ass, so he went ahead and said, "At the morgue, you didn't list any guardians or next of kin. You said you have no surviving family members, is that right?"

Debbie nodded.

"Does your dad have any friends that can help take care of you?" he said as gently as possible.

"No," Debbie answered softly. She saw the coroner's reaction and did not like it.

"What about friends at school? Anyone there that—"

"I can take care of myself."

"Well, Debbie, you haven't been. And there are certain things you just need a grown up for. Like making sure—"

"I can take care of myself," Debbie repeated. "I'm not going to leave this house and go live with some stranger. And I don't know anyone who would...who I..." Another hard cry interrupted the sentence.

He allowed this wave of grief to subside, then started up again on an entirely different tack. "If you don't mind, Debbie, I would like to look at some things. I promise not to disturb anything. But I think I should look at your dad's papers and things just to see if I can help you and see where you stand. Is that okay?"

"He kept the bills in there," she said, pointing to what would have been a junk drawer in most kitchens. "He also has a box, a metal box in his closet. But I think that has mostly to do with when he sold the farm."

The coroner stood up, cleared the table, and turned on more lights. It was now dusk and would quickly turn to night. He gave Debbie a small plate of watermelon and told her to get comfortable, maybe even turn on the TV. Then he began sorting out the life and times of Delwin Coomb.

After a good hour of sifting through the papers, the coroner walked into the dead quiet living room. Debbie was back in her dad's La-Z-Boy curled up and clutching his jacket like a toddler clutching a blanket.

"Debbie, can you come into the kitchen with me for a few minutes, I want to go over a few things with you."

Debbie padded into the kitchen, seeming more like a frail grandmother than a young, stout teenager. The coroner, seeming lighter and happier, followed. Together they sat down at the kitchen table where he had placed two slices of pie. A few stacks of documents lay between them.

"Before I get started, I have to ask you something," said the coroner. "What kind of grades do you get in school?"

"Mostly A's, I guess. I got a C in PE. Why?"

"Well, I need to know if you are smart enough to understand all that I am going to tell you."

"Okay," said Debbie through a mouthful of pie. "I'm not dumb. Just sad."

The coroner nodded politely in response. "Debbie, it appears you and your dad have been living off a monthly stipend from the investments he made when he sold the farm. This money is all dividend income, meaning the principles of his investments are preserved and growing. Do you understand what I am saying?"

After a brief pause, Debbie answered. "I think so."

"You know how interest works in a savings account?"

Debbie nodded.

"Well, that's what your dad and you have been living off of— the interest he gets from his holdings."

"Is that bad?"

"Well it depends on how much that interest is and how long you can expect to receive it. But in your case, I assure you, it's not bad."

"How much is it?"

"Well, as far as I can tell, it's nearly two thousand dollars a month.

"Is that good?"

"With your expenses—I mean how much you pay for groceries, gas and electricity—it's nothing to sneeze at. Some people work fifty or sixty hours a week for far less."

"I always thought we lived kinda poor. At least compared to people on TV."

"Your house is paid for. You have no real bills except these here, which don't really add up to much." He pointed to the smallest stack of papers on the table, then looked Debbie in the eyes. "Debbie," he said, "your dad was a wealthy man, especially for these parts. He lived modestly, however, which is a blessing for you, since you do not want people around here thinking you've got money. He paid his taxes, paid his bills on time. I can't find any loose ends or anything odd—"

"Teddy from Teddy's Tavern keeps calling me and saying…" Debbie stopped to stem another round of tears. This time she was successful. "He calls and says my dad owes a bar tab."

"Well, Debbie, you can afford to pay it. But I wouldn't be telling him or anyone about your finances, okay? That's really important around here. Really important."

Debbie nodded.

"It's too late now, but tomorrow morning, what I would like to do is get you set up so you can pay bills, get groceries, and, well, get you set up with the dailies. How does that sound?"

"And I stay here? Take care of myself?"

"For now, yes. But that means you have to take proper care of yourself."

"Can we pay Teddy so he'll stop calling?"

"Yes, we can pay Teddy, too," the coroner answered, smiling. "We'll also have to talk about school and guardianship. This money is a blessing to be sure, but it also means we—you—are going to have to make some decisions about the next couple years until you turn eighteen. But for now, why don't you get snuggled into your dad's chair and I'll bring you another slice of pie and a glass of milk?"

"Okay. Thank you." The news of her financial good fortune seemed to have zero effect on Debbie, but the coroner's gentle comfort and his wife's good cooking had obviously helped.

While in the kitchen, the coroner called his wife again before returning to the living room with seconds of dessert. The call was short, the tone better. Debbie sat up in the La-Z-Boy and began to eat while the coroner sat down on the long, puffy couch. "Do you think I should spend the night?" he asked softly.

"Okay. Yes. Please," she answered without hesitation.

"I don't mind. But I have to tell you that even though I'm supposed to be off work, there's a small chance that I may get a call in the middle of the night and have to leave."

"What for?"

"To do what I did for you and your dad," the coroner replied.

Debbie sighed as she considered that what had happened to her a few days ago might happen to someone else tonight and someone else tomorrow. And the next day, and the next, forever. What a wicked world this must be, she thought with a despair deeper than her well of tears. "Have you...? I mean, has anyone died on the side of the road like that before?"

"Debbie, people die everywhere, and all the time."

Debbie began to contemplate the realities of death beyond her personal experience. The coroner drew her back to the present. "You don't want to wear out that chair. I know it was your father's and you'll want it around for some time. You should try to rest your head on your own pillow in your own bed. What do you say? I'll sleep here on the couch and you go sleep upstairs in your nice bed."

"What's it like having to pick up dead people all the time?" Debbie asked, ignoring the coroner's suggestion. "Do you ever get there and they're still alive? Is it ever a mistake?"

"Being a coroner can be very sad and difficult sometimes," he confessed. "But, you know, everyone dies sooner or later. My job is to help when that inevitable thing happens. And helping feels good. It's still sad. That part doesn't really ever change. But helping people when something like this happens—I think it's a good job."

For perhaps the first time that evening, Debbie looked openly into the coroner's eyes. She liked how it felt. It felt safe, and safe was big. "Thank you," she said.

"You're welcome."

Holding her dad's jacket, Debbie went to bed. "Goodnight."

"Goodnight."

He waited for Debbie to reach the upstairs before he went and tidied the kitchen. Then he called his wife for the third time. As great a wife as she was and as great a mother to his children as she was, Laurette would not allow Debbie to come stay with them. They could make room for her—you can always make room for someone if you really want to. But as the daughter of a successful black doctor in the south, Laurette had had private schooling all her life. She had been the lone black girl in a school of snotty, cruel Scarlett O'Hara's. Every one had gained their fortunes from the sweat and misery of her and the coroner's ancestors and brethren. So in spite of the picture the coroner painted of Debbie and her circumstances, and in spite of his polite persistence, he could not take Debbie home. Some things just took too long to forgive.

5

FORTUNATELY FOR ALL INVOLVED, the phone at the Coomb house never rang on the night the coroner stayed over, and his pager never beeped. Technically, it wasn't a night off since he spent it on the swallowing couch of a recent client. Still, it was better than a three a.m. call to go scrape chunks of human outside a curve in the highway.

His body's alarm clock woke him sharply at six. Quiet as a thief, the coroner made a pot of coffee and then carefully folded the grandmotherly quilt he had slept under and replaced it on the back of the couch. He waited nearly two hours for Debbie to appear downstairs. She did not. Reluctantly, he climbed the stairs. Halfway up, he heard her crying. He stopped.

"Debbie," he called out. "I'm making breakfast. It will be ready in a few minutes. Please come down and join me."

The coroner walked back down the stairs and returned to the kitchen where he made up some eggs, potatoes, a can of Heinz beans, and toast—things he had brought with him the night before. There was bacon in the fridge, but it smelled suspect and he tossed it out. Even if it were fresh, he would not have cooked it. A coroner will not eat a dead man's food.

By the time this good ol' fry up was ready, Debbie still had not made an appearance. He grabbed a tray he found leaning sideways against the fridge and delivered Debbie's breakfast to her just as Delwin had done dozens of times before. At the top of the stairs, he called out softly, "Debbie? I'm coming in now. I made a breakfast you'd be proud to eat."

"Come in, please." She didn't sound too bad. The crying had thankfully subsided.

"Good morning," the coroner said as he entered Debbie's cheery-white and-yellow-room. It reminded him of his daughter's room. The only real difference being the posters on his daughter's bedroom walls were of black artists and celebrities, and the posters on Debbie's bedroom walls were of white artists and celebrities. "Mornings are rough, I know," he said. "But if you eat, you'll feel better. We have a busy day ahead of us. You're going to need your strength."

"Okay. Thank you," she said. She had tears on her face but had stopped crying.

"You're welcome. If I leave you to it will you come down soon, dressed and ready to go?"

She nodded while raising a fork of scrambled eggs to her mouth. Her hair was an absolute mess, but at least it was clean.

"Do you need help with anything?"

"No," Debbie answered with a full mouth. "Do you?"

The coroner didn't quite know how to take that. Was Debbie offering to help? If so, that was an excellent sign that she was moving through her grief. "I'm okay. See you downstairs in a few minutes then, right?"

She nodded her head.

He looked startlingly deep into her eyes and said, "You have to show me you can take good care of yourself if you want to stay in this house." Then he walked downstairs, not waiting for a reply. He wanted to give her something to think about. He was on a mission now and he felt like whistling. While lying on the couch the night before, he had decided that he would look into making Debbie an emancipated minor, which meant he would have to commit to checking in on her several times a week, maybe even spend the night here on occasion. Whether he'd go through with this decision depended on how the day went with Debbie. He would be studying her closely. Surreptitiously, but closely.

As county coroner he'd made friends in the court system, but he had never been one to take advantage of that. Today would be different. He would have to find someone he could discuss Debbie's case with. He had lost all faith in the local foster care system, and was willing to go the extra mile to keep young Debbie Coomb out of it. He had been called out to three county foster homes over the past two years. The first was to pick up a foster dad whose kids loved him so much that they drowned him in a bathtub. As near as the coroner could tell, the foster kids had opened a dozen Benadryl capsules and poured them into foster dad's nineteenth and twentieth beer of the day. While dad was passed out, the three scrawny, bruised, and malnourished kids—two boys and one girl, not one over the age of fourteen—dragged all two hundred pounds of him across the peeling hardwood floor and into the bathroom. There they stripped off his clothes and somehow managed to get him over the side of the overfull tub. Then they held him under until the bubbles stopped. The coroner found him that way—face down in a dirty bathtub filled with water. The coroner saw the bruises on the kid's necks and arms. Big bruises. Hard to miss. Each kid had "the look" people in law enforcement see far too often. He learned from the cops and the kids that foster Mom, who was mostly nice, and also abused by the same man, had been kicked out of the house for spending too much of the county's money issued to cover the kid's needs. The coroner listed the cause of death as "accidental drowning due to severe intoxication." He left out of his report that he found slivers in foster dad's ass and a high concentration of diphenhydramine in his blood stream. The poor little murderers with their sad eyes and purple-and-gray bruises were shipped off to another adventure as wards of the state.

Calls to two other foster homes were to pick up deceased children, one of whom was the little girl who helped her brothers drown her last foster dad only six months prior. This new and improved foster dad had accidentally broken her neck. He admitted he was a little rough with her when she resisted being put to bed early for misbehaving. The coroner did everything he legally could to send this guy to death row, but the county lab botched the handling of the foreign DNA found inside the poor thing, and a plea bargain of involuntary manslaughter barred the way for justice. He spent less than five years in prison.

The last call was to pick up a little boy who had been mauled to death by his foster neighbor's pet, Bullet, a large, mud-colored mutt who lived on the end of a long, thick, chain. He'd had a mean streak beaten into him. The little boy made the mistake of going after a toy truck that had rolled into Bullet's perimeter. Usually a toy that ended up in Bullet's territory would just sit there eternally tempting children like a dolly in a minefield. What the coroner didn't know was that peer pressure from the other kids sent the little boy after his rusting Tonka. The kid sure as hell didn't want to retrieve it, but by the end of it, he really had no choice, or so he thought.

Retribution was served by a state patrolman shooting the dog in front of the kids. His partner yelled at him for not putting the kids in the house to protect their innocent little eyes. "Well, hell," the patrolman replied in front of the kids, "they just watched the dog eat one of their own; you'd think they'd want to see him put down."

So, yeah, as far as the coroner was concerned, he wasn't going to make Debbie's situation worse by making her a ward of the state in a financially strapped county.

After a day of errands, impromptu meetings, favors happily granted, and paperwork pushed through, Debbie Coomb was granted emancipated status exactly four days after her father's tragic death. Delwin's checking account was put into her name and she had ordered a debit card. She had her picture taken for a state ID, and she would receive a monthly stipend of fifteen hundred dollars a month until she turned eighteen. Suddenly, Debbie was the youngest person of means in her county by a good fifteen years. She and the coroner agreed to have a house key made for him, and he expected he would be dropping by the Coomb place quite often.

He would have never gone through with it had Debbie had not stepped up her game. She didn't cry once during the hectic and tedious day. She went out of her way to be helpful and appear responsible. At lunch, Debbie offered to pay. And when the day was done, she offered to write a check for the gas the coroner used running her around. She was sincere, but the coroner also thought she was eager to write her first check. He let her do it— for practice, and to build the habit of paying her way. She made small talk about getting back to school. She looked forward to English and history (*US, this time, instead of all that ancient world stuff...*), but not having to tell her school friends that her father had passed. She managed to relay this concern without a single tear. When they went shopping for a handbag and a wallet, Debbie picked something reserved and inexpensive, almost masculine. Though, to be fair, the most expensive handbag for sale in Wilburn was under forty dollars.

After a long day that seemed to do Debbie much good, she and the coroner headed back to Wilburn in his black county coroner's wagon. Debbie reminded the coroner to stop at Teddy's and pay "that creep" on the way home. Debbie now had a small wad of tens and twenties tucked inside her new wallet at the bottom of her new bag. She gave the coroner five twenties. "He should give you change. It was eighty-something," she instructed, taking her new pseudo-adult status seriously. The coroner obliged.

He parked in front of the tavern, stepped out of the wagon and sized up the place. He didn't like it. It was an ugly, good ol' boy joint with a confederate flag covering the only window. Nailed to the top of the building's facade was a sheet of plywood with "Teddy's Tavern" painted on it in unimaginative block letters. A dusty brown couch with flattened cushions and one armrest sat on the sidewalk next to the tavern's entrance.

As is always the case when the watering holes are few and far between, Teddy's Tavern served a diverse clientele. One or more road-worn Harleys could routinely be found parked on the sidewalk in front of the tavern, and sometimes as many as a dozen. A college kid's subcompact could occasionally be found parked a safe distance from these black hogs, along with the requisite pickup truck and the occasional Case or John Deere tractor belonging to a farmer who couldn't wait to switch vehicles before getting greased in Teddy's cool, dark shack. Teddy's offered the worst elements of a dive bar along with a few redeeming ones: cold beer on tap, chilled mugs, and a jukebox with a halfway-decent selection of rock and country no fresher than 1978. Delwin had frequented the place because some of the regulars were friends of his since he was a boy. Besides, it was within walking distance to his home, and what semi-regular drinker can't appreciate that?

The coroner took out his wallet, removed his county coroner badge, and clipped it to his shirt pocket. He hoped it would be enough to ward off any trouble already drinking inside. He doubted that any person of color had ever walked through the peeling red door. He wanted to make damn sure he walked out the same way he walked in.

After one long minute, the coroner returned to his wagon looking none the worse for wear. He put his badge back in his wallet, gave Debbie fifteen dollars change, and drove to her too quiet home.

"Can you come inside?" she asked as he pulled into the gravel driveway. "For a minute at least?"

"Sure thing," said the coroner.

Debbie was visibly relieved by his response.

She led him up the walk, then unlocked and opened the door into the cool living room of what she would always think of as Daddy's house.

"You want a can of pop? Maybe a sandwich?" Debbie asked, surprising the coroner.

"Sure, that sounds great," he said, following her into the kitchen. "Laurette packed you some sliced ham, and I put a loaf of bread in the box on the drain board."

"I used to make my dad lunches all the time. And I told you how he taught me to do breakfast, too, though I ain't never had a can of beans for breakfast before. Did you get that from the army or something?"

The coroner took Debbie's ability to maintain a casual conversation as a good sign. Light conversation driving around town was one thing, but to resist sliding back into tears in the home where her father's now-permanent absence could be felt acutely was another.

"Nooo," he said with a small chuckle. "My wife and I went to England before we had children, and that's how they served breakfast at one of the places we were staying. It was a B&B. Bed and—"

"I know what a B&B is. I just never heard of a can of beans for breakfast before," Debbie said as she gathered sandwich fixings and placed them on the counter. "Maybe in England B&B stands for beans and breakfast."

The coroner's eyebrows jumped high. Was that an honest to goodness joke?

Debbie noticed his look of surprise. "They tasted good, that's all I'm saying. I was afraid they wouldn't because I never seen such a thing, but they tasted good mixed up with the eggs and browns."

"Yep, that's the best way. Mix 'em all together into one bite."

The coroner opened the door to the fridge and realized he should have stopped for milk and a few things.

"You're going to need a few basics before Liberty Market starts delivering. I'll bring some by before I leave for home."

"There's no need," she answered. "We get milk, eggs, and butter delivered on Fridays, at least we used to before…" Debbie remembered walking down the highway, finding the out-of-place object jutting from the weeds on the side of the road, recognizing it as the ankle and foot of her dead Daddy, and all the rest.

No crying this time, but a few tears salted the bread.

"Let's sit at the table, shall we?" the coroner asked, trying to keep things upbeat.

Debbie answered by following his suggestion.

He brought two cans of soda from the fridge over to the table. They both took the same seats they had used the night before and quietly began eating.

"Debbie, I think you know how bad I feel for you."

She nodded.

"And I took a big risk today getting your emancipation so the state doesn't send you to a foster home. But I think I made the right decision." He looked her right in the eyes with seriousness softened by compassion. "But if you don't take good care of yourself and do all the day-to-day things we grownups hate doing, then I made the wrong decision. And then I don't know what."

"I know," she said. "I don't want to let you down because you been so kind to me. Sometimes I don't know if I can make it. I just don't know, it's so…"

"Overwhelming?"

"Exactly."

"Well, you got to take it one day at a time, no more, and sometimes less. I mean if you have to—to get through it, to make it—you take it one minute at a time. Whatever you have to do to make it into your bed at night and back out in the morning, you must do. And I don't need to tell you that it won't be easy. You understand?"

Debbie didn't answer because she knew she had no choice.

"And I mean this with everything I got. Under no circumstances do you tell anyone about your money. You're a rich young lady now. People are going to wonder where it comes from. Play dumb, play deaf, and don't go buying anything fancy that makes you look rich. At least not for a while. I will stop in once a day for starters, but I can't do that forever. Debbie, I am sorry to say that today, we ended your childhood. And you have no choice now but to be an adult. I'm really sorry about that."

Debbie was taken aback by the seriousness in the coroner's voice. It dawned on her that maybe emancipation was not a consolation prize for losing her father. It wasn't just eat all the ice cream you want and stay up as late as you want. It was the grind of responsibility, and she was too young and naive to really know what that meant. The coroner pulled a small notebook and pen out of his breast pocket and began writing. When he was finished, he handed it to Debbie.

"What's this?" she asked.

"Homework. I will be back tomorrow to check it and give you some more. Be prepared, don't let me down."

Debbie read the note.

Homework for Debbie Coomb—Week 1

1. Use the yellow pages to find a housekeeper who has her own car, cooks, and can start right away. Pay no more than $25.00 per cleaning. Get references, give to Sam.

2. Keep the doors locked and never open them unless you know who it is on the other side and you really want them in your house.

3. Call Liberty Market and set up a weekly delivery. I made you a grocery list. You can add groceries to it, but NO CANDY! Pay them by check when they arrive.

4. When a bill comes in the mail, send it off the next day paid in full. If you get a bill and you do not know what it is, call Sam.

5. You must call me every day, rain or shine, no matter what. If you have any problems, questions, anything—CALL SAM, ANYTIME!!

Samuel Miles

555-6459 home 555 5699 work

"Your name is Samuel."

"Yes, it is. I guess we were never properly introduced. You can call me Sam."

After they had finished their sandwiches and sodas, the coroner helped Debbie clean up. Together they walked to the front door, neither wanting to part company, but the coroner knowing he really must. They hugged tightly for many seconds, squeezing more tears from Debbie. She felt saved in his arms and knew that feeling would end when he released her. And he did, slowly, in deference to her state.

Then, Samuel Miles, the coroner of Paro County, quietly took his leave of the Coomb house. On his way to the car he said a silent prayer for her safety and healing. Then he drove away, thinking about all he had to do to help Debbie succeed. He would stop off at the market and coach them on what to do when she called. He would also stop in at the county social services building and arrange for a social worker to return with him. He would establish a contact at Debbie's high school. He had shown her how to read bills and statements and write checks, and had generally accepted the responsibility of making sure Debbie would make it. He planned on doing as much as possible from behind the scenes so Debbie could feel a sense of ownership and accomplishment with regards to her new life. Still, he figured he would be spending quite a lot of time at this old farmhouse on the outskirts of Wilburn.

That night, while out scooping another human roadkill off the highway and into a body bag, a drunk driver slammed into a police car parked behind the coroner's wagon, crushing him between the two vehicles. Coroner Samuel Miles died a few minutes later. And the cycle of death and ache and life rolled into another set of hearts.

Chapter 5

1

THE CORONER HAD BEEN a kind angel of death to Debbie. He had breathed life into a home desperately needing it. After he left, everything got too quiet too fast. The living room wallpaper with its strawflower bouquets was designed for a lively room. That print now emphasized the stillness. Shadows falling at intervals on the puffy couch emphasized abandon. And the sounds you never hear in a house full of life—a light switch being flipped, footsteps on a thin runner, the buzz of the refrigerator— all contributed to a gloomy tattoo that reminded Debbie of one terrible thing: she was alone with a devastating completeness. And there was no hint that this depressing rhythm Debbie now marched to would ever change. She clung to the promise that the coroner would make good on his word and that she would see him soon. She couldn't wait.

The next morning broke gloomy with storm-beckoning winds. Debbie found herself switching lights on wherever she went and leaving them on when she left the room. If nothing else, her father's house would not sit in darkness. She could combat her newfound fear of the dark, but her primary fear, the one steeped in grief and crawling with dire implications, would not be so easy to defy. It was the fear of being all alone today, tomorrow, forever. It dogged her and nipped at her heels if she stayed in one room for too long. Her penchant for lingering in the living room curled in her father's easy chair only made it worse.

Fear followed her into the kitchen where she pulled from the fridge the leftover pie—not a great breakfast choice for a freshly emancipated teen. Not a surprising one, either. She grabbed a fork, sat at the table, and began looking over the coroner's instructions. She read and ate, and when finished with both, went over to the kitchen telephone. It sat on a small, darkly stained table originally intended to be a nightstand. She thought about calling the coroner, but what would she say? That she had pie for breakfast and had not done anything on the list? She decided to wait.

Debbie picked up the thin Wilburn phonebook Delwin had kept on the nightstand's low shelf. She took a pen from a pencil cup covered in white-and-gold contact paper. Debbie tried not to think back to the time she and her dad had made it from a pony beer can one rainy afternoon. She returned to the table with pen and Yellow Pages in one hand and the phone in the other. There were seven listings under Housekeeping, one of which had an actual ad: "Tidy-Rite Housecleaning—Affordable Prices—Ask about our Sparkle Guarantee!" She wrote down the number and promised herself she would call, *as soon as I wash the pie dish for Sam,* followed by, *right after I lie down for a spell,* and after that, *maybe after lunch—it'll give me something to do.*

After rationalizing her procrastination, Debbie left the kitchen for a midmorning nap. She stopped at her dad's La-Z-Boy and contemplated going up to her room versus curling up in Daddy's chair. The choice made her realize she was already getting used to Delwin being gone. She did not like that one bit. She was not yet ready for acceptance. During her earliest throes of grieving, she could still cling to a fractured and dysfunctional attachment to her dearly departed. But acceptance led to detachment—killing hope and making the tragedy god-awful real. She retrieved Delwin's jacket from her bed and returned to his chair. There, she curled up and cried herself to sleep—again. Her last thought before drifting off was, *better not let Sam catch me like this.*

Hours later, Debbie was startled awake by the ring of the phone. Foggy from too much sleep, she forced herself to run to it. She knew it would be the coroner, and couldn't wait to hear his voice. "Hello?"

"Well hi there, cutie," Teddy Eel replied.

"Hello," Debbie said with obvious disappointment.

"Where's my money, Delwin's lit-tle gir-ul?" He sounded just a notch past drunk. His t's came out like hard d's, and he over emphasized every syllable in effort to sound superior to a grieving teenager. Teddy's orneriness was in full force. "I ain't just gonna forget, you know," Teddy continued. "I run a business here, Lit-tle Gir-ul! You better under—"

"I came by yesterday with the coroner and paid you—he paid you," Debbie interrupted with a dash of her old petulance. "I waited in his car right in front. I saw him go in."

"No, he ain't," spat Teddy, which sounded like 'noey-a-unt.' "Coroner's a coon. You think I'd let one of them in my bar? Is that what you think, lit-tle gir-ul? Don't play with me. Your daddy was a good man, and I know he wouldn't have raised no penny filcher. You're trying to steal from me."

"No I—"

"I WANT MY MONEY, DAMMIT!" Teddy yelled.

But was that really what he wanted?

"No sir, I'm not a penny filcher," Debbie tried to explain. "I saw him go in with my own eyes. He put his badge on and everything. It was around three o'clock, maybe a little later. Maybe you weren't there. Maybe he left it with someone."

"I'd know if a coon come in my tavern. And one ain't come in. They know better. And my hundred bucks ain't here." Evidently Teddy charged interest on tabs.

Debbie didn't know what to say, so she remained quiet. Teddy broke the brief silence by shouting, "DON'T LIE TO ME, DEL-WIN'S LIT-TLE GIR-UL!"

He wanted to make Debbie cry, wanted to *hear* her cry.

The way Teddy spat his venom through the phone stung Debbie. What was he getting at? Did he want more money? The coroner wouldn't mislead her, of that she was certain. She battled back tears.

"I'll bring you more tomorrow," Debbie offered.

"Why shou—"

"I promise. I will bring you some more money tomorrow, and then you can leave me alone."

Debbie hung up the phone before Teddy could reply. His words had formed a blade that poked and churned her ache. She returned to Delwin's La-Z-Boy holding her gut as if she were stabbed and bleeding. She picked up her father's jacket and held it against her face. She breathed in the scent and cried the words *Daddy* and *No* until she fell back to sleep. No steps forward, two steps back.

2

AFTER TEDDY'S LATEST PHONE call to the Coomb home, Debbie fell back into a hard sleep. In the middle of the night, she woke, ate, went to the bathroom, and then went back to the La-Z-Boy where she slept hard some more. Sleep was fast becoming her drug. A form of anesthesia. It saved her from the heaviness of reality and the adult status she was beginning to regret even though she could hardly fathom its ramifications. When the coroner returned, she decided that she would confess her failings and ask for his help. Maybe he could stay the night again. If he did, she would promise to do all he asked of her. She would cook for him, too. She would do whatever he wanted as soon as he came back—*I promise with all my heart.* She was afraid that if she called him so soon he would be disappointed—maybe enough to give up on her. She needed him too much to let that happen.

Curled tightly in her dad's La-Z-Boy with her feet tucked against one armrest and her head resting upon the other, Debbie had become intoxicated by sleep. The sound of car wheels on the gravel driveway did not wake her. Nor did the footsteps on the walk up to the home's stubby porch. It was the knocking on the front door that shocked her wide awake.

"Daddy?" The word pierced the quiet living room. A transient in dead air. She couldn't help herself. The first waking seconds from a hard sleep could still trick her. Then reality engulfed Debbie like a sodden blanket. She hurried to open the door and let the coroner in, not bothering to check first like she had been warned. Death had thrice done Debbie wrong, but she did not know it yet. She opened the door.

"Well hi there, Del-win's lit-tle gir-ul!" Debbie's eyes grew wide. She tried to shut the door in Teddy's face, but in an instant, he was not only in the house, but standing too close behind her. Debbie's throat tightened until it was hard to breathe. "Now you can shut the door—lit-tle gir-ul," he whispered, inches from her ear.

Teddy Eel looked like what he was. He had three upper teeth in the front of his mouth, one made of silver. Half of his back teeth had rotted out, thanks to a steady diet of drug smoke and hard alcohol. His remaining bottom teeth were held in place by peanut-brittle-looking hunks of gunk. He was gaunt and perpetually sweaty, which only partially explained his smell. His yellowed, wife-beater T-shirt stunk like a dirty hamper. His skin tone was the color of an underarm stain, and his neck had half a dozen Skittles-sized moles, as did his chest, which sported a burnt forest of gray-and-brown hair. He was thirty-five but looked a hard fifty.

"You want more money, Teddy?" There was no hiding the fear in her voice. "I'll give you all I got. Wait—"

"You call me Mr. Eel!" Teddy barked, still inches from her ear. Debbie clutched her ears. "Why are you—?"

"Come on, Debbie," Teddy said as he kicked the door closed. "Delwin used to say how smart you was." He locked the door, which to Debbie felt like a kick in the gut. She inched toward the center of the living room and away from Teddy Eel.

"I know you want money," Debbie answered. "I'll go get it right now and then you can—"

"Wait a minute, cutie. Yeah, I come for my money. I also come to pay my respects. Everyone at my tavern liked your dad a whole lot. And we all feel terrible about him dying like that and leaving you all alone." Teddy looked around to make sure he was right about her being alone.

Ordinarily, Debbie would have seen through Teddy like a fruitcake through cellophane. And then she would have run out the back door hoping the drunken barkeep couldn't catch her. But all she managed to do was inch farther into the living room while trying not to choke on his cruelty.

"If you ever need anything, just give your Uncle Teddy a call, okay? Delwin would have wanted that." That was complete bullshit, and Debbie knew it. Delwin would have preferred Debbie live a long and happy life without degenerates like Teddy Eel ever crossing her path, let alone slithering inside his house.

"Got anyone here to take care of you? Help you out? Watch over you? 'Cause if you don't, maybe I can help. Make sure you're okay and all. We could be friends. I could watch out for you. What do you say, cutie?" Teddy walked to the couch, fell back onto it, and then stretched out his legs and put his hands behind his head like he was the fucking man.

Debbie stood frozen in the middle of the living room. She could not stand the sound of Teddy's voice. The way he sounded drunk and angry on the phone was bad enough. But his attempts to sound benevolent revealed something sick and slimy. This, coupled with the way he looked at her, rattled Debbie's grief and stoked a fear that was already a maelstrom. She felt exposed, as if caught outdoors in her undies. He smiled at her like they shared a secret.

She prayed silently for the coroner to come quickly. *Please, Sam.*

"I'll go get your money, Mr. Eel."

"Call me Teddy. I was just playing with you earlier. In fact—"

"I'll get your money," Debbie repeated. She walked past Teddy toward the kitchen. He lunged. Debbie let out a shrill cry as Teddy snatched her by the arm and flung her hard onto the couch. He jerked his arms out and back as if he had successfully completed sleight-of-hand trick, then sat back on the couch and scooted close until his hips touched hers. All at once she realized that the fear of being alone was nothing compared with having your isolation broken by this horrible man. She could only look down. Debbie went from feeling caught in her undies to feeling completely naked with nowhere to hide. She wasn't sure what Teddy would do if she stood up again. Even worse, she wasn't sure she could stand at all.

"Look at me, lit-tle gir-ul," Teddy said, too quietly. "Think I'm gonna hurt you? I ain't gonna hurt you. I'm gonna help you." Teddy softly moved Debbie's hair off her face, caressing her cheek as he did so. Never in her life had she wanted her father so much. And never before had the finality of his demise felt so real. *I really am all alone,* she thought. Teddy's eyes pierced her. His touch foreboding, like the tongue of a poisonous snake sniffing delicious fear off the skin of its prey.

"Gonna let me take care of you, cutie?" Teddy whispered. "Gonna let Teddy ease your burden, some? Come on now, look it me."

Debbie could not. This pissed him off and he shouted in her face, "I AINT NO ELEPHANT MAN, FOR CHRISSAKE!"

Debbie remained paralyzed next to him. She could not look at him, even if he held a gun to her head and demanded it. She kept looking down while he stroked her tearstained cheek and soft hair.

"You're shaking," Teddy said, resuming the low voice that made Debbie queasy. "Afraid? Ain't nothing to be afraid of. Teddy's gonna take care of you. Make you feel good and safe. Tomorrow you're gonna ask me to stay—just wait and see." He leaned into his prey until his fetid breath was on her cheek. "Let me lead this dance," he whispered, "and everything'll be all right. I know you're new at having someone besides your daddy take care of you. Just leave it up to Ted here, okay?"

Debbie responded with trembles and tears. She willed for the sound of the coroner's wagon on the driveway gravel.

Of course, it never came.

Teddy stopped caressing her face long enough to thump her temple hard with his bird finger. "O-K?" he shouted an inch from her face.

Debbie shuddered and then shook her head no.

And then Teddy Eel moved in, violently taking possession of the Coomb house and all its contents, including a young, helpless, grieving, teenager.

Debbie pleaded. She fought with all she had, wondering all the while why God and the coroner had forsaken her. Teddy's tight skin seemed impervious to scratches, bites, and blows. He just egged her on, telling her she was doing a good job of getting into it. He questioned her about the pain he was inflicting. Debbie refused to answer, no matter how hard, how crushing, how deep the pain was. He pulled tufts of her hair out as he moved and manipulated her body. He tossed her around on the couch and threw her on the floor. Teddy was too jacked up to finish quickly or easily. Before it was over, Debbie, too, had begun to pull her hair out.

When he was finally done, he told her to stop sniveling and get him a beer. And then he spat a brown loogie on the living room floor and said, "Go wait in your bedroom until I'm ready for another dose of your high-energy snatch. You almost wore ol' Teddy out. Gonna have to teach you some things, Delwin's lit-tle gir-ul. Gonna teach you how to sing and dance like a real pro."

He never brought up the money again.

3

Debbie was kept in her room. Occasionally, and with increasing regularity as time drudged on, Teddy sold her by the hour to his patrons. And the town did nothing. How could they not know?

Had the coroner not died, things may have turned out differently for Delwin's daughter. And if long ago Israel had a Roman prefect with the balls to stand up to an angry mob hungry for crucifixion, what then?

Under the gender weaponry of one Theodore Eel, Debbie went from being a grieving, brokenhearted teenager to being just plain broken. Devastating in its sadness, this innocent girl who had been loved tremendously by a good man and pitied tremendously by another, now lay splayed and pinned like a dead specimen of nature's blessings—a butterfly killed and mounted under glass so men could enjoy its delicate beauty at their leisure. Years later when Debbie got a computer and joined the internet, she learned her plight was an industry.

Chapter 6

1

THANKS TO TEDDY'S NEWFOUND avocation, he began spending a lot less time at the "Tavern in the dirt" and a lot more at the home of the late Delwin Coomb. Teddy's older, slower, and uglier brother Clyde picked up the slack at the bar and doubled as a guard at Debbie's house with what Teddy dubbed "pussy privileges." A padlock on the door and a few boards nailed to the window frame were all they needed to keep Debbie imprisoned at the top of the stairs. It took a little over a week to thoroughly shatter her what was left of her soul and will, at which point she accepted her fate during the quiet moments, but not always during the disquiet ones. She became pregnant, and Teddy, being the man about shithole town that he was, knew a "doctor" who was willing to solve that problem, as long as he was paid up front with a little quality time with his patient. The man, who had lost his medical license by accepting carnal payment from women who had neither insurance nor cash to pay for his services, terminated Debbie's pregnancy and put her on the pill. He was handsome, clean-cut, and in his forties. He kept a few regular patients, mostly working girls. His large American sedan served as his medical office, with a well-stocked pharmacy in the trunk. The Wilburn police knew about him, but no one ever complained, so they ignored him. On a few occasions, they even passed his number on to poor women who needed *that* kind of medical attention and who could only barter for payment.

Luckily for Debbie, if indeed she could ever be described as such, borderline illiteracy kept Teddy from opening anything but familiar-looking utility bills mailed to the Coomb house, so he was therefore ignorant of his concubine's wealth. He figured that forging any of Delwin's checks would only send the law to the Coomb house. Why risk the steady cash flow from Debbie's growing clientele? He alone answered the few calls that came in, one of which was an inquiry as to why Debbie Coomb had never registered for her junior year of high school. Coincidentally, Teddy picked Florida, Deborah Fairchild's home state, to explain Debbie's whereabouts. *She left for Opa-locka with her boyfriend and his family. They're churchies, so I'm sure you'll get a letter or a postcard or something. I'll send a note off with the rent that you're asking about her. Thanks for calling.*

2

THE EX-DOCTOR WHO ADMINISTERED Debbie's contraceptives in exchange for bodily access pitied her enough to give her a supply of downers for the emotional damage and painkillers for the physical. They served to keep her uncomfortably numb when the torpor of shock was not enough. The first chance she got, Debbie took all the pills at once, hoping to quit the battlefield entirely. But all that did was make her semiconscious for most of a day, during which her plight took on a phantasmagoric quality. When she left the pills in plain sight, any one of her abusers would take them. So she got good at hiding them and lying about having anything other than what they had paid Teddy to take. It was a requirement for making them last. Given she rarely wore clothes and her assailants had full access to her from head to toe, they believed her without fuss. She always saved a few pills for Teddy's morning call, however, because he was the first, and because he was in charge. The drugs helped Debbie suffer through her nightmare, and because of that, the ex-doctor was the closest thing she had to a friend during this time.

She wondered about the coroner quite a bit while in captivity. *Did they kill him? Scare him away? Was he just lying about coming back to check on me? Did he die? Did he forget me?* She eventually settled on this last one after driving the others around for a while. Although she sometimes heard quite the ruckus downstairs, she figured she would have known if the coroner was at the center of it. *Why would he still care? After a few hours back in his family's arms, he probably forgot all about me. Who could blame him? Look at me—look at me now.* This last thought never failed to make her cry. It was a sign of life inside a young woman who was otherwise dead to the world. She would have found it comforting to know that during Coroner Samuel Miles' last minute on Earth, Debbie was the one he worried about most.

3

THOUGH TEDDY TREASURED THE memory of his first assault on Debbie, things had gone downhill from there. Submission just didn't do it for him after consuming and validating the raw fear of an innocent, helpless girl. But that didn't mean he was about to lay off. Hell no. He was in charge, after all, and though the beauty of his pinned butterfly began to fade in his eyes, she was still his possession.

Teddy often used Debbie in the late morning before the tavern opened. Afterward, he would send his brother Clyde in to make sure Debbie and her room were cleaned up enough for business. Clyde was gentler than Teddy could ever possibly be. He understood what was going on. He just wasn't sure how wrong it was, since the whole town seemed to be in on it. Clyde was never one to speak up or question things. Just like Debbie's own future captive, Howard Feck, Clyde Eel pretty much always did what he was told. Along with being slower and gentler than his brother, Clyde's libido ranged from faint to tepid. In the months of Debbie's servitude, he used her only twice, both after being pressured by Teddy. *If ya don't go fuck her now and then, she won't ever respect ya or listen to ya.*

One cold gray afternoon, Clyde was just waking up from his place on the living room couch as Teddy scuttled down the stairs in faded yellow underpants. His chest was blotchy and sweaty. "You'd better get up there Clydey. She's looking like she's gonna throw up or something.

"Did you hurt her?" Clyde asked nonchalantly, as if he were talking about a worn-out toy.

"Nah, I don't think so," Teddy replied, grabbing his pants off Delwin's La-Z-Boy. "I gotta get. Beer truck's coming today, and if I ain't open when it—hey, Clydey, I almost forgot…"

"Forgot what?" Clyde asked as he sat up on the defiantly puffy couch, rubbing his face and resigning himself to the start of another day.

"I forgot to feed her yesterday. In fact, I'm not sure when she ate last. Make sure you feed her good, okay? That may be her problem. I ran her and hadn't fed her. Shit, we don't want her getting sick."

"I'll feed her, Teddy-boy."

"Feed her something good. Fry up some baloney and eggs or something. Don't just give her Twinkies, for Chrissake."

"How about coffee pie? I got biscuits left over from—"

"No damn coffee pie! Jesus, Clyde, you dumbshit. Give her something rib-sticking, okay? I went to the store. Ought to be something in that kitchen for her. We gotta protect our investment. Our racehorse ain't gonna win no races on damn coffee pie and Twinkies. For Chrissake, Clyde, think for once. Least try, you dumbshit."

Clyde didn't get Teddy's analogy. As he saw it, their customers merely demanded a reasonably priced female with a pulse—the rest was gravy.

"How 'bout a TV dinner?" Clyde asked.

"You're thinking. About damn time, too, dumbshit brother o' mine. TV dinner'd be fine. Now get up and check on her. Shit, she could be up there puking right now. If she is, you better clean it up good. Place already stinks. I gotta get. Be a good dumbshit brother and don't let me down."

And then Teddy Eel walked out of the Coomb family home for the very last time.

4

CLYDE WENT UPSTAIRS AND casually walked into Debbie's room. She was naked and uncovered, with one wrist tied to the bed frame—a sign Teddy had been with her. The restraint was merely a prop Teddy insisted on whenever he used her. She was covered in sweat, both hers and Teddy's. Her hairline was black with sweat, and she had little bruises and scratches all over. Her fingernails dug into the palms of her hands. Her knuckles were white. Her toes splayed then relaxed, splayed then relaxed, over and over. Debbie stared at Clyde like a freaked-out lab animal. If Delwin were to walk into the room, he would not recognize this beastie the Eel brothers had whooped out of the flesh of his poor, grieving daughter.

"Hey, Debbie," Clyde sounded like he had just bumped into her at the supermarket. "You okay? Teddy thought maybe you're gonna be sick or something. I'm gonna untie you, but you know the rules. You can't hit me or scratch me, okay? No biting neither. If you do you know what I'm gonna do, right?"

Debbie nodded.

"All right now. Don't fuck with me. I'm suposed to make you breakfast," Clyde said in his casual and agreeable tone. He loosened the thin extension cord that bound her to the bed frame. Debbie lowered her arm and rubbed her wrist against her damp abdomen. She clutched the mattress with her other hand, as if to keep from falling out of bed. She was dizzy from the terrible activity Teddy forced on her while having nothing to eat for over twenty-four hours.

"You don't seem like yourself."

Clyde Eel, lord of the understatement.

Her anger always returned whenever Teddy was in her room. And it caused Debbie to hyper-focus on the one thing worth her attention these days—how to escape from these monsters. How to kill them. "I think I'm going to bleed again," Debbie lied to Clyde.

"Aww, now you know Teddy don't like that." Clyde sounded as if Debbie menstruated on purpose.

"I'm sorry. Can I go get some toilet paper or something? I need to use the bathroom, too."

"Sure, why not?" Clyde had nothing to fear since every window Debbie could access was nailed shut, and Delwin's room had been padlocked to keep Debbie and the customers out.

"I'm supposed to make you breakfast." It was an inch past noon. "You want a TV dinner? We got Hungry Man."

Debbie had had more than enough hungry men, thank you. "Can I have eggs?" she asked, feeling out Clyde's acquiescence.

"Aww, eggs takes too long. I don't want to wash a frying pan and—"

"Clyde?"

"What?"

"Today—today's my birthday," Debbie said, then looked at the floor.

"It is?"

It wasn't. Debbie had no idea what day of the week it was, let alone the date.

She nodded briskly and Clyde gave in. "All right, I'll make you eggs, since it is your birthday and all."

"Thank you, Clyde." She tried to sound relaxed despite the lingering anger over Teddy's recent visit and anxiety over the lies she was feeding Clyde. She desperately wanted to sound calm lest she scare him off. "You've always been nice to me. Thank you."

"It's okay." With a brother like Teddy, Clyde was not used to compliments.

"Clyde?" Debbie sat upright in her bed and held the filthy top sheet against her naked sweaty body.

"What?"

"Do you think that since it's my birthday and all, I can eat downstairs in the kitchen?"

"Huh?"

"Can I eat in the kitchen with you?" Debbie resumed. "I'll be good. Teddy don't ever let me leave my room except to go to the bathroom, and well, being my birthday, I thought maybe…maybe I could eat with you at the kitchen table like a regular person."

Clyde slowly mulled over the idea. It was against Teddy's rules to let her out of the bedroom except for her toilet. But it was her birthday, and she hadn't given him any trouble since the early days of her imprisonment.

Like a regular person.

"I can even do the cooking. I remember how to cook eggs. I cook eggs really good." Debbie hoped this would close the deal.

"All right, I guess so. Just don't give me no trouble, okay? You know what happens when you start giving trouble."

"I promise," Debbie said, trying to contain her relief. A glimmer of hope entered her heart. As if the escape she constantly fantasized about could actually happen.

"All right, go do your business in the can, and I'll get the downstairs locked up. Teddy would kill me if you took off on him, and you know how Teddy can be."

Yes, unfortunately Debbie knew all too well how Teddy could be.

Clyde watched Debbie walk to the bathroom before he headed downstairs. Teddy had removed the doorknob from the bathroom door. Debbie pushed it closed and it creaked back open a few inches.

She relieved herself and then gave herself a quick cleanup. She wanted a thorough washing, but was afraid Clyde would change his mind if she were out of sight for too long. She darted back to her bedroom. Returning to her room always gave her a sense of how bad it smelled. She went to her bed and picked up her flattened pillow in its filthy pillowcase. Somewhere in the pillow was a small hole. Debbie rooted for it, found it, and stuck a finger inside. She fished for the pills she had stashed for this occasion while squeezing the outside of the pillow with her other hand. She pulled out nine pills, a combination of painkillers and sedatives.

Naked, she walked over to her dresser. She held the pills in her hand as if they were precious and fragile. Her possessions atop the dresser had long ago been usurped and replaced with empty beer cans, cigarette butts, and a few condom wrappers left by the more cautious violators. Her drawers had been cleaned out except for the topmost, which held a few sleazy pieces of lingerie some men would make her wear and the summer dress she was wearing when Teddy first introduced her to hell. She refused to wear any of those pieces. She looked around, saw a very large men's shirt in one corner, and put it on. It went halfway to her knees. She buttoned it, tucked the pills into the front pocket, and walked downstairs.

Clyde stood waiting near the bottom of the stairs. "Hey, you got dressed," he said with mild surprise.

"Is that okay?" Debbie asked. She stared at the floor for fear of seeing what they had done to her father's house. At least she was dressed and out of her room.

"Sure, suit yourself. I just ain't hardly seen you with clothes on before. Almost didn't recognize you," Clyde said.

Debbie didn't know what to say to that.

"Come on, get cooking. If you tell Teddy I let you down here, I'm gonna punch you till you puke."

Debbie's amped nerves chipped away at her hope. "I won't tell, I promise." She walked toward the kitchen. It felt weird—familiar and yet forbidden at the same time.

She entered Delwin's now filthy kitchen with Clyde following lazily behind. The last time she saw it, it was nearly spotless. Now every surface was covered in beer and soda cans, garbage, abandoned dirty dishes, and an archive of takeout containers and wrappers. "I'll wash a pan. What should we have with our eggs?"

"I think there's some baloney in the fridge, if you want to fry that," Clyde said in his predictably docile tone. He sat down at the kitchen table. "Don't forget toast."

Dirty pots, pans, and plates stacked higher than the faucet filled the sink. It made washing a single frying pan difficult. She managed to rinse one overly used iron skillet that she remembered as her dad's favorite piece. She tried to push those memories away and began to think that she would fail, that her emotions would come screeching out, and Clyde would end up punching her in the gut until she couldn't breathe. She repeatedly bit her lip to quell the emotional pain brewing within.

Debbie put the grease-coated skillet on the stovetop and went to the fridge, just like the old days. The beer was on the wrong shelf, and there were moldy leftovers in containers she didn't recognize. A small stack of poorly wrapped baloney and an unopened package of individually wrapped American cheese sat in front of a few refrigerated relics left by Delwin and the coroner. Debbie grabbed the cheese, the baloney, and a carton of eggs, then set them on the funk-covered cutting board next to the stove. She began cooking her captor breakfast. She didn't hate Clyde nearly as much as she hated Teddy and all the others who came to use her. But still she hated him. She hated him for his complicity, for being a foot soldier in Teddy's army of rape. She turned to look at him sitting at the kitchen table. He paid no attention to her, just sat there staring straight ahead like a robot with rundown batteries. Another point in Debbie's favor.

After striking out on finding a clean plate in the cupboard, she went back to the sink and quickly found two medium dirty dishes and a slightly melted spatula. She scrubbed them moderately clean and set them next to the stove. Then she dropped two stale pieces of white bread in the old family toaster. She turned her back toward Clyde, reached into a pocket, and pulled out what she hoped were the keys to her freedom in the form of nine little pills. Four were tablets that would have to be crushed. She placed them on the cutting board, put one thin plate on top of them, then quietly pushed down hard. She heard a small snap and glanced guiltily toward Clyde. He remained sitting at the table staring at nothing in particular. She lifted up the plate and looked at the pile. One pill had broken in two and the others were stubbornly intact. That wasn't good enough. How could she break them into small enough pieces without stupid Clyde catching on? She looked around feeling trapped by the situation. Then she remembered the fan above the stove. She turned it on, hoping it would drown out the sound of her crushing the pills. The old greasy fan started noisily. Debbie pushed and turned the plate over the pills with considerable force, feeling them crumble into what she hoped were small enough pieces.

"Why the noise?" Clyde called, spooking Debbie. She abruptly turned to him.

"It's the fan. I didn't want it to get smoky in here." Debbie sounded like a lying child.

Clyde looked at her for a few long seconds. The toaster popped its contents and Debbie jumped. He cocked his head. "You feel okay?"

"Just not used to being down here," Debbie answered.

"Maybe you should go back—"

"I'll be all right. I just need some food in me, and I'll be better, I promise."

"You sure? You seem sorta—"

"Breakfast is almost done," she blurted. "I'll go back up after I eat, I promise." She turned back to the stove. Clyde called her name again. "Debbie?"

Panic jumped up her throat. *Please let me stay. Please—please let me stay down here.* "Yes?"

"Toast is done."

Swallowing the panic back down again, Debbie watched him return to dull gazing. She double-timed her efforts to get the drugs mixed into Clyde's food. The pills were reduced to grains and gravelly white bits. It would have to do. Debbie scooped some eggs onto her plate and then dabbed up the grains with her finger and sprinkled them into the remaining mixture in the skillet.

Next, she grabbed the capsules from the shirt pocket and speedily opened them above the frying pan. She watched the narcotic dust fall into Clyde's breakfast. Glancing furtively at Clyde, Debbie stirred his eggs, blending in the cocktail of downers and opioids. She added a couple more slices of cheese to help bury any pharmaceutical taste, then poured the mixture onto Clyde's plate. She turned off the fan and delivered breakfast to the table. It was easy to tell which was which since Clyde had twice as much food on his plate and Debbie's was slightly underdone.

"Don't forget the toast," Clyde offered.

Debbie hadn't. She picked up the toast with one bare hand and grabbed a tub of margarine from the fridge with the other. She was mildly afraid that while her back was turned, Clyde would pull a switcheroo with the plates—as if he was hip to Debbie's plan. She needn't have worried. Clyde had tucked into the meal before she had even sat down.

Watching him cautiously, she joined him and forced herself to eat.

"Too much cheese," Clyde critiqued.

"Sorry."

"Still good, though," he said with his mouth full and open. "Better than I would have done."

"Thank you," Debbie said. She ought to be famished but anxiety over her desperate grasp toward freedom had destroyed her appetite. She hoped she was going to need her strength, so she quietly made herself eat everything on her plate, which wasn't much to begin with. She took her time as Clyde happily shoveled the food and drugs into his wide mouth. "Can I clean up the dishes?" Debbie asked, after eating the last little morsel off her plate.

"I guess so. Just don't make it too nice. I don't want Teddy thinking I let you down here."

Debbie took the breakfast dishes to the overloaded sink and didn't know where to begin. She set the dishes down and opened the dishwasher, releasing a foul, organic stench. It was packed full of dirty dishes caked with mold.

"It don't work—the dishwasher," Clyde said as he sucked bits of egg, baloney, and narcotics from between his teeth. He looked at the clock. "It's later than I thought, Debbie. You better get back upstairs. Probably gonna get business soon, and I don't want anybody seeing you down here."

Debbie was visibly crushed.

"Come, on, now. I let you down here for breakfast. That ought to be enough."

Enough for whom?

"I'll leave your door unlocked if you stay in your bed," Clyde offered magnanimously. This was not much of a consolation since they rarely locked it anyway.

Not wanting to push her luck, Debbie surrendered yet again and went back upstairs to her room. She crawled onto her filthy bed and pulled her knees to her chest. Rocking back and forth, she anxiously awaited to see if her plan was going to work. Nearly an hour later, hope faded and she gave in to sleep.

5

DEBBIE FELT LIKE SHE had just nodded off when a faint knock on the front door woke her. *Shit. This could ruin everything.* There was a second knock, then a third, then the sound of someone trying a locked door followed by a muffled shout. Then silence. Debbie's throat tightened.

Had it worked? Had it actually worked? It was too good to be true. *Clyde's just probably in the bathroom,* she told herself. She waited out the silence to make sure the visitors were indeed gone before she got out of bed and tiptoed to the hallway. The lights were off downstairs and yet Debbie could see between the boards over her window that it was dark gray dusk outside.

"Clyde?" The word hung in silence.

Please, God, let it work.

"Clyde?" she said a little bit louder.

Silence.

Debbie went to the top of the stairs and looked down into darkness. She thought she heard something. It was a wet click followed by a soft whistle. It had a consistent rhythm. She had never heard it before but was almost damn sure it was the sound of one passed out Eel. Debbie suddenly felt giddy with the promise of escape.

"Clyde?"

Click, pause, *whistle* was the only reply.

She flipped the light switch at the top of the stairs and darkness fled.

Confidence crept skittishly back into her heart. Debbie tiptoed downstairs. *Click*, pause, *whistle* was still the only sound she could hear besides her own thunderous heartbeat.

Clyde sat with his head and upper torso slumped over one end of the puffy couch. Debbie walked around him, keeping out of snatching range in case he suddenly came to life. She watched his slack face to see if his eyes would open.

Click, pause, *whistle.*

He was south of comatose but far north of deep slumber.

Debbie stared at him. She stared at his gentle, stupid, complicit face. She saw Teddy in coitus in that face, and somewhere inside her, seeds of rage sprouted in bitter soil. She looked at his rubbery parted lips and saw every mouth that had been on her during the past months—every stinking mouth, vicious with criminal hunger—and the seedlings of a victim's rage grew to saplings. She looked Clyde up and down from head to toe and saw in him every man who had used the wicked destruction of her innocence, her spirit, her *life* for their amusement. And in her spoilt heart the saplings of rage grew into a dense forest shaking from the howling winds of retribution. She wanted to leap on top of him like a big wild cat and tear him into hamburger. But the promise of liberation influenced her actions—barely, but enough.

With a severe sense of purpose, she calmly but steadfastly walked into the kitchen. After a brief metallic rattle, Debbie returned with the large black iron skillet she had used to cook Clyde's last meal. She walked to the side of the couch where Clyde appeared to offer his head in sacrifice. His posture made him look utterly ridiculous. Debbie held the skillet low and at arm's length. Grease dripped from its lowest point onto the carpet. She set her hate to boil. With both hands on the handle, she raised the iron pan as high as she could. Her eyes widened, her mouth opened. Taking a full breath of air tinged with Clyde's BO, Debbie exhaled a scream and brought the skillet straight down on to the crown of Clyde's greasy head. She gave it everything she had. All the defensive energy that had been kept tightly coiled within her and that she had been unable to summon while being assaulted suddenly released itself in one swing, one scream. The impact cracked Clyde's skull clean open. It sounded like a big, clapperless bell falling on rotted wood. The blow stung her hands. Finally, a pain she could appreciate. Debbie raised the skillet high above her head a second time. She screamed again and thrust the iron pan down so hard that her feet left the ground. She heard a bright "crick" as Clyde's neck broke. Again, Debbie savored the sting from the skillet's reverberating handle. She could tell by how Clyde's head now hung at an unnatural angle over the side of the couch that she had indeed broken his neck. One more swing and it would probably fall right off like an overripe persimmon from its tree. The house returned to silence. No more *click*, pause, *whistle*. Clyde Eel was now in need of a coroner. Debbie was almost free.

Almost.

She returned the well-seasoned murder weapon to the stove, went down the short hall past the fridge, and into her father's downstairs bathroom. The same bathroom where, years later, Howard would politely await his fate. She wanted a towel but the closet was bare. Debbie went to the back porch and fished a couple of dirty towels out of a pile of filthy laundry. She returned to Clyde's body and threw the towels over it without fanfare. It was too early to celebrate. She returned to the back porch to search for the tools required to complete her task. Sadly but not surprisingly, the place had been looted. She dug through the mess, hoping to find the twenty-two caliber rifle her dad used for shooting skunks and other trespassing varmints.

It was gone.

She looked around for other lethal weapons but came up empty. Then, behind sheets of dusty spider webs, she saw a five-gallon can of gasoline sitting against the wall. She put her hand through the sticky webs, grabbed the can's handle and shook, the fuel sloshing around inside. Not a lot, but hopefully enough. It bumped heavily against her leg as she walked into the kitchen, but not so heavy as to dissuade her. She set the can down and rooted around until she found matches and a few kitchen rags. After a few seconds of deliberation, Debbie darted down the hall and up the stairs to her father's room, hoping she could find some shoes to put on and maybe even a pair of jeans.

"Shit," Debbie said aloud. In the excitement, she had forgotten that the Eel brothers had padlocked Delwin's bedroom. Hearing her voice in the quiet reminded her that it was now okay to speak aloud whenever she wanted. It felt weird but good.

At some point, Clyde was supposed to lock her in her room while he went and relieved Teddy at the tavern. She hauled ass back downstairs, running against the clock. She wondered how hard it would be to take the shoes off a dead guy, and found that Clyde wasn't wearing any—just a pair of holey socks. She looked around the filthy garbage-strewn living room until she found his work boots lying next to her father's La-Z-Boy. Intentionally avoiding Daddy's chair, she sat on the couch and put them on. "Thanks for the boots, asshole," Debbie said to the dead man one cushion over.

It felt good to say that aloud.

And despite who they'd belonged to and how poorly they fit, it felt even better putting them on. She tried to remember the last time she had worn shoes and figured it was back when she had been out with the coroner.

Debbie found Clyde's jacket on the floor by the couch. She grabbed it and returned to the kitchen. She decided she might as well put the jacket on now to get used to its funk. It went almost to her knees and the sleeves ended inches past her fingertips. She quickly folded the sleeves back until her hands were mostly exposed. She grabbed the matches and rags and stuffed them into the jacket pockets where she felt something cold and metallic.

A set of keys.

Instead walking down the dark highway carrying a heavy gas can, passing by the spot where she had found her father's corpse, she was going to drive. The tavern was about a mile away, and Debbie had had some driving experience, albeit as a child on her daddy's lap on straight country roads leading nowhere. Without hesitation, Debbie grabbed the gas can and headed out the back door. Lugging the gas can she loped down the back steps and then suddenly fell to her knees.

Whatever hit her was cold and sharp. She felt it not just on her face but down her throat and in her lungs. She had been trapped for so long in that bedroom made fetid by filthy linen, cigarette butts, junk food detritus, half-empty beer cans, sweat, and rape that breathing the clean cool air of the outside had stunned her deeply. The fresh air and open space soothed her, renewed her strength as she knelt in the empty and unkempt backyard. Tears fell cold on her cheeks beneath the vast, dark sky. There were no stars, but she made a wish anyway. Then she rose, committed to her quest.

She crept around to the front of the house. The only car parked in the drive was a white-and-gray primered van. Delwin's pickup had been sold by Teddy the week he had moved in. Debbie opened the driver's door, heaved the gas can over the seat, and climbed in. She thought about just driving away—somewhere— anywhere. *But this was Daddy's house, dammit.* On the inside, it had become something else. But from the outside, it looked like the happy home of her childhood. She felt it more than she could see it in the dark. And she knew that this was where she belonged—once she got rid of the infestation. Debbie shut the van door.

She went through a few keys until she found one that entered the ignition easily. She turned the key and nothing happened. She turned it again with the same result. "Shit," she said aloud, only this time it didn't feel good. *Was it a dead battery? Did the van even run?* It must, since Clyde drove to Teddy's Tavern and back every damned day, and there were no other cars on the property. She kept trying and failing. *Start, damn you. Start, you stupid thing.* She shook her head, stomped Clyde's big boots, and turned the key harder. She was about to give up when one boot accidentally stomped the brake pedal and the starter turned. A few whines later, the engine roared to life.

Thank you, thank you, Go-. I mean, thank you, Daddy.

Now she just had to figure out how to back out and turn around. She quickly realized that the easiest and quickest thing to do by far was to drive over the rose bed and turn around on the wide, neglected front lawn. She found the headlight switch and put the automatic transmission (another blessing) into D. She quickly lifted her foot off the brake and the van immediately moved forward—too fast. She hit the brake hard, causing the van and everything in it to lurch forward with a loud rattle. Next, she struggled with the steering wheel until the front wheels turned right. She eased her foot off the brake this time, and the van moved at a soft angle. She turned the steering wheel again and learned it turned easier if the van was moving. The tires easily absorbed the rose planter's red-scalloped edging as she drove over a couple hybrid teas and onto the grass. Debbie continued turning the steering wheel until she had maneuvered the van back onto the driveway. She pulled to the highway and stopped awkwardly. She looked to her left. There were no headlights in that direction, so Debbie turned right and hit the road hard, causing the gas can to fall over onto its side. Debbie's lucky streak continued as the lid held tight and gas did not spill. She headed to Teddy's Tavern with a smile born of determination, liberation, and revenge. A smile no living man had ever seen.

Chapter 7

1

PER USUAL, WILBURN'S MAIN Street was mostly abandoned—a couple lazily parked pickups one of the few signs of life. Debbie stopped the van well before the tavern, then pulled half-assed toward the sidewalk. She looked up the street. Its emptiness felt good, the solitude comfortable. It allowed her to focus on her mission. As she wondered how best to burn down Teddy's Tavern without any of the occupants escaping, a loud, deep pop punctured the silence without warning. Debbie jumped out of her seat for a brief moment, during which time her foot left the brake pedal and the van began moving. She had to look down to find the pedal before jumping on it with one of Clyde's big boots. Once again, the van lurched to a stop. The loud pops kept coming. Instead of ducking for cover, Debbie froze, panicking in earnest as the sound of successive, reverberating bangs filled the street. She looked down the street and saw, silhouetted by a Confederate flag glowing against the neon beer light in the one window of Teddy's Tavern, a man straddling a big motorcycle—the source of the outburst. She watched him rev the bike, making the thunder grow, then slow until it exploded into backfire. Apparently satisfied to have shaken the dust off the town's rafters, the man rode away. Away from Teddy's. Away from Debbie. He was lucky.

She put the van into park and tried to calm down. The returning quiet helped. In the dark, she could just make out Teddy's name hand-painted on the plywood sign nailed to the top of the building. She started to get angry and began rocking back and forth in her seat. It was good. Probably the best feeling she could experience at this moment. She needed anger right now as much as she needed anything, and she knew it.

In a single move and with both hands, Debbie hoisted the gas can onto the wide dashboard. It lay on its side, half hanging over the engine housing. She tried to unscrew the lid but it wanted nothing to do with being opened. "Righty-tighty, lefty-loosey," she reminded herself aloud as she tried the cap again. It wouldn't budge. She sat there looking at it. In her mind's eye, she saw a hundred random flashes of so many bad things done to her for Teddy's amusement and profit. Debbie's anger grew to an infestation. The forest was shaking again—the winds of retribution and the scent of freedom had returned. And with it came the severe sense of purpose and calm that had guided her in the killing of Clyde Eel. Using both hands, she wrestled with the gas can lid. The lid turned. Debbie loosened it until gas dribbled down the engine housing and spread onto the floor. *Fine, spill all you want, just don't catch fire until I'm ready.*

The smell of gasoline filled the van and reminded her of Delwin. She hadn't realized she missed that smell until just then. She could have indulged in that scent-born memory for many minutes but knew it could prove devastating. She shook it off.

Debbie backed the van down the street until she had put a good hundred yards between it and Teddy's Tavern. Suddenly inspired, she hopped out of the van, went around, and opened its two back doors. She got back in and fastened her seat belt.

Debbie was feeling slightly more positive about living, and if she was going to die, she didn't want it to be alongside her abusers. Satisfied with the escape route she had given herself, she moved the van's shifter back to D.

Debbie white-knuckled the wide steering wheel and then stomped on the accelerator. The van lunged forward. She felt her body pushing back into the seat from the force of the acceleration. She would remember that feeling for years. She saw the tavern's dingy exterior zoom closer—first dull and safely distant, then dangerously close and harshly lit by headlights.

The grimy couch where Debbie had expected to find her daddy that terrible morning flashed into view before disappearing beneath the windshield. The door to Teddy's Tavern, red and blazing from the headlights, rushed toward her. She noticed that the paint had peeled away around its handle. The van bounced violently over the curb, causing her teeth to smack together—she barely escaped biting off a piece of her tongue. Debbie closed her eyes just before impact. The van launched into the building with the noise and violence of a compressed hurricane. The seatbelt choked her momentarily. The steering wheel gnawed at her gut as she struggled to hold it. Later, her fingers would be stiff and sore when she exercised them—a pleasing reminder of her grip on vengeance.

The van jerked up and down, left and right, while still perpetually lunging forward—wrenching its way into the center of the tavern. The structure, poorly built and poorly maintained, crumbled and caved around the vehicle. Debbie's body tensed and flinched from the violent clamor of the collapsing building. The van's front end now tilted awkwardly on the wreckage it had just created. Forward progress had finally been halted by a logjam of plywood, two-by-fours, tables, chairs, barstools, and bodies. The vehicle shook in protest—noises foreign and strident filled the air all around Debbie—the rumble and shriek of a stuck vehicle straining to accommodate a floored accelerator; a cacophony of wood and glass, bottles and cans, carpet and paper, flesh and bones tearing to pieces under the hot, oily destruction of a Debbie's missile. Underneath it all, she heard country music coming from a tinny jukebox speaker.

Debbie was unable to take her foot off the gas pedal. With the engine at full throttle, the van, unable to move forward, fishtailed. Its rear tires screamed and smoked in vain. A man trapped underneath the vehicle tried to avoid being burnt by the engine's belly. Debbie heard him scream and thump as he was mauled to death by a drivetrain in overdrive. Above the squealing tires and racing motor, she heard more screams, the sound of glass rain, and the dry cough of splintering and falling wood. She opened her eyes and looked around Teddy's Tavern, a place her dad knew as well as anyone. Only it didn't always look like this, she imagined. The place glowed eerily red, thanks to the tavern's Confederate flag now clinging to one shining headlight. Debbie saw galaxies of dust particles, prisms of mayhem, and a kaleidoscope of splintered lumber—partly painted dull blue, partly raw and unfinished. Headlights reflected off pockets of broken glass and spotlighted two men whose postures indicated that their demise was imminent and excruciating. Beer sprayed out from somewhere to her left, raining gold liquid and white suds onto the windshield. She could smell burning tires, beer, gasoline, and a cool, stale, cigarette smoke-tinged odor that reminded her of her father and his jacket. Debbie heard screams and cussing rising in pitch, the latter sounding familiar.

Still, somewhere in the background, a Southern voice twanged through the juke:

You're more than a honkytonk angel to me
In bed and in my truck

When I'm dancin'

Or outta luck

You're more than a honkytonk angel to me

She had forgotten all about the gas can until Teddy Eel's yelling cut through the chaos. "CLYYYYDE! WHAT IN THE HOLY FUCK OF MARY AND JOSEPH HAPPENED, YOU SONOFABITCH?!" Teddy's voice grew closer as he navigated through the rubble and toward the van, apparently unscathed. "Fuckin' CLYDE! You fuckin' dumbshit! SHIT! You fucked us all up a good one now you fuckin' dumb—"

Upon recognizing his concubine behind the wheel of his brother's van in the middle of his bar, Teddy shut the hell up, though his mouth remained open. He and Debbie locked eyes for several long seconds during which much was conveyed. She gave Teddy a sick smile, then quickly fumbled loose the seatbelt and hopped into the van's cargo area. Teddy pushed his way through the tangle of two-by-fours and wooden shards that used to be his tavern.

Crouching in the middle of the van, galvanized by violent hatred, Debbie stared Teddy down. She stared at him as he made it to the driver's side door and tried to open it. He wanted to crawl inside and kill her—more than anything in the world—but the wreckage kept the door from opening more than a few inches. Being slight of build and greasy as a carp, he nearly succeeded in squeezing himself through the narrow opening. Stuck halfway in, he cussed and spat and hurt himself trying to get to Debbie who was just a few agonizing inches out of reach. Debbie half laughed and half cried wildly as she watched Teddy struggle maddeningly to free himself, furious to reach her. Keeping her eyes on a snarling Teddy Eel, Debbie backed toward the van's rear doors on all fours. The gasoline puddle at the base of the engine housing had spread into a narrow rivulet running down the center of the cargo area. Debbie stepped out of the van, reached into Clyde's jacket pocket and pulled out the book of matches. She lit the entire book and tossed them onto the thin rill of gas. Fire sped toward Teddy. In a single *Fwuh*, her captor's face disappeared behind curtains of flames. Debbie ran across the street, listening intently to the screams of wounded, trapped, and dying patrons above which rose a shriek of epithets from Teddy's foul mouth. Before Debbie could reach the opposite sidewalk, the gas can exploded. A smoky fireball bloomed out of the van's rear doors accompanied by a hot blast of air that shoved Debbie to the ground as if she had been bounced from hell by the devil himself. Teddy's profane screams turned to screams for help and then pure screams of pure agony. Debbie stood and turned to survey her accomplishment. Smoke from the explosion cleared to reveal a snapping, roaring fire that soon drowned out any screams at all. Another, bigger explosion startled her into weeping and shaking. The experience of a grieving daughter, trapped, tortured, and enslaved, caught up with her in an instant—igniting a fiery explosion of its own inside her withering heart.

Once again, Delwin's daughter was a party to death. Any ache from these deaths, however, was not Debbie's to bear. For Debbie it was enough just trying to accept the fact that the unbelievable dream of liberation and revenge had come true this very instant. She could no longer be all the things Teddy told her she was. She no longer had to do all those terrible things. She could go back to being Debbie Coomb, daughter of Delwin Coomb.

Or so she thought.

2

TEDDY'S TAVERN BURNT DOWN to the ground in record time. Amid the ruins were the ashes, bone fragments, and teeth of

Teddy Eel and seven patrons. Five of the seven had committed crimes against Debbie. It was only a matter of time before Teddy would have introduced the other two to what he jokingly referred to as the town pump. From across the street, Debbie watched the fire, sheltered in darkness provided by an awning in front of Cliff's Bike Shop. The smoldering hull of Clyde's old Dodge van—the first vehicle she had ever fully driven—remained surrounded by flames and smoke like a skull in a burning helmet. Both trucks from the Wilburn Volunteer Fire Department showed up and focused entirely on saving the buildings on either side. Not a single soul noticed Debbie standing in the shadows across the street, and some had been to her room. She had stopped crying and now leaned against the bicycle shop window, struck how the firemen let the tavern burn while saving all around it. She still couldn't believe what had happened. The further she looked back in time the more surreal and unbelievable it all seemed.

Once upon a time, she had been an innocent girl named Debbie Coomb—raised by a doting and devoted father named Delwin. Then he died and she was alone.

And then the coroner came and helped her. He was wonderful. And then he abandoned her and she was alone.

And then Teddy came with his violence and cruelty and army of rape and...and...

And *they killed me*, she thought, finally. That was the closest she would ever get to giving it a name worthy of the pain. *They killed me and I was alone with the pain of dying. But not the killing. They killed me and kept my dead heart beating so they could come back and kill me all over again and again.*

And again.

The killings were fast and hard and suffocating and wet. But the dying was slow—agonizingly so and brutally painful and lonely. The physical wounds had grown numb, but her heart and her soul acutely felt every attack. And she would never forget. Although there would be times when she wished she could.

Watching Teddy's Tavern burn to the ground was profoundly therapeutic. The heat, the roar, the smell—there was no doubt in Debbie's mind that she had done the right thing. Watching the fire department letting it cook to ruins confirmed it. But as the flames died down, so did Debbie's fever of liberation and revenge. That old bully fear began inching over her again like a creeping shadow. She needed to go home, but then what? She had a dead body waiting for her and a front door that let men in to try their hand at killing her for a while. What the hell was she going to do about that? She had nothing with her except the clothes on her back and the useless crap in Clyde's jacket pockets. Still, she had a growing feeling that she needed to leave.

"Excuse me." An old fireman in full turnouts now stood before her. He seemed to come from nowhere. She looked at him for a long moment, and then looked down. The visor of his helmet cast a shadow over his face leaving only his mouth and square jaw visible.

"Did you see—" Upon recognizing whom he was addressing, the fireman stopped. *Couldn't be, no way,* he tried to tell himself as he stared at Debbie from the shadow of his helmet. But those eyes—*that girl with the faraway eyes*—he used to sing to himself up and down the stairs that lead to her room. Those eyes had to be her eyes. But the rest didn't look right. She was completely out of context, being dressed in a man's shirt, jacket, and boots, and standing across the street from a structure fire.

Debbie recognized him as well.

The fireman looked at her. She wanted to be invisible. "Was that you?" he asked, jerking his head toward the dying fire behind him.

Debbie shook her head no and gazed at Clyde's enormous boots. The fireman sighed audibly. He was considered a good guy all the way around by friends, family, and fellow firefighters. He never thought he was hurting anybody by paying to plunge into the inviting purse of a working girl. He'd been with a dozen hookers in his lifetime, and they were all the same in his eyes—including Debbie. Now, seeing the girl with the faraway eyes dressed and at his job brought the weight of the crime home to him.

"How did you get here?" he asked softly, like a social worker addressing a skittish runaway.

Debbie didn't reply.

"Do you know—do you recognize me?"

Debbie nodded and then hung her head once more.

The fireman stared at her.

"No more," she said, shaking her hanging head. "No more."

"I see that."

"Everybody—tell them. Tell them no more. Ever."

"I understand...I'll do what I can. You know I never meant to hurt you or nothing...It was just...I don't know if I can explain it...I guess you'd—"

Debbie shook her head, silencing the fireman's confession. It was bad enough to be at the center of his sin. She shouldn't have to provide absolution, too.

The fireman looked Debbie up and down and noticed she was scratched up and battered-looking. "You're pretty banged up. You should be seen to."

Debbie was oblivious to her injuries until the fireman had pointed them out. It was hard to tell which were from her plight and which were from her liberation.

"No." There was power behind that word and the fireman felt it.

"You need to get out of here, then," said the fireman. "Where you got to go?"

"Home."

"Is it safe there?"

Debbie shrugged her shoulders. She wasn't sure what was waiting there for her other than Teddy's dead brother.

"How you going to get there?"

"Walk."

The fireman reached inside his turncoat and pulled out a sooty, yellow flashlight. He handed it to Debbie butt-end first. She took the flashlight and stuck it deep into Clyde's jacket pocket. "Walk on the left side of the street so you can see oncoming traffic," advised the fireman. "Don't be obvious. And be careful."

Debbie didn't respond.

"What are you going to do if you got..." the fireman paused, "...people waiting for you back home?"

Debbie thought about this in front of him, still looking at the ground between Clyde's boots. She shrugged.

"I'll drive by as soon as I can. If I see any—company, I'll drive them off. I promise. People will get wind of what happened here soon enough—they'll understand it's over, believe me. You be careful now." He expected Debbie to acknowledge what he had said, but she just turned and started walking home.

"I hope you'll forgive me," he called. "I never meant any harm," he added, though mostly for his own ears. The fireman watched Debbie go, wanting to do more to assuage his guilt, but afraid he would only make it worse.

Chapter 8

1

WALKING ALONG THE HIGHWAY and close to home, Debbie spotted two pickups in the driveway. She turned off the flashlight and crossed to the far side of the road before cautiously continuing on. This part of the highway had no streetlamps. The moon was nowhere to be found. She was in near-complete darkness. As she got a little closer, she could just make out, standing between the trucks, three dark figures with three cigarette cherries hovering around them like slow fireflies. They spoke in hushed tones broken by loud laughter from one. Sound carries well in darkness. Clyde's boots made it difficult to walk quickly and quietly, but Debbie did her best. She hugged the line of knee-high weeds on the shoulder and was prepared to drop and hide in them if need be. The weeds dipped down into a muddy ditch just like the one her father had died in on the other side of the road. She had a flash of fear that if she fell in the ditch, she would die, too. She made it past her home, then crossed back over the highway and disappeared behind a scrubby hedgerow of oleander and laurel that marked one boundary of the Coomb property. She was fully prepared to spend the night there if she had to. Once she was far enough down the hedgerow to where she could see both the back of her home and the three men, she crawled into the hedge, knelt among the branches, and waited.

2

As Debbie spied on the scene, she was startled by a distant, familiar noise—the sound of the back screen door winding open and swinging shut. She looked and saw someone running from the back corner of the house, down the side, and around to the front where the figures stood smoking in the dark. Debbie watched, frozen. The quiet voices suddenly took on a panicked cadence. She made out the words, *shit, no fuckin' way*, and *sonofabitch* mixed liberally into the hurried conversation. She watched the three cigarette cherries dive independently to the ground followed by the group of men jumping into their trucks. They wasted no time driving away from the house and toward Teddy's Tavern where yet another surprise awaited them. Once their tail lights were the size of sunflower seeds, Debbie crawled out of the hedge and fled across the lawn and into the house. She closed the back door behind her and then leaned against it trying to catch her breath. The running had not winded her, but the fear had. She locked the back door and tried it twice, making sure it was indeed secure. The kitchen and hall lights were on just as she had left them. These, along with the light at the top of the stairs, filled the living room with shadows. She lit the flashlight, entered the shadowy room, and saw Clyde, still dead and still slumped over one end of the couch. The towel covering his head had been removed. Clyde's face remained hidden in shadow. That was just fine. Debbie never wanted to see it again. She scurried to the front door, making a wide berth around old Dead and Ugly.

The front door was still locked. She turned off the porch light and stopped herself from turning on the living room lights. While the brightness would make the dead body on her couch seem less creepy, it would also reveal her presence to the outside.

She didn't want to face Clyde. Yet she couldn't resist shining the flashlight on him. He didn't look too bad—for a dead guy. He didn't look too good, either. His head was flopped over the couch arm, making him look like a giant, well-loved ragdoll refusing to sit up. Drying blood had matted the back of his hair. It looked like an overripe plum had been squished into his scalp. His mouth hung open, and half an inch of tongue had lolled out. His eyes were open slits and his nostrils had dark rings around them. Blood must have found a way out through his nose. She looked at the rug below him. There was a small, perfectly round dark spot directly below his face. Now that Debbie had taken all this in, she found it hard to look away. After a few long seconds staring at a dead man, her first (but not last) murder victim, her co-kidnapper and rapist, she crept upstairs, staring all the while at the corpse on her couch. She returned a moment later with the smelly, stained sheet she had been forced to live on during her days in captivity. She snapped it up over Clyde's body. As it slowly billowed down, she guided it over him. *Lights out, asshole.*

Flashlight in hand, Debbie walked to the kitchen and retrieved the skillet she had used so effectively on Clyde's numb skull. Before heading back upstairs, she checked the locks again and turned off the remaining downstairs lights. She hoped it would let it be known that Debbie Coomb, daughter of Delwin, would be used no more. Business was officially closed—for good.

With the fireman's flashlight in one hand, and the skillet in the other, she went to her father's padlocked bedroom door. With the same force she had used on Clyde, Debbie tried to murder the hasp and lock with the skillet. The impact sent another shockwave deep into her palms and past her wrists. It did nothing to the lock. Iron on steel was much harder than iron on Eel, and now Debbie knew the difference. *How many people could say that?* she wondered. She raised the skillet high above her head and swung it down a second time. She managed to take a small chunk out of the doorjamb, but that was it.

The hook from which the lock hung was far too snug against the jamb to properly swipe at with a frying pan. But the hinged part of the hasp was far from flush. After a brief study of the obstacle, Debbie shoved the skillet's iron handle as far as it would go into the narrow opening between the hasp and the doorjamb. It was a tight fit. She then managed to get fingers from both hands between the lip of the pan and the door so she could try to pry the hasp loose. Not giving a damn about her knuckles scraping painfully against the door, Debbie pulled and grunted and begged for the hasp to come free. There were probably a half dozen more suitable makeshift crowbars in the house, but she really didn't want to head back downstairs unless absolutely necessary. Besides, the skillet had served her well in dispatching Clyde, and was fast becoming her weapon of choice. After some struggle, Debbie was rewarded by the sound of first one, then two nails being pulled from the doorframe. The groans were like cheers of encouragement, giving her the strength required to remove the hasp and free the door. Both nails slipped free, and the hasp they held now hung stupidly from the lock. There was nothing now to stop her from opening her father's bedroom door—except the fear of what she might find inside. Last she saw it, the room was full of Delwin's *life*. She had no idea what to expect now. What was Teddy's method of destruction up here in Daddy's room? Was it anything like the disaster downstairs, which was so bad that a dead body looked at home? For Debbie, it took more courage to open the door to her late father's room than it did to look at the dead asshole downstairs.

After many long seconds with her hand on the door, Debbie turned the knob and gently pushed. The squeak of the door on its hinges pinched her heart. She thought about how the sound of her father's door opening and closing had been taken for granted and yet meant so much. Its absence meaning even more. Then the smell of Delwin's room hit her. Tears flowed. Ache bloomed. Distant memories of her upbringing rushed at her like phantoms freed from purgatory. She found herself estranged from them. All those pleasant, bucolic memories of a spoilt and precocious daddy's girl fit uncomfortably because the last three months of Debbie's life made them irreconcilable.

Light from the hallway poured into her father's room and Debbie could not believe what she saw. The room looked frozen in time. She threw on the bedroom light switch. The bright bulb in the ceiling fixture confirmed that, for whatever reason, Delwin Coomb's bedroom had been perfectly preserved. Debbie had no idea why and could care less. The truth was that Clyde had lost the key to the lock the same day he had put it on, and Teddy had more important things to focus on.

She entered slowly, as if walking into a memory. The two top drawers of the tall dresser were partially opened, as if Delwin had dressed here this very morning. The old, maple-framed bed was neatly made. Two pictures sat on the matching nightstand between the bed and the wall. One was of Debbie at three years old, sitting atop her daddy's shoulders in front of a faded blue truck. Her small hands were holding Delwin's forehead. He was beaming in the picture, and little Debbie was laughing. The other picture was Debbie's eighth-grade graduation photo. In it she had her hair pulled back and wore a yellow dress with a crème-colored lace collar. She looked young and innocent, full of promise and ready to bloom into a young lady. From this picture, Debbie had to look away.

She took in every square inch of the room, but avoided that eighth-grade picture and a mirror opposite the bed. Delwin's room looked like—like Delwin's room. Like he would return to it at any moment. Debbie was floored. She laughed aloud, then put her hands over her mouth in a failed attempt to stop the laughter's transformation into weeping. Perhaps she once was that little girl in those memories that now felt otherworldly. Debbie stood there, laughing some, and crying a lot. The preserved room was almost proof that the vicious few months before tonight were just one, long, nightmare in slow motion. It never really happened like it did. Then she remembered the corpse with a nosebleed and a broken neck hanging off the couch downstairs. The fantasy was over. The pain was true. *Out there*, she thought.

But not in here.

In here, she thought, *I am safe, and I am home*. She allowed in a few simple, purely joyful memories. Not "the time we went to Disneyworld" memories—though she had those, too. They were plain memories—sitting on Daddy's lap in his La-Z-Boy, smelling him, cuddling him, watching TV together. Memories of him holding her hands so she wouldn't fall when she jumped up and down on his bed. Memories of walking together down the long gravel drive to fetch the mail.

These were the true memories of a true childhood. And they were framed in despair because Debbie knew that this room was as close as she would ever get to being in her daddy's arms again.

She went to Delwin's pajama drawer and opened it. She grabbed his favorite pair, light-blue with ship's wheels on them. Not wanting to leave the room in case it really was just a dream, Debbie forced herself to take a long, hot, shower. She scrubbed clean the cuts and scratches she had earned in her escape, washed away the scum of her violators, and scalded the scars of her captivity. It was cathartic, and would become a ritual often repeated. She returned to her dad's room soaking wet and clutching his PJs. Not about to use the towel she had used as a victim, she instead dried herself off with a couple of Delwin's clean T-shirts. Then she slipped on her daddy's pajamas and crawled into his bed. She got in slowly—torn over whether to muss it or preserve it.

He made this bed, she thought.

Debbie could smell her father ever so faintly on his pillow, and that decided it. She got in fully, pulled the covers to her chin, and fell fast asleep with tears in her eyes.

That night, in the midst of Debbie's slumber, Delwin came to her the way ancestors sometimes do. He stroked her weary head and brushed the hair from her eyes, just like he had when he was alive. He whispered things into her ear that entered her softly and folded into her dreams. And then he left her to sleep and heal— and to ache.

Chapter 9

1

THE NEXT MORNING DEBBIE awoke to a serious contradiction. She was a little girl arising from sweet slumber in Daddy's big bed. She was also a victim waking from a prolonged and unbearable horror she would feel in her muscles and on her skin for quite some time. She couldn't bear to touch herself anywhere except her hair, which felt alien because it was clean. At this moment, the extent of her wounds were unfathomable. She sat up in her father's bed and took in his room all over again. Its preservation was beautiful but melancholy, and it was all she had in the way of healing—a bittersweet reminder of what once was.

She sat up, closed her eyes, prayed to Delwin, and attempted to rein in her pain. With eyes closed, the sight, sound, and feelings of her hell came rushing back with such force that she hyperventilated and nearly vomited. She opened her eyes quickly, and the horror subsided—some. She closed them again and tried hard to remember the actions of her liberation. Painful memories fought liberating ones for her attention, making her swoon, but she rode it out and was able to take it. Though her victory held little glory, she found herself energized by the vivid memory of killing Clyde with her own hands and destroying Teddy and his world. She had assumed control, wrested freedom, and exacted revenge—the ultimate victim's trifecta. Healing, however, was another matter entirely.

In light of this, Debbie's subconscious began shutting down her heart. It did this with the best of intentions, as if each new day forward depended on it. Over days measured in moments, Debbie's broken heart retreated into deep shadow.

She could not celebrate her freedom, nor did she feel like hiding in the undeniable solace of her father's bed. She had spent enough time in bed, thank you. Debbie decided that the best thing she could possibly do was to make the house a home again by picking up where she had left off. But what waited for her down there besides the body and the mess? What about the men? What if they were outside? What if the police came? Could she recover her home from a house of ill repute? Would news of the tavern fire be enough to stop the traffic up to Debbie's front door? Would the fireman keep his word and get out the message that Debbie was through being used?

Teddy was actively evil, Clyde passively so—this Debbie knew. But she did not understand that the rest were just men looking to get off, and thanks to the late Teddy Eel, they had the means to do so at a good price. The owners of the random hands, mouths, and cocks used on Debbie were okay with prostitution, but not kidnapping and rape. When violence and captivity are prerequisites for entertainment, the ugly business behind the cage, the tank, and the mattress is not usually discussed. Since Teddy had successfully destroyed the young woman's spirit prior to hanging out his shingle, his customers took Debbie's participation and lack of resistance as earnest acquiescence. While they would miss the easily accessible sex, they weren't about to resort to Teddy's level of cruelty and criminal activity to recover it. That would be just plain stupid. It was a good ride, and a bargain to boot. Good things never last. Just ask Debbie Coomb, who for months after her nightmare ended lived with the fear that the men would come back.

They never did.

Still dressed in her dad's PJs, Debbie headed downstairs. She immediately checked all downstairs doors and windows to make sure they were still locked. Twice she walked right past the covered body without looking at it, the second time on her way to the kitchen. A dead body on your couch was bad, *but*, Debbie thought, *the state of this kitchen is a whole lot worse.* Somewhere underneath all the filth and detritus were pieces of her life. At least they were there when Teddy arrived to roost, rape, and pimp.

Focusing on the materials of her previous life helped Debbie divorce the present from the cruel crimes of her most recent past. She ate half a loaf of bread straight from the bag while searching for signs of that old life. After an hour of concentrated effort, Debbie had recovered from beneath a stack of unopened mail, the coroner's notepad with the important numbers written on it, a booklet of checks, and the phonebook. Sitting down at the kitchen table where only yesterday she had shared breakfast with the dead guy in the living room, she opened the phonebook and went right back to finding a housekeeper. Debbie returned to the ad that read: "Tidy-Rite Housecleaning—Affordable Prices—Ask about our Sparkle Guarantee!" She called and ordered two housecleaners, explaining how she and her dad had been out of town and had come back to a disaster. Then she asked about the Sparkle Guarantee. After checking all the windows for signs of trouble, Debbie tested her freedom by going to the back door and walking out into the cold morning air.

Just a few feet from the back door, Debbie stood and looked around at the world. Then she walked in small circles, feeling the cold air on her face and the half-dead Bermuda grass on the soles of her bare feet. Things often taken for granted—the arguments of blackbirds, a cold breeze tingling bare skin, a blue sky marred by unremarkable clouds—each became a profound symbol of freedom for Debbie. She wanted to be outside all day but wasn't about to let the presence of the late Clyde Eel void her Sparkle Guarantee. She went to the sloped cellar door against the house and found it held in place by an old rusted lock she remembered from her childhood. This time Debbie had the luxury of taking her time to find the right tool for the right job. Going through her dad's well-looted workbench on the back porch, she managed to find a dirt- and rust-coated screwdriver and a pipe wrench she hoped would make a decent hammer. The door had sufficient dry rot so the lock surrendered with next to no struggle. This simple act fueled a refreshing sense of self-reliance—something Debbie would come to savor. Freeing the lock was the easy part. Debbie knew the hard part would be getting Clyde on down to his new home.

It took Debbie more than an hour to move two hundred and fifty pounds of dead weight the forty feet from where Clyde died to where he would rest in peace (or turbulence, for all Debbie cared). In the first thirty minutes, Debbie had moved Clyde maybe eight feet. The hard, unnerving, and intimate work of pushing by hand an overweight corpse stirred Debbie's mind into coming up with an easier, less grotesque solution. She rolled Clyde onto the sheet that once covered him, then removed the hallway runner from the hardwood floor. With both hands, Debbie grabbed one end of the sheet and pulled Clyde's carcass down the hallway, out of the house, and down the cellar steps. By the end, she was wet with sweat and her head ached. It was a lot of exertion for someone who had eaten so little and accomplished so much.

Debbie returned to the kitchen and ate a large helping of whatever she could find that wasn't spoiled and didn't require preparation. This meant baloney, cheese, and some Neapolitan freezer burn. Then she went back to her dad's room and napped until startled awake by a knock. She prayed to Daddy that it was the folks with the Sparkle Guarantee.

It was.

2

DEBBIE, STILL WEARING HER father's pajamas, walked the two Tidy-Rite housecleaners through the downstairs rather professionally. It wasn't the worst they had seen, but it was certainly a runner up. To the housecleaners, it looked like the aftermath of one heavy-duty college party that must have lasted an entire semester. Every surface was covered with trash sitting on top of something dirty—dirty plates, dirty linen, dirty floors, dirty shelves, dirty tabletops, and dirty magazines. Empty chip bags and cigarette packs lay nestled between empty boxes of cupcakes and off-brand Twinkies. Greasy white paper bags had been wadded up and tossed into corners. Flatware, dried-out food, and dishes had been grease-welded together into disgusting sculptures. Soiled paper plates were grease-glued to surfaces. Pizza boxes full of used paper towels and petrified pieces of crust were stacked window-high against one wall. A hundred little folded pieces of foil and paper were strewn across the floor and hidden between seat cushions. Countless empty beer bottles and cans were strewn everywhere, nearly a third of them had been repurposed as ashtrays and spittoons. Every coffee mug Delwin had ever owned was in the living room half full of chaw spit, instant coffee dregs, and clots of greenish mold. Even china teacups that had never before left their hutch were now chipped and scattered around, used as ashtrays.

Working at a pace designed to get the most out of an hourly wage, it took the two housecleaners three days to make the downstairs habitable. On day four, a single cleaner came back to do the upstairs bathroom and Debbie's former bedroom dungeon. She was a scrawny, coarse-skinned, stale-smoke-scented woman named Doris. Debbie's room had trapped in its walls and fabrics the stench of crimes committed there, and Doris recognized it. "You know, Miss, are you sure you're all right? 'Cause, you know, there is something not right with that room," she said.

"I was out of town and came back to it like that. Can't you just clean it?" Debbie answered. She wasn't up for conversation, period, let alone discussing her bedroom. Doris wasn't sure there was enough Simple Green in all of Paro County to camouflage the stink. Downstairs, which had the benefit of halfway decent air circulation, the chemical-clean smell of cleansers, deodorizers, and bleach all but completely erased the smells trapped there. Debbie's bedroom smelled worse. It smelled of abuse and neglect and worse things.

"I sure will try," Doris replied. She had been through enough hell and had watched enough daytime talk shows to feel qualified to dispense therapy to those who needed it but hadn't asked for it. After a short awkward pause, Doris tried again. "Miss Debbie, is that your room?"

Debbie did not reply.

"I guess it has to be since the big room looks like it must be your dad's," Doris said, mostly to herself. "Miss Debbie, are you okay? Wanna talk? I kind of think I know what you're going through. I used to have this boyfriend and one time him and his buddies…"

"It's not my room, okay? My dad and me came home from vacation, and it was like that. I just want my Sparkle Guarantee. Can you do that or should I get someone else?"

"Young Miss, I can clean the worst, just takes time, that's all. But if I were you, I'd be happy just to get rid of that smell. I took the boards off the window—hope that was okay— but the window itself is nailed shut. Won't open."

Debbie hoped that by not responding, the conversation would die quickly.

"You're going to want that window open."

Debbie continued to ignore her.

"Ever think about getting new carpet?" Doris persisted. "That and the drapes—getting new ones would help a lot."

"What color?" Debbie asked. She had no clue where carpet and drapes came from or how they got in your house. But it did sound nice.

"Not white, that's for sure. I never understood white carpet. What about a nice green, like an Irish green?"

"Okay, how long will it take?"

Doris chuckled. "Heck, what are you asking me for? You need a carpet store."

Suddenly embarrassed by her ignorance in the ways of flooring, Debbie's growing agitation with the nosy housecleaner could no longer be contained. "Well, if you can't do carpeting, why did you ask if I want new carpets?" Debbie barked. She could not remember raising her voice like that to someone ever before. It seemed to work. The domestic mumbled an apology, shook her head, and went back to work.

The next afternoon, Doris came back to finish up. It could have been done in a day, but she took her time. Besides, she really wanted to help this girl while her daddy was away. It was obvious that she was lying. Of course, it was her room, and, of course, what happened in it must have happened to her. Maybe not only her, maybe there were others—cousins, sisters, who knows? Some sins grow like ivy. Doris decided to catch young Miss Debbie in her lie. Then, she could fix her just like they fix damaged women in between commercials on daytime TV.

"Miss, you want me to save your night things?" Doris asked, innocently enough from the top of the stairs. "I think throwing 'em away'd be a shame. I can sew up the torn ones if you—"

Debbie sat up and squeezed the La-Z-boy arm rests. "I already told you yesterday. THAT is NOT my ROOM!" She glared icily at Doris who was standing at the top of the stairs holding a stained white camisole in her hands. "Can't you follow simple little directions like CLEAN and THROW AWAY?" Debbie yelled.

"Sorry, miss," Doris said contritely. "I didn't mean nothing. Just trying to, you know, help. I don't think it's healthy for you to..."

"Don't think, okay? Just don't. You're a maid. A stupid, no-class maid. I imagine if you knew how to think you'd be doing something else for a living. But you ain't. You're just a stupid, dumb, no-class maid. So stop talking and go clean that room. That's what my daddy's paying you for. And please do it with your dumb mouth shut." Debbie knew she was being cruel and hurtful, and within her pain she was fine with that—no, not just fine, invigorated. It scratched quite a mean itch, and Debbie immediately wanted to scratch some more.

Doris abandoned the talk show therapy idea and instead turned the knife. "Fine. I'll just go ahead and dispose of *your* undies, then," Debbie exploded. "THOSE ARE NOT MY THINGS!" She noticed that the housecleaner suddenly looked embarrassed, even afraid. That coupled with the energy of anger thrumming through her body fascinated Debbie. There was a feeling of exhilaration reminiscent of the day she set herself free. "What is wrong with you? Don't you listen?" The question pinched Doris's own bruise. "Those are not my things, and that is not my room. If you wanna take them home so you have something new to wear when your man kicks you around, go ahead, be my guest.

Now dammit, do what I say and shut your dumb mouth and clean my daddy's house like I told you. I want my Sparkle Guarantee!"

Debbie was almost panting, now. She was surprised at how effortless it was to be cruel toward the housecleaner. It was hard to stop. "And if you can't clean my daddy's house with your mouth shut, then GET OUT!"

Stunned by the castigation issued from the young snot with a checkbook, Doris thought, *I hope they got her good*. She knew that the bad thoughts against Debbie were mean, and the most she could hope for.

Doris could have gotten a few more hours out of the Coomb house, but enough was enough. She finished dutifully and went downstairs to leave. Watching Doris head out, Debbie recognized a victim's aura. She felt a sudden twinge of guilt over how she had acted—another new emotion. "Are you done up there?" Debbie asked, trying to sound considerate.

"Yes, all done," Doris nodded. She stood only a few feet from the door. She wanted badly to get in her car and light a cigarette.

"Okay, well, thank you. I know that probably wasn't a very fun job," Debbie said. She got up from the La-Z-Boy and handed Doris a check covering a full day's labor.

"I done worse before," Doris replied. She took the money without making eye contact.

"Um ..." Debbie wanted to make up for being mean, but had little to say and was unable to apologize. "What's that in your hair? It looks nice...sort of nice."

"It's not nice, Miss. I just use it to keep my hair up when I'm working," Doris said, self-consciously touching the ugly, uncomfortable hair clip at the back of her head.

"I like it," Debbie said, in part because she wanted to be kind, but also because she had already said it was nice and didn't want to admit otherwise. Doris did not respond.

"I'll give you ten dollars for it," Debbie offered.

"Miss, you can get these for a buck at the Woolworths," Doris replied.

"But I want that one—ten dollars, okay?"

Debbie insisted. Doris agreed, feeling that if she didn't, it would cause a problem. Plus, she just wanted to get out of the house and out of this awkward conversation with the young woman, whom, she now noticed, didn't look so young behind the eyes. She certainly didn't sound like a young woman when she said those mean things. Debbie took the hair clip from Doris's scalp before Doris could remove it herself. The move scared Doris a little. Debbie bunched up her hair and placed it atop her head. The way it pulled her hair hurt, but in time Debbie found the pain satisfying. As if pinching her skull kept her mind from wandering to a past that would hurt even more.

"Looks nice on you, Miss," Doris lied. She waited for Debbie to write a ten-dollar check, then walked out the door.

3

ONCE THE HOUSE HAD regained its rural, middleclass order at the hands of the housekeepers, Debbie had very little to do. She had ordered a pile of groceries and had them delivered to the back door by an old gent in a small truck. Thankfully, they had never seen each other before. He kindly advised Debbie that he smelled a dead animal nearby, probably under the house. And if the man of the house found it and threw a little quicklime and rock salt on it, it ought to take care of the odor before it gets any worse. Debbie was grateful for the advice but did not show it. Immediately after the old man left, she called the Liberty Market and tried to order both. Liberty Market recommended she try a hardware store. She did, they delivered, and two days later the pungent smell of Clyde's putrescence had all but disappeared.

The job of curing Clyde's carcass allowed Debbie to stay busy for a couple hours. But aside from putting groceries away and ordering clothes and other essentials out of catalogs, Debbie did not know what to do with herself. So she ate, gained weight, ordered new clothes, and ate some more. With her sedentary lifestyle and predilection for junk food, she gained weight surprisingly fast. Before Delwin died, she was slightly heavy for her age, though certainly not unhealthy. She lost weight while enslaved, so it was understandable that she gained her first fifty extra pounds in a little over two months after regaining her freedom. Her second fifty took only slightly longer, and it came with a bonus prize—she could now look at herself in the mirror without painful memories stabbing through the looking glass. The more she gained, the better she hid. The better she hid, the better she felt. By the time she had gained her third fifty, she was all but unrecognizable to herself and, she later found out, to the entire town of Wilburn on the few occasions she left her home. Men did not look at her. People ignored her. It was as if the more space she took up, the more invisible she became. This, despite her penchant for wearing the ugliest housedresses in all of catalog-dom. The invisibility added to Debbie's sense of freedom, which often felt fragile and tenuous until she had grown into a 350-pound force to be reckoned with. Her attitude during this time evolved as well. Her treatment of Doris was a mild precursor to how she would end up treating all in her path, whether they were serving her or just happened to be nearby. In a small town where fucking with each other, sometimes with little provocation, was not uncommon, no one fucked with Debbie Coomb. Not anymore. As it should be.

During this time, Debbie spent many hours in Delwin's bedroom. Here, she reverted to a broken-hearted young woman taking small comfort from her surroundings. Outside that room, Debbie became a ruined work no longer in progress. As she grew into a beastie in both stature and demeanor, all signs of potential common to young people were replaced by revulsion, resentment, and on rare occasion, pity.

4

ASIDE FROM HER PHYSICAL transition, Debbie's first few years of regained freedom were unremarkable. Weeks would go by without her ever opening her front door. Deliveries and any business she had were nearly always taken from the back door. She had followed the Tidy-Rite maid's advice and put new carpet in her bedroom and in the living room. She enjoyed the process, which included an antagonistic surliness toward the carpet layers. She ordered a big TV and watched safe things like game shows and shopping channels. She never watched the news but had baseball and football on during their seasons because the sounds reminded her of Delwin. She cooked eggs at least once a day and ate all kinds of nuke-able frozen food—all kinds except Hungry Man, that is. She overfed her sweet tooth with cheap pop, kid's cakes, and cheap ice cream. She could afford premium confections and beverages but remained ignorant of them, thanks in part to the limited selection at her disposal. She subscribed to a zillion magazines and catalogs, and spent much of her day dealing with mail. She kept the house spotless herself but still had the Tidy-Rite people come every two weeks. She could be very rough on them and she rarely saw the same housecleaner twice. She hated Christmas and Halloween with a passion. No one ever came to the door during the holidays, which was just as well.

Months went by before she ever ventured into town. On her first few trips, she walked to the abandoned lot that had once been Teddy's Tavern. She would hang around for up to an hour, staring at the charred lumber that rose up through the weeds. Then she would turn around and go straight home. She studied the ruins of Teddy's Tavern from many angles. She watched it evolve into a weedy lot hiding the artifacts of the incident—broken glass, nails, chunks of charred debris, pieces of plumbing, and bits of melted tire. When the bike shop across the street closed down, it put her in an extra-dark mood for a week.

By her mid-twenties, Debbie had become sadistically self-sufficient. She had figured out how to do all business from within the house, including all forms of shopping, from groceries to appliances. And this was before the Internet. When she did leave the house on an errand, it was because the pain had built up to sufficient levels requiring release. And that release came in the form of abusing those she encountered.

Debbie Coomb had the means to get what she needed to exist, but not what she really wanted, which was to be fifteen and innocent again, with her daddy alive and well. She could not find those things in the Yellow Pages or in catalogs, and they couldn't be purchased by check. So she remained stuck. Stuck with the pain and memories of being broken, and not a single tangible idea about how to fix herself.

She cut her own hair, which she religiously kept trapped in the dangerous looking hair claw she had bought from Doris the domestic. When it finally broke, she went crazy looking for another. It had to be ugly and painful, though Debbie herself would not have used those words to describe the device, much to the dismay of the drugstore clerk charged with helping her find the right one.

She had no friends, only contacts whose relationships were fee-based. One taught her to drive and paid dearly for it, another sold her a car for a hefty commission he wasn't sure was worth it. One delivered a new television set; another attached it to a cable. Each gave Debbie the opportunity to scratch her itch through salvos of acrimony. They all left with check in hand, swearing they would insist on hazard pay if they ever had to do business with Debbie Coomb again.

Years later, when the internet came to small towns, Debbie embraced it not just as a solution, but also, per chance, as salvation. It gave her restless, pain-soaked mind and aching, broken heart something to do. And like so many internet newbies, she soon felt let down by the whole experience—she never won anything of value by clicking the right answer, punching the bouncing monkey, or being the 211,244th person to visit this or that website. The only free things she ever received online merely served to plug up her computer until she finally had to order a new, "faster than yesterday's but much slower than tomorrow's" computer. She burned through three personal computers in a little over a year.

She eventually found the same chat rooms Howard frequented—a lonely-hearts exit off the information highway. At the same time, she had become hooked on a handful of daytime dramas. She loved and pitied the tragic victims, vigorously hated the villains (to the point of damaging the TV on occasion), and generally became swept away by the storylines. If any scene became too sexually charged, she would abruptly turn the channel. It was these hackneyed characters and plot devices that taught her how to act with alleged suitors on the other side of the wire. Soon she became a chat room regular. Actually, she became about six regulars in six different rooms. Debbie was always a part of each identity. She was *DebbieDelight* in marriedbutlooking, *DebbieDaytime* in flirty30s, *DebbieDuchovony* in an *X-Files* room, *WebDeb* in HotAsianConnections, *Debbie4Dessert* in

BBW&luvinit, and *Lil_Debbie* in Luv2Flirt, which was where she had met *HappiHoward*.

She found it easy to establish cyber-relationships. Subconsciously she was desperate for healthy human contact, something she did not know how to acquire nor maintain. In what were really typed cries for companionship and healing, Debbie soon began using chat rooms to ruin good men—to make the functional dysfunctional, just like her. It was a never-ending catch-up game of payback toward the opposite sex.

She would participate in digital intercourse via email and chat to get her cybermates to open up to her and confess their crimes of the heart. She learned how to save pictures of pretty women found on various websites and attach them to an email, claiming it was a so-so picture of herself. She would accept all promises, and affirm she was, did, and liked everything her cybermates wanted a woman to be, do, and enjoy. She often struggled reading their sex chats, however, so she would just read the last couple words and respond with oohs, ahhs, yessss's and the requisite—I'm cumming. To spare herself from actually having to type her own sexual replies, she kept a text file full of pornographic descriptions and responses that she could copy and paste into a chat window. For Debbie, this made the conversations far less sexual and much more like a word game. She would do this day in and day out until those pursuing her believed they had fallen in love—through typing. Then she would move in for the kill—breaking hearts and promises, egos and spirits—through some seriously twisted mindfucking. She would then meet another round of desperate, dysfunctional, or merely curious and bored individuals and repeat the process. Her success in hurting people depended on how closely they matched their chat room persona. She managed to merely irritate a housewife posing as a thirty-five-year-old male truck driver who had a thing for chubby women. But she absolutely destroyed a science teacher who was trying to meet the hot Asian teen of his dreams in between posting convoluted essays confirming alien encounters.

In time, remotely breaking hearts was not enough. Typing in caps wasn't nearly as satisfying as real, honest-to-goodness screaming into someone's face. So Debbie began to arrange meetings with her computer-based consorts.

Howard Feck was the third man she had lured onto her property and only the second one to make it into the house. The first refused to get out of his car. Debbie confirmed his suspicions by punching and kicking his vehicle when he locked the doors. He backed right onto the highway, narrowly escaping a serious accident, and drove away, vowing to never again use the internet for sex.

Her second date made it inside and up the stairs, where Debbie finally came out of her shell. He slipped past her as she tried to lock him into her old bedroom and then badly twisted his ankle bolting down the stairs. He hobbled to the front door, only to find it locked. Debbie caught up with him in the kitchen as he searched for the back door. Hitting the back of his head with the iron skillet was meant to initiate a timeout. But he kept squirming, so she kept hitting. Soon she had lost her place in time and space and could have sworn she was killing an Eel brother all over again. She kept swinging until his face had turned to hash. It was an accident. Debbie knew him only by his chat room name: BigDave88. She felt bad for killing him, and for hiding the body in the cellar. She felt worse because of all the emotional business that had remained undone. She parked his car behind Wilburn Grocery and left the keys in it. Within hours, someone had discovered it and taken it home. So it wasn't a total loss.

This was the Debbie who had locked Howard in the bathroom. He should consider himself lucky—he'd been inside the Coomb house for more than twenty-four hours and had yet to meet the iron skillet or Debbie's old flames rotting away in the cellar.

Chapter 10

1

TWENTY YEARS AFTER BURNING Teddy's Tavern straight to the ground, Debbie awoke having forgotten about the houseguest locked in the downstairs bathroom. It wasn't until she used the bathroom herself that she had remembered the events of the day before: Stumbling upon Howard at Webspresso's; improvising the the poor sickly roommate trap; Howard's embarrassingly urgent need to use a bathroom, and Debbie locking him inside it. She wondered what was going through his mind. She dressed and went down to check on her hostage.

Howard had spent the night with his head and shoulders tucked under the bottom shelf of the towel closet. He found comfort in confined spaces. Debbie put her ear to the barricaded bathroom door and made out a faint, dry snore. Something about that snore irritated her. She felt that he should be awake and panicked instead of sawing lumber with apparent ease. Debbie pounded three times on the bathroom door. It was answered immediately by a distinct *ka-donk*. She had no clue it was the sound of Howard being startled awake, hitting his head on the underside of the closet's bottom shelf, and then ricocheting back onto the hard tile floor. He was shaking off pain and grogginess when he heard the fist on the door again. *DUNT-DUNT-DUNT!*

"Hello?" he croaked from the bottom of the closet. "Who is it?" He scooched out and sat up. Slowly and painfully waking, he surveyed his surroundings. His mind showed him Crayola drawings of how he got there.

Debbie could not believe it. The guy had been locked in a bathroom overnight by a stranger in a strange house in a strange town, and he had the gall to answer a knocked door from inside this predicament with a polite *who is it?* She was just about to improvise some mindfucking when Howard spoke again. "I'm sorry, I don't know what happened."

God, what a pathetic fucker.

"Miss Coomb? If you're there, I accidentally locked myself in and I couldn't get out and I guess you forgot about me so I…" Howard's dismal apology went on, though Debbie had stopped listening. She was too preoccupied with the realization that Howard did not understand that he had been kidnapped.

How do you successfully imprison a man so pathetic he thinks the actions against him are his own doing? The situation had completely caught Debbie off guard, and took the winds of vicious payback right out of her sails. Victimizing someone who mistakes abuse for mishap takes all the fun out of it. What the hell was she going to do now?

Maybe if she let the rabbit loose from its trap, it might help her come up with a plan. Debbie grabbed the chair she had wedged under the bathroom doorknob and returned it to the mudroom. She locked the back door, took the key out of the deadbolt, and placed it in her housecoat pocket. Then she walked back into the kitchen, got out her favorite dual-purpose iron skillet, and began to make breakfast—for two.

Howard's pitiful apology and explanation ended as it began—asking if anyone was there. He sat on the floor looking at the door he had failed to open the night before. He thought he had seen the doorknob jiggle slightly during his confession. He definitely had heard footsteps coming and going outside the door. Feeling he was probably pushing his luck, he tried the door. It opened easily with a click. He walked into the kitchen relieved his ordeal was over but upset over how he had ruined his first night in Deborah's home. He had no idea what to do or what to expect next.

Entering the kitchen, he saw Miss Coomb at the stove. Her back was to him. He began to apologize. "I'm really sorry, Miss Coomb. I don't know what to say. I accidentally locked myself in your restroom. I called out for help but…"

"Want some breakfast…Howard?" Debbie thought of several cruel names she could call him. But for some reason, she did not say them aloud. She found this puzzling.

"Sure, I guess. If that's okay." He added sheepishly, "Only I can't have any milk."

"I see." Debbie had added milk to the scrambled eggs, cheese, too. It was the Clyde special, hold the tranquilizers

"What about cheese? Can you eat cheese, Howard?"

"Cheese has milk in it, so I'm not supposed to eat cheese. If that's okay."

"And if it's not okay, then what, you going to run home to your lactose-free house?"

Howard could not tell if Debbie was joking or not. Debbie was not quite sure herself. She surely did not like the off-balance feeling she got from a guy who should be freaking out over being kidnapped.

"Can you eat toast?" Debbie asked not so nicely.

"Not supposed to have butter," Howard replied. "It has—"

"Dairy. I know. You can't eat anything that has to do with cows. Can you have jam? As far as I know, jam's got nothing to do with cows."

"I can have jam. Yes, that sounds good—thank you very much," Howard said, wanting to sound agreeable. "I can have margarine, too." he added. "Margarine has no milk in it that I know of. I have margarine at home all the time." Howard hoped this exciting bit of news might cheer up Miss Coomb. She seemed unhappy over his special dietary needs.

"Then you can make the toast. Jam is in the fridge. I don't have any margarine, only butter."

"That's okay. I don't mind my toast dry, even. That's how I had it growing up."

Debbie looked at Howard as he handled the bread with both hands and put it into the toaster. It was just shy of a glare. She couldn't believe she was cooking Howard Feck breakfast instead of cooking his goose.

"I already put cheese and milk in the eggs, and I'm not making another round. So it's up to you whether to eat them or not. I also made hash browns. You can help yourself to the coffee."

"Okay. I like coffee and toast together. Thank you kindly, Miss Coomb. It's what I normally eat for breakfast anyways, except for the coff—hey, what's Deborah eating for breakfast? How's she doing? You think I could—"

"Deborah's fine. She's having the same thing as you and me."

"How is she feeling? Is she still sick? I know when I get sick real bad I can—"

"Deborah. Deborah is on the mend."

"Oh, good! Maybe I can take breakfast up to her?"

"Maybe." Debbie appreciated this idea, but she had already locked up the bastard once and he didn't get it. "Sit down and eat first. It's ready."

"Yes ma'am." In his boyish politeness, Howard sounded a bit like the well-behaved son from a fifties family sitcom. Only coming from a skinny, oily man in his thirties with greasy hair and an unhealthy pallor, it didn't come across all that sweet. "The toast isn't done yet, Miss Coomb."

"So I see. You can get it when it is ready, okay...Howard?" *What is wrong with me? Why do I keep using this pathetic bastard's name instead of shithead, fuckhead, assface—anything?* Debbie bit her lumpy lower lip. *What am I waiting for? Breakfast? With him?*

Howard sat in Debbie's spot at the kitchen table, and much like Clyde before him, stared into nothingness as he waited for food to appear. He had taken Debbie's cup of coffee, cheating death in the process. Debbie growled under her breath, retrieved a fresh mug, filled it, then served the meal. Howard's plate contained only hash browns. The toast popped up, Debbie said she would get it, and Howard jabbered something with a mouth full of shredded potato.

They ate in relative silence. Neither of them were particularly quiet eaters, and both recognized this in each other but not in themselves. Howard, rarely the first to finish anything, cleaned his plate just before Debbie, who had twice as much food. "There's more browns...Howard."

"Yes, please," Howard, as the good sitcom boy, replied. He was trying to please. The way she said his name made him feel like he was in trouble. Not having dinner the night before, and only potatoes and toast in a kitchen that smelled strongly of breakfast had made him awfully hungry.

Debbie went back to the stove. The fact that Howard should have been waiting on her instead of the other way around added to her frustration. She picked up her trusty iron skillet and took a good look at the back of Howard's ill-shapen head. Debbie felt an urge that was both reassuring and familiar. Walking back to the table, she passed behind Howard and casually popped the back of his skull with the skillet—just to see how it felt. Howard's head and shoulders flung forward.

"Oww!"

"Sorry about that…Howard," Debbie said in an unapologetic tone. "I gotta watch what I'm doing. You okay?" She was satisfied with the test. The tap of the skillet on Howard's head was just the right velocity for practice. And that made her want to do it again.

"That's okay," Howard said, rubbing the point of impact. "It was an accident." Witnessing the accidents of others gave Howard a sense of belonging.

Debbie spooned the remaining hash browns onto Howard's plate, and on her way back to the stove, smacked him one more time. Due to the angle and her attempt to make it seem accidental, the blow was milder than she had intended. "Ha. Can you believe I did it again?"

Howard grunted and then turned and looked at Debbie. She was smiling. "Maybe you need a smaller frying pan, Miss Coomb," Howard offered.

"Nah," Debbie replied. "This pan is a lifesaver. I don't know what I'd do without it."

She watched Howard scarf down his second helping. He was undoubtedly hurrying so he could run upstairs and meet his ailing sweetheart. A couple greasy white curls of potato had bounced out of the pan and landed atop his head. He was unaware of this, and Debbie did not bother to mention it. As she studied them, she subconsciously reached up and touched her own unique scalp adornment.

2

THE SECOND HOWARD FINISHED eating he started talking about the magnificent Deborah Fairchild. Debbie listened. He went on about her picture. He went on about how sweet and kind she was and how she would never hurt a fly—*even if it landed on her birthday cake*. He hinted at her naughty way with words, giving Debbie a wink that looked like he was possibly suffering an embolism. As he enthusiastically went on and on describing the many attributes of his dreamy love, Debbie began to realize that he was rhapsodizing over her polar opposite. Even though she had invented the Deborah that Howard now waxed on about ad nauseam, she had not realized until this moment that Debbie Coomb had created the antithesis of who she had become. It was quite the revelation there in the kitchen where her daddy used to make her breakfast and dinner, where the coroner sat her down and pointed her toward a possibly bright future, where she had drugged Clyde Eel, killed the last man she had caught, and where she had just cooked and shared breakfast with Howard Feck, who was madly in love with everything Debbie Coomb was not.

Fuck.

Confusion to anger, anger to pain, pain begets sorrow, and back to anger we go. She grabbed the iron skillet and walked over to the table. She could have bashed his stupid head in right then, right there, but she did not. And she did not understand why. Howard saw her approaching and lowered his head. Debbie sat down opposite him and put old ironside on the table as a peacemaker she had no qualms about using. And then she proceeded to tell Howard all about the fake Deborah.

"Deborah Fairchild is me, Howard. What do you think of that?" Debbie started. "Does that break your heart? Have you lost your boner? Tell me, Howard. Tell me how that makes you feel?"

Howard took on the look of a bewildered child. It was not nearly enough. Debbie leaned in. "Or maybe I should tell you that I killed Deborah Fairchild with this here frying pan. How does that sound Howard, you stupid, shitting fuck? I killed her last night because I just knew that if she found out you didn't quite look like Robbie Fucking Benson, and that instead you looked like—like THAT," she pointed a finger straight at his face, "she would die of revulsion. So I put her out of her misery for ya— what do you think of that, Howie? How does that make you feel? I want to know!"

Howard sat there in stunned silence, his bulging eyes had turned red and watery. Soon, Debbie hoped, tears would flow.

"Miss Coomb?" He looked at the murder weapon on the table and not at Debbie. "You didn't really—" Howard stopped and smiled. He clung to his version of Deborah with the same myopic affection Linus Van Pelt held for The Great Pumpkin. He exhaled a goofy laugh. "You almost got me good that time, Miss Coomb. You wouldn't really hurt her. She's your roommate. You said yesterday that Deborah wouldn't care if I don't look *that* much like the picture in the email." The timbre of Howard's voice had a hee-haw quality to it as he defended a reality the foundation of which trembled. "And I know Deborah pretty well, let me tell you. Pictures don't matter, even if I do look..." Howard trailed off, his low self-esteem opened wide midsentence like a lily to the dawn. The cruel crow voices, never gone for long, had returned. "You wouldn't hurt Deborah—would you?"

Something in her eyes told Howard that maybe, just maybe... Then he remembered his first impression of Miss Coomb back at the coffee shop. That first impression had induced fear.

Debbie scowled at him. She knew she should wallop Howard right then just for defending and praising Deborah Fairchild. But she wasn't sure she wanted to. *Why the hell not?* she thought. *I just cooked the man breakfast, and he showed his gratitude by swooning over the fake I created, who,* (she now realized) *is everything I will never be.*

And never want to be! she reminded herself.

Was he not worthy of death by frying pan? Confusion wrestled aggression inside Debbie's unsteady mind. She grew sullen. Her demeanor had suddenly turned dark and Howard found this troubling indeed. He nervously considered aloud poor, sickly Deborah Fairchild, waiting upstairs for her knight in shining polyester. Debbie interrupted his lament. "SHUT UP!" She pounded the iron skillet on the wooden table like an oversized gavel in a cartoon courtroom. "SHUT UP! SHUT UP! SHUT UP!" It was very effective. Howard jumped in his seat and put his arms over his head. Debbie glowered at him. He sucked his lips into his mouth as if trying to make his face incapable of producing sound. His nose whistled softly as he breathed.

Debbie lowered her voice, tilted her head down, and stared up into Howard's bulging eyes. "Howard. Listen to me because I am only going to say this once. If you refuse to understand me, I will hit you very hard with this frying pan."

Howard nodded like a little boy accustomed to heavy scolding.

"Deborah Fairchild—is me. Her picture is as real as the one you sent me. The emails and chats and all her words came from *me*. And if I hear you pine about your Little Deborah ever again, I will pick up this iron skillet and hit you right in the face as hard as I can. Even if you remain quiet like you are now, I may still pick it up and bash your face in. I have done it before, Howard, and I know that sooner or later I will do it again."

Tears finally flowed from Howard's eyes. Not because he was afraid of Debbie's wrath, but because his heart was finally breaking. It was as if the one true love of his pathetic life had died right there in front of him, just out of arm's reach. He looked at Debbie, all 350 pounds of her wrapped in a housedress with a print clearly inspired by a paint store explosion. He looked at the torturous device holding her hair away from her face and ears. He looked at a mole she had peeking at him from between chins. It seemed to wink at him when she talked. He looked at her small, swampy green eyes and the lines of anger and despair surrounding them. He looked at her enormous, ill-defined bosom heaving slightly. He looked at her hairy arms and huge hands and chewed fingernails. Through tears shed for the lost, libidinous Deborah Fairchild, Howard Feck faced the real Debbie for the first time.

As he sat there crying, his mind broke down the situation into small, digestible chunks. Howard knew he was a pitiful excuse for a man. He mostly saw it in how "normal" people reacted to him, or, more often, ignored him altogether. Now, studying Miss Coomb, he was able to draw a parallel from which he understood her to be likewise pitifully unloved and lonely. Sad, too. In Debbie, these traits were intertwined with an anger and capability foreign to Howard. Still, he recognized her condition and felt bad that someone else had to suffer such a fate. Until now, Howard had thought he was the only one, and it gave him a martyr-like sense of duty. Yet, here in the kitchen of the Coomb house, he had found another victim of crippling self-loathing and discontent. Only Debbie was angry over hers, while Howard looked upon his as merely his lot in life, and, therefore, his contribution to humanity. *Let birds and angels shit on me, leaving the worthy free from such humiliations.*

"I'm real sorry." That was the extent of Howard's response to Debbie's revelation. Another mighty curve ball just when Debbie was once again feeling dangerously comfortable at home plate. She looked at Howard and raised a forearm off the table with her open palm facing her. It was a simple, "what the fuck?" gesture. She had just busted Captain Pathetic's heart right in the chops, and his response was a teary, *I'm sorry*? Again she thought about using the iron skillet on him just out of principle.

"You're sorry?"

"Yes." Howard wiped the tears from his cheeks and eyes and then looked at his hands before wiping them on his pants. "I guess I had it coming. I mean, I sort of lied to you with that picture I sent. I know I don't really look like that guy. So what you did was no worse than what I did to you. And since—"

"Wait a minute, shitfuck," Debbie interrupted. "I didn't mean a single word I wrote you. I wrote every one just so I could hurt you."

"But they didn't hurt. They felt good. You cared."

"No, I didn't care. I was just setting you up for later."

"Well, still, it felt really good. Even if you did make some of it up."

"All of it, Howard!" Debbie shouted. "I made up every word. Behind every word was the intent to hurt you—bad. Do you understand that?"

Having to defend her premeditated cruelty further stymied Debbie. Howard was a fool, of that she was certain. But he was also no typical man with a short sensitive tether between cock and heart that could be plucked to arousal and then snapped like a rubber band stretched too far. She needed a moment to wrap her brain around the situation.

Howard continued. "I liked what you said on the computer— some of it a lot." He looked at her coyly when he spoke those last five words. Debbie subconsciously shook her head.

"To tell you the truth, Miss Coomb," Howard confessed. "You could have sent me a real picture of you, and I still would have replied. Probably still would have driven all the way down here in my blue Geo to come and surprise you, too."

Snap went Debbie once again. Only this time it was not the snap from calmness to violence. It was a snap from control to sudden and unquestionable defeat. For now she was not going to hurt him, and that was all she really knew.

"All right, Howard, to your room," Debbie growled with exasperation.

This statement reminded Howard of life with Gramma Helen, and he let slip a smile. "You mean you're going to keep me after all this?" he hoped aloud.

Debbie sighed. "I need to think." She sounded beat for the first time in a long while. "If I don't, I'm just going to wallop you with my favorite frying pan to get you to quit looking at me like that." She gave one last hard look at the heavy iron skillet. She thought again about dishing out abuse, but her heart just wasn't in it. She rose, pulled Howard up by his shirtsleeve, and then walked him to the stairs. She was on him so quickly that he resisted at first, not knowing what she wanted from him. She manhandled him up the stairs like a bad little boy in a dangerous home. He went quietly. "Unless you want me to hurt you," Debbie said between gritted teeth, "you're going to keep your mouth shut while you're in your room. You're going to keep quiet."

Howard had no idea why he was annoying Miss Coomb, but he was. He had not yet had enough time to fully process his fate, and he felt that Deborah and Miss Coomb were somehow interchangeable. So the woman dragging him up the stairs was also the woman he loved. And a woman who loved him. He was comforted by the thought. At the door to what Miss Coomb referred to as his room, Howard thought about asking her if he should take a shower first, in case she came in later to seduce him.

"Miss Coomb?"

"What?"

"Who's Robbie F-word Bensen?"

Debbie tossed Howard into her old bedroom like a wet towel into a hamper. She locked the door and returned to the kitchen.

Howard landed in a heap against the bed. He stood up and straightened his clothes, then sat down on a corner of the mattress. He took in his new room. The walls were white and bare, the carpet an Irish green. There was a tall chest of drawers next to the window. He decided he did not have permission to open the drawers, but could not resist the window. He went to it, pulled back the off-white curtains, and looked out upon an unfamiliar landscape of Downtown Wilburn off in the distance. It looked dusty, dilapidated, and nearly deserted. Closer by he saw the wide dirt lot of the Lone Tree Trucking Company with its few out buildings and a small house trailer, the interior of which Howard briefly wondered about. Normally he would have been content to study all that he surveyed, but his thoughts kept returning to Deborah and Miss Coomb. He sat down on the bed, put his elbows on his knees and his face between his hands. He sure was disappointed—no doubt about that. He had fantasized often about Deborah and all the naughty things she had said she wanted to do and wanted done to her. He had brought himself to orgasm many times while picturing his cutie in X-rated action. But with the beauty of this faux Deborah came pressure. He would have to be on guard to make sure he did not repulse any of her refined senses. Even if she was going to call the shots, and even though he was good at following directions (though he had never done so naked), that was a lot of pressure for a guy like Howard, and he knew it. In the back of his flat mind, he knew he would have had to be perfect. And perfection was just not in the cards for the Howard Fecks of the world.

In light of all this, Miss Coomb was looking all right. Her lack of beauty and numerous imperfections made her accessible, or so Howard thought. Miss Coomb also seemed to excel at giving orders, and that was important if not downright essential for any relationship with Howard Feck. Perhaps most interesting of all, those deliciously naughty words that were the basis of his sexual fantasies with Deborah came from Miss Coomb's mind.

Howard was beginning to feel that things were working out pretty darn well. Turns out that his broken heart had a zipper, and it had begun to zip itself back up. He lay back on the bed smiling over the new promise of companionship and intimate contact. Howard Feck was hopeful.

As Debbie cleaned up the kitchen, she found herself deeply preoccupied over her new domestic situation. *Why is Howard really here?* She had not invited him and was not so sure she ever would have, at least not this early in the game. What was she supposed to do with him, just kill him and throw him in the cellar with Clyde and BigDave88? That seemed almost trite. As much as she wanted to, she couldn't kill every horny, lonely man she met on the internet, could she? If nothing else, the cellar would fill up. She reluctantly accepted the fact that unless Howard really messed up, she was not going to murder him. Letting him go, however, would amount to admitting defeat in the violent battle between the sexes. She would have to keep him. If he fussed or resisted, then maybe she could kill him, or at least wallop him back into shape like a junky car. This concept revealed a completely new horizon for Debbie. It had been nearly twenty years since she had burned down Teddy's mission. Since then, she had hardened painfully into a cruel, lonely, broken person. It was what she knew. And there is comfort in what is known.

But was keeping a pet around like Howard something she even wanted? Other than the obvious bonus of having someone at her disposal to unload on—both physically and mentally, what else did he bring to the table? Debbie went down the list: She remembered from their chats that he complained of asthma— *probably allergic to that fungus withering on his upper lip.* He didn't smell too bad. He was house broken, though barely, it seemed. He's little and probably wouldn't eat much. She perked up a bit and thought, *he doesn't seem to mind being locked up, that's a biggun.* The truth she danced around was simply this: It felt good to have a little more life in this big, sad home.

Debbie told herself that if she did keep Howard, she would have to be careful. He looked cheaply made and not built for abuse. If she added another body to the cellar, she wanted to be purposeful about it. No accidents. She decided a little physical abuse would be okay as long as it didn't require medical attention or the cellar. That seemed reasonable. Besides, after the Eels and before BigDave88, Debbie's goal was, once her victims of the heart and the hard-on were properly broken, to let them crawl away like prey that could not believe its luck. Keeping Howard could help her get back to realizing that goal. Debbie never considered the choice as kidnapping since Howard seemed okay with being kept. In her mind, kidnapping involved restraints. It had a smell. And she should know.

3

DEBBIE KEPT HOWARD. FOR six years, she kept him. For the first month, he lived mostly in the bedroom with the door closed but rarely locked. This was much easier on both of them. Then, after weeks of building trust, millimeter-by-millimeter, Howard was allowed out of his room for most of the day and sometimes even at night. But nights could sometimes be extra difficult on Debbie, and Howard had learned the hard way that it was often best to stay in his room after dark. When he had learned her name was Deborah, though she only went by Debbie (or else!), he took it as a sign that maybe she was, in some undiscovered way, more like her sex-dynamo alter ego Deborah Fairchild than she was willing to admit.

She was not.

During these early days, Howard thought about asking if he could leave. But leave for what, exactly? A job where his coworkers often seemed disgusted with him? A mundane overly simple job that his peers thought he was terrible at? (He did secretly enjoy reading the labels and packing slips from the boxes he unpacked to see where they had come from, which was nearly always China.) As quiet as the Coomb house was, it *felt* less quiet than Gramma Helen's lonely home. At least at Miss Coomb's he had a bona fide relationship with someone in the flesh, *and* she was the opposite sex. Better still, it was a relationship with a sexual and romantic history. Even though Miss Coomb would sometimes go days without saying more than two words to Howard, they made eye contact on occasion, and she cooked him three meals a day. Heck, he was used to being quiet for Gramma Helen, especially on Sundays. Plus, sooner or later, they would end up commingling, right?

Right?

In time, they both grew comfortable around each other, and brief casual conversations, not unlike what you'd hear in a married couple's home, became routine. They rarely touched each other out of compassion or friendship, though Debbie occasionally punched and slapped him (both would agree he had it coming). Debbie cooked, Howard cleaned. She fired the Tidy-Rite people, and Howard became the primary outlet for her pain and suffering—most but not all of which was verbal and emotional. As time moved on, weeks would pass where Debbie only raised her voice in disgust or command and not in cruelty.

Howard and Debbie had breakfast together, they had dinner together, they watched movies together that Debbie picked out. Sometimes Debbie would talk and Howard would listen. Other times they both would talk and no one would listen. Occasionally, they would both laugh, though usually at Howard's expense. They would argue, too. Sometimes hushed, darkly cruel, one-sided arguments. Sometimes loud, clownish, evenly matched but short-lived arguments. Worst of all, sometimes physical arguments, where Debbie went for the easy win through violence. To Howard's credit, he never hit back, though he often tried futilely to defend his person.

Less than a full year in, their relationship had hit a comfortable plateau. It had evolved into something that, to an outsider, looked like a marriage that was spark-less but true. They had their habits, their compromises, and their TV shows. Howard watched football on Sundays during fall and winter, and baseball during spring and summer. While he did not care for sports, he liked making Debbie happy, and Debbie liked the sound of the games on TV. On Friday nights, Debbie would cook (heat) fried shrimp and Kraft dinner. She never grew past latchkey cooking skills—heating, reheating, and preparing a few three-step dishes with egg or hamburger.

They had their first night out about a year after she had captured him. It was at Webspresso's for coffee. Debbie made damn sure the barista knew that if Howard's drink was made with milk, she would drag him by a piercing of her choice to attend Howard's inevitable aftermath.

Howard and Debbie sat by the window. They had no use for the computer lounge, since neither went to chat rooms anymore. On the day Howard showed up in Wilburn, all of Debbie's various chat room personas had disappeared into the cyberspace-time continuum.

Sitting together at a sticky, white wooden café table, Howard tried to reminisce aloud about how they had met at the café with secrets on their minds. Debbie did not reciprocate. Howard figured it was just as well, since that night had ended poorly for him.

Then Debbie looked out the window to the empty lot across the street. She became lost in (memory) thought. Howard had learned to be quietly invisible during Debbie's pensive moments. He sat quietly, not drinking his lactose-free caffeine beverage for fear the noise might set off his rotund sea-mine date in the orange, pink and lawn-green housedress. He was just grateful to be out of the house and happy to look out a different window at a different view. He made the most of it, and after taking in the panorama, he decided to focus on the empty weedy lot that had captured Debbie's attention. It sat between two vacant buildings—one a former five-and-dime, the other a former stationary store. Both had limped out of business after getting caught in the shock wave of a distant megastore bomb. Somewhere lost in the weeds between the two buildings was a faded plastic wreath with a white ribbon and a mush of faded, dust-stained plastic flowers. The ribbon used to say "Beloved Father" in a pretty, gold-colored script. It was left by an aching family who neither knew nor cared about their beloved's habit of stopping by the Coomb house for a "quick and dirty" after closing time. Howard stared intently at the empty lot, trying to extrapolate whatever meaning Debbie seemed to find there. She turned to him and spoke morosely. "There used to be a bar there. An ugly place. One night—the same night I learned to drive—it burned down. I saw it. It was noisy and hot and bright. You could hear beer kegs exploding inside, and a couple times, beer exploded right out of the place in big white sprays. Fire trucks came, and all they did was spray water on the buildings next to it to keep them from burning too. They didn't even care that there were people inside. Because—because they were bad people inside. And they had it coming."

"They were?"

Debbie sipped her coffee, then turned back to the lot. "They were. They were bad, evil people who had it coming. They were from hell and proud about it. That's why flames took them. Fire claimed them and took them straight back to hell."

Debbie added after a pause. "Hell abated into the ashes, and no one was left. Hell abated."

"I'm sorry," Howard said. He was mildly confused by Debbie's dark little story.

"Sorry for what?"

Howard thought for a long moment, searching for the safest answer. "Sorry about your daddy, I guess. Mine died in Viet Nam. I think I told you—"

"Why did you say that, Howard? You think my daddy was a part of that? You think he was in there when it burned to the ground? He wasn't. He was already gone, and not to hell, either. Daddy had nothing to do with it, except he liked to drink there sometimes, 'cause it was the only place."

Howard looked down, stayed quiet.

"Let's go home," Debbie said.

The date was over, and despite the change of scenery, Howard was relieved. He noisily drank a few hot sips of his coffee, wiped his mouth, then met Debbie who was standing and waiting near the door. They got in the Cadillac and drove in silence around the few downtown streets and some country roads before heading home. Howard was grateful for the bland scenery made ashen by the falling night. The evening had ended peacefully with each going to their respective rooms at the time Debbie specified. It was the only date either of them had ever been on. Each, in their own way, and for their own reasons, was grateful the night was uneventful. Though Howard had privately clung to the hope of intimacy, he was content with not being struck or yelled at.

4

AS TIME SOFTENED HIS living conditions and strengthened their relationship, Howard was allowed to possess a few books and magazines. Both enjoyed reading, and in a new ritual, they would go to the megastore down in Shipley once a month to get reading material. This was followed by a trip to Web's for a coffee and a chance to peruse their new purchases. Debbie was less the master during these outings, and Howard less the pet.

On most nights, they could be found sitting on the couch, sharing disproportionate amounts of popcorn and watching TV. It was the only time Debbie ever sat on the couch, and once the popcorn was gone, she returned to the worn nest of her father's La-Z-Boy. One night, she did not return soon enough, and it gave poor Howard ideas. There, in the living room lit only by the television and a floor lamp near Delwin's chair, Howard's libido had come down with a small fever. He started asking a few questions that mildly hinted at sex. Debbie responded neither by hitting him nor sending him to his room—a good sign. Then he started referring to his chats with the lusty Deborah Fairchild. Debbie felt a twinge of unstable pride as Howard politely praised her ability to *get a man thinking things*. She responded outwardly by looking at him without frowning. When Howard brought up a few specifics, she rolled her eyes and said, "Can't you just quietly watch the TV?"

Howard took this as a green light. Softly, he began to stroke her upper arm fat. Debbie let him. Her libido was screwed up— arousal was still cloaked in pain and subjugation. But the need for skin-to-skin contact was elemental, so she let Howard touch her. He moved to the shoulder. Debbie tightened but seemed willing to see where this was going. He stroked Debbie from her shoulder to where the long rise of her breasts began. Debbie continued watching some actress driveling away on a talk show couch while Howard grew. He felt it start in the middle of his abdomen and, like syrup, it flowed down the center of him and into his balls. He grew some more. His libido whispered promises of pleasure and release—the kind Deborah Fairchild wrote about in those emails and chats back before he had truly met her. He was overtaken by a growing, musty glow. Then Howard slid his hand down Debbie's large left breast and gave it a clown horn squeeze right on the end. Debbie did not oblige with a honk. Instead, she jammed her elbow right into his nose. It started bleeding profusely. Then she swung her forearm down and smacked his warm hard spot with her fist. Howard gasped. She searched his lap for his scrotum, found it, and began choking it. Howard screamed at a pitch rising above what humans could hear. The air left his lungs, and he could not get it back for many seconds. He shuddered in pain against Debbie's arm as her hand relentlessly squeezed his sack, filling him with bright agony as his nose bled down his shirt. Contorted from the pain, he leaned on her, which caused Debbie to tighten her clutch, which in turn made him lean on her even more. Howard could no longer see anything but a blazing, sharp, white light. He sucked air through his nose, causing gobs of blood to shoot down his throat. He started to choke. After what seemed like an eternity, which was really only a handful of seconds, Debbie let go. Howard crumpled to the floor at the foot of the couch. He bumped her legs on the way down, so she kicked him while he lay there writhing. Drops of blood mixed with snot and saliva dribbled onto the carpet. Howard was on his side in a fetal position, whimpering and wheezing *I'm sorry* like a frightened, beaten lickspittle. Debbie stood up and kicked him right in the ass, twice, then bent down and hit his face a couple times with an open hand—punishment for making her hurt him so badly. Red handprints bloomed on Howard's sickly-white cheek. Debbie wiped blood off her hand and onto her dress, where it blended right in. Howard's chest moved inches up and down in an attempt to recapture his breath. She grabbed him by the collar, pulled him to his knees and then let go.

"Why? Why would you do that Howard?" Debbie yelled, sounding hurt and disappointed. "I was having an okay night. Why did you have to go and spoil it? You're a fucking spoiler."

Howard kneeled, genuflecting to his violent goddess. He fumbled for his asthma inhaler and hoarsely cried hymns of remorse. Debbie was surprised to learn that seeing Howard bloodied and whimpering in pain did not make her feel any better. In fact, it made her feel worse. "Because I love you," he whispered shamefully to himself.

"Come on," Debbie said, as if calling a bad dog to its crate. "Come on, Howard."

She yanked him to his feet by the shoulder of his shirt, and took off for the stairs, half dragging him behind her. She took the stairs at a trot. Howard stumbled and bounced behind her best he could, lest Debbie lose her grip and cause him to fall and break his neck. She reached his bedroom and threw him in. Howard left the ground entirely before landing against the footboard. Debbie walked in, stepped on his shoeless feet, and then went around to the far side of the bed. She bent over and lifted up the entire bed frame in one clean and jerk move—letting out a raging scream as she upended it. The mattress and box spring spilled onto the floor. The frame landed unsteadily upside down on top. Debbie now looked like a shaved, housedress-clad bear raiding a campground.

She went to Howard, who had jumped to hug a wall when his bed went flying.

She glared down into his eyes. "Don't touch that bed. When I come back that bed better be just like it is now, or you will pay with so much hell, you'll beg me to squeeze your marbles like you made me do tonight."

Howard gave a brisk, sweaty nod, then looked away. He was peeing and he sure as hell didn't want Debbie to know it. She left and returned a moment later to throw something at Howard's face. It was his asthma inhaler. Though Howard desperately needed a whiff or six, he dare not move except for his labored breathing. Debbie locked the door behind her and then calmly returned to her TV show as if she had merely put the cat out during commercial. A few tears fell down her face. She brushed them away like flies.

The following afternoon, Debbie unlocked the door to Howard's room and threw in a plastic wrapped baloney sandwich—dry—and a wet rag to clean himself. Debbie found Howard sitting on the floor against the wall opposite the overturned bed. He had changed into a fresh pair of tighty-whities and a clean T-shirt. He had dried blood on his face. He was reading a special edition of *Knucklebones Magazine*. He looked at her and gave a cheery "Good morning," as she opened the door. She let him use the bathroom while she inspected his room, looking for anything that could make her angry. Earlier, after his genitalia had quieted down from Debbie's death-squeeze, Howard had masturbated while reminiscing over one of Deborah's naughty chats and the feel of Debbie's breast. His spasms of orgasm were accompanied by a long-lasting dull ache deep and low in his body. Later, after dinner in his room (another dry baloney sandwich), he was allowed to fix his bed.

Chapter 11

1

THE SPRING BEFORE DEBBIE had turned forty, she and Howard had been together over five years. Their relationship was more burl than blossom, but it continued to grow in its own gnarled fashion. Time had introduced a small measure of security into the relationship. Out of that security, Debbie's biological clock began to make itself known. It would go off just as she was going to sleep, and its tick was the first thing to greet her in the morning. The clock—sometimes it was soft pink, other times light blue—would not be ignored. Its tick-tocking *Bay-bee, Bay-bee* and cooing alarm evoked images of her childhood with Delwin—mental pictures that seemed lifetimes ago except for the backdrop, which had not changed much over the years. Debbie found herself unable to look away from these mental images for they were joyful, though framed in great sadness, like a blind man's vivid dreams. The clock promised healing and happiness, wholeness and immortality. The promise was true—Debbie felt that, saw it, even. It was not a hard promise to keep. But it would be easy to break.

When Debbie closed her eyes in bed at night, she would pray-talk to Delwin. She asked him if he wanted to be a granddad.

She apologized for the grandchild's father, but pointed out that aside from the coroner who had abandoned her, he was the nicest man she had ever known—

—*except for you, Daddy. He never did it with me, though he wants to. He shows me respect like you always said ladies deserve. He does what he is told. I think he would be really nice to her*—she caught herself—*him…whatever.*

I miss you so much Daddy. I miss your love. I miss seeing it in your eyes and feeling it between us like water between the tules. I remember it good, though. I remember it really good—too good. So good it hurts so I make myself never think about it. I'm sorry about that. I hope that where you ended up you never forget how much I love you, Daddy. Crazy how bad everything went after you left. I'm really sorry.

Daddy, I want a baby, I just do. I want to be a mommy just like how you were my daddy. And maybe—maybe if I have just one child, it can have your eyes and your hair and smell a bit like you. Maybe our child can even look like you. Maybe you can come back to me in this child. Like in a movie. We can hold hands again. We can laugh. We can fix everything that went wrong. I know that's probably too much to ask you for, Daddy. I know you probably can't come back like that. But maybe—maybe you'd want to? And maybe you'd be okay if I went and had a baby and you can, I dunno, send me love so I can be a parent exactly like you? Maybe if I had a baby I can think about you again without crying. Maybe I can miss you without it hurting so goddam much. Maybe it'll fix things.

Maybe.

These were the things Debbie confessed to her late father as she sought permission and guidance on the ultra-serious quest for parenthood.

Debbie would also ask herself the same question millions of young women asked themselves as they lie awake in their beds at night—*Does he love me?* She attributed this question to her father. It was what *he* needed to know before Debbie could accept the tender promise of progeny. She began to think about Howard. He would be a huge part of this. It would be his chromosomes she was going to use. Was that smart? Did she have a choice? *Howard Feck's chromosomes—now there's a topic,* she thought, and nearly smiled. *Does he have the type of chromosomes required to have a little baby girl, and if so, how many did he have? How many do I need? What if his chromosomes are broken or damaged—then what? What if his chromosomes make me sick?* Debbie drifted off to sleep picturing Howard as a father. She did not know it but she was smiling.

2

DEBBIE USED HER UNYIELDING gruffness to get a doctor's appointment that day down in Shipley. While Debbie did not want to be in the room while they examined Howard for his breeding risk and potential, she felt she had no choice. Although never outwardly acknowledged, Howard was still technically her captive, and he was never out of Debbie's sight in public, except for bathroom breaks during which Debbie hovered unnaturally close to the men's room door.

The highway to Shipley sliced through farmland dotted with decaying, rural American buildings. Power lines trimmed one side. Modern, brightly stuccoed farmhouses appeared scattered across the landscape haphazardly surrounded by dull, bulky farm equipment and shiny, sleek SUVs. Red flashing lights hung high above intersections where towns had sprouted but failed to grow. *Town* was too big a word for these hubs, and *village* too pretty. They were nothing more than four corners of rundown buildings stubbornly standing as they served the most dusty and anonymous parts of America.

Debbie parked in a dirt lot in front of a shotgun cottage hollowed out to hold rows of groceries. A plywood sign atop a dented, rusty pole stood in the center of the lot. The sign announced 4 CORNERS MARKET in large, shaky, hand-painted letters. Underneath, written in a swirl, were the words, "We don't know where Mom is but Pop's in the Cooler!" Debbie and Howard emerged from the Cadillac and walked into the market, Debbie walked back out with a Mountain Dew and a Mexican pastry full of false promise and Howard with a Seven-Up that she made him pour half of out before getting back in the car. Leaving the mandatory dust cloud, they pulled out of the dirt parking lot and continued onward until a proper town popped up out of the flat brown farmland. The big white car dove into the city limits and parked in front of a brick building with a flat roof covered in white rock. Squat, opaque, amber-colored windows circled the one-story building just beneath the eaves. Two glass doors bearing long Lucite handles marked the entrance to the Shipley Medical Building. Debbie turned off the engine, looked at Howard, and broke the silence that had accompanied the drive.

"I want to have a baby," she said.

"Where?" a stunned Howard replied.

Debbie ignored the response. "I need to see if you are healthy enough so I can become pregnant. And don't get no ideas just because I said that."

"Okay, I won't."

"Listen," Debbie said. "We go in there and fill out forms and talk to the doctor. We say we are married. Howard and Debbie Feck, okay?"

Howard smiled a stupid, contented smile. "Okay."

"And I do the talking. You just sign where I tell you to and do what I tell you to, okay?"

"I'll be good, Debbie," Howard promised. "I used to go to the doctor a lot with my Gramma Helen."

Too many things ran through Debbie's head. Some she did not want to think about. A singular thought called *BABY*! broke through them all. She opened the heavy car door and stepped out. Howard followed suit, taking longer per usual. They walked around the long front of the car and eventually met up at the grille.

"Remember to keep your mouth shut," Debbie huffed.

Arm in arm like husband and wife, they walked into a large waiting room broken into two wings. At the apex of the wings and opposite the front door, there was an open glassless window that looked onto a cluttered office area. At the bottom of the window, a forehead framed in dark curly hair bobbed in and out of view. Debbie walked up to the window. The receptionist politely raised a "wait-a-minute" finger as she spoke into a telephone headset. Debbie noticed the young woman was pretty, so she looked at Howard to see if he had noticed the same. And if he did, what was his reaction? Howard was busy studying the titles on a rack of medical pamphlets—looking for anything that might ring a bell. Debbie looked back to the receptionist and, feeling surly in the face of young beauty, told her pointedly that she had an appointment with a Dr. Coe. The receptionist had had enough experience working with the public to recognize that she should stand down to the large woman with the winking neck mole and orthopedic hair contraption. She wanted to roll her eyes, but instead put her call on hold. "Is this your first time here?" she asked, politely.

"Yes," Debbie answered, gruffly.

The receptionist handed Debbie a clipboard holding a dozen pages printed on blue paper and said, "You will need to fill out and sign these forms. What insurance do you have?"

"Cash. My husband has an appointment, too. His is first. Do I need another set of forms for him?"

The receptionist smiled and handed Debbie a second clipboard with forms attached. Debbie snatched them and then chose two seats equidistant between the receptionist's window and the nearest patient waiting to be seen.

Having received next to no health care in her life, Debbie drew a straight line down the "no" column without reading any of the questions on the form. Howard's paperwork, which she filled out on his behalf, took time. Many of his yes's required written explanations. Normally, Debbie would have cut to the chase and not even bothered with Howard's many ailments and their complicated descriptions. But this was why she was here—to find out if Howard's sperm would kill her or her baby, or barring that, make either of them sickly. She had Howard sign his forms and realized it was the first time she had ever seen his signature. It was thick and round and looked slowly written. She learned that he had a middle initial "E" and that his grandmother's maiden name was Yancy.

Debbie delivered the forms to the receptionist and then stood there, as if waiting for a grape to be peeled. The receptionist suggested she have a seat and wait until the nurse called her and her husband's names. Debbie huffed and returned to Howard, only he wasn't there. His seat was empty. She looked around, saw a few sick schlubs, but none were Howard. She looked through the front door—nothing but sidewalk, grass, trees, and cars. She looked back to where they were sitting and Howard was there, as if he had never left. Only now he was staring into a magazine on his lap. The thought of Howard's escape had inflamed Debbie's choleric nature. She glided back to him on a wave of fresh anger and sat down hard next to him. She slid her large hand underneath the magazine and clamped down on his leg just above the knee. Howard's ass left its seat.

"What are you doing?" Debbie whispered angrily. "I didn't tell you you could get up, dammit. If you mess this up I will—"

"Howard Feck," drawled a female voice.

"Here," Howard croaked, clearly in pain.

Debbie let go. They looked toward the voice and saw a short, stout nurse filling the bottom half of a doorway. The nurse sized Howard and Debbie up without a smile.

"Come on," Debbie said. She held him tightly by his wrist and guided him to where she expected to find all the answers to all her questions about—BABY!

3

SOMETIME AFTER HOWARD AND Debbie had been taken back to see Dr. Coe, folks in the waiting room heard a distant commotion. In a corner exam room, Howard, stripped down to his skivvies and slouching on an exam table, tuned out an argument between Debbie and the doctor. Dr. Coe, short and thin with bright eyes shining from an old man's face, stood between Howard and a counter, sink, and cabinet combo. Debbie glowered and towered over them both. She was angry over Dr. Coe demanding Howard generate a semen sample from the privacy of his home and not in the bathroom or anywhere else at the Shipley Community Medical Offices. Debbie insisted that she was not about to drive all the way back to Wilburn just so Howard could jack off into a plastic cup, and then drive all the way back to Shipley so someone could see what bright stuff his dreams were made of. He could just go to the restroom, do his dirty business, and return. The doctor explained that that was not how it was done unless you were in the army. Debbie gave a retort on how she didn't give a rat's ass how it was done, army or not. She had been gesticulating with her meaty arms and had accidentally knocked a medical tray off its stand and onto the floor. Two vials of Howard's blood fell and rolled to the doctor's feet. The doctor raised his voice at Debbie, telling her to calm down or she would have to leave. Debbie bit her tongue—visibly—and bent down to pick up Howard's donation to her cause. She apologized through gritted teeth and insisted again that she would gladly pay extra so that Howard could step into the bathroom "just for five minutes—I promise," as if Howard were Old Faithful. Then Debbie asked if there were some medical procedure that could remove a sample of Howard's semen. The doctor avoided discussion of any alternative and, out of sympathy for poor Howard, acquiesced to the traditional method right then and there.

"You can do it in here," said the good doctor. He figured that given the various and sundry bodily fluids spilled in the exam room over the years, one more wouldn't matter. "I'll return in fifteen minutes, Mrs. Feck." Howard heard what the doc had called Debbie and smiled. "You can stand in front of the door until the sample is in the cup," Dr. Coe finished.

"I'll stay on this side of the door, thanks," Debbie replied. "I'll make sure no one comes in."

"I'm sure you will." The doctor looked at his watch. He pointed to the clock above the door and said he would return at quarter 'till, giving Howard exactly thirteen minutes and twenty-six seconds to orgasm into a cup.

The doctor turned to Howard and said, "Good luck, son," with sincerity and concern over Howard's long haul, not just the next few minutes. He left them to their business.

Debbie chose to stay behind because she did not trust Howard to do it without messing something up. He would no doubt miss the cup, or Lord knows what. She steeled herself for the pitiable sight of Howard Feck shucking his own corn.

"All right, Howard, get busy. I'm going to hold the cup, and when you're ready, nod or grunt or something."

Howard sat crinkling the paper sheet that covered the exam table. He wasn't sure he could perform under such pressure, and was afraid to say so. He'd had countless orgasms, but, except for what he referred to in his mind as "the supply room disaster," he was always in his bed or in front of the computer. Now he *had* to orgasm, and do so while his drill sergeant captor/wife in her Rorschach-patterned housedress hovered over him to catch his release.

"Why are you shaking your head, Howard?" Debbie demanded in an angry whisper. "Now it's your turn, okay? I take care of you, feed you, clothe you, buy you books and magazines. The least you could do is put your sperm into a cup for me."

"What if I can't?"

"Then I'll kill you, that's what."

"You're not helping," Howard whined.

He looked as virile as a wet cracker. Debbie wanted to hit him. But he was right, she wasn't helping.

"Take him out, time's a'wasting," Debbie said quietly but firmly.

Howard reached into his underwear and fumbled for a penis intent on hiding. Lacking tumescence, he had little to pull out. Debbie sensed this—read it on Howard's face as much as the way his hand looked lost and lonely inside his briefs.

"Stand up."

Howard did as he was told.

Debbie went to him. Howard cringed. But instead of hitting him, she slid her fleshy hand past his waistband and into his shorts. And a stunned Howard began to grow—quickly.

"Close your eyes."

He obliged, then made a short, soft guttural sound.

"Shhh," Debbie said curtly. She pulled down his underwear and breathed a small sigh of relief at the sight of Howard's nonthreatening genitalia. His penis had awakened quite happily. She began stroking it with the accuracy of a professional, unaware of the muscle memory at work.

Howard's soft little mind quickly surrendered to the situation, and a brilliant, warm fever overtook him like a rapidly growing infection. The fever started as a hot brick against his crotch and swelled quickly into his abdomen, expanding like the spidery cracks of a busted windshield. He climbed quickly to his peak. With her free hand, Debbie held the specimen cup at the ready. Howard's entire body convulsed in contribution. Debbie caught it, screwed the lid onto the cup, then washed her hands to the sound of Howard wheezing—and crying. Howard was crying. Instead of being antagonized by this, Debbie momentarily thought it sweet. She brought Howard a couple of tissues from the wall-mounted dispenser. "You can open your eyes now."

"Thank you, thank you so much, Debbie," Howard said. He wasn't referring to the tissues.

"It's okay," Debbie said. "Thank you, too, I suppose. It's your stuff we need. Now, you better hope it's in good shape."

Howard held the tissue in his hand. His penis, still out of its childish, white cotton scabbard, drooped down farther and farther in time with his pulse.

"Can I hug you?"

"Put that thing away and I'll think about it." Despite Debbie's awful past, the act of bringing Howard to orgasm so she could have a baby was not a terrible thing for her. Although she performed it perfunctorily, she felt a small zing of power from her ability to make Howard do that so quickly. She did not want to follow that power toward its source. Such a trek could prove painful. However, the interaction had taught her that the loud ticking of her bio-clock was capable of distracting her mind from the dark, terrible thoughts it sometimes refused to turn off. Still, the satisfaction of human interaction in a region where love mingled with sex strained her thin tolerance. The event was not terrible, however, and that centered Debbie a little. She looked at the clock and saw that they still had almost ten minutes to spare. She thought about going to find the doctor but decided it would be best to wait quietly with Howard, who had stopped crying but seemed shaky, dazed, and very, very relaxed.

"I never...I never ever felt anything like that before, you are—"

"That'll do, Howard," Debbie instructed. "I'm glad you liked it, but I don't want to talk about it. So don't you bring it up."

"Okay."

"We still got things to do," she reminded him.

As Howard basked in his afterglow, Debbie quietly waited for the doctor to return. Now that it was over and all was quiet, her first intimate encounter since her days as a captive prostitute triggered a dull rumble of memories, emotions, and questions. Behind them lay the void carved by Delwin's demise. She felt the rumble rise and fall gently around the bedrock of procreation to which she clung. She went back to her mental list of questions and answers as that low rumble sought her attention. Her position was precarious, but with a great view toward a future construed as salvation. As Debbie mulled heady changes and possibilities abound, she was interrupted by a knock on the door.

"Come in," she said.

Dr. Coe walked in and couldn't help but notice a change in both of them. Howard looked empty headed and sleepy. Debbie looked less oppressive.

"Thank you very much, doctor," Debbie said. "The specimen is on the counter right there."

Tilting his head down to look over his reading glasses, Dr. Coe confirmed Howard's deposit. "Mr. Feck, you can get dressed now.

And I suppose we can move on to you now, Ma'am," the doctor said, turning to Debbie. "When was your last pelvic exam?"

"It's been some time."

"Pap smear?"

"Same."

"Well, if you want to get pregnant, don't you think you should see an ob-gyn? We can do your pap and pelvic, but you'll need to meet with someone who specializes in women's health and prenatal care. Who's your gynecologist?"

Debbie hesitated long enough for the doctor to understand she did not have one.

"We have an ob-gyn here two days a week. I would advise you to make an appointment at the front desk for her—name's Dr. Sanders. She's quite good. I assume you'd rather see her for your pap and pelvic?"

"I want it done now. How long does it take?"

"How long? Mrs. Feck, haven't you ever had a pelvic exam? It only takes a minute or two once your—"

"Okay, do it now—please." Debbie and Howard missed the briefest look of concern on the old doctor's face.

"All right. I'll need to get a nurse. Mr. Feck, please get dressed. I'm going to need the exam table."

Howard nodded. He wished he could close his eyes just for a few minutes. Debbie glared at him for having to be asked to get dressed twice by the man who was to bless their fertility. He dressed and moved as far away from Debbie as possible in the small room.

Dr. Coe opened the door and summoned the same nurse who had called them back from the waiting room. "This is Claudia. She will assist."

Claudia immediately got busy. She went to the counter and pulled from a drawer a sealed packet of longer-than-you'd-think-necessary swabs, a little container to hold the sample, and a tube of gel to facilitate the procedure. She laid these on a tray, and then retrieved one of the most frightening-looking things Debbie had ever seen: a stainless-steel speculum. Debbie wanted to ask what that barbaric-looking device was for, but didn't dare. She insisted on acting cool and calm, despite how she really felt. She figured it was the only way to get through this. It was a step toward her promised future and that's all that really mattered. And yet fear started bubbling up inside her.

Until now, Debbie had assumed that the examination "down there" would be superficial. Such was her ignorance of her own body and the capabilities, biology, and health practices of her gender. Like a kid focused on dessert, her research online focused mostly on delivery and infancy, and very little on pregnancy itself. She had yet to grasp what, as a woman, she must go through for a proper exam—strange fingers deep inside her (once again), staring eyes and the heat of the lamp penetrating her eternally open wound. These were the methods of cursory investigation that would help determine the ability for this unhealed woman to hold, grow, and discharge life.

Debbie believed that as long as she could avoid certain memories, she would get through this with nary a whimper. But that stainless-steel pterodactyl's beak looked impossibly uncomfortable. And she had yet to learn it expanded.

Born out of maternal desire, Debbie believed that when the tools of the trade coldly entered her, stretching her open with professional indifference instead of profane wantonness, she could prevent herself from reliving her nightmarish past. Such a belief was more foolish than Howard's greatest missteps because Debbie's scars were deeper, and her wounds were more serious than anything Howard Feck had ever suffered. Debbie believed that to get through the exam she only need summon and then focus on the squishy feelings of maternity that her bio-clock fed her. She regained those feelings easily enough, but, now that she was the subject of examination, they failed to consume her effortlessly like they usually did.

"You can lay up here, miss," Nurse Claudia said, having converted the general exam table into something more gynecological. "Underwear off first, please. Shoes too. You can pull your dress to your knees once you lie down and get your feet in the stirrups."

Stirrups? Debbie looked at the exam table and saw nothing that looked like stirrups. She saw two steel ovals on arms in mid air and assumed that was for her to hold onto while the doctor did his painful business.

In spite of second thoughts about what she was getting herself into, Debbie continued to participate calmly. She took off her underwear modestly and with less effort than you would think for a woman her size. She sat on the table, and just as she was about to rest her hands in the stirrups, the nurse helped Debbie lie back and placed her feet where they belonged.

Getting into such a vulnerable position was all it took. Lying there, she tried to suppress a thick, *oh no, here it comes* feeling, burdensome in its familiarity. Her position coupled with her view of the ceiling caused the dull rumble of memory to grow sharp as knives eager to stab. She closed her eyes. It didn't help. She heard the doctor's voice and felt his presence between her legs. He said something about cold and pressure, and then Debbie felt both as the speculum entered her like a cold steel rail into pliable earth. A deluge of devastating feelings and memories Debbie had never shared with anyone threatened to escape and swamp the room. She gasped as the doctor went to work like a professional who knows exactly how such an exam is performed but has never received one. Wounds opened wide and dark. Heavy emotions and mournful thoughts flooded Debbie's heart and mind. She began to cry. Tears of pain and shame streamed down each side of her face, puddling in the folds of her ears before falling onto the table, blotting its paper covering. She inhaled a sob, held it, then another, then fought for breath as the doctor finished.

The nurse and doctor looked at each other. They both knew that they both knew—Mrs. Feck was crying over a far greater pain than a pelvic exam. The doctor softened toward Debbie considerably. Nurse Claudia, who had been at her side the whole time, held Debbie's hand and told her it was all right.

Yeah, right, Debbie thought, amid the cloying haze of her escaping pain and regenerative sorrow. Claudia looked at Howard, who stared at Debbie with a look of confusion and concern. *Is she supposed to be doing that?* The nurse motioned for him to come and comfort Debbie. He went to her awkwardly, hyper-aware that she was exposed to the doctor. Mimicking the nurse, Howard took Debbie's other hand and looked down into her face just as it exploded into a squall of sobs and tears. He did not know what to say, or why Debbie was crying so.

"Debbie? You okay?" he tried. "You need something? Want a soda or a candy bar? You want to go home?"

Debbie continued to wail uncontrollably.

Howard turned slowly to memories of his Gramma Helen standing by his side when he was getting something lanced. "Don't think of the pain, Debbie," said Howard, dispensing his late Gramma's advice. "Wish it away and say, 'thank you, God, for this day.' Then the pain will go, a new day will grow, and chase all your hurts away." He sang this in a nursery rhyme melody. It was Gramma Helen's little mantra of comfort and sympathy whenever Howard hurt himself growing up. It came with hand movements.

Having come too close to the undercurrent of painful memory, Debbie, spinning and thrashing, was swept away by the dark, powerful flow. She could see the safety of her physical surroundings in the same way that someone pulled to sea by a riptide could still see the shore—so close and useless. Dr. Coe, Nurse Claudia, and Howard stood by, watching with concern. The nurse motioned for the doctor to leave the room, and he did. Debbie gripped Howard's and Claudia's hands, squeezing them through each wave of sobs as if she were in labor—and she was—trying to deliver her pain from the shadows and crannies of her broken, twisted self. After several minutes lying there with her legs spread as wide as her housedress would allow, Debbie fought her way out of that cold, awful undercurrent. Slowly, steadily, she regained herself.

She let go of their hands and fought for composure. The nurse put her own hands to her heart, Debbie put hers to her eyes. Howard handed her some tissues. She got up and put her underpants back on as swiftly as she had taken them off. She looked like she had been held underwater for too many seconds. Howard looked straight down, afraid that whatever else he did, it would only make things worse.

"Excuse me," Debbie said. "Sorry."

Claudia offered an expression of compassion. Howard looked at Debbie with a deep and sincere curiosity over what had just happened, and then resumed looking at the floor. He vacillated between reminiscing over his first hand job and the serious episode that had just ended. He went back to his few feeble attempts at pitching woo to his captor and her violent responses. A light bulb in Howard's brain grew a little brighter, for a moment anyway. *Amazing what getting the pipes cleaned out can do for you,* a fresh little devil chimed somewhere in his mind.

Debbie, meanwhile, was staring at a freshly closed, paint-peeled cellar door that had appeared in the middle of an ugly field inside her mind. The door held back all the things that had ambushed her while being examined. It looked like the door behind which rested the bones of Clyde Eel and BigDave88. Only it was in a field of tall dead grass, gray weeds, and sharp rocks. The cellar door used to be far away from where she went in her mind, except on occasional restless nights. She got along dysfunctionally but adequately at such a safe distance. Now, she realized, the path to motherhood went right by it. And with its busted lock and flimsy weathered latch, the door could easily fly open again, releasing shards of pain that would fly right at Debbie like bats from a cave. Debbie forced herself to turn away from that cellar door and to the present outside herself.

"The doctor will want to talk to you briefly before you go," said Claudia. "I'll bring him in."

"All right."

The nurse asked, gently, "But first, Mrs. Feck, do you want to talk a little about what just happened? There's help available. I know groups that meet—"

"I want to talk to the doctor."

"Yes, but I just thought that—"

"Don't. It's nothing. I need to go. Where's the doctor?" Had the nurse not been a part of Debbie's baby-making plans, she would have been rebuked far more severely.

4

ON THE PEACEFUL DRIVE home, evening fell, Howard slept, and Debbie's mind wandered miles from the road. Her breakdown in the doctor's office had released some of the pressure caused by a world that had turned on her. It gave her room to roam inward to the past, though not deeply so. For the first time in a long time, Debbie acknowledged the weight of what she had endured and how she carried it around like Jacob Marley carried his chains. Acceptance would allow her to leave behind some of that crippling burden. Debbie didn't know this outright but she felt it indirectly and it guided her thoughts like a subtle rise in the land alters the path of the lost. But, Debbie felt, *acceptance means they win.*

She looked forward and saw hope—something she had not seen since Delwin died. This hope was wrapped up in a soft pink blanket with a beat of its own and a face she could not see. It was the hope of salvation from pain and redemption from what she had become.

Memories and experiences she could not deal with along with the pressure of her loudly ticking bio-clock forced Debbie into believing that the only way to get from point A to point B-aby was to change—right here, right now. In lieu of forgiving, Debbie decided to forget as best she could. And that meant quelling certain emotions and pain and the behaviors they cultivated. Her bio-clock also reminded her that she was on a schedule, dammit, so her transformation would have to be quick.

I have to forget about it. Let it go. Forget them. It never happened. There were no Eels in my house, only Daddy, and now Howard—and he's harmless. And I sure as hell don't know any coroner. I do this for you, my baby. My past is gone for you. My hands are clean. My...my...(she tripped on the word)...my body is clean. My heart is clean now, too. You, baby, and me...we are the only things inside me, even though you're just a promise. One I intend to keep. You are beautiful and I am free and we both are strong. I am free. And I can have you. I am okay. And you will be okay, too.

I will have you. And you will have me. And my past...My past is gone. My past is clean. It. Did. Not. Happen. Not like it did, anyway...

Will you let me have you? If you let me make you inside, Mommy can change her past forever. Deal? My past for your future? Is it a deal, baby? Debbie patted her stomach and smiled a smile that felt tender but looked sad.

What past?

A whispered cackle burst from Debbie's lips. The noise caused Howard to stir, but not to wake.

What past?

See? You're already making things better, aren't you? And still only a promise. Thank you, baby. You are so good to Mommy. So good. No past. No pain. Just you and me.

And Howard.

You and me are clean.

And we are strong.

What past? Debbie cackled aloud again, and Howard stirred once more but did not wake.

I am okay. I am okay. I am okay, she repeated the mantra for miles. If asked, she would have said it was the truth.

I am okay, baby (girl).

What Debbie couldn't do for herself, she believed she could do for her baby. If the symptoms went away, if only into hiding, then surely the cure would fill the void. *Only say the words and I shall be healed.*

I am healed.

I am okay.

And pain, wrapped in a pink blanket and harbored under a red dawn, secretly smiled its wicked, rotten smile.

Mommy is healed, my baby.

I am okay.

Thank you.

Debbie stopped at a lonely intersection beneath a single flashing red light swaying in the wind, and she believed herself suddenly healed by a baby living as a promise in the ether. As long as she behaved as though she were healed, she was. Which meant she faked it. And she faked it pretty well, at least for a while.

5

HOWARD AWOKE IN THE soft glow of the Cadillac's interior lights. He was small enough and the Cadillac front seat big enough for him to curl up nicely for his nap, using the passenger door armrest for a pillow. Sleeping comfortably in a car cutting through the dark felt dreamy and secure. It brought back memories of being a little boy tucked under the stiff warm wing of Gramma Helen. He was still under the influence of his thoroughly deep release. When he relived it in his mind, he felt oozy inside. And a little embarrassed.

He looked at Debbie. She had the silhouette of a stout truck driver with a big bug on his head. Howard looked fondly upon this image. Debbie was now his sun and he worshipped her.

Howard sat up. He looked out the large windows and saw the scattershot lights from stars above and farms on the horizon. He looked back to Debbie. He felt comfortable and decided to break the silence and initiate conversation—a move he had sometimes been punished for.

"Debbie?"

"Hello," Debbie said with a smile. She was ready to exercise her new attitude, her newly found way.

"How are you?" Howard was on the ball enough to gauge the present temperament of his beastie lover.

"I am okay," she said with intentional yet dim cheerfulness. Then, after a short pause, "How are you?"

"I feel really good. I hope that's all right."

"Are you hungry?"

"You know," Howard sounded like he had just made a brilliant discovery, "I am. I am really hungry. How about you?"

"Sure. There's a Tracy's on the way home. How about we stop and get dinner?"

What choice did Howard have? Still, it was nice to be asked. "Okay. I've never been to a Tracy's. Driven by 'em a few times, but never stopped."

"Me neither, the place always looked too darn…" *happy*, she wanted to say. "I don't know, it didn't look right. But we're going to come up on one, so it looks like tonight we give old Tracy a whirl." Debbie sounded as if her world was a peach. Howard looked at her sideways.

"Debbie?"

"Huh?"

"Can I ask you something?"

Debbie thought about this. It was easy enough for Howard to get outside her narrow zone of tolerance, and she wasn't sure she was ready to test how okay she really was. In honor of her ticking bio-clock, she decided to meet this challenge with grace and airiness.

"Go ahead," Debbie answered. "But I'll tell you right now I don't want to talk about the doctor's office."

"I know. I just want to say thank you. That was really wonderful back there. I mean it. I have never had anything like that, ever. And, my God, it was—it was super-amazing."

"You're welcome. I'm glad you liked it." Debbie wasn't sure if that was true or not.

"Have you ever done that before?" Howard asked, innocently.

Debbie paused again. She could get angry and put Howard back in his little box, or she could choose acceptance and answer in the affirmative.

"No," she lied. "And you know I don't want to talk about that. You liked it, leave it at that."

"Sure, Debbie. Thank you, though. Thank you for everything. You made me happy and you're taking good care of me. And I don't even have to work or nothing. So thank you."

Howard put his hand in the middle of the split-bench seat. Debbie briefly looked at him, then took it. It was a hard but loving grasp. Each unknowingly sighed over this simple act. All the way to the Tracy's parking lot their hands lay together innocently, Howard's too sweaty and Debbie's too dry.

I am okay.

6

FROM THE PARKING LOT, Tracy's Restaurant looked warm and cozy—you could even say it glowed. Inside, a grid of powerful fluorescent tubes blazed harshly above pods of flamboyant orange and magenta booths. It was so bright, Howard and Debbie had to squint upon walking into the restaurant from the dark parking lot.

They sat in a booth as far away as possible from the other patrons. On any other evening, the mere ambience of the joint would have been enough to raise Debbie's ire. But tonight she would be as cool as the Cadillac's AC.

Howard had experience with loser-magnet diners, though none quite as garish as the Tracy's between Shipley and Wilburn. This, along with his fascination of the mundane, allowed him to feel quite content sitting across from Debbie, whose housedress blended right in with the restaurant's color scheme. Howard continued to silently reminisce over his orgasm. It caused him to smile in a way that made him look mentally ill. Debbie had seen that smile before. Normally when she caught him in such a state, she would slap him upside the head as if he were an old television with a dodgy picture. But this night she merely looked away.

After several minutes with the same expression on his face and one corner of his mouth wet with drool, Debbie decided to get Howard talking. She had things she wanted to discuss, and Howard was her only option aside from the skinny, dirty-haired waitress who had vanished after leaving two shiny, sticky menus on their shiny, sticky table.

"Howard."

No response.

"Howard."

Still no response. Just a fixated queasy smile above vacant eyes.

Debbie grunted in mild frustration then whacked Howard gently on the side of his head with a menu. He came to life like a ventriloquist's dummy with an arm fresh up its bum.

"Howard," she said again, a beat after the whack.

"What?" Howard asked, as if he had been available the whole time.

"You ever thought about being a daddy—being someone's daddy?"

Howard glazed over again as he searched the half-full shelves of his mind. "No." As always, he was telling the truth.

"Why not?" Debbie needed to know this.

"I don't know. Was I supposed to?"

"Yes, Howard," Debbie answered. "Haven't you ever wondered what your baby would look like or feel like in your arms? What it'd be like to walk around with your little child calling you 'Daddy' and looking up to you, like…like you were everything good in the world and you could do no wrong? Don't you want someone to love you no matter what you look like? No matter what people think about you or say about you or done to you?"

"You know, I never thought about it. It does sound nice the way you say it. But…"

"But what, Howard?" Debbie started to showed signs of irritation, and Howard knew that could put the kybosh on the meal.

"But," Howard continued. "I already have someone who loves me. I have you."

Debbie would not allow herself to be affected by this statement. Pity, that. "Howard, that's different." She had begun to reset the conversation but was interrupted by the waitress.

"Ready to order?" the server asked dully. She wore a brown-and-yellow smock that must have come into her possession when she worked at an entirely different restaurant.

Debbie quickly opened her menu. "Just a second—don't go anywhere." Going by the pictures on the menu, Debbie ordered decisively, "I'll have the Tracy's Chicken Fried Steak with mashed potatoes, extra gravy, cheese toast and fiesta salad; and he'll have Salisbury steak with fries and Tracy's corn medley. Two Dr. Peppers, please."

The waitress scribbled something on her green pad and said thank you in a tone intimating that there was no way in hell the order was going to come out right. Then she disappeared again, allowing Debbie to return to the matter at hand.

"Howard."

"Uh-huh?"

"Do you remember the way you loved your Gramma Ellen?"

"Gramma Helen. There is an H."

Who cares?

"Helen. Helen," she repeated. "Do you remember how much you loved your Gramma Helen?" Debbie gave the H in Helen extra emphasis.

Howard went back to those half-empty shelves in his mind and returned with an armful of memories from his childhood.

His deep love for Helen came from the same tepidly emotional place that gave his life much of its pathetic shape. It was not as profound as Debbie's love for her father. But for Howard, it was as deep as things got, and the memories warmed his heart.

"Yeah," Howard said. "Gramma Helen used to snuggle me, tuck me in. She'd even give me breakfast in bed when I stayed home sick—sort of like you used to do, only she didn't lock me in. She would wipe my tears away when she put iodine on my sores or when she made me drink bean oil for my tummy. Now that I think about it, Gramma Helen was everything to me. She celebrated all my Christmases and birthdays and even threw me a party when I graduated. She also—"

Debbie sensed Howard would reveal every sweet *Gramma Helen* memory if she allowed him.

"So Gramma Helen loved you as much as you loved her?"

"She loved me a lot. More than anything, I think. It was just me and her, you know. She didn't have to, but she raised me after my dad died and my mom ran off to be a stinker hippie. She even—"

"Howard, listen," Debbie interrupted.

"Okay."

"Howard. Imagine if you were like a Gramma Helen to a little boy or girl (*yes, please—a girl*) of your very own? Imagine if you were a father." Debbie said the word father with much reverence, and something clicked in Howard's brain.

"A father," Howard repeated with wonderment. "Howard Feck—a father." The vexing smile returned to Howard's dopey face, only this time Debbie looked at it without a sense of revulsion. For perhaps the very first time in their bizarre relationship they both felt the same wondrous thing at the same time. It was a moment to cherish.

"Does this mean we're going to get married?" Howard asked.

"Why, I think we're already married, don't you? We've been together for some time now, and we don't fight much anymore—thanks to you, mostly."

Howard positively beamed in response to this. Debbie decided to go all the way.

"Howard, I'm going to level with you. Now please listen carefully, okay?"

Howard sat up straight. "Okay."

"I know I'm…I can be…crazy sometimes. I know I've hurt you. Hell, let's face the truth we never talk about—I kidnapped you and locked you up. And I know that's not okay. And, well, you've been very good about it. Even during times when I was real mean to you. You went along, and in a way, that was maybe the nicest thing you could have done. And I want you to know…I want you to know, Howard…I appreciate it."

It was the best she could do.

"Okay," Howard replied. It seemed to be enough.

"And I'm going to be nicer to you. At least I'm going to try. Some of this will depend on you, of course."

Debbie took in a big breath, and then finally said what needed to be said. "And I'm sorry. I'm sorry for when I hurt you. You don't deserve to be hurt, Howard." Debbie stopped there lest she cry again.

Howard showed no sign that he was still paying attention. But he was. He had listened intently. And while he may not have entirely grasped the significance, he did understand that it was hard for Debbie to say these things. So instead of saying the first thing that came into his head, he purposely paused and thought about what he *should* say. He said what he believed to be the nicest and richest contribution to the dialogue.

"Friends?" he asked, smiling.

Debbie looked at him warmly. She found eloquence in his simple response, and was once again made happier by Howard's natural inclination to make things easier for her.

"Friends," Debbie answered, moving her hand across the table for Howard to take. He did so after looking at it for a second or two. She gave it a shake that reverberated up Howard's arm, and then let go.

"But not just friends, okay?" Debbie said. "We're married, Howard. You and me. Married. Look what we've been through. We're made for each other in some ways, don't you think? I mean you like me taking care of you. You *let* me take care of you, and…" Debbie suddenly realized it was a short list. "And you don't have to worry about nothing."

Howard nodded and issued a gleeful snort.

"I mean what would you be doing, Howard, if you weren't here with me?"

Life pre-Debbie and post Gramma Helen felt long ago and otherworldly. Howard had to think about the question. "Well, I'd probably be back in the receiving department at Burke's where I used to work," Howard answered, as if it were a test. "Maybe I would have made manager by now. I used to play the lotto; maybe I would have won it. I'd still be in Gramma Helen's house, though I am kind of glad not to live there anymore. It was kind of a sad place after she died. I wonder what happened to it."

It wasn't quite the answer Debbie was hoping for, but she nodded as if to say, *See? Aren't you better off here with your extra-large psychopath girlfriend-wife-guardian-kidnapper-punisher?*

"I know," Howard blurted.

"What?"

"I'd be watching *Gilligan's Island* and *The Three Stooges* in the afternoon when your judge shows are on. I know I'd be doing that."

"All right, Howard. I'll make you a deal since we're friends, okay?"

"Okay."

"Pick one. I'll split the hour with you."

Howard thought for a long moment. The choice between Curly Howard's slapstick and Mary Ann in short shorts was nothing to sneeze at. After more seconds than Debbie expected, Howard finally gave his answer.

"*Gilligan's Island.*"

"Gilligan it is."

While Howard and Debbie continued to share their most pleasant conversation to date, their waitress reappeared, having gathered two ghastly hickies while she had been away. She dropped off something that bore no resemblance to their order, along with a pile of cold cheese toast.

"Close," Debbie said as the server disappeared again. Howard tucked in, clearly in need of sustenance. Debbie, too preoccupied to eat much, picked at hers. She considered sending the mess back but decided that the new Debbie would do no such thing. When they had finished eating, the waitress brought them the check and their beverages, which, while late, were accurate. They both drank them down—it was by far the highlight of the meal.

Chapter 12

1

IN THE DAYS THAT followed, Howard and Debbie entered the happiest part of their lives together.

Debbie recognized this new plateau and congratulated herself for keeping her past dead and buried. It was essential to her quest for motherhood. If only she had realized that healing required more than just pretending to have never been wounded.

Though he had no ring, said no vows, signed no certificate, and shared no bed, Howard Feck was, according to his keeper-wife, married. Even Gramma Helen would have found that surprising. Being a husband gave Howard a faint flicker of self-esteem. He was more at ease with himself in subtle ways. He showed an increase in devotion to his spouse—something that tried Debbie's newly formed patience. Intimacy between them, however, was relegated to occasional handholding and brief casual contact. Howard savored each, and they sent a little charge down to the place where Debbie had touched him at the doctor's office.

When Dr. Coe's nurse phoned, she had nothing but good news. Both blood tests came back with nothing unusual—they were even the same blood type. And Howard's sperm was deemed healthy and normal, though the count was a little light. Debbie was so happy she almost sprung her hair claw. Once he realized that the news implied another sexual encounter, Howard shared in the excitement and immediately went to the bathroom mirror to fix his unfixable ink-stain hairstyle. He walked away feeling as he always did after primping—that he had only made things worse.

They celebrated the green light for conception with dinner at the Chuck Wagon, Wilburn's version of a fine eatery. It was no Tavern on the Green, but it was a giant's stride better than their last dinner out. They even shared a bottle of overpriced, cheap champagne that went right to their heads, making them giggle and coo about the adjustments in living arrangements required to accommodate a family. The phrase "a family" made Debbie very tender inside, while Howard's champagne high made him giddy and loud. On three separate occasions, he told Debbie, "I love you, wifey-do" loudly enough to annoy other diners. They ended the night at Webspresso where they talked about baby names, baby clothes, and the myriad of baby accouterments Debbie had discovered on the internet.

Howard waited patiently over the next several days until the ovulating kit Debbie had purchased indicated her reproductive system was at the ready. The kit suggested a peak window of five-days, during which Howard had twelve orgasms, each by the hand of Debbie and all more clinical than sensual. Debbie performed the act not out of love but out of a need to control the situation. Howard didn't care. He was getting off by the hands of the woman he loved for Christ's sake, and that was a good and dirty blessing as far as he was concerned. The encounters were always the same. Debbie sat on Howard's bed while he stood next to her with his pants and underwear down around his ankles. She would seize his little bishop with one hand while holding a dainty china teacup in the other. The teacup had sat in the dining room hutch and was once used as an ashtray by Teddy Eel. Debbie chose it out of a subconscious need to ceremonialize the act.

Howard started slowly and ended in quick shudders. Debbie would then walk quickly to her room, shut the door, and attempt to insert Howard's stuff into her reproductive tract using a large medicine dropper. Her first two attempts were comically awkward. Because of her size, the stubbornness of a vagina grown accustomed to neglect, and that universal friend and enemy— gravity, it was quite a feat to get the fix where it needed to go. On her back with her spread legs resting against a wall, Debbie shook the upstairs as she tried to get the little doggies home. By day three, Howard was light in his loads, which strained Debbie's new pleasant facade. She had read on the web that papayas, carrots, and green leafy vegetables helped increase sperm count, so she made damn sure Howard's diet was overloaded with them. Howard was not a fresh fruit and veggie kind of guy, but he acquiesced the best his digestive system would allow.

Two ovulation cycles later, and after his nineteenth and last volley into the teacup, Howard was ready for a break. He didn't want it to be the end of his sex life with Debbie, and had he played it smart, he probably could have bargained for a less industrial encounter, since she was now at the mercy of her bio-clock and willing to do nearly anything for procreation. Nonetheless, Debbie had rendered him with professional accuracy, and he had thoroughly enjoyed it. Still, a hug or pillow talk between orgasm and nap would have been nice.

A few weeks after Debbie accepted Howard's last contribution to her dream, she missed her period. The dipstick from her home pregnancy kit showed two rich purple lines, confirming that life anew had sprouted inside her. They returned to Dr. Coe, as Debbie needed to be positive. The doctor spoke to her as if she were pregnant, and he gave her a load of pamphlets and a prescription for prenatal vitamins. He also warned her about depression—a nod to what had happened last time he had examined her—and told Debbie she would now need to see the staff ob-gyn, who would be happy to provide prenatal care throughout the pregnancy. Once again, she insisted on waiting for the results. The doctor explained that the home tests were almost always spot on, and the official test went to a lab, so she had no choice in the matter. Debbie surrendered and left quietly, emotionally, and with a tentative happiness. Howard was hoping to ask about a weird itch under his left armpit but never got the chance.

2

Before Dr. Coe's nurse called to relay the good news and remind Debbie about scheduling an ob-gyn appointment, Debbie had already known in her heart that she was pregnant. She suffered no morning sickness but felt sleepier than usual. While she lay awake in bed, tired but restless, rhapsodies about the large promise with the tiny beating heart played in her head.

Debbie had read enough on the web to know that prenatal care was important. But she thought that even routine visits would require her being exposed and penetrated and that was wholly unsettling. It could also bring her dead past back to life. Remembering or even acknowledging what she now pretended had never happened was surely bad for gestation. Especially if it gave her anxiety or depression, which the doctor had warned her about. So in a way, not seeing an ob-gyn was prescribed. Debbie was confident that if they only knew what these exams would do to her, and, therefore. her baby, Dr. Coe and his nurse would agree.

3

"HOWARD, GET OVER HERE," Debbie grumbled unpleasantly from her father's bedroom. It was a Tuesday morning around 7:00, a little over three months into Debbie's pregnancy. Howard was nowhere close to awake.

"Howard!" Debbie yelled again.

Howard stirred, rolled onto his back, and grabbed his morning hard-on. He managed to croak, "Hmmm? Debbie? Are you calling me?"

"I said get in here, Howard." Then, before he could ask, she added, "I'm in the bedroom."

Howard wondered what he had done wrong. It seemed early for trouble, but it would not be the first time he started his day in the doghouse. Still, ever since Debbie had been on the path of procreation, things had been pretty good.

He knew that walking into Debbie's room with a boner stretching the crotch of his jammies would only fuel her anger. Yet holding it with both hands wasn't making it go away. He couldn't help it. They were best friends.

"Howard!" Whatever bee Debbie had in her bonnet at this early hour seemed to have quite the stinger. He got out of bed and started for Debbie's room. He placed one hand over the obvious bulge, hoping Debbie would not see it. "Coming Debbie," he said meekly. He did not know what awaited him. It could be wildly violent, emotionally cruel, or just another castigation. Of all the possibilities, sex was nowhere on the list. He slunk into her room like a good victim.

"Come here, Howard," Debbie said in a devilish voice that made Howard want to run. "Quit looking like that and come here, goddammit."

Howard obliged. When he got close enough, Debbie snatched him hard like a circus bear who'd had enough. She had him by his

T-shirt and pulled him on top of her so his face was tight against her breasts. Howard could not breathe, but he could hear. "Listen, Howard. I am going to do something to you, and you are going to promise me you'll keep your eyes closed and not say a goddam word, got it?"

Deep in her cleavage, Howard nodded briskly. He had about twenty seconds of air left in his lungs.

"Got it, Howard?" Debbie asked again, raking his face against her alpine bosom. He nodded again.

Howard was standing bedside, bent over with his face deep in Debbie's flesh. He held onto her thick upper arms for balance. His hard-on was far worse than when he had walked into the room, and to top it off, he was genuinely afraid he was going to suffocate to death. Debbie grabbed him by the scruff of his neck and pulled him free. He gasped deeply twice, but surprisingly did not ask for his inhaler. In fact, it was the furthest thing from his mind. Debbie pulled down her baggy pajama top and her breasts lolled out. Her arms were positioned in a way that made her bosom stand tall and round and surprisingly firm, given Debbie's size. She saw a lustful hungry look cross Howard's face that she did not like, so she roughly pulled Howard to her in another smothering grasp. "Kiss them, Howard. Both of them. Kiss them, goddammit."

Howard began kissing them best he could, considering he could barely move his face. Debbie backed him off a little so he could roam her hills with his mouth. "Get the tips, Howard. Shut up and put them in your mouth before I pull your hair out." Debbie was not yelling, but she kept the same devilish tone. Howard, who had said nothing since he had entered the room, was getting off on her demands, but not as much as Debbie was.

It took some time for him to find purchase. The terrain was vast and unfamiliar. He felt the tense, puckered flesh of an erect nipple against his lips and accidentally moaned. Debbie hit him openhanded on the side of the head. "I said be quiet, Howard, and I mean it."

Pregnancy, it turns out, had made Debbie horny. And just like her anger, she wielded it with indomitable force. The profound need to experience the remarkable act of love and nature was what got Howard into Debbie's life to begin with, and lo these many years later, Howard's original goal was finally being met— with a vengeance.

Debbie's surging hormones pushed her desire beyond the reach of her many sexually related demons. As long as she kept commanding Howard to please her, she denied her mind the fertile silence required to summon them. Howard's work on her body was making her pliable to intercourse, which she wanted badly for the first time ever. She writhed and moved Howard's face around her chest, occasionally helping to stuff mammary flesh into his stretched mouth.

Debbie turned to see Howard's erection arching his pants away from his body. She grabbed it and said, "What's this, Howard? What do you have in here, huh?" She felt it and squeezed it, sussing out its size and density, despite having stroked it before— it was how she got to this moment, after all.

Howard knew better than to answer.

Debbie pushed his face down between her breasts again and demanded he take it out and shut up, even though he had yet to say a word. He was suffocating again, and Debbie meant to keep it that way until his penis was freed. She would not help Howard with this task. With his upper body balanced on his flesh-buried face, Howard used both hands to open his pajama pants. He completed the task with only eight seconds of oxygen left in his lungs.

She let him up briefly, and he managed to gulp half a breath before she pulled him down on her again. She wanted him there because she wanted to examine his genitals without him seeing.

She remembered from attempts at conception that they were nonthreatening. Still, she wanted reassurance before going any further. She allowed him to adjust his head so he could exhale through his nose and sniff down more air.

Debbie let go of him, kicked the covers off her legs, and said, "Howard, shut up and get between my legs. I need you to do something." She pulled him off her breasts again, and he accidentally made an audible suction-release sound. He kept his eyes closed, expecting to be hit. "Howard, goddammit, I said get on the bed down between my legs."

In a single motion, he jumped onto the bed and landed on his knees squarely between Debbie's thighs.

"Pull down your pants, stupid," Debbie barked. The devilishness was still in her voice, but impatience was the dominant tone now because inside of Debbie, the little creatures that rule the body during sex were rioting at the gate. Howard had barely gotten his pants to his knees when Debbie seized his cock with her hands and glided it into her. She wrapped her strong meaty legs around his bony weak ones. She had her hands on his dull-knife shoulder blades. Again she shoved his face into her flesh as she pushed and pulled him in and out of her. He flopped about in submission like a gangly, unbreakable, thinly-stuffed animal being roughly handled. All the while, she kept telling him to shut up and push, shut up and go slow, and just shut up.

Howard did not make a peep—until he came. He could not help this. He loved Debbie, and the only other time he was with a woman in this way, she leaped off him the instant he freefalled from plateau to orgasm. He made a series of shallow wheezy gasps that he tried to suppress against her breasts, and then exhaled in one large sob. Tears, saliva, and sperm flowed from him to Debbie. And Debbie, good sport that she was, did not hit him. There was only one smallish problem. Howard was finished, and Debbie was not. She took his sobs, told him it was okay, even rubbed his back. Then gently (for her), she pushed Howard up so she could look at him. She sighed.

Howard breathed heavily, causing a booger to dart in and out of his nose like a tiny eel in a cave.

"Go to the bathroom, Howard. Clean yourself up and come back. We're not finished."

It was one of the happiest days of his life.

Chapter 13

1

SEVEN AND A HALF months in, Howard and Debbie had finished refurbishing Howard's old bedroom (Debbie's old dungeon) and overstocking it with an array of baby-related items. With the room now destined for their child, Howard finally and gratefully moved into Debbie's bedroom (formerly Delwin's). It was the final consummating act of their marriage.

Debbie showed obvious physical signs of being with child. Her stomach stuck out farther than usual and was now rock hard. Her breasts seemed to rise off her chest in a gravity-defying manner. Her face was paler in some parts and blotchier in others. The famed pregnancy glow did make her look younger, and the extended breasts and belly forced her into maternity clothes that were an improvement over her standard shapeless, splattery-patterned couture.

She was often uncomfortable, but not so much that she questioned the wisdom of her sage biological clock. Discomfort and concern for the baby overrode her libido. Plus, when lying down now, she had the mobility of a laden sea turtle in wet sand. So Howard and Debbie's sex life quickly returned to the nothingness from whence it came. Howard did not complain and considered himself blessed for the few weeks of lovemaking they enjoyed. Intimacy now solely existed in the form of spooning in slumber and Howard massaging the pain out of Debbie's various body parts. Contact with so much flesh stirred him, and after Debbie fell asleep, he would lie next to her in Delwin's bed and secretly masturbate.

By the end of the third trimester, Debbie was very cranky again. She was more than ready to have this child, and now that the big day was only a week or two away, fear in the form of regret slid into her psyche on hormone-greased rails. Debbie's regret was multifaceted, but primarily had to do with her substitution of proper prenatal care with advice found on various websites. That regret turned to terror one night when the internet revealed to her the multitude of things that could go wrong in a pregnancy. The information was there all along, but she somehow missed (ignored) it until now, when she could go into labor at any time. From spina bifida to gestational diabetes, from exposure to German measles to toxoplasmosis, the successful delivery of a healthy normal baby seemed not just dubious but a nearly impossible feat worthy of headlines.

The fear generated from those afflictions paled greatly to that inspired by the freakish bogeymen of expectant mothers Debbie had uncovered going one click too far. Images of conjoined twins, prehensile tails, parasitic twins, mermaidism, and cyclopia filled her computer screen. The internet teemed with documented cases of Mother Nature's gruesome streak. It was too much information impossible to unlearn. And it sent Debbie right over the top. Not having had a single ultrasound on her uterus, Debbie realized that she had no idea what was in there. And if the web was any indication, she could be carrying something out of a horror movie.

Debbie was no longer sure about the sweet pink bundle she imagined snugly curled up in her womb. Already wound tight from surging hormones and the physical impact of pregnancy on the body, the reality of something going dreadfully wrong hit Debbie like a ton of pink-and-blue bricks. She began crying and expressing fear as she stared at a webpage of freakish humans trapped in old black-and-white photos. Each, she realized, started out as a bright little promise in the womb of a new mother, proud and tender. Howard rushed to Debbie's side upon realizing the depth of her conniption. She sat at the computer, trembling and crying, unable to tear her eyes away from these fringe examples of the miracle of life. Howard looked briefly at the computer monitor, saw the pictures of grotesque figures and immediately switched it off. He began stroking Debbie's back and doing his best to soothe her.

"It's okay, Debbie. Don't look. Don't look at those yucky pictures. There's no reason."

"The baby," Debbie managed to say.

"Our baby's fine. I mean, look at you and me. We made it out okay, didn't we?"

Debbie gained no comfort from these words. Howard tried again.

"Every person in this world was born and made it out fine or they wouldn't be here," Howard reminded her. "Remember how you used to say there's too many darn people in this world? Well, they were all born, just like you and me. The doctor said we were fine when we started this. Why should that change now just because you saw a bunch of scary pictures?"

"I want to know," Debbie sobbed. "I want to know everything's okay."

That seemed easy enough to Howard. "Then let's go to the doctor, and have him look. He'll tell you, just like I am.

Everything's okay—okay? Then you can stop worrying and go back to making that baby of ours. How does that sound?"

The thought of action soothed Debbie a little.

"We can call the doctor and drive down to Shipley tomorrow and put you on that thing where we can see the baby, okay?"

"Ultrasound."

"Ultrasound. That's right. Ultrasound. We can go get an ultrasound. Remember how we saw on the computer that they can print out a picture of the baby while she's still in your belly, and we can take it home and frame it, and you can put it by the bed and—"

"I want to go now."

"Now? It's too late to go tonight, Debbie, I'm sure of it. The doctor won't be in 'til morning. I'm almost positive."

"I want to go now." The tone of Debbie's voice made it clear that this was not a request. "We're going now, Howard. Go find my shoes and get our jackets. We can go to the emergency room at the county hospital. I want to know what is in my belly and if it ain't right, I want it out."

Howard stared at Debbie. Action seemed to be the tonic required to settle down her fear and anxiety. But what of providence, and the frightening power of a mother's intuition?

"What are you waiting for, dammit?" Debbie was beginning to sound like the insufferable Debbie of old. "Let's go. Get my shoes. In fact, get my overnight bag, just in case—" Debbie did not want to finish the sentence. It ended with *in case they have to pull a monster out of my belly.*

Mercy, she thought, *what have I gotten myself into?*

Howard stumbled into action. Debbie grabbed him and pulled him roughly to her. She looked into his eyes and said, "I need you, Howard. I need you to help me right now. I'm scared. Be with me if it goes bad. And be with me if we get to come home and everything's all right."

"Sure, Debbie. I'm just excited to get a picture of our baby and take it home." Howard's enthusiasm helped Debbie move further away from this new bad place in her mind. A place where carnival freaks in fetal positions waited underneath the smooth skin of distended bellies.

2

THE DRIVE TO PARO County Hospital failed to draw Debbie's attention away from bogey-infants. "Howard, say something," she demanded, as Howard looked out the passenger window onto the dark, lonely landscape of rural America past its bedtime.

"Okay." Howard started up his imagination as if he were turning a stiff hand crank on a rusty Model T.

"Howard!" Debbie yelled.

"Okay. I'm thinking, Debbie. I'm trying to—hey, how 'bout the radio? Want me to find some music for you?"

Debbie sighed. She knew Howard wasn't cut out for this. "Just tell me again that it's okay."

"Want to hear some country?"

"Tell me, Howard!" Debbie barked with an undertone of panic. "Tell me the baby is okay or I'm going to drive this car right into—"

"The baby is fine Debbie. I know it is." Howard said this matter-of-factly. Inside, he was flustered over the responsibility of keeping Debbie from losing it. "I mean, you did everything just right. You ate right, you rested, you didn't do anything wrong. You just got a little ways more to go. Then you can see her."

Her.

This word stuck out like a blossom on a thorn bush.

"And you'll see that she—"

She.

Another bloom.

"—will be perfect. You'll look into her eyes without a arm and holding her care—"

"What?" Debbie looked at Howard and nearly drove off the road by accident.

"I mean, the baby will be fine, and you can hold her in your arms without her hair—I mean, a care—and she looks into her eye—ahh—I mean your eyes—sorry."

"How come you said 'she'?"

Howard thought for a few seconds.

"How come you said 'she'?"

"I don't know, I…it just came out like that. I guess that, like I feel she is okay, I feel like she is a she, too. A baby girl."

A baby girl.

Debbie liked this concept. It validated her wish and gave her something bright to cling to amid grainy black and white fears and a Cadillac tearing through the night on an unlit county road. Somewhere on that road there was a hospital. A hospital whose clientele was mostly car accident victims, injured folk on their way to jail, and the untouchables of America.

"Debbie?"

"What?"

"I just know it's going to be all right, just you wait and see."

"Promise?"

"I promise with all my heart."

"I hope you're right, Howard," Debbie said, sounding a tad more like the new and improved version he had quickly grown accustomed to. "You better be right."

"I am right, Debbie. I don't know how I know, but I know. And I'm never one to believe in myself like I believe in others. It's just…this is different. I don't know why but it is. I see you holding your baby—*our* baby—and taking her home and cuddling her and raising her and the whole thing, just like it was for you and me—only without the sadness."

Debbie dared to believe it. She wanted it so bad. "Thank you, Howard," she said. "You know, kidnapping you was maybe the best thing that ever happened to me."

"And lying to you about being handsome was the best thing that ever happened to me," he snorted with lovey-dovey glee.

Debbie looked at him with mock superciliousness. "You lied to me, Howard? Why I thought you lied to that tarty Fairchild girl with the dirty mind?"

Howard snorted again, deeply, almost triggering an asthma attack. "It was your mind," he said playfully. "It was a cute girl's picture, but it was your mind. And given the choice, I think I came out ahead. Especially the way we are now." Howard smiled, big.

For a long minute, there was only the sound of the Cadillac's tires on the road and a dim whistle coming from Howard's nose every time he inhaled. He reached across the long bench seat until his hand reached Debbie's leg. There he rested it, having to shift his frame over to close the gap between them. The conversation and the feelings it summoned were enough to keep Debbie's mind off that weather-beaten cellar door behind which a stack of mad scientist imagery now lurked among the demons from Debbie's time in captivity. All were tucked away behind that flimsy barrier—until they arrived at Debbie's dark tower, her Avalon, her Oz: the all-too-gloomy Paro County Hospital.

Chapter 14

1

THE HOSPITAL WAS A large, square, six-story concrete block building rising above flat, barren farmland. Under the quarter-moon night, sodium-vapor streetlights guarded dirty rundown cars and various government vehicles. The place looked as inviting as a dilapidated prison. It was rural America's version of the mad scientist's castle and laboratory. From the outside, one could easily assign a nefarious quality to the cold, isolated structure looming out of shadows broken by thin, ochre luminescence. It was even scarier inside. Like many government-run agencies serving the outcaste, it was poorly funded and, therefore, poorly staffed with the poorly trained.

The Cadillac pulled into the parking lot at a good clip, making full use of its suspension as it bobbed noisily across the sidewalk. Debbie cruised through the ER parking lot and found it full except for the last row, which was heavily marked by signs reading Physician's Parking Only. The row was nearly empty. Feeling like a shiny big Cadillac would not look out of place there, and not giving a damn if it did, Debbie parked.

Howard and Debbie bustled through the automatic doors of the ER. The strong smell of piss, wet linen, and rubbing alcohol hit them like a punch. Unsettling noises boxed their ears, and unforgiving fluorescent lights strained their eyes. The soundscape of the ER waiting room was a mix of wicked, phlegmy coughs, crying babies, wailing children, and moaning adults. The tinny din of an old TV perched high in a corner and parked on a foreign language station mixed with these noises, ensuring that even if everyone awaiting treatment died in the chairs they sat in, the waiting room would still thrum obnoxiously.

Debbie quickly surveyed the bright rectangle room packed with rows of uncomfortable chairs with hard plastic seat buckets suitable for hosing down. Members of the sickly ensemble occupied them. A small number were empty. Some of the sickly had surrounded themselves with piles of plastic-bagged belongings, as if homesteading. There was no way in hell Debbie was going to queue up behind these sick, wounded, and crazy, dirty bastards. And no way in hell was she going to sit her fat pregnant ass down in one of those contaminated chairs, either.

At a counter across from the entrance, a thin Filipino nurse sat at an old metal desk with standard-issue medical office paraphernalia. Behind her there was a pair of doors with small, square windows and a sign that said, *No Admittance* and *No Entrar*. Debbie immediately knew that she needed to be on the other side of those doors as quickly as possible. She considered barreling past the nurse but knew that could backfire on her in a place like this. She opened her large, purple, old-lady purse and pulled a few twenties from the wallet inside. Seizing Howard's arm, Debbie stormed up to the nurse who had just stuck a thermometer into the mouth of a shaky old sot seated beside the desk. The nurse looked up, ignored Howard, and in a thick accent told Debbie to fill out a card from the stack on the counter. Debbie glowered at her. It had no effect whatsoever. She quickly stepped away, filled out the card, and returned to the nurse who was now writing something on a clipboard. The old, weathered drunk was still sitting there, shaking like a paint mixer. Speaking in short, halting phrases, the nurse told the old man to go have a seat until they called his name. Despite the nurse's dismissal, he just sat there, vibrating his thrift store sports coat and filthy dress slacks. Either he didn't understand or he couldn't stand up. The nurse pointed toward the rows of chairs and barked, "Go sit DOWN! Over there. People waiting. Go!" She repeatedly motioned with her arm to help the man understand he needed to get out of the chair he was shaking in. As he tried to push himself up, Debbie decided to help. She grabbed his jacket collar and pulled the man off to the side. The old man groaned like he had been kicked in the gut. The battle-hardened nurse looked at Debbie and snapped, "Hey! Miss! You no touch. No touch patients. You touch patients, I call security. They throw you out. HARD!"

"Sorry," Debbie said with great restraint. "I thought he needed some help."

"You not the nurse. I AM the nurse. He need help, I help, not you. Okay?"

With her eye on the prize and the growing feeling that this was exactly the kind of joint where the horrors of birth that had sent her here came into the world, Debbie surrendered authority to this tough, wiry woman. "Sorry," she said, not sounding sorry at all.

"Okay. You should be sorry. Sit now. Give me the card." The nurse took the card before Debbie could hand it over. She read it quickly, then asked Debbie, "When last time you feel kick?"

"I felt her kicking in the car on the way here."

"You been chick for anemia?"

"Look. Here's the deal," Debbie said. "My baby is due in a couple weeks, and I need to see her on an ultrasound and make sure she's okay. Here's a couple twenties. Take me back there now, okay?" Debbie set the cash on the nurse's desk. The nurse immediately put her clipboard over it.

"Nu-huh," said the nurse. "You no insurance." Then leaning closer to Debbie, "Fifty. Fifty put you ahead a dose sick people out there."

Debbie put another twenty on the clipboard. "Keep the change, lady. Just get me to a doctor."

The nurse picked up the clipboard and the cash on both sides of it magically disappeared. She picked up the phone, pressed a button, and spoke so fast Debbie could not tell if it was English. "Okay lady. They come they get you. Right now."

A dozen seconds later, another skinny, brown-skinned nurse who could have been the first one's twin came through the double doors and motioned for Howard and Debbie to follow her through the double doors. The nurse took Debbie to a "room" with three curtains for walls and a fourth that was solid and held a few valves, outlets, and archaic medical devices housed in pale-green anodized metal. A hospital bed filled the rest of the space. Folded at the foot of the bed was a faded blue-and-white hospital gown. In the exact same accent as the triage nurse, the ER nurse told Debbie to strip, put on the garment, and lie down and wait. Then she disappeared through one of the curtains, never to be seen again.

On Debbie, the hospital garment was more bib than gown. Debbie's corpulence made it impossible to tie it behind her considerable backside. She thought about sending Howard to the car for her overnight bag, which contained maternity pajamas, but after all these years she still struggled with letting her kept man go free—even for a much-needed errand. And if she did send him to the car, Debbie figured he would have an impossible time returning to her bedside. She imagined Howard hurting himself on purpose as a way to get past the tough triage nurse she had bribed, such was his unique brand of chivalry. Despite feeling extremely uncomfortable with so much flesh exposed, she did not mention the overnight bag, and Howard, who was busy making himself dizzy on the doctor's swivel stool, didn't think of it. Looking terribly uncomfortable, Debbie laid back and waited.

And waited.

And waited some more.

The smell here was less pissy and more antiseptic—*at least that was something*, Debbie thought. The lighting was equally intense, but the sounds were considerably better. There seemed to be only one, maybe two wailing young ones. The sounds of groaning elderly were replaced by that of a lone, ill madman jib-jabbering nonsensically. A woman in the next compartment burst into long colorful strings of profanity every few minutes. A multitude of irregular beeps and boops, dings and pings coming from the various pieces of health monitoring equipment replaced the waiting room's blaring TV. These electronic sounds sat above the other noises like a bad guitar solo. Occasionally, a monotone lead vocal would chime in atop all of this, repeating the words "doctor" followed by a name, then "code," followed by either a number or a color (blue seemed popular).

Debbie had turned her thoughts inward again. Surprisingly, Howard sensed this and knew he had to say or do something.

"Debbie," he said finally. "Debbie, are you sure you want to be here right now? This doesn't seem like the place for us, or the place to have the uterus sound."

"Ultrasound," Debbie corrected. "Christ, Howard. Can you please remember it's called an ultrasound?"

"Sorry. I'm just saying—you know—remember how you picked that one maternity place in Merritin for when the baby comes? Remember we saw it on the internet, and it was pretty and had nice rooms all set up for babies and new mommies?"

"Merritin is too far away, and it's a birthing center, Howard. They don't have an emergency room."

"I'm just saying. I'm not sure you want to have our—"

"We're here just to make sure the baby is okay. I'm not going to have her here unless…" Debbie paused. Stopping certain thoughts was like stopping a freight train by standing in front of it. The heavier the thought, the faster it flattened you.

"I'm sorry, Debbie," Howard said. "Like I keep saying, and I mean it with all my heart, the baby is okay. She is fine. But now I'm getting worried about you. I've been to a lot of medical places but geez, this one—this one is not right."

Howard paused. He had never seen Debbie look this sad, this afraid before.

"Heck, Debbie," he continued. "You can tell too, can't you? This place seems like a crazy-person place and not a healthy place to be in at all."

Debbie sighed. Howard was right. She looked at him with a face that had all the makings of someone about to cry. "You mean it looks like the kind of place where freaks are born. Is that what you're saying?"

"No. No, no, no. That's not what I…"

"You think we ended up here because maybe I do have a freak in here," Debbie said, rubbing her belly. Before Howard could answer, she quickly took her hands away as if she had touched a hot stove.

"Debbie, look at me." Normally, taking in Howard's physical attributes raised more health issues than they diminished. But Debbie had some love for him, at least her version of love. She looked at him mournfully.

"I don't know why," Howard said. "But I know that the baby inside of you is fine. Right as rain on Mondays. So no more crazy talk, please? I know it's a girl and I know she is fine, okay?"

Howard believed with childlike sincerity that he was telling the truth, which helped Debbie relax slightly. After a few moments of silence, he spoke again. "We've been waiting here a long time. What time is it?"

Debbie looked at her zirconium-encrusted watch. "It's half past twelve. We've been here an hour."

Howard tried to sound strong and capable, "All right, Debbie. I'm not going to let them forget about you and our baby. I'm going to get a nurse or a doctor or someone to come and look at you. I have been to the emergency room many times, and I never had to wait this long for someone to come and at least take my temperature."

Debbie spoke. "Howard, I don't need you getting lost on me. I got enough to worry about without wondering where you ended up. These rooms all look the same, and…" Debbie stopped. She could tell by the sudden change in Howard's posture that he was getting up the nerve to make himself useful. And she was certain it would prove disastrous. "No, Howard," she snapped. "I forbid it. You stay here. I'll go."

"You can't go, Debbie. You're naked."

"What do you call this?" Debbie lifted up the small garment from the breasts it failed to harness.

"I call that naked." Howard was driven, and it sent some chemical to his brain that seemed to make it work better.

Debbie held back a sardonic chuckle. This was no time to let Howard have his first upper-hand experience. "Look, Howard…"

"No," Howard said, reflexively putting up his arms in anticipation of a smack. "Please, Debbie. You look for a minute. I have been to doctors and hospitals a lot. This is my…I'm comfortable in these places. I know how it works, how to get their attention."

Howard looked at Debbie and pleaded sincerely. He spoke words born from the bottom of his heart. "Debbie, let me do this for you. I need to. I can. Please let me take care of you. I promise I'll come right back."

Debbie searched inside herself for the bio-clock that had gotten her into this mess. She found it ticking away nonchalantly and awfully close to that damn cellar door behind which freaks of birth lay writhing like infant bogeymen. And behind them lurked a long line of ugly, naked, angry male-demons and, lastly, a sad, dead father. The clock winked at her like something out of a Walt Disney cartoon. She looked Howard in the eye. "Promise you won't get lost?" she asked.

"Promise."

"Promise you will come back?"

"Promise. I could never leave you no matter what."

Debbie looked affectionately toward her broken stick of a man demanding to care for her in this moment of doubt and fear. Howard felt on top of the world—like a teenager gaining permission to drive to the store for a gallon of milk. Debbie noticed that a light bulb appeared to have come on somewhere not too far behind Howard's bulgy eyeballs.

"Debbie, you got to go potty?"

"I'm nine months pregnant Howard. I *always* have to go potty."

"What about sick? Could you make sick?"

"What? Can I make sick?" Debbie thought about slapping him. She resisted. "If you mean throw up, then no. I'm upset, but I ain't going to puke on you. Now you better hurry before I—"

"The thing is," Howard said confidently, "they don't like people making sick or having an accident in the emergency room. That'll get 'em over here in a jiff if I tell them you're about to make sick, and you haven't even seen a nurse yet and you don't even have one of those plastic vomit boats to catch it."

Debbie looked at Howard with a queasy admiration. "You want me to throw up for you, Howard?"

"Well, if comes to it, it might help us get someone over here to get the…ultrasound going."

"Well I have to piss like a racehorse, if that helps."

"Good enough for me. Wish me luck."

"Go get 'em, hubby," Debbie said, admiring the peculiar way Howard seemed to have risen to this occasion. He disappeared behind one of the curtains, and as if on cue Debbie's mind led her back to that awful cellar door. She knew if it opened, there was a very good chance that she would puke her guts out all over the place from here to the waiting room. *That ought to make Howard happy*, she thought.

2

HOWARD STUMBLED BLINDLY THROUGH the curtains and into a world he felt more comfortable in than any other. He had always been a good patient and knew what doctors and nurses wanted to hear. Though the smells were more pungent here than in the doctor's offices and private hospitals of his youth, they made Howard feel at home. He surveyed the large room. A substantial circular kiosk stood at the center—the nurse's station. It was surrounded by people in scrubs and smocks buzzing about. They came and went like obsessive worker bees building combs and filling them with honey. Of the curtained "rooms" along the emergency room perimeter, only one had its curtains pulled open. It revealed an emaciated, worn-out-looking old man sporting a nasal cannula and a hospital gown he could lose himself in. He lied in a bed that had its head adjusted to a sitting position. Howard, smiled and waved. The old man appeared to stare at Howard with glassy, unblinking eyes. His mouth was open and surrounded by gray stubble. He did not wave back.

Howard shrugged, then turned and aimed for an open section of the nurse's station. He took one step and walked right into the path of an orderly pushing a large medical gizmo on wheels.

"Pinche Baboso," the orderly huffed, swerving to avoid the collision.

"Sorry sir," Howard said, stepping back.

The orderly pushed on, insulting Howard's manhood in Spanish as he passed.

Incandescent lighting within the circumference of the nurse's station gave it a soft glow, putting it in stark contrast to the harsh fluorescents lighting in the rest of the ER. It gave the middle-aged nurse standing in the middle of it an aura of peace. Her old-fashioned white nurse's uniform and cap complimented her milk chocolate skin. She noticed Howard approaching, stopped what she was doing, and asked, "What do you need, sir? We are very busy."

Howard took a breath and spoke in one long exhalation. "My wife is here because she is worried about our baby and she has been back here for over an hour and hasn't even seen a nurse and I think she's going to get sick and if she doesn't get to a bathroom I think she's going to have an accident and she's not dressed and no one gave us a urinal or one of those little plastic vomit boats or nothing and…" Howard paused to refill his lungs.

Sensing that he would just keep going if she let him, the nurse started talking before he finished inhaling. "What's wrong with your baby, sir?"

"Well, nothing. I don't think, anyway. She's still inside my wife. I mean, she's pregnant. My wife, I mean, not the baby. She's not born yet. The baby, I mean."

"Got it," the nurse replied patiently. Where's your wife?"

"Um," Howard looked at each curtained room. It was like looking at a circle of petals from the center of a flower. Damn if he wasn't confused over which one held Debbie.

The nurse looked at him. "I am sorry, sir, but we are extra busy tonight and short on staff so—"

"I think that one there," he said, pointing to the right one. "We're next to the lady who keeps cussing."

"Why do you think something's wrong with your baby?"

"I don't know. My wife just thinks there is."

The nurse generously placed aside the six other things she needed to be doing and focused on Howard. "Name?"

"Howard."

"Not your name. I need the patient's name."

"Well, we haven't really named her yet. We don't know if it is a—"

"What is your wife's name?"

"Oh. It's Debbie Feck."

"Thank you." The nurse looked at different clipboards scattered on her side of the counter. "Now where is she again?"

Howard pointed quickly to the right set of curtains before his mind could confuse things.

"Mr. Feck, please wait here one second." The nurse turned to a post lined with plastic pockets holding orange folders. She examined the column of folders, pulled one out, looked at it briefly, then put it back. "I don't have a Debbie Feck registered back here. Did she check in with the triage nurse outside?"

"Yes she did. In fact, she even gave her…" Howard managed to stop himself from telling the nurse that Debbie had bribed her way in. "I think she may have used her maiden name. But the thing is, I know she is going to be sick all over the place, and she is a very big woman. He emphasized this by standing on his toes and spreading his arms. "And let me tell you, you don't want her getting sick back here, unless you got something she can get sick into."

"Mr. Feck, this is an emergency room. That's what people do back here—they get sick."

Howard paused briefly at this retort, then offered, "Yes, but all over the floor and stuff?"

"Everywhere," the nurse answered unequivocally.

Howard felt let down and he showed it.

"What's her maiden name?"

Uh-oh, Howard thought. He was not prepared for that one. He knew Debbie's real last name, didn't he? Why sure he did. He scrunched up his eyes and searched his mind like a kid searching for a clean sock in a messy bedroom. The name Fairchild kept coming to him and he knew it was wrong.

"Sir, don't you know what your wife's maiden name is?"

"Yes, I do. I'm just…I'm just…(*Come on, stupid mind—oh to heck with it, just tell the truth.*) I'm nervous. I'm sorry, ma'am. I get nervous real easy and when I do, I don't think so well. I'm sorry, please forgive me. I just want to get my poor wife some help. She's not doing so—"

"Okay." The nurse believed Howard. As a good nurse in a bad hospital with a dangerous clientele, it was critical to know when someone was telling the truth. And Howard looked like the kind of guy who got nervous a lot and was bad at lying.

"As soon as I can get a nurse to sit here for five minutes, I'll come over and see what's going on, okay?"

"Coomb!" Howard shouted at the nurse. She looked at him superciliously.

"Pardon me sir? What did you just say?"

"Coomb. Debbie Coomb. That's her name. C-O-O-M-B. My wife's name is Debbie Coomb. I got it. Coomb."

"Debbie Coomb. Okay. Thank you." The nurse pulled from somewhere below the counter a small stack of what Howard called vomit boats. "Take these with you. We're out of the large ones, so here's a handful. Try not to get any on the floor." The nurse smiled as she said this last bit. She thought it amusing that Howard tried to persuade her with a puddle of bodily fluids.

3

LEFT ALONE, DEBBIE'S FEAR over the contents of her belly had created a dark cloud over the curtained room. She just wanted to get the (*baby*) thing out of there so she could go home, crawl under the covers, and die. *This is what I get for hoping*, she thought.

Howard returned to find Debbie lying flat with wet, closed eyes. "Debbie? You okay?"

"You didn't bring anyone, did you, Howard?" Her eyes remained closed.

"No," Howard said. "I got some vomit boats though." He tried to make that sound like an attractive consolation prize but he knew better.

Debbie opened her eyes, looked at Howard, and then looked at nothing in particular over his left shoulder. "Baby's been kicking. A lot." Debbie always ran her hands over her belly when she talked about the baby. Now her hands lay motionless at her side. "Did you at least talk to anybody out there?"

"Yes, I talked to a really nice nurse who promised she'd be here in a few minutes."

"Well, that's something, I guess."

"She meant it, too. I could tell. I know doctors and nurses."

"I don't," Debbie said, staring at the invisible nothing to Howard's left. She sounded far away. She looked pale.

"Can I feel the baby kicking?"

"If you want to. Go ahead."

Howard rubbed his hands over Debbie's large distended belly while she craned her neck, looking as far away as she could, just like when she was a captive whore. Whore. Debbie sometimes used that word on herself when she was severely depressed, when the demons of memory danced a gaudy jig on the main stage of her mind. It was self-mutilation of the psyche and the soul. When angry, she used the words "prisoner" or "captive" to describe her place in her past. Under no circumstances did she ever use the word "victim." That word implied that she had lost and they had won. No matter what state of mind she was in, the concept of them winning and her losing was unbearable. She need only remember the look on Teddy's face, framed in the flames of the tavern fire to remind herself that she had not lost. The memory of that moment still had the ability to energize her all these years later, though upon turning a new leaf in her quest for motherhood, she had banned the thought of it. Nowadays, she had no past with Eels. That was the deal she made with her baby. Now that was in jeopardy too.

Howard kept his clammy hands on Debbie's tight white belly skin. Her hospital gown was pulled up and to the side like an ugly kerchief. The baby was kicking up a storm. He could actually see the movement pushing against her skin. Howard seemed to be whipping the thing into a frenzy as he frenetically rubbed the dome-shaped womb.

"Stop it, Howard. Enough. You're behaving as if I'm some sort of carnival prize." Debbie adjusted her gown while Howard cowered in admonishment.

"Sorry, I guess I got carried—"

"Hello, are you Debbie Coomb?" It was the nurse Howard had spoken with.

"Yes, I am," Debbie answered.

"I'm Esperanza, the charge nurse. Your husband here said you are feeling ill and are worried about your baby."

"Yes, that's right. And I have to go to the bathroom really bad."

"We can take care of that. In fact, I wouldn't mind getting a sample while you're at it. Come with me. I'll walk you to the bathroom."

Debbie got up awkwardly with help from the nurse. Howard offered assistance a little late, and in exchange received a slap on the hand from Debbie.

"Well, I see they gave you one of our custom-fit gowns," Esperanza said, trying to lighten the dark atmosphere that filled the small space. "Hang on one second. Let me see what I can do about that." The nurse stepped out of the room and quickly returned with an appropriately sized gown that she handed over to Debbie. "Here you go."

As Debbie changed, Esperanza turned to Howard and said, "Sir, why don't you wait here. Unfortunately this is the kind of hospital where you shouldn't leave your belongings unattended. Ms. Coomb will come with me."

"Feck," Howard insisted.

"Excuse me?" said the nurse.

"Her name is Mrs. Feck. Coomb is her maiden name, remember?"

Esperanza smiled at Howard. Debbie glared at him. They left together with Debbie muttering an apology.

A few minutes later, Esperanza and Debbie returned. They were talking comfortably with each other, and Debbie looked far more at ease than when she had left.

"Debbie, why don't you get up on the bed? Mr. Feck, you can help her. I'm going to get an ultrasound machine, and we'll have that look."

"Thank you, Esperanza."

"Mm-hmm," Esperanza answered in a soothing, two-note melody.

"You look like you're feeling better, Debbie," Howard said as he helped her back into the hospital bed.

"She's nice. I like her. She said the fact that the baby is kicking a lot is a good sign. She said babies who have big problems don't normally kick much at all."

"I think she's nice too."

Esperanza returned with a machine that looked like a communications prop from an old science fiction movie. As she rolled it up to Debbie's bedside, the same orderly who almost ran over Howard pushed in an old television on a tall, rickety stand. Nurse Esperanza began connecting the devices together before plugging them into a wall socket behind the head of the hospital bed. Snow faded in on the TV as the ultrasound machine's cooling fan whirred to life. A squeeze bottle like those used for mustard at a hot dog stand sat in a holder on the side of the machine. Esperanza picked it up and warned Debbie it would be cold on her belly.

"What is that stuff?" Howard asked.

"It helps the ultrasound pick up the image of your baby," said the nurse. "Okay, Debbie. Go ahead and pull your gown up to your breast line."

Debbie did as she was told. The nurse covered Debbie's lower half with a blanket leaving only the white fleshy mound of her abdomen exposed. Esperanza squirted farty glops of thick opaque gel onto Debbie's womb. Then, taking what looked like a microphone from a sci-fi communicator, Esperanza squirted another dollop of goop onto its flat metal head and smeared it around the big belly until it was evenly coated.

"Ready to see your baby for the very first time?"

"I am," Howard answered, unable to contain his excitement.

"I'm not sure I'm ready," Debbie said. "Esperanza, I'm afraid. What if…"

"It'll be okay," the nurse replied, soothingly. "You can keep your eyes closed if you like, and I'll take the first peek. Then you can look. I don't want you to be afraid. That won't help any of us."

While the nurse was providing gentle reassurances, Howard had moved closer to her bedside and had taken Debbie's hand. She squeezed the bejeezus out of it for comfort and punishment. Howard winced dutifully and obviously.

The good nurse in a hospital to be feared turned a big dial and threw a couple switches. The snow on the television screen became softer and grayer. Numbers and letters appeared on the screen's four corners. Then, from the salt-and-pepper flickers, a form appeared. The head was obvious and large. The rest looked like a pot roast with a lumpy sausage coming out of it.

"Oh my goodness," Howard gasped in awe.

Debbie squeezed his hand even harder, but Howard did not notice. He was dumbstruck by the image that came and went as Esperanza moved the ultrasound wand over Debbie's belly. Howard's mind gathered itself and formed questions he thankfully did not say aloud, lest he stir Debbie's fear into violent action. *Is the baby okay? Why is its head so big? Is the lumpy snake the umbilical cord? If so, does it look right?* He stood there with his hand in a vice, staring at the TV screen. Esperanza knew silence was troubling, and although she was still trying to look at everything to make sure there were no surprises, she knew the expectant parents could not wait any longer.

"Debbie? I see your baby. Your baby is beautiful."

"Really?"

"Really. Wouldn't you like to see?"

"I'm not sure." Aside from confirming or dispelling the horror that had brought Debbie to this place, looking at her baby would make overwhelmingly real the promise, the risk, and the reality of motherhood. She was to be a mother and bear a child that would need her like she needed her daddy—a word that filled her with joy turned to suffering, bringing along with it a multitude of "what if" and "what then" questions.

"It's okay, Debbie," Nurse Esperanza reassured her. "You'll feel much better if you look."

The nurse looked at Howard as if to say, *C'mon, husband, do your job. Help your frightened wife.*

"She's beautiful, Debbie," Howard offered. "I think she looks like me."

That worked.

Debbie opened her eyes and stared at the screen as the nurse moved the wand to different positions, offering Debbie different views of her child.

"See? There's the head, there are the arms. Look at the little fists tucked under the chin. There are the legs—whoa! Did you see that? It just kicked."

"I felt it." Seeing the baby kick in snowy black and white while simultaneously feeling that kick internally created an odd sensation of duality. Debbie put one hand over her mouth. "Oh my God. Is it okay?"

"Yes, I think the baby is just fine. I can't tell for certain if it's a boy or a girl. Do you want to know?"

"Yes," they both answered simultaneously.

"Well it's hard to tell from this angle, but I don't see a penis so…"

"I told you," Howard uncharacteristically boasted. "I just knew it was a girl."

Debbie beamed and clutched her heart. *The promise is true, thank you, Daddy.*

"Well, now, I can't be certain. You really need to see the ob-gyn and have them take a look. They should be able to tell you the sex and they can also take some measurements and make sure the baby's growth is on target."

"Can we have a picture please?" Howard asked, excitedly.

"I'm sorry but this machine doesn't print pictures. But the one in Maternity does. In fact, if you don't mind, I'd like to see about getting you up there while you're here. There is a staff ob-gyn available and it is probably the nicest part of the hospital. A whole lot nicer than down here, anyway."

"Sure. Okay," Debbie answered. She was unable to take her eyes off the TV. "Go back so I can see her face. Please." Debbie wanted to be polite to Esperanza.

"Sure." The nurse surreptitiously tried to get a look at the entire contents of Debbie's uterus to make sure things were as they should be. She wasn't sure they were, but uncertainty was no reason for alarm. Esperanza returned the wand to where they could see the head in profile. They could easily make out a baby button nose and long eyelashes that thrilled the room with every blink. Looking closely, they could also make out a spine and a skull as the ultrasound device looked through the baby's flesh as well as the mother's.

"Look, Howard." Debbie sounded happy again. "She is adorable. I don't believe it. She's perfect—just like you said she would be."

"Yes, sirree. She sure is," Howard said. "Her head's kind of big, but she still looks great."

"What do you mean her head looks big?" Debbie snapped, yanking Howard by the hand she still held clamped. "Is there something wrong with her head?" Debbie asked the nurse. "What does he mean by that? Tell me!"

"Heck if I know," Esperanza said. "The head looks fine to me. Remember, both of you, babies have heads that are big in proportion to their bodies. Your baby's head looks perfectly normal to me. I don't think there is anything to worry about."

"What do you mean *think*? Can't you say for sure?"

"The baby's head is fine, Debbie. Relax. Please," Esperanza said. "I think your husband is the only one in this room with a problem with his head." She tried to make this sound like a joke, but Howard thought she was perturbed over him upsetting the apple cart. He was right. "If you don't mind, I think we should get you admitted into the maternity ward where you belong. I sure could put this bed to better use. It appears there is nothing wrong with any of you. You do not need the ER. You need an ob-gyn to help make sure these last days go smoothly for you and your baby. And they have a much better ultrasound machine up there that can print out pictures."

"Sounds good to me," Howard said, trying to save face.

Esperanza turned off the machines, retrieved a small towel, and handed it to Debbie to wipe the goop off her belly. She looked deep into Debbie's eyes and with an aura of Zen said, "Congratulations. It was nice meeting you both. Take good care of each other. That's all a family ever needs." She left the room, went to the nurse's station, and picked up the phone. A chatterbox do-gooder maternity nurse named Penny answered. Penny did not want the peace and calm on her floor disturbed by another druggie loon from the ER with a bad egg in her stomach. Thanks to Esperanza's reputation, Penny believed her when she said the patient in question was not crazy or on drugs, and that her baby looked fine on the ER's antiquated ultrasound. Esperanza also reminded her that she was managing a dozen agitated patients compared with Penny's three dozing ones. The discussion was a formality—Debbie Coomb would soon be arriving on the fourth floor whether Penny wanted her or not.

Esperanza was honest with Penny about her assessment of Debbie and her pregnancy. She did, however, leave out one thing. There appeared to be something else besides a baby in Debbie's womb. She saw it but could not make out what it was. A harmless growth? Something malignant? An organ that looked strange due to the size and condition of the mother? She knew that focusing on something she could not define would only cause problems until someone with more expertise could give it a name. And that someone would soon be examining Debbie up on the fourth floor. As always, she did the right thing and did not mention it. Esperanza was not just kind, she was also smart.

Chapter 15

1

THE FOURTH-FLOOR MATERNITY WARD was by far the nicest part of Paro County Hospital. And even then it was just a thin veneer of nice over the drab, utilitarian architecture of a county building. Here, the antiseptic smell was hardly noticeable, and there was not the slightest whiff of urine. Instead, a light powdery smell somewhere between matronly talcum and Johnson's Baby Powder scented the air. Nurse Penny was at the elevator anticipating Debbie's arrival. Penny took the wheelchair from the orderly who had taken Debbie to Maternity and began pushing her slowly down the quiet corridor. Howard followed behind. They passed a few open doors revealing neat, empty rooms. The place was quiet, especially compared to the cacophonous humanity of the ER and its waiting room. Nurse Penny started asking Debbie questions without leaving space for answers. She had taken Debbie's chart out of the back pocket of the wheelchair while continuing to push it with her hips. She read the chart aloud to herself and titched and tutted. The threesome passed by the soundproof viewing window of the nursery. On the other side of the window, Howard saw three tightly wrapped bundles of joy in plastic bassinets, and several empty cribs and incubators lining the nursery's back wall. He snuck a wave to the oblivious infants.

"You know," Penny said, "Merritin Maternity is only an hour and a half from Wilburn. What made you come to us?"

"I—"

"No insurance?"

"We—"

"Well, let me tell you a little secret," Penny continued. She had returned the file to its pocket and was pushing the wheelchair with her hands again. "Even if you don't have insurance, there is no hospital that will turn a pregnant woman away. Not that you made a bad choice in coming here. We mostly have the same doctors they do."

"Can—"

"It's just that our emergency room is no place for a pregnant woman—in my opinion, at least. No place for any woman that doesn't make a living 'tween her legs." Penny snorted at her own joke.

She continued alternating between slightly condescending questions and unfunny jokes. Debbie tried several times to interrupt, but Penny simply paid her no mind. Then, as they entered a tiny room at the end of the corridor, something very curious happened—Howard spoke up. "Miss Nurse Penny, please stop talking," he said with a raised, trembling voice. "My wife has something to say."

Penny stopped talking, but her mouth remained opened. Looking hurt, she turned to Howard, who immediately felt bad. He looked over Penny's shoulder to gauge Debbie's reaction. She was smiling, proud that her husband, in his own way, had taken another baby step forward to help her. The smile faded when she heard Howard apologize. "Sorry, Nurse Penny. It's just that my wife is trying to tell you something. Sorry."

Penny pouted.

Debbie was fine with it. "Look, Nurse. I just want to have a proper look at my baby and make sure she is okay. I'm sorry I didn't get prenatal care, but the pregnancy has been very smooth, and I've been monitoring it on the internet"

"The internet?" Penny said, this time not trying to hide her disdain. There was a brief duel of silence, which Penny broke. "Can I ask you some questions while the machine warms up, Ms. Coomb?"

"Yes, of course," Debbie said, rolling her eyes.

Penny exhaled like an accomplished passive aggressive. "Is this your first pregnancy?"

"Yes," Debbie lied.

"I mean, including any accidents or miscarriages or anything like that?"

"Yes."

Penny's long look intimated that she knew it was untrue. The questions went on and on. A form of punishment, Debbie thought, followed by—*you want punishment, lady? I can give you that. Won't be passive, though—but it'll be aggressive.* The thought made Debbie feel uncommonly guilty—new mommas surely did not think such things. In an effort to keep her new self intact, Debbie gave what she thought were the best answers, regardless of truth or ignorance, to Penny's many questions. Too many minutes later, Penny began the ultrasound using what looked like a very modern machine.

Debbie did not shy away from the images this time. Instead, she found herself hungry for another look. Penny rolled the wand over the head of the fetus and announced to the room what it was. She navigated the wand, pressed keys on the machine, and made notes on Debbie's chart. Meanwhile, Debbie had shifted her focus from the entire baby to its little heart throbbing away at a healthy clip. Debbie found it discomforting. Even when Penny zoomed out to see the entire fetus, she could still see that dark, tiny, thumb-tip-sized heart pumping away in cut time. It seemed unfair that this organ would have to beat without rest for most of a century if its owner was to live a full life. The tiny heart had another task as well: to replace Debbie's broken one. Indeed, Debbie had a lot riding on that throbbing gray smudge on the screen. An awful lot.

Penny continued the exam. She saw the growth Esperanza had seen, only she saw it much more clearly. She was surprised Howard and Debbie had not asked about it. To Penny it looked like a second placenta, abnormally large, and lacking a fetus of its own. To be sure, she would have to study it with the ultrasound, which would no doubt alarm the parents to be. So Penny punted. She left the discovery of the malformation to the doctor. "Do you want to know the sex?"

"Nurse Esperanza said it was a girl," Debbie answered.

"It is. Not a hundred percent sure, but I haven't been wrong yet. Congratulations, both of you," Penny said sincerely. She had returned to her old chipper, motor-mouth self.

Debbie smiled and suddenly seemed lighter in presence. "Is her head the right size?"

"Absolutely. I even measured it."

Howard, having removed the wheelchair without being asked, now stood in a cranny at the foot of the bed in the cramped room. He looked at Debbie with relief. Penny clicked a button on the ultrasound machine and it spit out two images on the same kind of paper used for gas pump receipts. Debbie took them both.

"And everything else?" Debbie asked.

Shit. Penny was a lousy liar. "As far as I can see, your daughter looks perfect. We have a wonderful doctor here tonight," Penny offered, avoiding what might not be okay. "Dr. Srivinihinirisan.

I'm the only one on the floor who can pronounce her name. Since you're here, she'll want to take a look at you and your baby. She is very gentle."

Howard nodded yes, as if it was his womb being examined. Debbie wasn't sure she needed any further examination. Penny showed her everything was fine. No monsters, just her baby (*girl!*) with that tiny beating heart dark with blood. So why not get up and leave? She had twice received the confirmation she was seeking. She felt better. Everything was okay. She refused to take her eyes away from the grainy pictures of her daughter. If she did, she was afraid she might return to that foreboding cellar door in its desolate field, rattling against its lock, though not from the wind.

Penny left the room to retrieve Dr. Srivinihinirisan. Howard went to Debbie's bedside. She was staring at the grainy pictures of her womb with an expression he had never seen her hold so completely. He had seen flashes of it now and then—most often when she cried in her sleep, which she often did. But now, instead of fragments of expression inspired by dreams, Howard saw it fully formed, and it was beautiful—mostly. Despite how Debbie felt inside, with her eyes on her child-to-be, she possessed externally a loving serenity. It emboldened Howard enough to reach for one of the ultrasound pictures. Debbie jerked them away, reconsidered, then surrendered her least favorite.

"She is beautiful, Debbie, just like her mommy," Howard said, looking at the hazy image of life anew. "Can you believe that the baby you see in these funny pictures is living inside you right now? Wow."

The profundity and beauty of new life where there was none before had Howard mesmerized. "It doesn't get any closer than that. No sirree. Amazing. Just amazing." He could not stop shaking his head in reaction to the black-and-white proof that the miracle of life had moved through him and a turkey baster and into Debbie.

Howard's good words caused a smiling Debbie to rub her free hand across her belly. Only she had forgotten that it was still covered in ultrasound goop. She wiped her hand over and over on the back of Howard's shirt until it was mostly dry. Howard appreciated the contact. It felt like she was rubbing his back out of love, and in a way she was. She loved the fact that he was there for that too.

"Thank you, Howard. You did good," Debbie said as she finished wiping her hand clean. "I don't think I would have done this without you."

"Heck, I enjoyed it," Howard said. "Thank you too, Debbie. This really is something. You made a baby." Howard sounded impressed, like someone had baked a difficult cake. Without thinking, he bent over Debbie's slimed belly and gave her a hug. She allowed it. She even put her formerly goopy hand on him in reciprocation. She also raised the hand holding the picture so she could keep looking at her prize.

"You were right, Howard," Debbie said as he lay over her like an oily rag. "Nothing wrong with her. Nothing wrong with the pregnancy. Everything is just great, just like you said it would be. I know now. I know I can believe in you. I can trust you."

Howard sighed.

"She's *okay*," Debbie whispered to herself. "My dad was the last person I ever trusted, Howard. That was so long ago. Two lifetimes ago. There was one other but he disappeared. Can't trust someone who disappears. You going to disappear on me one day, Howard? One day, when I really need you?"

"Never," Howard responded. The word was muffled by Debbie's neck flesh. "Never in a million, billion years. I would never leave you. And," he pushed himself up so he could look into Debbie's wet eyes, "I could never leave our baby girl. No way could I leave either of you. We been too much to each other. Been through too much too, though maybe not all of it together."

Howard pulled his inhaler from his pants pocket, shook it, then took a hit off it. "I know you think you been real mean to me, Debbie," he continued with all seriousness. "Especially in the old days. But the truth is, you were never mean to me the way people were when I was in school, or at work, or anywhere but home with Gramma Helen. Or home with you," he added. "I know what real mean is. You know there are things that hurt worse than getting beat up?" (Oh, yes, Debbie knew this very well.) "There are things that take ten times longer to heal than a bruise, if they heal at all, that is.

"People used to be *really* mean to me," Howard confessed. "They *meant* it. They wouldn't hit me because they said I was too gross to touch. Some did, but the real mean ones didn't. They hurt me so bad, Debbie. And no one bothered to stop them. They could have if they wanted to. And no one ever really knew how bad it hurt except me, and if they did they loved it. They laughed about it and told people who I thought were my friends. But they weren't my friends because they laughed too.

"I love you, Debbie. You were never *really* mean to me. You have a temper—that's for sure. You got angry a lot in the old days, but heck, I probably would too if I had…if I had to live with me." Howard laid his head down on Debbie's bosom and she accepted him lovingly. It was the first time he had felt her breasts against him without it feeling sexual. He was crying softly, now. "I mean I have no choice but to live with me. You have a choice. And you let me stay. I will love you till the day I die, Debbie Feck, and I won't never leave you. Even if you asked me to, I wouldn't go. You'd have to kill me to keep me away from you and our baby girl." Then, after a couple beats, "And even then I'd haunt you."

"I love you too, Howard." Even in the tenderness of the moment, they were hard words. Perhaps because she wasn't sure they were true. "Thank you for staying with me and all," she said. "I promise I'm going to be nice to you for real."

"You already are."

"Well, I've been nicer, but that doesn't mean I've been nice. I want my baby to be proud of her daddy. I want her to trust you the way I trusted my Dad, and the way I now trust you, thanks to this," Debbie held the picture for Howard to see. "And I want her to believe in you the way I do now. And I do, Howard. I was freaking out back home, thinking my little baby girl had become a monster because…" Debbie paused to push back painful, conflicting feelings. "Because that's what I became and I was afraid that's all I could ever make. And you, for the first time I know of, you were sure. Sure that she was just a baby girl and that neither of us are monsters. You believed my pregnancy was a good pregnancy, even though I was convinced it had all gone wrong."

Debbie paused and wiped away a lone tear.

"That's what I'm used to, Howard—the wrongness of life. And now, I promise—I promise that I will (*almost*) always believe in you. That's all you need, sugar. And I've known that for forever, maybe. You just needed someone to believe in you and I do now. I got pictures here to prove why."

Howard sat up to look at the pictures again. He smiled and shook his head once more, trying to make sense of the magic. He did not notice, and wouldn't have cared if he had, that the lower front of his shirt was slathered in ultrasound goop from Debbie's belly.

Chapter 16

1

D R. M ATI S RIVINIHINIRISAN WAS not your typical county hospital baby doctor. Born in India and over-educated by American standards in Great Britain, she could have delivered babies in any hospital in America. Full of altruistic idealism, upon graduation she chose for her residency a poor county with a low birth rate. That was nearly thirty years ago. She had promised herself that as soon as her current crop of patients had their babies and her services were no longer required, she would move to a more beautiful and liberated part of the country. But her obligations never waned—there was always a woman who really needed her services. Plus, all the female doctors and doctor's wives made sure Dr. Srivinihinirisan was available when time came for them to contribute to the population. She split her work evenly between the modestly upscale Merritin Maternity and Surgery Center and the dreary Paro County Hospital. Debbie had picked a good night for her maternal freak-out.

The doctor was in her fifties, yet still ripe with exotic beauty. Her dark skin sustained few wrinkles, and most of those were caused by smiling—an occupational hazard when your job is bringing new life into an old world. She wore expensive, tastefully colorful blouses that peeked out from the collar of her white doctor's coat, which she always wore unless dressed in scrubs. Her accent was an amalgam of upper crust Oxford English and upper class Hindi. The severe and snobbish tone of the former was tempered nicely by the melodic lilt of the latter.

The doctor waited outside the ultrasound room until Howard and Debbie had completed their heartfelt confessions of love, forgiveness, and famous last words.

"Good evening, I am Dr. Mati Srivinihinirisan," the doctor said as she entered the small room. "People call me Dr. Mati. I must say you certainly chose an odd hour to have a picture taken of your baby."

"Sorry about that, Doctor," said Debbie.

"That's okay. We never close. In fact, I've done some of my best work at this and much later hours."

"I'm glad to hear that," Debbie responded with rare brightness. Dr. Mati had a Deepak Chopra-esque bedside manner, and it was powerful medicine.

"I understand from the nurse that you were worried about your baby so much that you drove all the way here from Wilburn and braved our legendary emergency room."

"That's right," Debbie replied, "but I see now that everything is just fine. Here's a picture if you want to see."

Dr. Mati looked at the picture and smiled, awaking the wrinkles on her face. "That's a very nice picture. Do you mind if I get a live view?"

"I guess not," Debbie replied. "Howard, get out of the way."

Howard returned to the nook at the foot of the bed. Dr. Mati pushed a button and the ultrasound came back to life. She piloted it like a top gun and within a few seconds had spied the second placenta, though never acknowledged it outwardly. Dr. Mati expertly mixed small talk with investigative questions about Debbie's pregnancy. But being sly herself, Debbie sensed that the doctor was being surreptitious in her investigation. Especially when it came to questions about pains dull or sharp, and tender areas, which made Debbie think of her emotional state, and a certain gray weedy field holding a weakly latched cellar door prone to rattling. Dr. Mati failed to divert Debbie's attention while she examined the abnormality. It was hard to miss next to the obvious child in Debbie's womb. And Debbie was afraid to mention the large amorphous mass Dr Mati kept returning to in her exam. She hoped the doctor would not mention it either. If that happened, then perhaps all was truly well, and there would have been no cause for fear and doubt in the first place. But, oh, that nagging intuition. That rattle in her mind. Dr. Mati complimented the couple on their beautifuly baby. Then she asked, "Would you like to hear your baby's heartbeat?

"Oh, yes please, Dr. Mati,"

The doctor pressed a button on the ultrasound, engaging a microphone on its wand. Grainy static blared from the device. It sounded like a cheap AM radio between stations. The device growled as Dr. Mati navigated the wand across Debbie's belly, seeking the baby's beating heart. Through the static, the beat came in loud and clear. *K'woop, k'woop, k'woop, k'woop* went the baby heart, rapidly and without any deviation in tempo. She moved the wand to a different location on Debbie's belly. Instead of the steady, singular *k'woop, k'woop, k'woop* from the baby heart, there was what seemed to be a second, softer version disrupting the syncopation of the first. It was the sonic equivalent of two turn signals blinking in and out of sync with each other.

This was bad.

This was the one thing Dr. Mati suspected but hoped would not be. The sound was unmistakable. There were two hearts inside that uterus. One was the pure baby heart Debbie saw as a metaphor for her healing. The other was folded up somewhere in the fleshy, alien-looking matter of the second placenta, clinically diagnosed as an accessory placenta. Debbie's womb had contained two fetuses. But twin number one (or was it number two?) had fused with its own placenta, something as rare as any of the horrors that drove Debbie to Paro County Hospital in the first place.

While Dr. Mati was superb in handling emotional pre- and postpartum women with their effusive hormones bouncing hither and thither, she also firmly believed that patients must know the truth, especially in matters of life and death. And a beating heart was considered life in Western medicine. The good doctor felt that her patient must know what was going on in her body. Then, as a team, they could rationally proceed on a path forged from this knowledge. This also meant that in a few hours, Debbie would have to perform the miracle of childbirth, delivering one normal, healthy baby with the promise of a long life, and its twin smothered in the very thing that was to sustain it until it could be placed upon its mother's breast. But that one had no mouth with which to root for a nipple, no nose with which to smell its mother's scent, and no eyes from which to shed its first tears. For one, birth meant life. For the other, death. Two sides of the same coin flipping madly and then landing on its edge. Not heads, not tails, but both. It was a push.

2

Dr. Mati quickly moved the wand back to where the healthy baby's heartbeat was most prominent. She let it sit there for many long seconds. The doctor sensed a growing agitation and fear lurking just below her patient's surface. The doctor hoped the rhythm and source of the beat would help Debbie settle into a more harmonious disposition and quell her fears. Dr. Mati could then calmly level with her. After all, the solution to this problem would deliver joy. The lofty pink promise made by Debbie's biological clock was about to come true.

Undoubtedly, the healthy baby Dr. Mati expected Debbie to deliver would soothe any ache associated with the death of its abhorrent twin. It was the hours preceding delivery that concerned Dr. Mati. The good, kind doctor, who had delivered hundreds of babies in her long, illustrious career as an obstetrician to the disadvantaged, had learned how to judge people pretty damn well—and quickly, too. Determining the emotional state and psychological disposition of her patients was, in part, what made her a great doctor. And Dr. Mati had accurately summed up Debbie as a tent stuffed full of damaged goods. A potential hurricane in a housedress. All of this would have been manageable if Debbie had not placed all her cracked chips on pink, betting that procreation would save her. Dr. Mati had seen this gamble before from middle-aged women whose dreams had never come true, or who simply needed a vessel to receive and dispense love. Dr. Mati had delivered dozens of babies wagered on similar false promises. And she had sent each one home wishing them the best, which she knew was relative. Now Dr. Mati was about to tell Debbie what no woman wanting her pregnancy ever wanted to hear. That there was a problem. But with Dr. Mati managing things, Debbie was in very capable hands.

Debbie stared at a picture of her baby, listening to a beat she could dance to. Dr. Mati turned off the device. She started with what she hoped Debbie would accept as good news. "Listen to me, both of you. I think we should deliver your baby—tonight."

Debbie's eyes grew wide with fear. Howard's grew wide with excitement.

"There is nothing to worry about. Your baby looks wonderful. However, inside your uterus is a second placenta. It is not entirely uncommon—Debbie, look at me, please."

Debbie had turned her head and stared at the ceiling tiles. *Now comes the news about monsters.* The rotted cellar door inside Debbie's mind shook once. Debbie's body shuddered involuntarily in response.

"Debbie, please look at me." The doctor was pleasant but authoritative.

Debbie looked at her.

"Your baby looks perfectly healthy," Dr. Mati continued in her best soothing voice. "I don't see any concerns there as far as I can tell from the ultrasound. Please understand that what I am saying has no effect on your baby. Do you understand me?"

"I do," Debbie managed after a few seconds.

"Based on my many years as an obstetrician, and based on the ultrasound we have just performed, your baby appears to be perfectly healthy and normal. There is no way to be absolutely positive since you haven't had an amniocentesis and I have not seen any bloodwork." Dr. Mati gave Debbie a subtly supercilious look. "I am expecting the results from your urine test shortly, and that will tell us a little more. But please know that I believe your baby is fine and will be delivered as such. I do not allow for anything less when I am in charge of the delivery. Understand?" Dr. Mati was being firm yet remained affable. Howard squeaked a "yay." Debbie appeared unconvinced.

"This is supposed to be a wonderful time for you," Dr. Mati continued. "You are about to partake in the greatest miracle known to the world. We are in this together, and we need to work as a team."

Debbie nodded. It seemed forced.

Dr. Mati continued, "You are at about forty weeks, and as you can see, there is not a lot of room in your uterus. So while we could wait for nature to choose your baby's birthday, I feel it is wise to err on the side of caution and deliver your baby now. The accessory placenta is taking up a lot of room and if it continues to grow, it could complicate delivery and increase the risk of a cord accident or hemorrhaging. So I think we should talk about having the baby cesarean, tonight."

Dr. Mati paused. All eyes were on Debbie while Howard stroked her swollen ankles. He was in a trance from the doctor's lilting-voiced lecture. Dr. Mati accepted their silence gratefully. It was far better than tears or anger or agitating questions. "Before we talk about how best to deliver your child, I want to make sure you understand the nature of your second placenta."

"Was it for a twin?" Debbie's question surprised Dr. Mati.

"Yes, exactly. How did you know?"

"Internet."

"Yes, in this instance, the second placenta is a sign that there was, at one time during your pregnancy, a twin to the baby we saw on the ultrasound."

"Where did it go?" Tension could be heard in Debbie's voice.

The short answer was "nowhere." It—for it truly was an "it" and not a he or a she—was still there. At least parts of it were. It had a heart beating a screwy little beat. That meant there must be a brain giving it instructions to do so. There probably wasn't much else, maybe a few other organs, some soft bones, and maybe a little hair to round out the gruesomeness. And it was all encased in big, ugly, twitchy, placenta number two.

Dr. Mati could not plan her words. Instead she just began talking, relying on mindfulness to guide her through the discussion. "Debbie, as you have said, there was a twin to your healthy baby in the womb. And unfortunately, that twin puts your healthy baby at risk."

Debbie remembered reading on the web about how some tumors in adults contained hair and teeth and bones that could have belonged to a twin consumed during gestation. Yuck.

"Your case is very unique, however," the doctor said. And your healthy baby seems to have played no role in the demise of the twin. Instead (*now through the heart of the minefield*), the twin appears to have been either enveloped by or fused to its own placenta, which no doubt arrested its gestation. I believe that is why the placenta is so large. That also means that the twin is still in there, and technically it is alive.

(*Snap—was that a trip wire?*)

I say technically because there is a second heart beating inside your uterus."

(*Twang—yes, that was a tripwire*)

"And when we deliver your baby and remove both placentas, that heart will stop."

That heart will stop echoed loudly inside Debbie's mind. The rotting cellar door flew open.

(*BOOM.*)

Debbie snapped like a Thanksgiving wishbone. Tears, words, and snot flew from her face as she flew into hysterics. Like shrapnel from a hand grenade exploding in a small space, pieces of Debbie's sanity flew around the room and bounced off the walls, ripping apart the peace Dr. Mati had established. About half of her words were unintelligible gasps and shrieks and sobs. In between these, Debbie vocalized how *fucking-piss-ant-brained* Howard was responsible for making her believe her pregnancy was fine. She demanded at the top of her mighty lungs to have the *thing* torn out of her belly and kept away from her daughter— if she was even still going to have a daughter after conceiving a *genuine fucking monster*. It was because of those putrid men that she couldn't have a real baby, like on TV. All she ever really wanted in this world was her daddy and a real baby and she knew—all along she *fucking knew*—both were fucking out of reach. The only thing within her grasp was a pathetic human with chromosomes so fucked up that he laid an abominable monster egg inside her, which he then tricked her into believing was a sweet pink progeny. Debbie then screamed a chorus about how she did not care how they did it—rend her into pieces if that's what it took. "Just get this fucking sideshow freak out of my belly and into the garbage can or a jar of formaldehyde or something. GET IT OUT RIGHT FUCKING NOW YOU HEAR ME DR. MATI-FUCKING-SONOFABITCHISTAN?!"

Debbie accompanied her quaint little siren song with a dance of sorts. Lying there, looking like a Ralph Steadman portrait come to life, she kicked at the father of the blob, who stood pinned against a cinder block wall far too close to the foot of the bed.

Dr. Mati, having delivered her share of poor helpless babies from the wombs of bipolar, schizoid, tweaking women, should have been better prepared. In her defense, no one could possibly be prepared for Debbie Coomb at her worst. Dr. Mati knew she had stepped on one of Debbie's tripwires the moment it had happened. She could see it in Debbie's face. But she had expected tears, cries, and a loud worry over the healthy child waiting to make an entrance. She did not expect this half-ton woman's megaton charge. Dr. Mati tried using her voice to diffuse the exploding pregnant woman, but it was like yelling into a jet engine. And she wasn't about to get sucked into that, thank you kindly. If Dr. Mati was to die this night, may it be by the grace of God, not the devil's fat aunt. After all her good work on behalf of the procreation of Western indigence, surely, God owed her that much.

The doctor remained a force of control and calm that could have parried with Debbie's over-the-top petitions if only Debbie were capable of listening. But Dr. Mati was not about to try and match Debbie decibel for decibel. The other maternity patients (including one with a black ribbon on the door—a sure sign of something beautiful gone terribly wrong) might forgive a patient for vociferously discombobulating, but not a doctor for joining in. Fortunately, Penny, who was back at the nurse's station, heard the explosion and called for orderlies and security to come, Code Hell.

Dr. Mati stepped slowly back toward the doorway. It was not a retreat. She wanted to signal someone at the nurse's station that there was a psychotic loose in the tiny ultrasound room. The doctor looked out the doorway and saw Penny running toward her and another nurse leaving the room with the sad, folded ribbon. Penny was out of breath by the time she made it to the end of the hall. Trotting down a long hall in comfortable shoes seemed to have done her in. A pleasant side effect from this was that Penny was too out of breath to talk much. "I called for security and some orderlies from downstairs. They're on their way."

A new sound, like a drum solo on dead skins, added to Debbie's screaming freak-out. It was enough to bring Dr. Mati's attention back to the ultrasound room. She looked in to find Debbie on her knees at the foot of the bed slapping and punching and throttling Howard with the ferocity of a circus bear that has finally had enough. Completely cornered, Howard was taking one hell of a beating. To make matters worse, he appeared to have taken self-defense lessons from the Three Stooges. He folded his arms over his head, giving Debbie free rein to punch his gut and ribs. When he involuntarily moved his arms down to protect his midsection, Debbie went to town on his face with open slaps and closed fists. He was bleeding substantially from his nose and a cut on his left cheek. Back and forth his arms went from head to abdomen, and back and forth Debbie's blows followed. It almost seemed choreographed, or at least as though they had done this a few times before. They had, but it had been a while.

"Debbie, stop this instant! Dr. Mati urged. "Get a hold of yourself and leave the poor man alone." Debbie didn't hear a word over her sobs of self-pity and screams of blame directed at Howard, who was now close to losing consciousness. Dr. Mati knew she could not overpower Debbie, even with Penny's assistance. She shouted for Howard to hit the ground. It was his only hope against the violence raining down upon him.

"Howard, drop to the ground! Drop to the ground! Now!" Dr. Mati implored. Dr. Mati turned to Mia, the little nurse who had come running from the sad room. "Mia, get the pepper spray. You know where it is?" Mia nodded and dashed back to the station. As she did, two large orderlies and one uniformed cop with baton at the ready came running out of the elevator.

Dr. Mati turned back to Howard, who now leaned against the wall with his eyes rolling back into his head. He had stopped bothering to defend himself from Debbie's insane rage.

"Howard, fall to the ground!" Dr. Mati yelled. "Fall to the ground!"

He didn't. He couldn't. He was pinned. Now, every time Debbie punched him in the face, his head snapped back against the cinderblock wall, giving Debbie a twofer on every wild swing. Dr. Mati, feeling she had to act lest she watch this man get beaten to death by his dearly beloved, dropped to all fours and scampered toward the foot of the bed. She stuck close to the wall nearest Howard and inched up close to his feet. Debbie, too consumed with her song of failure and her dance of rage, did not notice. Dr. Mati reached for Howard's ankles and pulled them forward, causing him to slide down the wall like a conked-out cartoon cat at the end of a chase. The back of his head smacked the cinderblock wall one last time, causing it to bounce forward, offering Debbie one last parting shot with her rocket right fist. He was unconscious now, for sure. Debbie started yelling something about not being finished and how he had better get his ass up right fucking now or—

THUD. THWACK. THOOM.

The two orderlies and the cop entered the room and in one fail swoop tackled Debbie, who flew backward, bouncing off the wall parallel to the bed before landing flat on the mattress. Her head solidly hit the bedrails, causing her to refocus on the bright knock of impact.

"She is pregnant! Be careful! Get off her belly," Dr. Mati commanded from her position on the floor. "Please do not harm the baby." If the rescue team had noticed Dr. Mati before she opened her mouth, it was as a fallen victim. "Take it easy," Dr. Mati instructed. "Hold her, don't hurt her. And do not hurt the baby in her womb."

Stunned by the tackle and the smack on the head, Debbie had finally shut up. One orderly lay across her chest, which had become exposed in the melee. The second orderly knelt on her legs. He had tackled her belly but had shot up and away from Debbie's uterus at the command of Dr. Mati. The cop, teetering between the orderly on Debbie's chest and her tear, saliva and mucus-caked face, held his baton against her throat. Howard lay unconscious against the opposite wall with two purple eyes swelling shut, a broken, bloodied nose, and half a dozen facial lacerations, thanks to a gaudy costume jewelry ring Debbie wore on her meaty right hook.

Dr. Mati pulled herself up and took charge of the scene. "Penny, get a gurney. No. wait. Penny, stay. Mia, get a gurney, right away. This poor man is in bad shape. Penny we should have a crash kit in here. Find it and bring it to me."

"The kit is behind the patient, I cannot—"

"Okay, then come here and tend to him. Get his vitals, be a nurse," Dr. Mati commanded.

Dr. Mati then addressed the orderly atop Debbie's chest, "You, sir, please get down off my patient and help the nurse get this man out of here and onto a gurney. Get him to the ER right away. Tell the charge nurse Dr. Mati says he needs to be seen immediately." Dr. Mati shook her head and sighed in frustration. "No, wait. Take him to the third floor. Tell a nurse you have a patient that came from my floor and he's crashing. Tell them I sent you. Go!"

"Dr. Mati, he's wheezing pretty badly," Penny said to the doctor. "He sounds obstructed. He sounds like either he's having a pretty bad asthma attack or he may have a collapsed—"

"Check his pockets for an inhaler. If he has one, use it. Does he need a bag?" Dr. Mati spoke quickly and clearly. She had a way of making sure people got her orders right the first time. Penny was accustomed to this, only under much different circumstances.

Mia returned with the gurney, having also had the foresight to grab Dr. Mati's personal medical bag while en route. She was very capable and needed little direction in crises. That did not stop Penny from parroting Dr. Mati's orders. "Mia, we are to get this man onto the gurney and take him down to three and tell them Dr. Mati sent—"

"I want Mia to stay here with me," Dr. Mati interrupted. "What are you waiting for, Penny? Get this man out of here."

The orderly who came down off Mt. Debbie looked at Dr. Mati as if she were a pain in the ass. Dr. Mati shot him a glance that made him feel like he needed to get busy.

"I'm still looking for his asthma inhaler, doctor," Penny sounded overwhelmed. "He's having a rough time here."

"Pull him out from the corner, Penny." Dr. Mati grabbed Penny by the shoulder and turned her so they were face to face. "Listen to me." Dr. Mati did not need to raise her voice to increase her command of authority. She did it through piercing eyes and increased articulation. "You cannot treat him if you cannot reach him. Please get him out."

Dr. Mati turned back toward Debbie and something caught her eye. It was a blue, plastic, L-shaped device—an inhaler for asthmatics. The policeman, still half on the bed restraining Debbie with one hand, held it out. "Here."

"Thank you, officer," Dr. Mati answered, taking the inhaler from him. "What is in it?"

"Albuterol," the cop answered. "It's pretty safe."

"Yes, thank you." Dr. Mati gave the inhaler to Penny. "Penny, give him four puffs. Shake it first."

Penny pulled Howard the rest of the way out from the corner, then gave a few quick shakes of the inhaler. She flicked the cap off with her thumb and opened his mouth enough to insert the business end. Four puffs later, Penny and an orderly put Howard onto a gurney, then quickly disappeared on their errand to save him from being beaten to death.

Dr. Mati went back to Debbie, who was heaving like a beast shot full of tranquilizers. The orderly tightly held Debbie's legs with his latex-gloved hands. She knew she was done for. The cop had removed his baton from Debbie's neck when he offered up his inhaler but kept one hand tightly on her shoulder.

"How could you do such a thing?" Dr. Mati asked with utter disappointment. "It is not his fault. Your baby is fine, as I told you. If you would have…"

Dr. Mati stopped herself. No use arguing or shaming a crazy person. And in this moment, it would have been impossible to convince Dr. Mati that Debbie Coomb was not insane.

"Officer, what is your name?"

"Patrick. Jack Patrick."

Dr. Mati spoke briskly again. "Officer Patrick, this woman needs to be arrested on several charges, including assault and battery, spousal abuse—perhaps even attempted murder—and causing such a disruption in a county hospital. You must have an offense for that. She will need to have a psychological evaluation once you have her safely in custody. Based on what just happened here, she is a danger to herself and others, which is my professional opinion as a physician. I will sign whatever is required to document that opinion and start the process of her being safely held and treated away from my patients."

"I will need your name, doctor," the cop answered agreeably. "And I gotta ask some questions. I'll have her picked up, don't worry. Paro County Women's Correctional is only a few miles from here. She could probably go straight there."

"First, this woman needs to have her baby, assuming she will agree to do so here and now. Debbie, do you want your daughter born in jail?" Dr. Mati gave her no chance to respond. "Assuming she cooperates to being taken into your custody now, we'll proceed with delivery, Officer Patrick. Once she has the baby and is stable, she can go, and I will answer any questions you have. If she refuses or resists in even the slightest fashion, then I will have her off my floor and she can give birth in your jail. Is that understood?"

"Uh, Doc, they don't—"

"Is that understood Officer Patrick? I would appreciate brevity given the circumstances. I have work to do if this woman cooperates and would like her baby's first moments to be spent in freedom instead of incarceration."

Dr. Mati quickly glanced at Debbie. Tears streamed out from beneath closed eyelids. The doctor looked at the policeman and blinked twice markedly. Of course she knew that Paro County Hospital was where female inmates delivered their babies, which the cop was about to point out to the very woman who delivered them. Dr. Mati shrewdly felt that had Debbie known this, her bargaining power over getting her to comply would be greatly diminished. Despite the violent and insane moments that had just passed, Dr. Mati still had the best interests of Debbie's child in mind. It took the cop a beat and a half before he got the hint.

"…Sure, doctor…"

"Dr. Srivinihinirisan. But you may call me Dr. Mati."

"Thank God," Officer Patrick said quietly.

Dr. Mati appeared not to appreciate his humor.

"Yeah, sure. Whatever you want," he finished.

"Arrest her now, please, for assault and battery so that we can have an officer on hand for her delivery and recovery. Do this now, please. Actually, wait—Debbie? Debbie, look at me."

The momentary loss of control and flash of violence irked Dr. Mati to no end. Witnessing such brutality against such a pathetic victim as Howard had made her feel decidedly bitter toward Debbie. The doctor never held grudges in her professional life and had held very few in a personal life of five and a half decades, three continents, and much living. But at this moment, Dr. Mati felt she would hold for lifetimes a grudge against Debbie for the brutal disruption and cruel behavior she had witnessed this night in the maternity ward of Paro County Hospital. While with child, no less. To salt things, Debbie refused Dr. Mati's order to look at her. Instead, she opened her eyes, briefly looked at the nothingness somewhere above her huge, exposed belly, then shut them tight again. She had stopped crying aloud and had stopped her song of man-hate the instant the three men had tackled her. But tears still flowed. And that would remain the case for a very long time.

Debbie moved her hands to her eyes. The orderly and cop jumped to prevent her movement. Mia shrank back to the doorway, standing away but near enough in case Dr. Mati needed her. Upon realizing what Debbie was doing, Officer Patrick and the orderly backed down. They continued to watch closely in case she bolted into violence again.

Debbie did not use her hands to rub her weeping eyes. Instead, like a child, she hid behind them. She sighed heavily, and wished she were long dead. Dead before she ever got pregnant. Dead before she ever met Howard. Dead before Teddy stepped foot in her house. Dead the moment of her father's passing so both could avoid the ache of surviving. For Debbie, the peacefulness of death now filled the thin space between salvation and redemption. But for Howard, she wanted something else. And then there was that awful thing inside. She wanted it to die, too, but she wanted that event to be separate from the death of her lovely daughter, whom now she wanted never to be born. *What's the use?* How could she bring such innocence into such a terrible world?

During her flight into brutal madness, her biological clock had disappeared. It had helped her into this mess, but now was either hiding in the waning shadows of her sanity, or had stopped ticking and, thus, simply ceased to be.

Dr. Mati continued to speak firmly, authoritatively. She was not going to lose control of the situation again. "Okay, Debbie, don't look at me. That is fine. Do you understand that we are still having this baby tonight? Either here or in jail."

Except for her heaving breath and two rivulets of tears down the broad sides of her face, Debbie remained motionless and mute.

"You are having this baby tonight because it is at risk. You have a choice—one of your last, I presume, since technically you are no longer a free woman."

I was free? Debbie thought. *I was free?* She let out a short huff over such an absurd presumption. *I was never free. Not since the day my daddy died have I been free, you stupid Indian. What do you know about not being free? I am the star of that show.*

"You can agree to have the baby through induction or Cesarean. Or, with Officer Patrick and Mia as my witnesses, I can rule you mentally incompetent and make the decision for you."

"Cesarean," Debbie whispered, hoarsely. She wanted the baby out quickly and as painlessly as possible.

Dr. Mati looked at her in silence. She would have ordered Cesarean. If Debbie went ka-boom again during labor, it could be disastrous for everyone. With a C-section, Debbie would be well sedated, thwarting the risk of any dangerous behavior. Dr. Mati did feel, however, that the miraculous pain and joy of natural childbirth could help Debbie heal substantially, though not completely. Unfortunately, Dr. Mati thought, Debbie had lost her right to experience such primal magnificence.

"Okay. Officer, you can arrest her now," Dr. Mati said without a hint of compassion. "Mia, please make the arrangements for a C-section in Suite B. You will probably have to call in a couple nurses from somewhere. Call the anesthesiologist first. They take so long to get here."

Mia nodded and went to get ready for the entrance of Howard and Debbie's daughter through a hatch to be carved in Debbie's womb.

"Orderly," Dr. Mati continued, "please stay with the officer and follow his orders until we get the patient into surgery."

"But I'm supposed to get off in thirty minutes," grumbled the orderly.

"Really?" Dr. Mati responded as she left to prepare for yet another beautiful and tragic birth.

Chapter 17

1

DEBBIE COOMB GAVE BIRTH. First, to the miracle of life. Second, to the shock of death. Virginia Violet Feck and her doomed twin both came into our beautiful and broken world just after three a.m. in a light-saturated, green-tiled surgery suite, while all around them, separated by cinder blocks cemented together, other humans were healing, dying, grieving, and copulating. Virginia and her twin entered a world full of opposites as icons of nature's ultimate opposite—birth and death. Ying and Yang made flesh. Spring and Fall made human. Joy and sorrow wrapped in thin blankets.

During the procedure, Debbie—raw in places, numb in others—remained awake, silent, and teary throughout. She experienced the birth of her daughter through a hazy swirl of sadness, anger, and a fading, desperate hope. When the cries of her daughter reached her ears, Debbie's crying became vocal again. Dr. Mati quietly said she was beautiful and healthy as she handed the newly born child to Penny to be examined and cleaned up.

Following Virginia's harsh welcome to a harsher world, Dr. Mati placed both hands inside Debbie's body to remove the lost one. She felt the pulse of its distinct heartbeat on the palms of her hands. Countless times before, those hands were the first to touch a life. This was the case here as well, and Dr. Mati was saddened by the knowledge that this life would soon cease, if, by perhaps too broad a definition, it had ever existed. She tugged the twin known as placenta number two away from the uterine wall. It did not come free. To make matters worse, the doctor felt the thing's heartbeat elevate as she attempted to separate it from its mother. Saying a silent prayer she reserved for birthing tragedies, Dr. Mati grabbed the heart-beating mass more firmly. She tugged and scooped until it surrendered to its executioner. Like a starting gun, its removal from Debbie's womb marked the beginning of the end for however much life was trapped inside. Mia held out her hands to take placenta/twin number two. While Mia held it, Dr. Mati examined it briefly, pulling back a fold to see if any salvageable life lurked inside. She quickly stopped. She said nothing. Mia felt the twitch of its pulse but little else. No angry newborn gesticulations, no heaving of breath. Just a strong and somewhat erratic pulse twitching through alien-looking tissue. Mia supplanted a rising repulsion with pity, and a reverence for life and death privy only to nurses, doctors, and paramedics. Dr. Mati whispered "blanket," and Mia wrapped it in a pink receiving blanket. She placed it in a clear plastic bassinette and then returned to help Dr. Mati clean and close.

The dying twin lay across the room from where Penny helped baby Virginia recover from birth. Virginia cried and snorted and gesticulated, hating the brightness, the openness, the cool dryness, and the myriad sensations her startled brain was forced to process after months of coming to be. Under bright lights where no visible defect could hide, Penny suctioned fluid from Virginia's lungs in order to help her breathe and live. No one tended to her twin who lay twitching and dying, waiting for the inevitable.

Dr. Mati spoke gently but emphatically to Debbie. "Once we aspirate your baby's lungs, which is normal, you can hold her. Would you like to do that, Debbie?"

Debbie shook her head no. The anesthesiologist relayed the answer to Dr. Mati, whose eyes showed she understood.

Each cry from the baby pulled harder on Debbie. In time, the weight of the cries became unbearable. But unbearable was once part of Debbie's routine. Dr. Mati gestured to the anesthesiologist to increase the sedation. It was her hope that through medication, Debbie would acquiesce to holding the lonely infant for the infant's sake if not the mother's. Of all the times we need our mother, there is none greater than in the first moments after being pulled from inside her. For the Dr. Mati Srivinihinirisans of the world, the sacredness and the pain of childbirth—both emotional and physical for both mother and child—remain freshly poignant, regardless of how many lives they have delivered into the world. So Dr. Mati cautiously softened her attitude toward Debbie. She was still greatly offended by the earlier events that had turned so violent and outrageous. Perhaps even more offended that she failed to maintain control. The seemingly native brutality of this new mother caused Dr. Mati to want the book thrown at her—hard. But as a fellow mother and fellow woman, she wanted Debbie to experience the joy of holding her newborn. Most of all, the baby needed to be held by her mother.

Nurse Penny surrogated for the time being, but she too wanted Debbie to accept the baby, who was already missing the sound, scent, and feel of her creator. Dr. Mati finished stitching up Debbie's shallowest wound, which allowed time for the sedation to work. She tried again.

"Debbie?"

"What?" Debbie sounded like a haughty teenager who had raided her parent's liquor cabinet.

"Your baby wants you. Do you hear her crying? Those are the cries of a healthy baby who does not care for her neonatal examination. Wouldn't you like to hold her and let her know that she is okay?" Dr. Mati spoke louder than usual. "She has grown accustomed to your voice, your heartbeat, your breathing. She even knows your smell. That baby you hear crying needs her mother. What do you say?"

"You know I don't like you, Dr. Mati Serendip-in-de-sand. This day was supposed to be different. Oh, so different. I wanted my baby. For months, I wanted her more than anything. And that's a lot. But now thanks to you—you and stupid Howard, it's all wrong." The pendulum swung and Debbie suddenly sounded frightened and vulnerable. "I'm afraid, Dr. Mati. You tell me everything is okay. Then you tell me I have something awful in my belly right next to my baby. Virginia. That's her name. Virginia Violet." The pendulum swung the other way. "Only she gets my last name, not Howard's, stupid jerk."

Dr. Mati and the anesthesiologist locked eyes above their surgical masks. Both were struck by the utter lack of joy in a room accustomed to it.

"He lied to me. He LIED! He had it coming, you know. Should have never taken him with me this far. He belongs in the cellar." Just as Debbie was about to reveal information that would implicate her in more than one murder, the pendulum swung yet again. "I want to hold my baby. Please. At least, I think I do. I'm afraid. Anybody…can you hear me? I am so afraid right now. More than usual."

Debbie's level of sedation made it difficult to maintain her train of thought. It was the one thing everyone in the room forgave her for.

"I want my Daddy. God, I want my Daddy. Will Virginia have a mommy or are you going to keep me away from her, doctor?"

The sentiment hit Dr. Mati hard. "I didn't have my mommy, and look at me." (And the pendulum swung again) "Where is she, doctor?" Debbie said accusatorily. "Let me have my baby. I want my baby, Virginia. She is supposed to be mine. It is supposed to be okay now. That was the deal."

"Please," Debbie added.

Dr. Mati directed Penny to deliver the child to her mother.

"Here you go, Momma. Congratulations," Penny said sweetly. It was hard not to be kind when holding a newborn.

Debbie awkwardly reached for her baby. Penny helped settle Virginia safely but not altogether gently into Debbie's arms. "Hi, baby," Debbie slurred tenderly as she stared into the pink round face of what was supposed to have been her future. The weight of the baby on Debbie's chest offset the weight of her heavy heart. "You. You are finally here. And you are amazing. Look at you. Perfect, aren't you? Just like the mean doctor said."

Debbie had stopped crying. After a long pause spent staring at her newborn's face, Debbie said to the room, "She doesn't look like me. She's beautiful!"

No one replied. Nurse Mia turned her head away and furtively wiped away a tear. Silently they all wished the best for Debbie. And all knew such wishes rarely came true.

"I wonder," she said to the child, "will you look like me when you grow up? It may be for the best. I may not look like much but I got what your granddad left me and you can have it. Every bit of it." Debbie looked up toward Dr. Mati who was finishing the last bit of work on Debbie's abdomen. The blue sheet used to keep Debbie from seeing herself cut open was down now. Doctor and patient looked at each other. Debbie spoke with alarming clarity. "I'm sorry, Dr. Mati. I'm a real mess."

Dr. Mati did not know what to say, which was a rare thing.

"She is perfect. You were right."

Dr. Mati smiled and nodded. Was she really going to have the mother thrown in jail where she would have to arrange for visitations with her bundle of joy and salvation? Dr. Mati was afraid so. She was forgiving, but Christ, Debbie had almost killed the father of her baby, and as far as she could tell, for no damn reason whatsoever. And what reason could there ever be to do such a thing? What would Debbie do if she grew angry with her child? Dr. Mati had faced similar dilemmas before. She looked into Debbie's eyes, glassy and soft from the sedation. She looked deeply, hoping for some silent guidance on the heavy decision she needed to make. Cherished for her unique no-nonsense compassion born from the ability to read the sufferings of women, Dr. Mati saw enough in Debbie's glazed eyes to change course—slightly. As an act of mercy, she decided that she would commit Debbie into the state hospital where she could be treated for her problems and where visitations would be easier and better. That, she felt, was the nicest thing she could do for both her patients, let alone their man, who was hopefully doing better than when last she saw him.

Dr. Mati spoke the truth, yet she could not help feel like she was faking it. "She is a beautiful baby. And I am not just saying that. All babies are beautiful, but she is something special. You should feel very proud."

Debbie, once again looking at the face of her daughter, said, "I owe you a sorry and a thank you." It was unclear if she were speaking to Dr. Mati or Virginia. Then Debbie looked straight into Dr. Mati's eyes once more and asked, "What happened to the other one?"

Dr. Mati rolled her lips inward and then spoke. "The other one is gone. You need not worry about that. Just hold your precious baby. Isn't this what you've been waiting for? What you've been wanting?"

"Was it born alive? Was it what you said it was?"

"Don't do this, Debbie," Dr. Mati cautioned. "Don't make yourself feel worse than you already do. Pregnancy and birth are truly difficult things. Given everything that can and must happen, it is a wonder we are born at all. You have a miracle in your arms. You have a precious gift. May that be your focus."

"Just tell me if it was born alive, so I know."

"Know what? I cannot answer such a question."

While they were talking and nearly forgiving each other, nurse Mia looked over at the odd, amorphously shaped thing wrapped in a receiving blanket with "Paro County Hospital" stenciled on it. The former twin/placenta *a la dos* looked a bit like the rotten, rubbery egg of some prehistoric reptile. Mia watched it, though it was not easy to do.

It's still beating. Mia said to herself. *I can see it.* The damned thing had been without oxygen for several minutes, and yet it was still slowly and rhythmically twitching from its heartbeat, as if begging for a chance to be born from the pall it was trapped within. Mia said a silent prayer for it. Whether she was just praying for a pod of random organs or an actual partially formed human thing, she did not know. She just prayed for its heart to stop beating the way one prays for the heart of a beloved to surrender to the final stages of cancer.

While Mia stared at the twin thing, waiting for that damned horrid twitch to cease, Debbie quietly focused on what it felt like to hold her very own baby. It was the first time Debbie Coomb had ever held a baby. She made note of how tiny the little fisted hands were, replete with tiny little fingernails on tiny little fingertips. She marveled at the incredible softness of the vernex coating the baby's skin. She loosened the blanket wrapped tightly around Virginia so she could peek at her body. It was soft and warm and blotchy from living in another. She noticed the faintest hint of buds on her daughter's chest, thinking that if all went well, they would one day have the ability to sustain life just as Debbie's breasts were, in that very moment, filling with milk in order to sustain her sweet Virginia. Debbie looked at her daughter's toes. Each a perfect reproduction. *So this is the miracle*, she thought. And she was right. In turn, that made her think of the imperfect life sitting somewhere in the room. *Did it die?* Debbie believed that the horrible and tragic offspring clearly implicated the source. But then, didn't the healthy, normal one do the same?

So confusing.

So sad.

So happy.

So what now?

Debbie held her hope in her arms. The nightmare that accompanied it was gone from her world now. Howard, too. After being so near each other day after day, year after year, fight after fight, love after…

Howard, too.

She had promised him fatherhood. And at the time, she meant it. Then it all went to shit just when Howard promised her everything was A-OK. And it happened right after Debbie really let Howard in, allowing herself to trust a man. A harmless, screwy little neener of a man named Howard Feck. And how was she repaid for that trust? *He lied. He lied about the very thing he insisted I trust him on.*

Or was he just wrong?

In Debbie's logic, if you were wrong, but you believed you were right and swore up, down, and sideways to that belief, having mistaken it for truth, then you were lying. So to Debbie, Howard lied about the most important thing in her world, and he had paid for it severely, though perhaps not unjustly. Life is a big deal, after all.

2

THOUGH SHE HARBORED ENMITY like a pond harbors mosquito larvae in July, she suddenly wished Howard were there with her. This truth flowed around her heart like warm grease.

"I shouldn't have been so rough on him," Debbie said to the room. "It's just that…you have no idea what he is like on a regular basis. He'd do anything for you, but not very well, and probably pee on the carpet getting it done."

No one remarked on what she was saying. Debbie continued.

"He told me I was the best thing that ever happened to him. And I'm a big, nasty, crummy bitch. I guess that tells you what kind of person he is." Debbie looked for Dr. Mati. "Is he okay? Can you let him in here to see me with my baby?"

"I told them to let us know what room they put him in after he stabilizes," the quiet Mia offered. "He was hurt pretty badly."

Debbie let out a single, long cry, closed her eyes, and spoke.

"I know what that's like. I was hurt pretty badly one time. One long time. It started when my daddy died. And ended…" Debbie opened her eyes, looked at Virginia, and sighed. "And I think it's ending right now, I hope. At least that's the plan."

"Men hated me," Debbie confessed. "They used their…they used themselves to show me how much they hated me, day in and day out. They hated me a lot. And they would not leave me alone. Weird to do that, huh? And all I could do was let them. I couldn't even show them how much I hated them back. They wouldn't let me. I would tell them, and they would laugh and show me how they could hate me even more—and then hit me when they were done, or close to done. They liked it when I fought back, especially Teddy. He was the first. And the last. Ironic, huh?"

These words were gently spoken, causing them to hang in the quiet room like funereal adornments in a nursery.

Debbie felt all eyes in the room upon her. It was another familiar feeling she did not like. She looked even closer into the face of her lovely daughter, seeking resolution in purity. "How could they, Dr. Mati, huh? My Dad and Howard were the only ones that didn't hate me. And they're both gone.

"I won't let any man hate my baby. I'll kill him. I know what it takes and I know how. Funny. That day was the best day of my life, until she came." Debbie kissed her daughter on her forehead. It had been many years since she had kissed anyone. She had never kissed Howard, even during the brief window of their torrid lovemaking.

"Death and birth, the two best days of my life. What do you think of that, Dr. Mati? What do you think of me now? Still think I was too hard on Howard? Maybe I was, but—what do you expect? What am I supposed to do? Let another one hurt me and laugh and get away?"

Dr. Mati had finished with her surgical ministrations. She continued to listen, silently, with compassion emanating from the eyes of her masked face.

Debbie continued. "I wasn't born with guardian angels like everybody else. God does not even know I exist. What am I supposed to do? Just let all of God's children feed off me like— like some pig that's only half dead?"

It was the first time Debbie had ever spoken about what had happened to her. As she confessed her sad truths and bitter despair, she sometimes appeared to hold the baby too tightly. Everyone in the room, except Virginia, watched cautiously, ready to jump in to pull the new perfect life away from the older broken one. The anesthesiologist was prepared to knock Debbie out if need be. It never came to that. As quickly as Debbie tightened her grip, she would relax it. Admittedly, it is hard to know just how firm the grip on one's future should be.

Her lament continued. "Sometimes I think God is personal. I mean, like, we each have our own, who listens to only our prayers and only has to watch out for just one person, and does godly things as God sees fit just for one. It makes sense, don't you think, Dr. Mati? It couldn't work any other way. I mean, how can one God listen to all the prayers in the world at once, and then choose who gets what?"

"I think my God was my dad. And he died. My God died. He was a good God, maybe the best God, but he died. So I had to fix things myself and go without all the godly things you all get to have. So forgive me if I'm not like you, okay?" Debbie raised her voice on that last line, and her eyes shifted from a piercing look at Dr. Mati to a hazy glare. Dr. Mati's expression remained hidden behind her surgical mask. But the compassion in her eyes held true. "I got my baby now. And I got my future back." Debbie looked around the room. "Where's the other? I don't want the other one in here with my baby. The other one is a devil. So that means this one—Virginia, she is my new God, huh, Dr. Mati? I got my God back, didn't I? Isn't that how it works? Please tell me how it works." Debbie kissed her baby's forehead again, slow and gentle.

"Then, please let us go home."

As Dr. Mati contemplated Debbie's questions and answers and their implications for the past, present, and future, Debbie spoke again, this time directly to Virginia. "This is a world where men do terrible things to you just because you're a girl and your daddy's gone. Oh, Virginia, oh, my baby girl, you'll have to be so careful." Tears fell from the mother's face onto the daughter's. Virginia reacted to the first few but accepted the rest as seemingly routine. She had no idea...

"I won't let it happen to you, baby. You'll see. And your daddy ain't so much like them. He has the gear and wants to drive, but he's nothing like the bad ones. And that makes him special. 'Cause bad ones are everywhere. And they won't stop—until you stop them yourself. It's amazing how much they can take from you when you already got nothing."

Had Dr. Mati not needed to wrap up and move her patient to post-op, they would have learned the details of Debbie's three biggest secrets—the ones out of the frying pan and into the fire. Plus, Virginia needed her neonatal care, not having the benefits that come from being squeezed through a birth canal. Dr. Mati also sensed that any further confessing could create legal and moral obligations she would rather not have to confront. She knew that Debbie was telling only truths.

"Debbie, your baby needs to go with Penny now where she can have her neonatal exam completed, and we can prepare her to go home. Meanwhile, you just had major surgery, and a baby. You have a lot of recovering to do."

Dr. Mati moved to Debbie's side, put her hand on Debbie's arm, and looked at her. Debbie kept her eyes on Virginia. "I am sorry for what happened to you. Words cannot express my sorrow for women like you on this planet. One is too many, and, unfortunately, there are millions. I will tell you that it is man's inhumanity toward women that drove me to become a doctor. Since I cannot make it better wishing that it never happened, my wish is for your healing. I am sure that life will be different for Virginia with you and your husband's influence and nurturing.

"Remember, Debbie, today you are a mother, not a victim. My wish is for you to accept fully and with an open heart the gift of motherhood. Own this wonder. If you do, you will leave here a better woman than when you arrived. And you will have made great strides on your healing path." Dr. Mati's soft voice and accent born from an ancient tongue made these sincere words sound like an incantation. They had the desired effect on Debbie, who was already well tenderized by medication and childbirth. Debbie deeply breathed in her daughter's scent, then surrendered her to Nurse Penny.

"As soon as we're done admiring this precious baby, we will bring her to your room, don't you worry," Penny said as she scooped Virginia from her mother's arms. "You just rest. You've had a big day."

They wheeled Debbie away to a quiet room down the hall. It was nearly four in the morning, and thanks to her pregnancy, she had not had a good night's sleep in many weeks—a warm-up for life with a newborn, no doubt. Debbie was sound asleep before they parked her in her room.

After the big wide door to the room closed, Debbie's father, Delwin, came down again like ancestors sometimes do. He put his head against his daughter's and cried tears that disappeared into her hair. He whispered things into her ear that became part of her dreams, including the words *Beautiful, Mother, Forgiveness,* and *Love.*

Chapter 18

1

WHEN NURSE ALMA SEARS heard the bitching and moaning coming from Debbie's room, she figured it was a good time for a cigarette. Officer Thoms, who had been assigned to the floor thanks to Debbie's incident the night before, agreed and joined her. Alma Sears had been a nurse at Paro County Hospital for more than twenty-five years and had hated all but the first five. She was a Vicodin, nicotine, and caffeine addict, and all but the nicotine had stopped making her feel good years ago. But if she stopped taking them, she felt worse. She was fifty-something but looked a wan seventy. She had weaseled her way into maternity because cleaning up baby shit was a lot better than cleaning up grown-up shit. She even connived a way for the state to pay for her labor and delivery training. She barely passed the exam, but that was sufficient for a job at Paro County. Few could stand working with Alma, so they were fine with her slacking off. It was understood that Nurse Alma and Dr. Mati were not to share the same shift.

Nurse Alma Sears was accurately briefed on the situation with mother Debbie Coomb, but she preferred the gossip version—druggie lowlife mom freaked out on the way to delivery and almost killed her boyfriend and infant, lucky to have one live baby of the two that were born. Based on this, she figured mother Coomb could wait the five goddam minutes it took to burn a Slim in the stairwell.

2

SEVEN HOURS AFTER GIVING birth, Debbie awoke with two hard pains on her chest and a searing band of fire below her navel. She came to on her back. Her breasts seemed to have been replaced during her slumber with something denser and heavier. These pains were much more immediate than the one she felt farther south. That one felt like a bad sunburn across a narrow swatch deep in the fold of her belly. It was the hard stones laying on her chest that filled her with exquisite pain and a yearning for release. She yelled for help, then discovered a little square box draped over the railing of the bed with the words NURSE and CALL on it. Debbie pressed the button. It lit up on the first push. A few minutes later, two people walked into her room—a nurse Debbie had never seen before and a sheriff's deputy following closely behind.

"I can hear you yelling all the way down at the nurse's station, Ms. Coomb, and I will not put up with it," barked Alma. "We all know what happened here last night. Officer Thoms is here on your behalf and he'll gladly teach you how to behave like a lady if you need a reminder."

Of course, Debbie didn't need a reminder on how to be a lady. She needed a first lesson. And Officer Thoms, who looked too old to be a cop in uniform and looked a little like Clyde Eel—had Clyde been allowed to reach old age, didn't look like he would be any good as a finishing school instructor. His bloodshot eyes, veiny, scarred-up nose, and beer belly made him look like he would be great at teaching folks how to hold down bar stools so they don't up and fly away. His policing skills had been refined over the years to just being in uniform and in the room. Sometimes that was enough. He figured that would be the SOP here, and if not, Billy clubs did not discriminate.

Debbie took one look at Officer Thoms and sized him up accurately. "He doesn't need to be here," Debbie said, pointing to the big ugly cop. "I'm sorry I yelled, it's just that—does he have to be here? I would like to talk about my female problems right now, please."

"Sorry, doctor's orders," said the old nurse. That wasn't exactly true. Dr. Mati had said a police officer needed to be on the floor in case the patient in room M-5 became violent. But the doctor had also said that Debbie Coomb should be treated with the same dignity as any other maternity patient, as long as she cooperated. Nurse Alma Sears felt the nuances of Dr. Mati's orders were inconvenient.

"Nurse, my breasts are killing me. They ache something fierce."

"Well, your milk has come in. Normally I'd have you lie on your chest, but you had to have a C-section, so you can't do that." Nurse Alma Sears made a Caesarean sound sinful. "I'll get you some ice packs. That will help the milk go down."

"But I want to breastfeed. Where's my baby—Virginia?" Debbie's face clearly showed fear.

Alma Sears was about to tell Debbie that an incarcerated mother shouldn't breastfeed when a woman who looked a lot like Nurse Mia walked into the room. "Everything okay? The call light for this room is still on," said Mia's sister, Nurse Leticia.

"Yeah, we're okay," answered Alma Sears. "Good of you to check on us, though." That was not what Leticia meant.

"I should have turned off the call light. I was just afraid of getting too close. You know…" Nurse Alma gave Leticia a look she did not care for.

"Why?" Nurse Leticia asked. "What's the matter? Is there a problem?"

"You heard what they said at shift change," Alma whispered. But not so quiet that Debbie couldn't hear. "You read the report."

"Hi, Debbie. My name is Leticia. My sister Mia attended the delivery of your baby. Congratulations."

"I want to see my baby. Why can't I see my baby?"

"I'll bring your baby to you, okay?"

"Please." Debbie remained agitated, fearful.

"First, I'm going to reset your call light, okay?" Leticia asked. "You're going to be nice, aren't you? If you are, we can keep your baby in here with you, at least some of the time."

"Yes, Nurse," Debbie said. "Dr. Mati said that would be okay. Please. I need to see her and feed her."

Leticia walked over to Debbie, reached across her and switched off the call button. She then opened the thick, blue curtain over the window behind Debbie's bed, revealing a bright but gray day.

"Alma, can you go to the nursery and tell them Ms. Coomb is ready for her baby? Also let them know she wants to breastfeed."

"I was going to bring some ice for her breasts," Alma Sears huffed. "Since she's going to jail, I don't see why you want to start with the breastfeeding anyways. Switching to formula will be hard on the baby. I thought you knew that."

Leticia answered Alma with a stern look. Then she turned to Officer Thoms, who had held the same expression since entering the room. "Sir, you can leave the room," Nurse Leticia said, authoritatively. "We will call you if we need your assistance. Until then, please stay out of patients rooms." Without a word, Officer Thoms turned and walked out the door a step behind Nurse Alma.

Chapter 19

1

WHILE DEBBIE AWAITED THE return of her sweet baby Virginia, Howard Feck, two floors below, was slowly waking in a room shared with a drunk driver who had slaughtered a tree with his pickup truck. He was young and loud and in a lot of pain—something to do with his knees, which were suspended in a traction device in a way that made the formerly drunken man look like he was frozen in a sitting position and then fell onto his back. Howard was on a lot of medication, and when they brought in his new roomie screaming in agony, he did not wake. Unlike maternity, this floor, dedicated to the bodily injured waiting out their healing and painful recovery, was hopping. Here, the mask of Howard's injuries made him run of the mill. Another victim of bad luck and bad choices full of stitches and painkillers and wearing darkly stained gauze.

None of Howard's injuries were life threatening. They were far from trivial, and on his pathetic physique, they looked much worse than they really were.

His mouth was wired mostly shut so his fractured jaw could heal properly. The wires, which ended above his ears, had two white Styrofoam safety-balls stuck on them so he wouldn't poke anyone's eye out or snag himself on anything. His right eye was all but swollen shut while his left was framed in a puffy purple bruise. His nose was crooked now, and would be for the rest of his days. But that was not the worst of it. The worst of it, Howard discovered almost immediately after waking, was the pain from just breathing thanks to a bruised sternum and two bruised ribs. There was nothing to be done about that except to let them heal at their own wounded-snail's pace. Until then, each breath felt like a frozen, jagged shard of glass ripping apart the center of his chest from the inside. To make things worse (with Howard, there always seemed to be something to make things worse), he'd had a couple of breathing treatments, since his asthma had reached an entirely new level during and shortly after his beating. His lungs were as clear and open as a brand new Sousaphone. With his broken nose swollen and caked with dried blood, he could only breathe through his half-wired-shut mouth. Breathing felt as if he were inhaling jagged glass shards. He was awake for only a few breaths before the pain of it made him cry. And, of course, crying made it worse. Then he remembered the original reason for being at the hospital.

The baby.

What about that baby? Did they send Debbie home? They must have. But—oh yeah, there was something else besides the baby, too.

Howard's pain and painkillers kept him from running a train of thought to where he could really understand how he came to be lying in a hospital bed where his face felt tight, thick, and odd, and breathing hurt like hell. He found the nurse call button. Reaching for it also hurt. Next to the call button, he saw something else. It was a Polaroid picture of a baby in a hospital bassinette. Written in neat handwriting on the border of the Polaroid were the words, *Congratulations! Virginia Coomb-Feck* with the day's date.

Virginia Feck?

Is that…? We talked about names but…My baby. I'm a dad!

With previously unavailable enthusiasm, Howard pushed the call button again. And again. And again, not knowing it didn't make a lick of difference.

It took several long minutes for a nurse to respond to Howard's call. This busy section of the hospital acutely felt the woes of budget cuts and requisite understaffing. The nurse who answered wore a plain yellow smock with splattered blood dried dark brown over the midsection. "What's the problem, sir?" the nurse twanged in a slow, nasally drawl.

"My chest hurts," Howard gulped, dryly. "When I brea—is this my daughter?" Howard pointed at the picture as the nurse sauntered toward him.

"I don't know," said the nurse. "Where does your chest hurt?"

"When I breathe," Howard breathed. "And all the time."

"You're due for your medication," the nurse replied. " It'll take a couple minutes to get it. Hang tight. How's the asthma?"

"Good. What about this?" Howard pulled from the bedrail the Polaroid of his baby.

The nurse picked up the picture from Howard's shaky hand. "Says Feck on it. Chart says Howard Feck. I'm guessing you're related. You expecting, Mr. Feck?"

"Yes."

"Well then. Congratulations. I'll be back."

The nurse opened the door and disappeared into a noisy hallway bright and busy with fast-moving staff and slow-moving patients. Then the heavy door closed, leaving the two wounded men in a moderate silence that Howard broke. "Can you hear me, sir?"

"Me?" said the DUI crash case. "Yeah, I hear you."

"I'm a dad."

"Congratulations," said Mr. DUI, as if Howard had just announced he had the clap.

"I mean just now. I'm a dad." Howard breathed, painfully. "A new dad."

"I said congratulations, boss."

"Thank you." Howard turned his attention back to the picture of his baby. Studying it helped take his mind off the pain. The room became quiet again with the faint sounds of the hallway bustle occasionally leaking in.

"Got any champagne over there? Anything to celebrate with?" Mr. DUI asked.

"No. Just a picture."

"Too bad."

The nurse returned to the room wheeling in a small tray.

"What'd you bring me?" asked Howard's roommate.

"Wait your turn. Please," said the nurse, trying halfheartedly not to sound unpleasant. "Mr. Feck. Your medication. Can you swallow okay?"

Howard gave it a dry run and was successful, though it also hurt. "Yes."

"Good. Because I have to squirt this. In your mouth. For the inflammation. It'll help with the pain."

The nurse instructed Howard to part his lips as much as he could and to swallow three times while she squirted in the liquid.

"Don't choke. It'll hurt. Bad." Howard did not need to hear this. Hearing the potential problems in any situation that involved him was usually enough to manifest them. But he held it together, partly because his focus was on his daughter, and partly because he knew he couldn't tolerate much more pain without losing consciousness.

"Now. The good stuff." The nurse held up the other syringe. "This will help. A lot. Four hours. Then more if you want."

She injected the painkillers into Howard's IV. He relaxed almost immediately. "If you need anything," the nurse pointed to the call box lying over the frame of the bed. She began to turn away but stopped. "Oh. Your wife gave birth upstairs early this morning. Baby is fine. Mother, too. You get feeling better. We can get someone. Take you up."

"I'm better." Howard slurred. "Can I go now? Please?"

"Honey. You're going sleepies. But I'll let them know."

Howard was asleep before the nurse had checked on his roommate and left the room.

2

HOWARD AWOKE THREE HOURS later with a maddening pain that refreshed itself with each breath. The pain from his jaw, nose, and lacerated face tried to keep up, but even those combined were no match for the pain his chest issued from plain, old, everyday breathing. After a few breaths had driven him to an intense wakefulness, he remembered the picture of his daughter. He looked around the bed and did not see it. He pressed the nurse call button and began to panic for fear the picture had been lost. Panic meant harder breathing and sharper pain. He tried to look over the edge of the bed to the floor but the pain prevented it. He rummaged through the bedding as best he could and found nothing.

I'll just go and see her myself. I don't need a picture. I'll get the real thing. I am her father after all. Howard smiled briefly in between breaths and said aloud to himself, "Gosh, I am a dad."

Painful minutes went by as Howard waited for a nurse and fretted over the missing picture of his daughter. Never once did he question why Debbie did this to him. Howard had sorted that out years ago. It had been a long while since he had suffered genuine (not casual) violence at the closed hand of his mate. But the conclusions from the incident remained the same—he was wrong and Debbie was angry because of it, or, at a minimum, angry because she felt "extra bad." He only wished it didn't hurt so bad this time. Even more, he wished it didn't have to be on the day of his daughter's birth. He almost cursed Debbie for that. Almost.

Eventually, the nurse reentered the room and went to Howard's bedside.

"Medication wearing off?"she asked.

"Yes. And I want to see my daughter. I had her picture here, and now I can't find it. I think I may have dropped it on the floor."

"Honey. Don't you want to wait? They won't take you loaded." This was not entirely true, but it was the path of least effort for the nurse.

"Then I won't go loaded. My chest hurts something awful when I breathe. But I need to see my daughter. Can't you understand?" Remarkably and without any self-awareness, Howard showed some grit. Could fatherhood have planted seeds of fortitude? "I'll take aspirin for the pain, then I can go see her. How about that?"

The nurse noticed something on the floor. She bent over, and returned holding the missing Polaroid. "Is this it?"

No, that's Deputy Dawg, is what Howard actually felt like saying. But he only nodded, which hurt less than talking. The nurse handed it to him. "How do I get to where she is?"

"All right. I'll call. See if anyone can get you. You'll need a wheelchair."

"Fine," Howard answered without hesitation. "Can I at least have some aspirin or something?"

"I'll see."

3

A LONG, PAINFUL THIRTY minutes later, or roughly five hundred agonizing breaths, Howard saw another hospital employee—a youngish man almost as thin as Howard, though covered in thin, ropy muscle instead of pasty, damp skin. Tattoos peeked out from the collar of his orderly scrubs and wrapped around his exposed forearms. The ink work appeared to be of the subpar variety created in penitentiaries or cheap motel parties. He had long, stringy, dirty-blonde hair. Its uneven length indicated it had grown out from a mullet. He pushed into the room a wheelchair with an antitheft sissy bar. He was very upbeat.

"You the one with the baby upstairs?"

"Yes, I am" said Howard. "Are you going to take me to her?"

"I am if your name is Harold Peck."

"My name is Howard Feck."

"Close enough. Hop in, bud. I'm Jammin' Dave. I'll be your driver over the next couple floors. Let's jam."

Jammin' Dave, who could have been Axl Rose's cheerier, well-adjusted brother with no signs of male pattern baldness, deftly maneuvered the wheelchair alongside Howard's bed and then dropped the bed's safety rail.

"You need a helping hand there, brother?" asked Jammin' Dave, spiritedly.

"I don't know. Maybe," Howard said. "I think I can stand up."

"Well, that's a start. Where does it hurt?"

Howard stopped to take a personal inventory of where it hurt. Jammin' Dave didn't feel like waiting that long. "Okay, let me guess," he said. "I'm guessing by those Styrofoam antlers and the extra holes in your face that someone did a drum solo on your mug, huh?"

Howard was not sure what Jammin' Dave meant, but that was okay.

"How did it happen? Doesn't look like road rash, and not enough damage to be a windshield. Piss off some bikers, maybe?"

"No." Howard did not want to tell Jammin' Dave what happened. Jammin' Dave seemed cool, and he was being cool to Howard, whose ego still clutched to the adolescent desire for acceptance by those he perceived as cool or popular. He didn't want Jammin' Dave laughing at him when he explained that his wife did this to him just before she gave birth to the baby he was about to see.

"Don't want to tell me, huh? It's all right man. I've been there. You ain't really a man until you've gotten your ass kicked so hard it hurts to fart." Ah, the wisdom of the Jam-Man. "You can be proud of your scars and bruises, man. Trust me, I know."

Jammin' Dave helped Howard into the wheelchair the best he could. This wasn't the part where Jammin' Dave really jammed. It was driving wheelchairs through a crowded hospital with speed, precision, and hardly any collisions. That was where Jammin' Dave jammed, and how he had earned his nickname.

"All right, Harold, you ready to fly?" asked Jammin Dave.

"Sure. I'd like to get there in one piece."

"Aw, I can't promise you that, man," Jammin' Dave replied. "But I can promise you'll arrive in the same number of pieces you're in now." Jammin' Dave laughed robustly at his own joke. Howard did not, which was a blessing, since laughing would have hurt like hell.

"You know," said Howard, "that nurse was supposed to bring me some aspirin or something. I hurt really bad, but I don't want it to get in the way of seeing my daughter."

"Who's your nurse?"

"I don't know the name."

"Well, nor do I my friend. I'm just the driver. We'll stop at the garage on the way to your new babe and see if they can hook you up. Cool?"

"Cool." It was one of the few times Howard had used the word in public without it causing him any grief. Howard liked Jammin' Dave and told himself he would introduce his daughter to him— the only parent in the history of procreation that thought this was a good idea.

"Let's jam, bro." Jammin' Dave grabbed Howard's IV bag, clipped it to a ring on the wheelchair's sissy bar, then made a "Vvvroomm" sound as he pulled into the considerable traffic of the Ortho-floor corridor. Above him, Howard sensed Jammin' Dave's head and shoulders weaving side to side as he pushed the chair faster than any other thing in the hallway. He used the entire width of the corridor to get around the slower people, carts, gurneys, and other wheelchairs. Howard heard the other workers call out "Jammin' Dave!" and "Hey, JD!" and, "Jam-Man!" as they passed by. It made Howard feel like a geeky girl riding shotgun in a bad boy's hot rod. It was damn near celebrity status and it helped keep his mind off his pain. It also made him feel that he was arriving to meet his DAUGHTER in ultimate style.

Jammin' Dave pushed the chair to the third floor nurse's station and made an "Errrch," braking sound as he stopped. A big, buff male nurse greeted him from the center of the semicircular station, "Hey, Jammin Dave."

With obvious adoration, Howard tried to turn his head to look up at the Jam-Man, but the pain stopped him. Jammin' Dave acknowledged the nurse with a head jerk.

"My man here was supposed to get his dose, but his nurse was a no-show."

"What's the name?" asked the beefy nurse behind the counter.

"Howard Feck." Howard jumped in only because he did not want the Jam-Man to get his name wrong in public. Bros had to cover each other that way.

Jammin' Dave lifted up Howard's wrist and read the name on the wristband.

"That's right," said Jammin' Dave. "Harold Feck. No wait. It's Howard." Then, addressing Howard, "I'm sorry, man. I got your name wrong back there. You should have told me. No disrespect—okay, man?"

"It's cool," Howard said affectionately.

The large male nurse and JD exchanged an "ain't that sweet" glance.

"My wife just had a baby here last night, and I'm on my way to see her. The nurse told me that I couldn't go see her if they gave me my medication because I would be too, umm, loaded."

The male nurse was looking at a computer screen while Howard talked. Jammin' Dave was having a hard time remaining stationary—like Mr. Toad about to embark on a new wild ride.

"All right, cowboy. Tell your driver to stay here. I'll be right back."

"You hear that, cowboy?" Howard said to Jammin' Dave.

"No, man. You're the cowboy," JD corrected. Howard looked mortified by his uncool faux pas.

"Sorry." Howard flushed with embarrassment.

"No worries, man. You got a lot going on. Plus, you need your meds."

After a brief, uncomfortable pause, the Jam-Man asked, "What's your baby's name?"

"I think it's Virginia."

"Cool, man. I popped my cherry to 'Sweet Virginia' by the Stones. Only it was another band doing it. GnR, I think. Anyway. Cool, man." This was a bald-faced lie by Jammin' Dave, but he wanted Howard to feel good on his way to meeting his daughter. What was he supposed to do, be honest and tell him it sounded like a granny name?

The large male nurse returned with a syringe and a cup of water with a straw. "Give me a smile, Dad, so I can get this in you," the nurse said. "This should take the edge off. When you come back, we can get you something stronger." The nurse squirted the medicine into Howard's narrowly opened mouth. "And here's some water. I know that stuff don't taste too good. All right, Jammin' Dave. Start your engines. Take him away."

"Right on." The Jam-Man made another peeling-out noise, which sounded a lot like his braking noise, only longer. Then onward they jammed.

4

As Howard ascended to his grace, Debbie descended in the adjacent elevator to her hell. Another hell. They briefly thought of one another as their elevator cars passed each other only a few feet apart. Howard's thoughts were positive as he rose to his occasion. Debbie's were darkly negative as she sank to her doom. Howard was riding shotgun with his new bud Jammin' Dave. Debbie was strapped to a wheelchair next to a lawman happy to use force as he saw fit.

In the lift, Jammin' Dave explained to Howard that they would have to keep it in low gear on the maternity floor since they were "all into babies and peace and junk like that." Howard said he understood, and that he did not want to wake his baby— and Jammin' Dave would not want to wake his wife. The Jam-Man chuckled at what he believed to be a joke.

The elevator doors opened onto the floor Debbie had just left. JD glided the wheelchair down the quiet hall to the nurse's station populated by two nurses deep in conversation. One ostentatiously held a cold pack against her wrist.

Jammin' Dave whispered to Howard, "Man, I could totally fly down this stretch if they'd let me. I mean there is *no* traffic. But they got a couple doctors up here that'll bust your ass till your crack goes sideways." Then he added, "If they catch you."

Cruising slowly down such an empty corridor seemed to squelch Jammin' Dave's manhood, perhaps even his integrity. "I might just have to light 'em up on my way back, man."

Arriving at the nurse's station, both nurses seemed to become instantly annoyed by the duo's presence.

"Someone ordered a dad?" Jammin' Dave chuckled at his levity. The nurses glared. "I have, uh, Howard, right?"

Howard nodded, proudly.

"Yeah, Howard Feck. His wife's up here. She just had a baby. He was told he could see her."

The one holding the dressing on her wrist spoke. "Not anymore she ain't," huffed Nurse Alma Sears. She meant to continue, but Howard interrupted.

"What do you mean she's not here anymore? She was born last night. Is she okay? What happened? Where is she?"

"You mean the baby?" asked Nurse Alma. "She's okay, I think. No thanks to your wife, that's for sure. She went psycho—what a surprise. Laid out one of our nurses pretty badly. I told her not to get too close after what she did to you, but she wouldn't listen. I tried to get the baby out of harm's way and she did this to me." Nurse Alma removed the compress from a hand accustomed to holding a fag. It now held black and yellow bruises. The first two fingers were quite swollen.

Howard put a hand to his temple, and, in doing so bumped the wires holding his jaw. Bright streamers of pain fluttered across the bottom of his face and down one side of his neck.

"Man, your wife did all of this?" Jammin' Dave said, with an open hand toward Howard's face. He sounded concerned.

Howard reeled. "Where did they take her? Is she okay?"

"She could be a lot worse. Better shape than you by the looks of it. She tore some sutures, and I told 'em she can go ahead and bleed to death, for all I care. I wasn't going to touch her after what she did to the other nurse. You should see her. She's a little thing, too. Lucky she didn't snap like a twig. She's in your wife's old room right now, as a matter of fact, trying to recover. It's not like I could help her since *your* wife crushed my damn hand." Nurse Alma Sears seemed to enjoy telling the disturbing news to a visibly shaken Howard. "They had to sedate her just to get her in restraints and get her out of here. You just missed her. Consider yourself lucky. Don't look at me like that. She wasn't bleeding too badly. They can work on her in jail where she belongs. They got EMTs there who don't put up with any crap."

Alma failed to mention how she contributed to the episode by having Officer Thoms forcefully restrain Debbie so she could take the baby away for her final neonatal exam—a requirement for discharge. Alma was less than clear about why she was taking the baby, and for how long. But she was quite clear that Debbie would soon be leaving for jail, where babies aren't allowed. So when Alma tried to take Virginia, Debbie fought to keep her. Upon hearing the commotion, Nurse Leticia arrived and tried to intervene. She paid a dear price: Strangled to near unconsciousness, a small chunk of her nose bitten off, and a chipped tooth from hitting the bedrail as she collapsed to the floor. The entire time Debbie was also squeezing and twisting Alma's hand as she tried to take the baby.

"What do you mean *jail*?" Howard asked, in disbelief.

"Paro County Women's Facility," answered Jammin' Dave, who decided he did not care for Alma Sears one little bit. She'd probably be one of the asshole nurses up here who would rat on him for jammin' down their hallways, too. "It's the women's county jail. Man. You know, Nurse, my man here has been through a lot." Jammin' Dave gave Nurse Alma a "c'mon, lighten up, you're killing the guy" look. Alma caught it and disregarded it entirely.

"How long will she be there?" Howard asked.

"Probably not long enough, if you ask me," bitched Alma.

"Hey, man, don't worry about none of that," Jammin' Dave said to Howard. "You didn't come up here to see your wife anyway. Nurse, this man needs to meet his baby, if you don't mind. What do we do to make that happen?"

"Is he clean? Any infections or anything?"

"Nah, man. He's clean." Jammin' Dave actually had no idea of that were true but figured it was likely.

Nurse Alma Sears took a moment to size up Howard and his escort. She spoke to the quiet nurse nearby who had found relief in Alma bitching and moaning to another set of ears. "All right. Jean, take these two to the nursery. They can't go in. But you can show 'em the baby."

Jean, glad to get away from Alma, who would no doubt remain parked at the nurse's station for as long as she could milk her minor injury, rose from her tall swivel chair and walked around to Jammin' Dave and poor, deflated Howard. She didn't say anything. Instead, she motioned with her finger for them to follow. Howard vacillated between despair over what Alma had spewed and eager anticipation over meeting his daughter. Meanwhile, Jammin' Dave had lost himself studying the tight curves of Jean's ass outlined by her trim-fitting pants. Jean was older, probably close to fifty. That mattered not one bit to Jammin' Dave.

Nurse Jean stopped in front of the large nursery window, turned around, and saw Alma checking them out. Jean looked at her party. JD and Jean made eye contact, but it seemed to affect her equilibrium, so she broke it and motioned with one hand for them to stay put as she headed into the nursery. Jammin' Dave used a different smile on her than on Howard. He made a few sexual innuendos about Jean while she was gone. Howard did not respond. Jammin' Dave followed them with, "Sorry, man. This is your big moment. I didn't mean to steal your thunder by talking about that nurse. You have brought us together, new Dad. I owe you respect, man."

A muted tap on the nursery window followed the apology. An infant, swaddled tightly in a white county hospital blanket, was being held up to the window by *who cares*. She was held at an angle so that Howard in his wheelchair could see her. Howard looked at his future made flesh. A future Debbie thought was hers. A future Debbie would come to think of as stolen from her by Howard, who had stopped breathing for a few wonderful pain-free moments while his brain and emotions processed what he was seeing.

Jammin' Dave's good intentions interrupted the moment. "Wow, there she is, big daddy. Your little Miss America. Congratulations, man."

Howard knew immediately that he liked being called "daddy." Out of the corner of his eye, he noticed Jammin' Dave had extended his hand. Howard took it and shook it. Sweet tears appeared around his eyes, and gravity brought them down his face. He was overcome. Upon seeing his infant daughter for the very first time, Howard's agonizing pain seemed to disappear, as if his nervous system had surrendered in adoration to the little living thing on the other side of the window. A thing not separate just remote. After a few moments bearing witness, Howard realized he could hear faint screams through the thick glass. Virginia's mouth was agape and she seemed to be a couple levels above crying. Howard looked at the nurse holding the child. She had a mask on, but in her eyes, one could sense perturbation. This was not lost on Jammin' Dave, who couldn't stop himself from saying, "Wow, man. Looks like she has her mamma's temper."

"I want to hold her. I want to hold her, please," said Howard.

Jammin' Dave, always the helpful one, looked at the nurse holding the infant. He waved an arm to get the nurse to look his way. He pointed down to Howard and then mimed rocking a baby. The nurse's eyes responded with a look that intimated "finally" and then walked away from the window.

"I think your wish is coming true, Big Daddy Feck." Jean came out of the nursery holding the screaming Virginia Violet Feck. She had on a yellow surgical mask just like the nurse who held the baby to the window. She had brought two more, which she handed to Howard and Jammin' Dave.

"Ah, man, now you can't see my smile," flirted the Jam-Man. He was too busy looking at Jean to notice that Howard's hands were shaky, and he was struggling mightily to fit the mask around the contraption holding his jaw to the rest of his face. By the time Jammin' Dave noticed Howard's dilemma, Howard had managed to get the mask tangled in the traction wires on both sides of his head. It was hard not to laugh at such a sight, but Jammin' Dave did not for two reasons: Howard's bruised ego and Jean's sweet ass. He let out a snicker to relieve the pressure, then prayed to his God that it wouldn't blossom into a spate of roaring guffaws. With Howard's mask hopelessly tangled in his jaw gizmo, Jean decided to forego protocol and handed over the screaming infant.

The first thing Howard noticed, aside from the volume at which his daughter produced sound, was how amazing she felt in his arms and against his pain-racked chest. It was more than a million times better than a heating pad or a hot water bottle, two things Howard loved when under duress. He noticed the perfection of Virginia's tiny face—a button nose right where it was supposed to be—soft elliptical eyes showing little dark circles between tiny white triangles. The forehead and cheeks, red from screaming, perfectly complimented each other. Howard wanted to kiss them. He felt things he could not articulate and didn't need to in order to gain from them understanding, love, and joy.

And he was changed forever.

And there was no going back.

What Howard did not notice was that within a minute of holding his daughter for the very first time, Virginia had stopped crying. She released a few whimpers and brays necessary to bring the screams to a full stop, like the last drops of blood from a congealing wound. And then she settled down to the kind of peace only babies experience. It was clear that she felt safe again after the shock of being ripped from the blissful solace of her mother—twice. The smell, the sound, the beat, and other things invisible to grownups that are the essence of an infant's universe had returned. Howard held her against his wounded chest and spoke softly to her. So it would be for father and daughter, but not poor mother.

5

VIRGINIA SPENT MANY QUIET minutes in her daddy's arms. She did two of the three things babies her age can do very well: She slept peacefully and she soiled her diaper. Her time in paternal bliss would have been longer, but Nurse Alma Sears interrupted them to remind Jean that Virginia was not the only infant under their care and Howard wasn't even their patient.

Howard was amenable to Nurse Jean taking Virginia back into the nursery. He figured she needed to be there, that nurseries were like greenhouses for babies. Jammin' Dave offered to leave Howard at the window so he could watch his baby for a while.

Then he took off his mask and walked Jean back to the nurse's station. He did all the talking, which was fine by the Jam-Man, and evidently fine by Nurse Jean as well. From the nurse's station, Jammin' Dave could see Howard painfully trying to stretch in the wheelchair to get a better view of his daughter. JD asked Jean if they had a couple of pillows or phone books or something to "elevate my man Howard's stature and accommodate his need to stare at his baby." Jean provided two pillows and a folded blanket. Jammin' Dave took them and, in a brotherly fashion, placed them under Howard's posterior. It was this act that clinched his opportunity to get to know Jean, who would accept this considerate younger man with the tight, tattooed skin as a virile and eager plaything. The Jam-Man and Howard were not the only ones on the maternity floor who thought today was a special day.

Elevated enough to properly see into the nursery, Howard smiled big, then frowned. Virginia was crying again. Not as bad as before, but she seemed to be ramping up. He looked for the nurse tending to Virginia and two other babies who were fast asleep. He spied her in the corner of the nursery with her back to the window. He could faintly hear the wail through what he guessed was bulletproof glass. It was actually sound proof—the cries were coming from the nursery entrance around the corner from the window. He grew anxious and concerned over Virginia's distress. He looked toward the nurse's station, saw Jammin' Dave, and figured he had been dumped for the quiet, petite nurse with the pleasant-to-look-at rear end. For the sake of his daughter, he would have to take things into his own hands. He tapped gently on the glass.

No reply.

He tapped again a bit more strongly.

Nothing.

Then he waved his arms frantically, and that hurt like hell.

Jean saw this and went to Howard. Jammin' Dave hung back and watched her walk away. Howard saw her coming and spoke. "She's crying her eyes out, and they aren't doing anything about it. Can I have her, please?"

Jean walked back into the nursery and returned with Howard's screaming baby. He still had his mask caught in the wires above his head like a kite in power lines. She ignored this and delivered the baby to her father. "Here you go, Mr. Feck," Nurse Jean said, quietly. "Time for Daddy to work his magic." Howard accepted the bundle of tears and fears and instinctively began rocking her as he whispered shushes, her name, and, lastly, "everything is going to be all right." Just like last time, Virginia's cries quickly morphed into mere whimpers that gave way to a contented silence. The nurse tending the infants appeared and gave Howard a bottle of warm formula. Howard fed Virginia like a pro, and Virginia ate like a champ.

6

IN THE BEST INTERESTS of Virginia Violet Feck and her nursery-mates and tenders, it was decided that Howard Feck would share a room in the maternity ward of Paro County Hospital with his daughter. Here he could comfort Virginia while convalescing. Alma Sears pitched a fit, bitching about how inappropriate it was to have a male patient *on her floor* and that of all the babies that had come through this hospital, the Coomb-Feck patient was least deserving of special treatment. Her argument fell on ears ringing from Virginia's piercing screams. So like most of Alma Sears' complaints, they were taken as just another load of tobacco-stained hooey. It helped an awful lot that the good nurses on the maternity floor felt badly for Howard.

"Hey, Big Daddy. I'm really glad to have been your driver on such an auspicious occasion. Congratulations, and thank you, man," Jammin' Dave said to Howard after he had helped him move to the maternity floor. Once again he had held out his hand. Howard teared up as he shook it. Jammin' Dave made a joke about how the meds will do that to a man. JD also promised he would try to visit before Howard checked out. "Maybe you'll do me the honor of wheeling you and the kid out, man." Howard agreed that would be a swell—err—*cool* departure. After Jammin' Dave left, Howard realized a tamer chauffer would be preferred for the sake of his daughter. He did not recognize this thought as another sign that he was already starting to think like a father.

Chapter 20

1

THE TELEVISION IN HOWARD's room got six channels, plus one additional hospital channel. On one of his visits to see his new pal Howard (and more importantly, Nurse Jean), Jammin' Dave revealed that every fifteen minutes the hospital channel played a lactation video that showed women's breasts at work. Howard was watching this video when a nurse walked in and asked if he was planning on breastfeeding. The nurse probably would not have noticed had Howard not looked so guilty when she entered his room. His subsequent fumbling of the clunky TV remote while holding baby Virginia didn't help any. The clinical images of women demonstrating how to use a breast pump and how to breastfeed a newborn were as erotic as an acne documentary. But Howard took what was available when it came to the female body. He had a natural curiosity that was not always voyeuristic.

That night, in his quiet maternity room, dozing off with meds kicking in and his child asleep in his arms, thoughts of Debbie snapped Howard awake. *What happened? Are they actually sending her to prison? How will I get home? Does she know I'm okay? Is she okay? How do I get in the house?*

He was concerned for Debbie's well-being. He loved her, and the child in his arms was hers too. *Perhaps more hers than mine, in some ways. This was Debbie's dream. I was just along for the ride, really. And now she was off to jail? For what? Because she hit a couple nurses? Certainly not because of what she did to me. I mean this was bad but you had to know Debbie.* Then Howard remembered the twin. An almost twin that was all messed up. *And I told her— promised her—that there was nothing wrong.* He looked at Virginia with her face pinched up into the sleep of newborns. *I was half-right. That's pretty good. The baby* is *perfect I just didn't know about that hitchhiker. Why did the doctor have to tell her anyway if they were just going to throw it away?* Howard had something there. Things could have turned out so very differently if Dr. Mati had kept from Debbie the bad part of the story. "But then," Howard thought aloud as he looked at his daughter, "I probably wouldn't be holding you right now, which feels amazing."

And I wouldn't have met Jammin' Dave.

And he wouldn't have met Jean.

And I'd probably feel a whole lot better when I breathe.

Fate is weird.

All these questions, plus the injuries, the meds, and the remarkable experiences of fresh parenthood finally caught up to Howard. He wanted to sleep. He rang for a nurse to help him put Virginia back in her acrylic bassinette next to his hospital bed. His injuries made that very difficult, and he did not want Virginia to slip out of his hands when he fell asleep. A nurse who was all business came in, lifted the baby from Howard, and placed her in the bassinette. Howard had a zillion questions about Debbie that he wanted to ask the nurse, but he was tired. They would have to wait.

Just as Howard passed through the threshold between consciousness and sleep, a loud, high-pitched noise shocked him back awake. It was Virginia, screaming her head off. She didn't work her way to a scream from stitches and sobs. She started in like a needle drop in the middle of an AC/DC record.

She was red-faced and open-mouthed, with even redder gums. Her eyes were so tightly squeezed shut, it looked painful. Her tiny fists on little bent arms pumped impotently in sync with her breath. She was something to behold—part baby jet engine swaddled in a blanket, part smoke alarm with its test button stuck in the on position. The pain this caused Howard was breathtaking, yet wholly different than that of his injuries. His daughter's fierce crying did not annoy him, it broke his tender heart.

"What's the matter, Virginia?" Howard said, although it was doubtful Virginia could hear him over her wailing. "You miss your mommy, huh? You hungry? Did you beep-beep your diaper?" Each word was lost under a peal of high-velocity infant screams. He could not pick her up without calling for the nurse. Even here in the most tenderhearted of venues, Howard sensed that he was still the one that no one wanted to deal with. So he decided not to bother the staff. He inched down and over to one side of the bed, just far enough to lay his fingers on Virginia's chest and belly. It worked. After a minute, she had quieted down and resumed sleeping off the stress of life outside the womb. Howard quickly fell asleep too, causing him to relax and accidentally break physical contact with his daughter. He slept the length of time it takes for a kid's balloon to lazily drift to the ground. Virginia awakened again, going off like a defective smoke alarm. Howard found a moderately uncomfortable position where he could sleep but not break physical contact with his daughter. An hour later, this was how Dr. Mati Srivinihinirisan found them when she walked into the room.

She looked at the baby and thought about the mother. She contemplated the enormous gap that now existed between these two closely related things. She thought about the arc from innocent being—unprepared yet eager for the mystery of life to unfold—to a being utterly corrupted and broken beyond repair. What a journey. What a reaction to the journey.

Dr. Mati looked at the father slumped over in a position that was no doubt uncomfortable to someone feeling fine, and probably just this side of agonizing to someone who had taken a serious beating. Suffering for his offspring—a keystone of motherhood throughout nature. It made Dr. Mati appreciate and respect the man she saw before her. To Dr. Mati, he looked like a one-hundred percent, bona fide A-number-one good father. Seeing him sacrifice his bruise of a body for his daughter's security and comfort rekindled the hope that Dr. Mati had lost when she found out Debbie was on her way to jail. That she was headed there because she had attacked the staff and a police officer with baby in hand, and not because of Dr. Mati's orders, mattered little. Sometimes the joy of pulling one life through another was erased by the sadness of sending that life home to a bad place, a bad parent, or no parent. But Howard had saved this one, and Dr. Mati meant to tell him so.

She lifted his hand out of the bassinette and helped him lie back into the bed. Howard cooperated like a half-wake child getting tucked back into bed after half falling out. With contact once again broken, the infant once again began to roar her powerful roar, which woke Howard immediately. He noticed Dr. Mati at the foot of his bed. He said nothing to her. Instead he reached for his daughter to quiet her down to something tolerable. Dr. Mati watched, smiling as he naturally but not gracefully tended and soothed his daughter back to a contented peace. Only after he had succeeded in soothing Virginia did Dr. Mati feel it appropriate to step in and help .

"Thank you, Dr. Mati." Howard said as Dr. Mati handed him the baby. He sounded like a stereotypical overtired new mother.

"Your baby knows her father," Dr. Mati said, emanating soothing happiness and esteemed pride. She looked at Howard and continued, "Parenthood comes naturally to you, Mr. Feck, and you seem meant to be a father for a little girl. I've been watching you. I know."

Howard blushed. "Thank you, Dr. Mati. She sure is a cutie, isn't she, though?"

"Absolutely. They all are."

"When can she go home?"

"I think the question is when can you go home?"

Howard took a beat and looked down at the baby in his arms. Though Virginia didn't look like her, Howard thought of Debbie. "That's a good question, I guess. Jammin' Dave thinks maybe tomorrow since I am no longer taking the IV stuff."

"Jammin' Dave? He is your doctor now? I think perhaps you should discuss your release with someone who has at least been through medical school. Besides, unless I have been getting it wrong all these years, that tube with the needle going into the back of your hand is an IV."

"I know. I mean I'm not taking the pain medicine through an IV anymore so I can be alert for Virginia." Howard looked down at his daughter and gave her an extra rock for emphasis.

"So then how are you feeling?"

"I feel fine, well, mostly. It hurts pretty bad when I breathe, though."

"Oh, it only hurts when you breathe?" said Dr. Mati through a good-natured smile. "Well, that sounds promising."

"Thanks." Howard smiled, too. "It doesn't seem too bad right now. Having her here," (another rock of the baby for emphasis) "keeps my mind off my pain, so that's good, right?"

"Well, it is not up to me. But I think that when you can pick up the baby, change her, and do all the things a parent needs to do for an infant, then you both can probably go home. Based on what I have seen so far, however, I do not think that will be tomorrow."

Dr. Mati saw a look of disappointment poking out between the cuts and bruises on Howard's swollen face. "We will see. It will be up to you, I suppose. Getting better sometimes takes hard work."

"Okay. Tell me what I have to do. Actually, can you tell me what happened with Debbie and everyone here last night?"

"I am glad you asked because we need to talk about it. But first, I think your baby is probably hungry. Can you press the call button and ask for a bottle?"

Howard managed to hold Virginia properly and push the call button at the same time. He then shifted in his bed slightly as if settling in for a bedtime story.

Dr. Mati sat at the foot of the bed and explained to Howard why Debbie was now headed to jail. And nearly every word was wrong. "All I know is what the nurses have told me and what is in the hospital incident report. Debbie is okay. However, one of my nurses looks about as good as you do, and that is serious business. Debbie assaulted those who were trying to help her. Those who supported her, including you. And she did this in front of witnesses while in a government building. And one was a police officer. She could be charged with a felony, and you may be a single parent for some time. Mr. Feck, I am very sorry to say this, but it may be in your and your daughter's best interests to keep Debbie away permanently, or until she responds to therapy for her anger and violence issues."

Howard grimaced. "I know Debbie can be rough, but if you are nice to her and don't push her buttons she's pretty good. Before we came here to the hospital to check on the pregnancy, I pushed her buttons. And she was already so afraid. She can get pretty rough when she is afraid—or angry, or frustrated, or when you do stupid things. And I think all those things were going on when she got mad at me."

To Dr. Mati, the only part of the beaten-spouse mantra he had left out was the part about how the abuser *really loves me and is a good provider.* She had heard this too many times before, though it was the first from a husband.

Howard continued. "Everything probably would have been okay if it weren't for that other thing you told her about in her belly. Why did you tell her that?"

"Because it was the truth. It was in her body. And she was to deliver it. Are you telling me I am responsible for this?" Dr. Mati moved an open hand up and down, calling attention to his numerous wounds. "Is that what you are saying, Mr. Feck?"

Howard could tell by her tone what the right answer was. "No. I'm sorry. I didn't mean for you to think that. It's my fault, I guess."

"It's not your fault! You cannot take the blame for what happened to you. That is ludicrous." Howard thought ludicrous was a big word for sad. In this instance, that definition also worked. "This is not about blame," Dr. Mati explained. "And let me say to you that if you are to be a good father, and I think you are going to be a wonderful one, then you must stop being a victim. Stop that type of thinking, for your daughter 's sake if not for yours."

Howard shrugged painfully. *Hard not to feel like a victim when it hurts so much.*

Before Dr. Mati could continue, a nurse walked in and handed Howard a small baby bottle filled with formula. Howard and the doctor thanked the nurse who, accurately gauging the tone in the room, reset the call button and quickly left.

"Mr. Feck," Dr. Mati said in her commanding but kind, sing-song voice, "what happened was Debbie's fault because it was in her control not to let it happen. I believe she suffered through some terrible things when she was a young woman. That is really a tragedy. But three wrongs do not make a right. I hope you understand this."

"I do," Howard said, though he didn't quite. "Is everyone okay?"

"No, they aren't, Mr. Feck. Leticia has a piece of her nose missing, and you should see her neck. I imagine it looks a lot like your chest. Even the officer got one black eye and one that hemorrhaged. He had to knock Debbie in the head with his baton to stop her assault. Fortunately, your baby was not hurt, which is a miracle because she was in the middle of the whole thing."

Dr. Mati sighed.

Howard sighed.

Virginia slurped.

"Now do you understand how serious this is?" Dr. Mati asked. "And how dangerous a situation it is for your baby?"

Howard nodded.

"So Debbie is now going to jail instead of Rancho Lucerne State Hospital, where she could have gotten treatment and have supervised visits with her baby. She will recover from her Caesarean there, and that is worse than I wanted for her, had she cooperated and not turned so violent again." Dr. Mati paused. She looked inward, and blinked once, slowly. "She almost killed one of my nurses, Mr. Feck."

Howard looked down at his daughter who had emptied the small bottle and was now sucking air out of it. Howard picked her up and laid her on his chest. Her warmth felt good against the pain.

"What about me?"

"You will go home and be a father to your child. You will have to figure that out. Young women less than half your age do it every day, so I'm sure you can manage. Do you have any friends who can help you?"

Howard shook his head no. At the same moment, Virginia decided it was a good time to burp warm, undigested formula onto her father's gown. Dr. Mati did not even blink an eye. "Well, you must figure out a way, okay? There are agencies that can help you. I will send a social worker to your room to discuss what is available."

"We'll be all right, I guess. Sure is going to be weird without Debbie, though. She wanted this baby real bad."

Chapter 21

1

OFFICER "YUKON JACK" THOMS, as he was known to old friends on the force and regulars on his beat, had his trophy in the back of his squad car. Debbie lay on her side on the back seat with her feet on the floorboard and handcuffs tightly holding her wrists behind her back. It was raining and gray, the kind of day that aggravated arthritis and depression. She was lying there in part because Officer Yukon Jack had just jabbed her in the gut a real good one with his billy club. Debbie normally would have weathered the blow just fine, had her belly not been split open the night before in order to bring Virginia and her nameless twin into the world. Yukon Jack's blow landed close to the jagged smile of stitches keeping Debbie's belly closed, causing her to almost faint from the pain. She didn't care. Unconsciousness sounded pretty good right about now. That punch was payback for the black and bloodied eyes Debbie had given him while he tried to restrain her at the hospital.

Debbie remained prone on the back seat, her mind thrumming. She was host to another merciless ache in bloom, only this time for the loss of someone still very much alive.

What will they do to my baby? My future? Is it because she's mine?

As Yukon Jack drove out of the Paro County Hospital parking lot, he didn't know that Debbie Coomb was bleeding out from her incision. It was slow, but steady enough that he was going to have quite a mess to clean up when he arrived at the sheriff's station. To make matters worse, Yukon Jack figured it was a good day to stop and get a bottle of his namesake to quell the "dull ache sonata" his arthritis played on his right hip every time it rained. She was probably asleep anyway, he figured. If she stirred when he stopped for his "arthritis medicine," then he would gladly teach her how to be a good perp and to never hit a cop no matter what he's doing to you.

He took the long way back to the station so that he could stop at a rural, rundown market where he knew he could shake a free half pint of whiskey. What should have been a thirteen-minute car ride from parking lot to parking lot became nearly forty-five by the time Jack stopped, committed petty extortion for a four-dollar bottle of low-grade hooch, took a few comforting pulls, and then hit the road again.

2

DEBBIE LAY IN THE back of the police car. Thoughts of Virginia being taken by force played in a loop inside her head. Rain fell from the thick gray sky, rat-a-tatting on the police cruiser like a machine-gun choir. Debbie was unaware that she was bleeding to death, even though she felt the dampness from her blood spreading across the thin gown clinging to her cold skin. She was cold both inside and out, and she didn't care.

While she waited for what was once her future but now was simply the end, there remained one distant, single spark of life available to her. With her eyes closed, she could almost see it. The spark was an old friend she had once known intimately.

Its name: Revenge.

Surrendering to the cold inside and out, Debbie faced that bitter source of heat in her mind. As she turned her attention to it, drawing closer to its presence, the spark turned into a single flame. The bright orange-and-red edges of the flame flickered with images of those she had battled, including the one who held her now. Within this, in the blue part of the flame, there was only one image.

Howard.

As she focused her thoughts and emotions more closely on that image, she could see that he was holding something.

Virginia.

Blood kept oozing from a small opening in her big surgical wound, and rain kept falling from clouds blocking out the sun, but Debbie was no longer cold. She clung to the blue flame in her mind. It fortified her and warmed her but provided no healing.

Debbie looked below the blue to the white center of the flame, the hottest part. Here she could make out the face of Alma Sears on a head slowly turning. As it turned, another face appeared. It was that of Teddy Eel. The head continued to turn until she saw Clyde Eel, followed by anonymous cruel faces in the ugly throes of selfish, brutal ecstasy. It hurt to look at this part of the flame. It was too bright, this hottest white. Debbie refocused on the blue with its glowing image of Howard holding HER baby in his clumsy hands. He did not look beaten, his image in the blue flame. He looked content, like his world was whole and healed. It seemed that the promise of salvation made by her biological clock had landed in Howard's lap instead of hers. If she could ask Howard a question, she knew his answer would be, "Debbie who?"

In the bluest part of the blue flame of revenge that moments ago was only a distant spark, Debbie's focus turned to HER baby in Howard's stupid, skinny arms. The baby looked happy. And that trebled Debbie's suffering. She knew if she could ask the baby a question, the answer would be, "Mommy who?"

"Mommy me," Debbie cried weakly, though she couldn't hear her own words over the falling rain.

"Mommy me," she said again.

Then Debbie lost consciousness.

She did not hear the car door open and close when Officer Yukon Jack returned from commandeering his bottle of sweet, cheap whiskey. She did not hear him start and rev the big police cruiser engine, nor the police radio, nor the slow, steady *plap... plap...plap* of the blood she once shared with her daughter as it dripped from her abdomen onto the back seat's vinyl upholstery.

She certainly did not hear Officer Yukon pulling into the police station. Nor did she hear him telling her to sit up as he stood in the rain next to the open back door of his cruiser. She did not hear him offer a love tap from his baton if she didn't get out of the car. Nor did she hear or feel the gush of blood and fluid burping out of the hole in her gut when Yukon Jack pushed one end of the baton slowly but firmly into her abdomen—a move designed to get her into an upright position. In fact, Debbie did not hear a single thing until the two paramedics who happened to be at the station dropped everything to try and save her life. Then all she heard was the flicker from that hot, blue flame whispering, "*Mommy who?*"

Shortly after that, the flame went out.

Chapter 22

1

THE DAY HOWARD FECK left Paro County Hospital with his sweet loud daughter was the best day of his life thus far. That wasn't saying much, but it seemed the start of an upward trend for the man. His natural ease as father to the "little loudmouth," as she was affectionately called by some of the nurses, and his ability to quickly quiet her down when shrieking at full throttle made him quite popular during his stay. So when Howard and his snuggly little smoke alarm were released, the maternity staff threw Howard and Virginia a small bon voyage party. They brought in a few homemade sweets, and gave Howard a bag of accessories that every infant and new mother receives upon their departure from the hospital. Howard thought the gift bag was prepared specially for him and Virginia, despite it containing a sample tube of nipple cream. Dr. Mati was there and had kept for Howard something very important: Debbie's handbag. She had kept it safe in her office since certain events prevented her from returning it to the rightful owner.

Howard gushed with sincere gratitude to anyone who would listen, especially Dr. Mati, who had delivered his little angel from the large demon. He also kissed Alma Sears' ass in an effort to make up for what Debbie had done. Leticia was still on medical leave—mostly because Dr. Mati did not feel it appropriate for a labor and delivery nurse to attend mothers and infants with stitches on her nose. No one present except Alma knew the truth behind Debbie's latest flash to violence, though a few, including Dr. Mati, had their suspicions.

Howard requested that Jammin' Dave be the one to pilot his wheelchair out of the hospital, and JD was happy to perform requests. Howard's shirt had disappeared sometime during his stay, so he wore a hospital gown over his pants with Debbie's purse tucked next to his side. On the way out, with Jammin Dave bobbing to and fro as he pushed from behind, Howard held his daughter tight against his chest, even though it still hurt like hell. His jaw gizmo had been upgraded to one with Velcro straps that was not nearly as interesting to look at but was far safer for baby, father, and anyone who got near the man.

Jammin' Dave pushed the chair slowly, at least until they were out of Dr. Mati's territory. On their way to the elevator, Alma called out, "Bye, Mommy." She would have sounded like a grade-school bully except for a throaty, raspy undertone that whispered rumors of lung cancer. Jammin' Dave looked at her without smiling. This meant Alma Sears was the only person at Paro County Hospital who could say they had seen Jammin' Dave without so much as a grin.

Safely in the elevator, Jammin' Dave spoke. "You know what, man? You're the first patient that let me wheel them out with their newborn. They usually let the old lady drivers wheel out the babies. And let me tell you, Howard, it is an honor, man." Jammin Dave put out his hand and Howard carefully reached for it while holding his daughter close. JD grasped it with fingers up and thumb clasping thumb—the classic stoner handshake.

"Thank you, Jammin' Dave," Howard said, smiling. "Virginia thanks you, too. It is really nice that you would do this for us. It's good to see you again—man."

"Hey, Howard, it's what I do," Jammin Dave replied. "I've been working on my three-sixties. You want me to give Virginia a little 'merry-go-round the rosy' on her way out?"

"That's okay," Howard answered. "She fusses easy." Howard sure didn't want to be a bummer to Jammin' Dave, but when it came to Virginia, he had grown an honest-to-goodness backbone. Perhaps it had been there all along and Howard had finally found someone worthy of exposing it.

"Aw, man. I guess father knows best," Jammin' Dave said, smiling of course. "Maybe when she is a little bit older, huh? Can I still be the first to give her a ride in a Camaro?"

"Do you have a car seat in your Camaro?"

"Nah, not now, man. You know, maybe in a few years or something. I want to take her when she can enjoy it."

"Okay, I understand." Howard wanted to say he was just kidding, but he wasn't. "Sure, Jammin' Dave. You can be the first one to give her a ride in a Camaro—man."

"Promise?"

"Promise."

The elevator opened, and Jammin' Dave made his signature tire-squealing sound as he entered the lobby. He then put it in low gear, much to Howard's visible relief. They rode in silence to the main entrance of the hospital. Jammin' Dave smiled and thought about his new dish—Nurse Jean—while Howard beamed like a proud parent on parade. The main doors opened as they approached, and out they went into the gray, drying day. Howard looked down at Virginia, tightly bundled in a county-issue receiving blanket, secure in her father's insecure arms. The world outside, cold but not bitterly so, seemed dreamlike and vivid—as if the late-model clunkers filling the ugly parking lot, the few barren trees, and the sagging power lines had all come to life and were about to break into song, Disney style. Howard serenely took all this in. It took Jammin' Dave to bring Howard a little closer to reality.

"Howard?"

"Hmm?" Howard answered as if under a magical halcyonic spell.

"Where's your car, man? I don't have to push you home, do I?"

The car. Debbie's car. Howard hadn't thought twice about the car since they had arrived at the hospital in the middle of the night almost two weeks ago. He struggled to open Debbie's purse while holding his baby.

"Jammin' Dave, can you look in my purse—I mean Debbie's purse—for car keys? We drove a Cadillac here. A big, white one. Pretty, too."

"What year?"

"I don't know. Pretty new, I think. At least it looks new."

"Seville or Eldorado?"

"Cadillac."

"Okay, Cadillac." Jammin' Dave opened the large handbag and found it was mostly empty, Debbie's wallet was there, some cruel-looking hair thingy, an old-fashioned plastic change purse, and there at the bottom, a thin set of keys, two of which sported the Cadillac coat of arms. JD put the purse back. He didn't like holding it, and it showed.

"Here's the keys, man. Do you know where you parked?"

"I don't. None of this looks familiar. I remember parking by some cop cars and ambulances, though.

"Emergency."

"Yes, maybe so." Howard was handling the situation remarkably well.

Jammin' Dave pushed them around the outside of the hospital and toward the emergency room parking lot. He moved briskly, creating a small breeze that stung Howard's healing face. Howard didn't care. He just hoped he would have a car to drive home. Otherwise, he feared that he and Virginia would have to stay at the hospital until someone decided to help him. As his shifting luck would have it, they found the car easily enough right where Debbie had parked it.

Jammin' Dave did the honors of strapping the baby into the infant car seat that Debbie had purchased months ago. Then he helped Howard into the driver's seat, which was set up for an enormous human being, not a wispy, wounded, waif of a man. Behind the wheel, Howard looked like a kid pretending to drive Dad's old Buick.

Clearly, Jammin' Dave did not like long (or perhaps any) goodbyes, so he kept his smile broad, his handshake brisk, and his parting words to a minimum. "Look, man, you're on your own now. If I can help, reach out. Jammin' Dave is always ready to help. Take care, Big Daddy."

Howard was busy playing with the seat adjustment buttons while Dave gave his brief but sincere farewell. By the time Howard had stopped screwing around with the controls and had lowered the window to say goodbye, the Jam-Man had already backed away from the car.

"Thank you so much for everything, Jammin' Dave."

"Hey, it's what I do. I'm Jammin' Dave, man." Jammin' Dave was already so far away that he almost had to shout. "Good luck, Big Daddy. See ya, Virginia. I'll have my Camaro painted by the time you're ready for a spin."

"How will I let you know when she's ready?"

"Call the hospital, man. Ask for Jammin' Dave."

And with that, the Jam-Man spun the wheelchair around, made his peeling out sound, and sprinted back into the hospital.

"Thanks again, Jammin' Dave," Howard said mostly to himself. He lacked the ability to express all that the Jam-Man had done for him. No matter. Jammin' Dave sort of knew. It was what he did. He was Jammin' Dave, man.

2

HOWARD SPENT MORE THAN ten minutes driving around the hospital parking lot looking for the exit. Finally on the road, he drove the big car painfully slowly down a straight highway. Although he had by turns become lost, confused, and turned around, by the end of the trip, Howard had begun to experience the joy of driving again.

By the time he got home, Virginia had been screaming for what seemed like an hour but was actually just several long minutes. Her cries were more than enough to rattle her father, who was already overwhelmed from having to drive an enormous automobile in an area he barely knew. He recognized Debbie's house as he passed its driveway. He then drove straight into town, went around a block, and headed back, putting on his turn signal as he slowed to make a left into the drive. Unable to judge the distance of the oncoming traffic and not leaving enough room for the cars piling up behind him to go around, he remained stuck on the road in front of the house, unsure what to do. After watching him pass up three juicy opportunities to make his turn, several drivers laid on their horns, causing Howard to drive on while his daughter screamed bloody murder in high C. It was three long miles before Howard came to an intersection with a four-way stop where he made a wide, lazy, illegal U-turn. Three long miles traveling thirty-five miles an hour on a road where fifty-five was too slow. Three miles leading a parade of pissed off motorists calling him names he couldn't hear but was used to being called. On the return three miles, he slowed to fifteen miles an hour for the last half mile, assuring he would not miss the driveway. He pulled in and parked, briefly struggling to remove himself from the car, and then struggling mightily and with considerable pain as he extricated his daughter from her car seat.

Without Debbie leading him to the front door, Howard felt like a trespasser. Once inside, things felt even stranger. Howard and Debbie had left the place in the middle of the night nearly two weeks ago. Now it was Howard and Virginia who had returned from that trip. As far as he knew, Debbie was in jail, paying in time the price for losing it. That's how Howard saw it. And because she lost it with strangers instead of a loved one, she would have to pay. Poor Debbie.

He called out more than once to see if anyone else was there. Satisfied that all was well, he sat down in Delwin's La-Z-Boy and tried to settle Virginia down. She quieted down but still seemed unhappy. Howard then realized that Virginia needed to eat. It had been over three hours since her last feeding, and he had learned before leaving the hospital that the infant cycle of feeding, sleeping, and pooping turned a full rotation every three hours. This was an estimate, an average provided by the nurses. But Howard took it as biological law. And he was in violation of it. He laid Virginia on the floor in the middle of the living room and ran outside to the Caddy to fetch the infant formula packed with his maternity parting gifts. When Howard returned to the front door with formula in hand, the doorknob did not turn. He could hear Virginia screaming inside, and yet here he was, locked out of the house. He panicked, tried the door again, panicked some more, then tried the door once more. He reached for his inhaler, and lo and behold, Debbie's keys were in his pocket. He caught his breath, unlocked the door and bolted inside. In front of Virginia, he found it important to act as if nothing had happened.

Howard painstakingly followed the directions on the formula jar and still managed to overheat it, requiring his daughter to wait until her meal had cooled down. He fed her on the La-Z-Boy where she ate too fast and baptized Howard with a voluminous stream of warm smelly liquid. Although he felt he'd had that coming, his mind nonetheless ran through a series of frightening scenarios. *I poisoned my daughter. She's contracted some sort of projectile spitting-up disorder. No, I just fed her incorrectly. I knew this would happen without a nurse to supervise.* With a crying wet daughter against a sore chest covered in congealing upchucked formula, Howard called the hospital and conveyed his fears to a maternity nurse. The nurse who had taken similar calls dozens of times before calmly explained that babies often do this sort of thing if they eat too fast or too much, and that Howard should feed her again. If it stays down, all is well. Virginia calmly ate her second meal then fell asleep on her dad's stinky, moist chest.

A settled baby gave Howard time to settle himself. He laid Virginia on the couch, ran upstairs, changed into clean clothes, and then returned with a bassinette loaded with diapers, onesies, blankies, binkies, hats, socks, soft books, and a few stuffed animals. Howard was back on top of the new parent game, and he did a good job of setting up a mini nursery downstairs in Debbie's house. He lifted Virginia up off the couch and went to lay her gently into the bassinette. She felt so good in his arms he couldn't bear to set her down. He sat in the La-Z-Boy holding his new, perfect, uncorrupted daughter, just as Delwin had with Debbie back when she was an infant and her mother was a dead woman swinging from the high beam in the nursery. Every family has their traditions.

Chapter 23

1

S HE WAS SUPPOSED TO be at the police station just long
enough for the right paperwork to gather the right words and
signatures, allowing her to enter the Paro County penal system
as an alleged perpetrator in custody. As far as Officer Yukon Jack
was concerned, she certainly was not supposed to bleed all over
the back seat of his cruiser. As far as Debbie was concerned, she
wasn't supposed to survive.

Yukon Jack had parked as close to the front of the station
as he could, which happened to be right next to an ambulance.
Debbie had come so close to giving up her ghost that the distance
of a few feet was all that kept her from reuniting with her father.

As Debbie lay in the ambulance with a hastily re-sewn abdomen
and plasma pumping into her veins, the paramedics were on the
radio arguing with Paro County Hospital about where to take her.
Paro County officially refused to accept her, thank you very much.
They had seen enough of Hurricane Debbie to last a lifetime. The
paramedics wondered how bad you had to be get turned away
from Abaddon General, as it was known in their group. They
immediately grew concerned for their safety, as if Debbie was some

slasher flick villain who could overcome life-threatening injuries in the name of a sequel. So the paramedics decided to keep Debbie alive but unconscious on the seventy-mile trip to Rancho Lucerne State Hospital, a.k.a. St. Lucy's, where the real hard-case, crazy bastards frittered away their days. Under the circumstances, it was Debbie's only option for incarceration and recovery.

The medics were supposed to be off duty after stopping at the Paro County Police Station to gas up their ambulance and get a cup of coffee. They should be headed home now, off to spend a rainy evening with loved ones inside their safe, warm houses. But Debbie Coomb was in their life now, so that all changed. With a 140-mile roundtrip in shitty weather before them, the paramedics decided they didn't care much for the person they were saving. Even near death, Debbie made one hell of an impression.

2

FOR HOWARD FECK, LIFE was great. The best. Six months into fatherhood, Debbie Coomb, the woman Howard loved, a woman who had been both decent and rotten to him over the years, fell onto the back burner of his mind, where she simmered on very low heat until thoughts of her all but evaporated. Consumed with his new life, it was easy enough to do.

Conversely, Howard was practically all Debbie ever thought about after being revived by the paramedics. How unfortunate for him.

3

HOWARD RECEIVED A LETTER in the mail from St. Lucy's the week he and the Virginia came home from the hospital. But he was too busy being a dad to open it. So it sat in a growing pile of mail he wasn't quite sure what to do with. Howard kept three piles of mail going by the kitchen phone. The smallest was bills—he never let that one grow. The second good-sized pile contained junk mail. He cleared it regularly by opening and reading each piece before throwing it out or acting upon it. The last pile contained mail about which he knew not what to do. It included financial statements, which came two a month, a celebrity magazine Debbie subscribed too, miscellaneous crap that probably belonged in the junk mail pile, and so forth. This pile was over a foot high and growing half an inch a month. Somewhere near the bottom of this pile was that letter from Rancho Lucerne State Hospital with a three-page questionnaire regarding Debbie Coomb. Howard meant to read it, but out of sight out of mind, especially when you're busy chasing down the pitter-patters of active little feet, hands, and knees. The right answers to those questions could have made Debbie's stay at St. Lucy's much more bearable. But then so would a decent blanket. The letter also included the hospital's visitation policies and details on how to contact St. Lucy's and move the ball toward Debbie's release, none of which Howard ever read. So while he was living in Debbie's house, sleeping in Debbie's bed, loving Debbie's baby, and spending Debbie's money (though not in any grand way), Howard only occasionally wondered what had happened to her, and if he would ever see her again. Little did he know, the answer to the last one loomed. And the answer was yes.

4

WHILE HOWARD HAD HIS hands full with fatherhood, upon her admittance to St. Lucy's, Debbie had her body thoroughly searched by strong women in white uniforms while large men dressed similarly stood by. They needed to make sure Debbie wasn't muling any drugs, weapons, or "miscellaneous paraphernalia," which was one of the items on the Patient Admission Inspection Checklist. Debbie, being unconscious for this, made the routine snappier and safer than usual. It wasn't until after they had examined her inside and out that they performed surgery to repair the tears in her womb that had caused her to almost bleed to death—damage inflicted by Yukon Jack's deft use of his baton. While St. Lucy's finest pumped life back into Debbie and made sure none would leak out, a nurse logged Debbie's surgical wounds, bumps, bruises, and unique markings onto an outdated, government-issued form. Then they strapped Debbie to a gurney, locked the wheels, and left her in a small room to recover from her physical wounds. There would be no recovery from her most wicked injuries, but the staff did encase these in a thick, gooey coating of tranquilizers and antipsychotics.

Upon learning of her admittance to St. Lucy's Dr. Mati submitted an Emergency Psychiatric Assessment Form, which helped keep Debbie in in the state hospital and out of prison. Dr. Mati felt strongly that, in regards to healing and gaining access to her daughter, Debbie Coomb stood a much better chance in a healthcare system as opposed to a penal one. St. Lucy's was both. The Emergency Psychiatric Assessment Form allowed St. Lucy's to hold Debbie for thirty days while a next of kin was notified. If the next of kin never showed up, then St. Lucy's, as a funny bone in the arm of government, could decide at its leisure what was best for Debbie and society.

Based on Dr. Mati's report, which was almost entirely based on Alma Sears' lies, St. Lucy's diagnosed an unconscious Debbie Coomb as bipolar, high-risk, psychotic, and extremely prone to violence. And so they medicated her according to her body weight and that terse, narrow description. Debbie lived in super-slow motion inside her mind during this time. Her desire to move dimmed, her desire to struggle against restraint dimmed even more so. It took everything she had to imitate pudding. Occasionally she would vocalize to the world outside, though rarely when someone was in the room. People came in to Debbie's tiny room only to change the tubes, wires, and bags connected to her body. Then they would check her restraints and physical wounds, and before leaving her as they found her refresh her Thorazine, Nardil, and Lithium cocktail. Twice a day, one large man and one large woman gave Debbie a sponge bath and handled her nutrition intake and waste outflow.

When Debbie's superficial wounds had sufficiently healed, they began adjusting her dosages in a way that gently encouraged alertness. Her first semi-cognizant memory included a haze of rain, the interior of a cold car, and a wrinkled monster with bloodshot eyes in a brown uniform. This monster had taken something important away from her. It was something she needed in order to live.

As Debbie's memory grew a bit stronger, it offered up its first real word since she had lost consciousness and ended up in a drug-induced limbo. It was a powerful word. The word traveled fast through the synapses of her nervous system and the chambers of her mind. Like a key, it unlocked memory upon memory, the combined force of which pushed the word past her lips.

"Baby," Debbie said aloud.

"Baby," Debbie said clearly.

"BABY!" Debbie shouted.

These unlocked memories formed more words, which rattled noisily in her Thorazine-fogged mind: *birth, life, twin, death, pain, take, gone,* prison, and then back to—*BABY.*

On and on more memory-words tumbled and fell into place.

Rain, ruin, RAPE, revenge-

The more words that rang out, the less Debbie wanted to hear them, see them, feel them.

—*Ditch, death, Daddy.*
Daddy?
Daddy?
Gone.
Teddy.
Home.
Clyde.
Dead.
Frying Pan.
Fire.
BURN.
DEAD.
Monster.
Howard.
Howard?

Virginia.

"Virginia!" she shouted loudly, though no one heard her. Not even the patients wasting away in adjacent rooms.

She gasped, became breathless, then nearly gagged on the emotions the memory-words summoned. She began pushing against the restraints on her wrists and ankles, twisting like a flatworm in the throes of vivisection. And then she fell back, exhausted, unconscious, numb in all the wrong places.

5

WHEN SHE OPENED HER eyes fully for the first time since entering St. Lucy's, she saw an older man dressed in white looking back at her, studying her. He spoke something about a welcome, and may have given his name. Whatever he said, it could not compete with Debbie's fresh understanding of how she got to wherever she was now. The doctor waited until Debbie's eyes revealed awareness before asking her simple questions.

"Do you know your name?"

"Debbie Coomb," she said, her voice confident but uncharacteristically distant, as if it had to travel a long way to get to her lips.

"Do you know why you are in restraints?"

"Yes. Howard."

"Do you know where you are?"

"Prison."

"Do you remember what happened?"

"Yes. Baby."

As Dr. Whitecoat began to fill in the gaps based on submitted paperwork he'd been given, Debbie shook her head no to many of the details. They were mostly lies as far as she was concerned. But to Dr. Whitecoat, these details were reality. They had to be, they were entered on official forms and signed by professionals in their respective fields. As a learned person whose career, livelihood, and education were formed by words on papers, Dr. Whitecoat held the reality of Debbie's situation in his hands. It mattered not that Debbie was there when the events had happened and Dr. Whitecoat was not because she did not have the paperwork, he did. Paperwork trumped everything. It had to, or the entire system to which Dr. Whitecoat had long been a part of and to which Debbie was their newest member would cease to function. It was a system predicated on forms, premade definitions, and little boxes checked or left blank according to written guidelines. Without the paperwork and the checks in the right boxes, Debbie and Dr. Whitecoat may not even exist.

All Debbie had were a bunch of cacophonous, hard- to-look-at memory-words. As long as no one gave Debbie a form and a pencil, and a dose of clarity through which to communicate, she would never have the paperwork required to back up her version of events which, sadly, while mostly true—a hell of a lot more true than Dr. Whitecoat's version—were not entirely true, either.

So began the mad dance between government-institutionalized psychiatrist and government-institutionalized mental patient. Dr. Whitecoat had the paperwork and knew all the steps. His job was merely to teach Debbie how to dance accordingly. St. Lucy's Dance Hall for the Demented was ready to teach yet another resident how to waltz back into sanity—guaranteed or your gray matter back.

In a jar.

6

AS THE MONTHS PASSED, Debbie learned to dance with her state-sponsored partner, Dr. Whitecoat. When she stepped too far from the little footprints she was to follow, usually through independence expressed as dissent, Dr. Whitecoat increased the medication and the isolation. She did not recognize her confines as hellish during such moments. She only knew that when the doctor resumed the dance lessons, much time had passed. And that only served to increase the distance between her and BABY.

When Debbie hit the right steps in the right order, according to a decades-old outline, she was rewarded with lucidity and the freedom to move around her nine-feet-by -nine-feet room. A room with white walls, another white ceiling Debbie grew to know well, and a stainless-steel toilet with no seat or lid. Near the ceiling, a wide but short opaque window let in sunlight or whatever it was that periodically shined through from the other side. A locked steel door with a thick pane of glass the size of an adult's face was the only way in or out. This was the new universe where the doctor and his interns came to evaluate Debbie, monitor Debbie, and, most importantly, teach Debbie how to dance with sanity and nonviolence.

Like most misdiagnosed or only part-time crazy psychiatric patients, Debbie valued lucidity more than anything else in this futureless, spongy world. Under such circumstances, the only place you could do any living was in your mind—a universal truth of captivity. Patients with roaming privileges could live outside their minds, trading (or stealing) sex and other contraband with fellow inmates and a handful of staff. For the nameless hulking figures in the maximum security wing where Debbie was a resident, the most they could hope for was living-dying, laughing-crying, fucking-killing inside the infinite mind.

As the months rolled up into a year, Debbie's ache for her daughter, her baby, her promised future, remained undimmed. Intermingled with this ache was the supreme need to once again experience the rapture of revenge. Unable to separate the pain of separation from the joy of holding her baby, revenge was Debbie's last really good time. That had been years ago, and it involved flames much bigger and brighter than the little blue and amber one that had kept her warm and focused in the back of Officer Thoms' cruiser. That earlier flame of revenge was so powerful it burned up a white trash institution and everyone inside it. Debbie wondered what this new one was capable of if she nurtured and stoked it.

And so she did.

The primary image flickering to life in that small blue flame's wicked shadows and comforting light was that of a plumply growing fruit hanging from a thin, weak, twisted branch. It was

Howard holding *her* baby. And that baby was looking at her father with all the love and trust in the world. Debbie knew that she was the rightful recipient of that love and that trust, but there Howard was, soaking it up like a cheap paper towel.

As Debbie trundled around her inner universe, worshipping the flame as it cast shadows like monsters in a child's closet, she purposefully avoided her heart, sensing it was where the ache, the pull, and the smell of her lost daughter dwelled vividly. So did memories of communing and bonding with Virginia, and of having her very own child take manna from her, literally sucking the ache from her breast. No amount of Thorazine, Nardil, and Lithium could diminish these poignant memories. Yes, with its broad cracks letting in cold, shifting winds, Debbie's broken heart was a place she dare not let the flame alight, lest it be snuffed out. But if she had, she would have known that in her heart she believed Howard would make a good father. He would know exactly what to do with all that love. And he would know perfectly well how to reciprocate and honor the gift of life he now held in his clammy palms and twiggy fingers.

She could only accept that Howard, that scrawny fuck with the crooked cartoon penis had started all this, anyway. He had laid the groundwork for opening Debbie's heart in the first place after it had been nailed shut by Teddy Eel's hammer. Howard had surrendered to Debbie completely, and that had caught her off balance. When she literally beat the snot out of him, fucked with his mind, and locked him up, Howard trusted that Debbie was only doing what was best for both of them. She had let Howard in, and worse still, she had reciprocated in her own fashion. And what did it get her, exactly? Everything she could remember about the events surrounding Virginia's birth, including the stuff she had to invent in order to connect those red hot dots implicated Howard, her pseudo-husband-turned-nemesis, the scrawny god of her destruction, the decimator of her future. And what of Virginia, the innocent little mommy's girl who was born for Debbie to raise and hold and feed and adore and, if at all possible, love? Virginia, spell it F-U-T-U-R-E. What of her? Howard had cursed her inception with his role in her conception. He had laid the seed of the monster that shared his daughter's womb, potentially corrupting her before she had breathed her first breath. He had promised and lied that her womb-work was fine. Healthy. Normal. And in the fragile, hormonal state of pregnancy, she believed him when deep down, a little voice and half a dozen websites told her otherwise.

He had done this to Debbie. *He* had stolen Debbie's future and was, at this very moment, cradling it against his sunken chest. *He* had sent Debbie off to St. Lucy's just so *He* could have the baby to himself. Debbie could have killed him in the ultrasound room of Paro County Maternity, but she allowed herself to be stopped. She should have/could have killed him right then and there, and then at least Virginia would not be in his stupid, skinny arms. If only. Then Virginia would be with her mommy. And wouldn't that give Debbie something to look at apart from the sea of tiny holes in the acoustic-tiled ceiling of her latest prison?

But that's not how fate played its always-winning hand. It had played it out differently, with a cast of characters out to get the hair claw-crowned queen. It was one big fucking conspiracy somewhere between chem-trails and Kennedy assassinations. And it all revolved around the man whom she couldn't wait to make dance herself. A man, if you could call him that, to whom Debbie would teach the iron skillet stomp in one lesson—one gloriously vengeful lesson. This was Debbie's new mission. To complete it, she knew she would have to become Dr. Whitecoat's most fleet-footed pupil.

ASIDE FROM PLOTTING HER revenge against Howard and the recovery of her future, current events for Debbie consisted of things like self-administered sponge baths and predicting whether her dinner would be served ice cold or lukewarm. It seemed as though all the patient meals at St. Lucy's were prepared in a Suzy EZ-Bake oven located in a far-away building.

Debbie was unaware that St. Lucy's had attempted to contact Howard via the postal service. Unfortunately and not unexpectedly, each communiqué had been abandoned in one of Howard's towering piles of mail while he remained fully absorbed in the raising of their daughter. Perhaps on some level, Howard didn't really want to know what had happened to Debbie. Perhaps Howard feared that Debbie would keep the baby all to herself and he would have to get permission just to hold her, care for her, love her, even.

Around Debbie's one-year anniversary at St. Lucy's, Dr. Mati paid a visit to Dr. Whitecoat. She had been remotely monitoring Debbie's treatment and was frustrated by the lack of progress and minimal details contained in Dr. Whitecoat's patient reports. She had judged him accurately and knew that he was incapable of thinking outside the checkbox. Dr. Mati never visited Debbie. She felt that it could cause more harm than good. Instead, she focused on convincing Dr. Whitecoat that antepartum and postpartum hormonal imbalances contributed greatly to Debbie's violence at Paro County Hospital. A simple blood test would confirm if Debbie's hormones had returned to normal levels, and if so, she should begin a regiment of proactive rehabilitation on a maintenance dose of antidepressants and nothing more. Dr. Whitecoat groused about the lack of a checkbox for hormones and wished silently that the doctor with the terribly long last name would stick to birthing babies and swabbing vaginas. But Dr. Mati was persuasive. She beat him down with knowledge delivered in a way that mesmerized the easily flustered shrink. Despite having no state hospital paperwork, Dr. Mati had one piece of parchment that Dr. Whitecoat had no choice but to respect: a medical degree from Oxford University. More importantly, Dr. Mati had delivered his two children. So when Dr. Whitecoat went home and discussed his day with Mrs. Whitecoat, she did not mince words over the fact that Dr. Mati Srivinihinirisan was twice the doctor he could ever hope to be, and if he had any sense at all, he would listen to every single word she had to say about anything.

Dr. Whitecoat implemented Dr. Mati's suggestions slowly. It was the only retaliation he had over this doctor he now resented. He agreed to adjust Debbie's medication, though seemed to take forever to wean her off the Thorazine. He eventually moved her from the maximum-security wing to a medium-security wing featuring larger rooms with slightly larger windows. Now Debbie could not only stare at the ceiling and walls, she could also stare at the crazy bastard across the hall.

Chapter 24

1

THAT CHAIR. THAT SPRUNG recliner with a broken handle, creaking springs, and cracked upholstery became the epicenter around which time passed for Howard and Virginia. First, in a series of seemingly endless three-hour cycles, then expanding to a comfortable eight-hour cycle suitable for a two-year-old tot leaving infancy behind in a whoosh. Virginia rolled over, crawled, and climbed right through her baby stage, and then walked right into her terrific twos with much on her mind and in her eyes. She had named the center of her universe "Da-Doh."

Of all the priceless gifts Virginia gave Howard naturally and without hesitation, there was one in particular that helped weave their lives closely together. It was the gift of finding your purpose. In being a parent to his daughter, Howard discovered what his contribution to the world was supposed to be. It was fatherhood, and it served him as much as it served Virginia. Like electricity to the guitar, Virginia changed Howard in a big way, forever. Not that anyone noticed, for they rarely left the house during the first two years of Virginia's life. Nested in the life that Debbie had set up with home deliveries, automatic deposits and transfers, and the marketplace of the world one "Buy Now" click away, there was little reason for the Fecks to go out. Plus, Howard hated driving the Behemoth Deville—though he could have ordered a fleet of Geo Metros had he paid any attention to Debbie's, and now his, finances.

Unable to take to the name Virginia, Howard called his daughter the Gingerbug. He was unfamiliar with the Stones' *Exile on Main Street*, and she just didn't look like a Virginia to him. But she did scoot around the house like a little bug, so by the time she had turned two, Howard and Debbie's daughter would not answer to "Virginia" the way she did "Gingerbug."

The Bug spent her days playing with Da-Doh. Since her first days at the hospital, Gingerbug needed her father. Not in any clinging way, exactly. It was more demanding than clinging. Perhaps this was something passed down from her forgotten mother. Like Debbie, the Gingerbug knew what she wanted and had no problems making sure the entire room knew as well. But unlike her mother, she was generously loving and gentle with Howard. Generous with a toddler's snickery laugh. Generous with hugs and drooly kisses. Generous with her responses to the many games of peek-a-boo, tickle monster, and gonna-getchoo that Howard performed over and over until both he and the Bug were tuckered out. Their days ended with the Bug resting on Howard's chest as he sat in the recliner, gently rocking until both fell asleep. Morning would find them cuddling upstairs in the big bed, Howard having no recollection of how he got there. Nor did he care.

Both slept soundly in Debbie's father's large bed, the very bed of the Gingerbug's awkward conception. They rarely spent any time in the bedroom he and Debbie had painstakingly made over to become a nursery. Howard didn't care for having his daughter out of sight, so the room became little more than a toddler supply room—a massive toy closet with bunnies on the walls and spongy yellow carpet.

Howard's culinary skills dovetailed nicely with the Gingerbug's palate. Cold cereal, hot cereal, toast, scrambled eggs, cold baloney or hot dogs with a side of something from a baby food jar were the well-worn parts of Chez Da-Doh's menu. The Bug loved it. She loved everything about Howard. And Howard loved everything about her, especially once she had grown out of the projectile spit-up and high-C caterwauling phase. A phase that now, two years later, Da-Doh reminisced over sentimentally.

Chapter 25

1

ROUNDING THE BEND TOWARD her second anniversary at St. Lucy's, Debbie received a gift from on high. It was a grand gift with enormous benefits and consequences. It came in the form of a government letter reeking of bureaucracy that had found its way to Dr. Whitecoat's inbox. The letter contained several paragraphs of large, cumbersome words swirling inside large, complex sentences. What it meant to Debbie could be summed up in one powerful word: FREEDOM.

The letter said in officious language that times were tough. The currency that flowed from Washington, DC, to the states was drying up, so states were obligated to redirect this smaller flow to the places and things that voters cared about most. And, well, state mental institutions were never a hot topic during an election year. So, St. Lucy's needed to make swift, severe cuts in staffing. Of course, staff cuts meant fewer patients, since the government-mandated ratio between the two remained intact. Plus, fewer patients meant less food, less laundry, less electricity, less *expense*. In short, certain patients from St. Lucy's would have to sane-up in a hurry because these cuts needed to happen by the first of the year.

Debbie Coomb offered a good bang for the cutback. Her release would also get Dr. Mati off Dr. Whitecoat's back, which would in turn make Mrs. Whitecoat happy if not proud. If Debbie assaulted or killed anyone, then it would be a law enforcement issue, and not St. Lucy's problem. Now wouldn't that be nice? Dr. Whitecoat was no dummy. This was a win-win.

In an effort to expedite things, the government provided a simple, two-page form designed to prove that a patient was no longer a loon but was, in fact, thanks to decades-old medicine and a brand new set of checkboxes, dandy as a summer breeze.

Just as Debbie had no say in her admittance to the state mental health system, she had none in her departure, either. Her parting gifts were far better than the ones Howard and Virginia received upon leaving their hospital. Debbie received a six-month maintenance supply of antidepressants along with a prescription for more, an address to a mental health clinic where she was to register for outpatient treatment, fifty dollars in cash, one phone call, and fifteen tranquilizers, just in case. They also gave Debbie donated clothing—which for her meant a tight-fitting pink Gabardine skirt-suit with black trim, matching scarf, and navy-blue slip-on deck shoes. They did not give her a brush or comb, however, so her natty attire combined with wild unkempt hair actually made her look crazier than she did in her hospital pajamas. And those had "Rancho Lucerne State Hospital" randomly stenciled all over them.

Then they set Debbie Coomb free.

Debbie never knew her release was government mandated. She merely thought Dr. Whitecoat had finally noticed that she was dancing a fine jig and therefore had no choice but to cut her loose. Her life was finally going to continue outside her mind. On a day like any other, as she lay there scheming vengeance, Dr. Whitecoat entered her room and casually told her that he was so impressed with her progress that he was going to release her—provided she stayed on her medication and continued to see a psychiatrist.

Yes, of course, doctor. Anything you say, you're the boss. You have done a remarkable job with me, sir. And Dr. Whitecoat, I only want to make you proud.

Dr. Whitecoat entered the room of a crazy person, and ten minutes later, he left the room of a sane one—at least according to the paperwork.

For those who had no next of kin available or willing to pick them up, the state provided minibuses to transport the suddenly sane patients to a shelter in one of three metropolitan areas a few hours away. Debbie took the bus but passed on her one phone call. She wanted to surprise Howard.

2

KNOWING THAT SHE WOULD soon be holding her little daughter made Debbie thrum with excitement, despite the antidepressants and apprehension. *How long had it been? Six months? A year?* Time is funny when you're a Thorazine zombie. Time is also a great source of anxiety—even for the sane—and therefore not generally discussed during therapy. When Dr. Whitecoat had told Debbie the good news, he had said something about two years having passed. But Debbie wasn't quite sure what he was talking about. Two years seemed an unfathomable amount of time to spend in a white room. Plus, she was too busy thinking about what this gift of freedom meant to worry about something as abstract as time. Again the thrill of freedom consumed her, this time as she climbed onto a short bus headed to Merritin, the drop-off location closest to Wilburn.

It seemed a lifetime ago since Debbie had left her daddy's home rightfully horrified by her intuition of what was growing in her belly. Looking around from her seat on the bus as it chewed up miles of two-lane blacktop, Debbie couldn't help but feel that the large expanse of world she was now riding through was an unwieldy, shifting thing. Now that she was outside her tiny, right-angled, sensory-minimized universe within the bowels of St. Lucy's, she suddenly felt vulnerable. She had grown accustomed to the secure, evenly lit, finite closeness of incarceration and was suddenly reminded that on its best days, the outside world was a scary place.

There were only two other people on this bus, the driver and a small black woman who rocked back and forth at a slight angle while frenetically thanking Jesus her Savior, her Lord on holy high. Debbie could have engaged her but instead chose to think about her fate, which she had renamed Virginia.

What if Virginia really has forgotten me? What if she cries when I take her from Howard? What if she wants her mommy's milk? I have none to give. Thoughts of Virginia turned to scenarios of rejection, so Debbie shifted her focus to the retribution she would extract from Howard. She wondered if the iron skillet would be clean or dirty when she picked it up to bash him over his greasy head. She wondered if maybe she should lock him in the bathroom where he had spent his first night in Debbie's world. She liked that idea quite a lot. Let Howard feel what it was like to be stuck 24/7 in a room with a toilet and not much else. She thought of the cruel details. How long would it take for him to starve? How noisy would that be? Would Howard go along with starvation as easily as he did all other things? Debbie's mind flashed on a series of images depicting Howard dying in comical agony. The images caused her to open her eyes wide and burst out laughing so hard she nearly shrieked. The sudden laughter breaking through the quiet ride caused the bus driver to shudder and pick up the speed a little. It made the woman saved by Jesus speed-pray under her breath and scoot closer to the window. Debbie noticed this, which made her laugh even more. Two hours later, the bus arrived at the shelter. The praying woman blessed the driver, avoided Debbie, and then disappeared into a society where she was just another homeless person with the cold, the hunger, and Jesus on her mind.

Before stepping off the bus herself, Debbie, in her ill-fitting pink designer suit, deck shoes, and clownishly wild hair, gave the driver a calm and pleasant "Thank you." He shuddered in response. She then approached the first stranger she saw and asked directions to the small town of Wilburn.

Chapter 26

1

WHENEVER GOD GAVE HOWARD lemons, he didn't say, *Let's make lemonade*, he merely said, *Oh, lemons*. Howard was unflappable not out of aplomb but out of resignation and a lack of expectation. This was how he had successfully adapted to life without Gramma Helen. How he had adapted to life as a victim of kidnapping. And now, how he was adapting to life with a baby.

With Virginia, Howard routinely experienced a profound joy that grew his character and fed his confidence, at least within the confines of his limited orbit. In return, he hadn't spoiled Gingerbug too badly, but there was still time. Her room was more enjoyable to play in now that he had used Debbie's credit cards to fill it with toys, including a tent made to resemble a castle, a playhouse made to resemble a castle, and other castle-themed toys. There was a hoard of stuffed animals on her bed. This was perfectly fine since Virginia still slept with Da-Doh in the master bedroom. They slept and snuggled well together. Each night Gingerbug would attach her sweaty body to Howard's exhausted one until they both awoke damp from sweat, their faces warmed by morning's light. Then they would begin their day of cuddling, eating, playing, and learning from one another. Such was their well-worn, well-loved routine.

So when Debbie arrived home one morning looking like a frenzied soccer mom having a horrific hair day, Howard didn't notice. She had walked all night along the highway, gathering blisters on her feet and burrs on her skirt from the weeds along the highway. She stood on the perpetually suffering front lawn watching flickers of life dance across the living room windows. Howard, meanwhile, remained oblivious to her presence. His eyes were on Virginia and their favorite morning toddler show *Teletubbies*. Earlier that morning, he had had a flicker of intuition that something was different this day. He thought that maybe a storm was coming. Or maybe Virginia was going to get sick, which she hardly ever did since they left home so infrequently. When Howard finally looked out the front window, Debbie had gone. He studied the front yard as if her presence had left behind a ghost. Finding neither storm nor ghost, Howard turned away from the window just as a loud thuddy bang issued from the back of the house. Howard jumped. Virginia heard it too. She turned toward the sound, then turned to her dad to make sure he was still there. Happy that he was, she returned her attention to Tinky Winky's search for his bag. Biiiiig Huuuug.

To Howard, the thud sounded like a car trunk slamming shut. But there were no cars behind the house, and Debbie's large Caddy, which was parked in the driveway, had a safety mechanism that made it impossible to slam. Satisfied that the half-dead lawn and thriving weeds were in their proper place, Howard walked to the back porch. Though his knowledge of the back of the Coomb property was not as intimate as that of the front, everything seemed to be where it was the last time he had looked. Howard then checked to see if the back door was locked, something he almost never did. It was.

Although that feeling of *something's different* remained, Howard told himself that everything was fine. He returned to the living room and joined the Gingerbug to watch the Teletubbies say goodbye as the baby-sun sank behind the hills of Teletubbyland. Virginia loved that part. Mesmerized by the image of the baby in the sun, she laughed with it and talked to it with her two-year-old voice and vocabulary.

Just as the sun disappeared below the Teletubbyland horizon, Howard heard another, identical, thuddy bang. The noise raised a lump in his throat. He looked out front again at the large, weedy locust tree across the highway and saw that its branches indicated only a mild breeze at best. Howard could not blame the noise on the wind, nor the trunk of a car. And that made the lump in his throat hurt.

Something's different.

Something's not the same. The day started the same—except for that slight, uneasy feeling Howard had awakened with. He reluctantly made the leap from *something's different* to *something's not right*. As he made that leap, he was startled by an unmistakable sound— a window being smashed to pieces at the back of the house. Howard's heart pounded against his ribcage. He grew weak in the knees with fear and panic.

"Whassat, Da-Doh?" Gingerbug asked in a bright, excited whisper. Howard looked toward the crashing sound. He could hear the gentle tinkles of glass fragments hitting the mudroom floor. "I don't know, Gingerbug," Howard answered, calmly. "Bad things. Yuckies."

Gingerbug looked at the funny face her dad made as Howard showed signs of worry. Then they both jumped at the sound of another rear window being smashed. The sound went on for several beats, as if a baseball bat had swung through the window and then raked over any remaining glass. The long, smashing sound held an uneven rhythm punctuated by the thumps of something solid hitting the window frame. Howard wanted to scream his girlish shriek but did not for the Gingerbug's sake.

Gotta be strong for the Gingerbug, he thought. *Gotta be brave. Gotta be the top bug. Da-Doh-bug.*

"Whassat?" Gingerbug asked again, playfully.

"I don't know, Gingerbug. Let's go upstairs," Howard said, scooping up his daughter.

Da-Doh Howard was much stronger than the old Howard was. The old Howard would have shrieked girlishly upon the shocking sounds of windows being smashed in his home. Fatherhood had made him a different man, all right, but he still remained one of the duller knives in the silverware tray. He had yet to realize that Debbie was the one smashing the back windows with psychotic glee. It was her version of a hound rolling in sweet shit prior to the hunt.

On his way to the stairs, Howard and Virginia heard the smashing of a third window. They tightened their grip on one another. Virginia sensed her father's fear but perceived it as a game and so was not afraid herself. "Whassat, Da-Doh? Whassat?" she asked again.

This time Howard didn't answer. Instead, he headed up the stairs, grabbing the TV's remote control on the way. It was the only weapon he could find on such short notice. All the useful weapons were in the kitchen but that was too close to the breaking glass sounds. In no way would Howard take a step in that direction. So he opted for the remote, which could only be considered a weapon if your opponent was a couch potato, and even then a passive-aggressive weapon.

Just as Da-Doh and the Gingerbug reached the top of the stairs, they heard the fourth and last back window shatter. Howard still could not fathom the source of the destruction.

He thought maybe it was a wild animal gone berserk or vandals thinking the house was abandoned. Holding Virginia, he entered her room, shut the door, and sat down on the edge of a bed that had never been slept in. On the way up, Gingerbug kept asking her question: "Whassat, Da-Doh?"

Da-Doh usually answered her right away. Why not this time?

Finally, Howard responded. "That is a bad sound, Gingerbug. Yucky sound."

"Yuck-ee," Gingerbug parroted. She liked that word.

"I don't know what it's from, though," Howard thought aloud, something he did often these days. Gingerbug liked it, and it strengthened Howard's thought process. "I don't remember seeing a car or anything out front." He silently thought himself a fool for not looking out front again to confirm or deny the presence of an automobile or bicycle or spaceship—something—anything—before going upstairs. He consulted the Gingerbug. "What should we do Gingerbug?"

"Yuck-ee, Da-Doh," she offered.

"It sure is. Yucky is right."

Then Howard got an idea. "I know. C'mon, Bug." With Virginia still tight in his arms, he opened the door, darted into the master bedroom, and went for the phone on the nightstand. It was a gaudy, cumbersome thing Debbie had ordered out of a catalogue that specialized in cheap, gaudy crap. The phone was faux French provincial, with a short, tightly coiled cord between receiver and base. The push-button numbers on the base were laid out in a circle to emulate an old-fashioned dial.

Howard sat on the edge of the bed and picked up the receiver with so much energy he yanked the telephone's base off the nightstand. The base now dangled in the air at the end of the receiver's cord. Howard tried to swing the base up and onto his lap by waving the receiver up and down. It looked like some sort of parlor game. Had he let go of Virginia he could have used two hands, but having grown so accustomed to holding her, it never crossed his mind. Finally, he put the receiver in the crook of his neck, and with his free hand, grabbed the dangling base. As he bent over slightly to grab it, he heard the smashing of another window—this one much closer. It had to have come from the living room. Howard flinched, causing the receiver to slide out from between his neck and shoulder. It spun to the floor. Like so many things Howard did, Virginia thought this was quite funny and she chuckled at her silly Da-Doh. Now Howard had the base but had lost the receiver. Meanwhile, the window-hating thing below was getting closer and would soon run out of windows. What then? Coming from the receiver's earpiece Howard heard the impatient "vonk vonk vonk" of a phone that had been off the hook too long. The sound harried him into rushing even more.

The telephone base now shared his lap with the Gingerbug. With her arms wrapped around Da-Doh's neck, she laughed and cooed at this new game. Howard inched the receiver up by walking the cord up through his fingers. The maneuver worked slowly but adequately until the receiver's earpiece hooked itself on the bottom edge of the bed frame. Howard tugged, yanking the cord out of the receiver. The vonking sound ceased. The receiver, untethered from its base, fell to the floor as the end of the cord flew up and hit Howard in the face. In that moment, he saw colored wires instead of a plug. It was still in the receiver. Howard had just broken the only upstairs telephone. The look on his face as he realized that he may have just now doomed himself and his daughter sent Virginia into full-squeal laughter. That laughter broke Howard's heart harder than Debbie had broken the windows. He fell back on the bed with the Gingerbug still in his arms.

"Fah down, Da-Doh," Virginia said gleefully, followed by, "Nah night, Da-Doh. Nah night," as she patted his sweaty head.

2

HOWARD CONTINUED TO HOPE in vain that the smashing of windows was merely an act of vandalism by some teenage thug who didn't know anyone was home. Finally letting go of Virginia, who was in the process of squirming free anyway, Howard rose from the bed to look out the bedroom window facing the front yard. Although the view from the second story prevented him from seeing the perimeter of the house, he caught a glimpse of something pink and black darting in and out of sight. Then came the sound of more smashing glass. *What was that? A stocking cap maybe? A scarf? If it's pink, maybe it's a female causing this ruckus. But what female could possibly have the gumption to…*

No need to finish the thought. Howard knew a woman with the balls and muscle to do such a thing. In fact, she used to live here.

"Debbie," Howard whispered. The implications were such that he sat on the bed and fell back once again.

Gingerbug laughed and repeated, "Fah down, Da-Doh. Fah down."

Shrouded in a fog of doubt and second guesses, Howard wrestled with the truth. He consulted his daughter as she rolled around the bed. "If it was Debbie, why didn't she just knock?" Howard asked aloud. "I would have let her in. Why all the fuss and noise and smashing windows? What is she mad about now? Maybe it's not Debbie, after all."

In either case, Howard wasn't sure which would be worse—Debbie in a rage or some stranger who had decided to treat their home as the world's largest piñata. It took just a few seconds for Howard to make the call that Debbie in a rage would be worse than any unknown terror, with the possible exception of acid-blooded aliens or a child-stealing biker gang.

He decided to shut Virginia into her playroom while he went downstairs and faced the music. His plan was to diffuse the situation, something he had never before attempted. Assuming it was Debbie he would be confronting, he decided to take a few extra precautions—that is, if he could find any.

"C'mon Gingerbug, let's go to your playroom."

"Ya-ya, Da-Doh."

Howard picked up Virginia and, hugging and smelling her, took her back to her room. He set her down in front of an elaborate Fisher Price castle, tossed some plush toys onto the floor next to her, then made a promise that was shattered by another window being smashed.

"Don't you fret none, Gingerbug. Da-Doh will be back in a jiffy to play with you. I have to go and…fix the yuckies. I'll be right back, I promise."

Virginia mostly ignored these words and the terrible sound coming from downstairs. She had become preoccupied with a large spider crawling around the upstairs of her plastic castle. Howard didn't see the spider. He took Virginia's attention on her playthings as a signal to skedaddle downstairs and address the window-hating phantom. "I love you, Gingerbug. Be right back."

Shutting the door behind him, he thought aloud, "Why's Debbie so upset now? She could have called. I would have picked her up."

Howard ran across the hall to the bathroom looking for something he could use to defend himself if necessary. He searched the medicine cabinet and the vanity and found a handful of disposable shavers. He grabbed three. Unfortunately, they would be as useless as the TV remote he had grabbed earlier unless the foe downstairs turned out to be a big, hairy toe. He carefully placed the disposable shavers with their dull safety razors in the front left pocket of his pants. The right held the remote control. He quickly looked around the bathroom once more then jumped at the sound of another plate of glass being reduced to shards.

Pathetically armed and starting to tremble, Howard began his timid descent down the stairs. The lump in his throat really hurt now, and hearing his pulse so fast and loud in his head made him screw up his eyes in an attempt to lessen the pounding. Halfway down the stairs, the final front window smashed, scaring Howard so badly he missed a step on the stairs and involuntarily blurted out some unrecognizable syllables. He steadied himself, then realized he didn't have his asthma inhaler. Howard's asthma had improved dramatically once he became a father—perhaps he was too busy parenting to think about having an attack. He felt for his futile weaponry, took one look back toward where he had hidden his precious daughter in the most obvious of locations, then continued down the stairs. Howard wished hard that he were better equipped mentally, physically, and weapon-wise for the looming confrontation. He desperately hoped he could rise to the situation and protect his little girl—a hope so strong it distracted him, causing him to miss yet another step and nearly fall down the few stairs that remained.

Then he wished he had given the Gingerbug another kiss, another hug, another nuzzle—just in case.

Reaching the bottom of the stairs, he noticed two obvious things. One was the cold breeze flowing through the downstairs thanks to the new modifications to the home. The other was that, yes indeedy, it was Debbie all right. For there she stood on the front lawn with a whitish, club-like object resting on one shoulder. She had not seen Howard yet. She was looking toward the upstairs as if she had sensed Virginia's exact location.

Howard thought Debbie looked nice. Her hair had grown some, and although it was quite messy, at least it wasn't pulled up into that painful-looking claw anymore. She had lost some weight, too. Of course, the last time he had seen her, she was busting at the seams with one-and-a-half babies in her womb. Howard was impressed with how she was dressed. Wherever she came from, it must have been nice, and it must have been really good for her. Perhaps their reunion wouldn't be too bad.

She probably just wants me to clean up the mess, that's all.

Howard walked straight toward the smashed window closest to her. Debbie stood a good fifteen feet back from her handiwork.

"Hi-ya, Debbie. You're home," Howard called out. He didn't want to sound frightened. Debbie hated that.

She looked at him. If he had startled her, she didn't show it. She made brief eye contact, took the weapon off her shoulder, held it at-ease, then took off around the side of the house. Not a single word did she say. But Howard saw undeniable recognition in her face. And something else, too. He wasn't sure what that something else was, but he knew it wasn't something good. Even though the last moment he had shared with Debbie was terribly violent (*she was just worried about the baby and had all those hormones*), and even though she had just smashed all the downstairs windows (*she sure is dressed nice, though*), his nerves had begun to settle after seeing her. At least he now knew what he was up against. He figured that he would take his punishment and then wait things out until her mood improved—just like old times.

Identifying his window-smashing adversary as someone he loved cleared Howard's mind, allowing a rather bold thought to enter: *I cannot let Debbie hurt me this time. Not now that I—we—have a daughter to look after. I can't let Virginia see me like that. I can't do that to the Gingerbug. She needs me.*

The thought grounded Howard with a sense of purpose. He knew he would have to stop Debbie before she started in on him.

He couldn't even give her the chance. This was what Da-Dohs did for their Gingerbugs.

Howard figured Debbie was somewhere around the back of the house so he headed to the back door. He made it as far as the kitchen before fear overcame him once again. It did not crawl back as implications of the moment further dawned on him. Instead, it flooded his very being, like an angry sea through a breached, weathered hull. He knew Debbie was back. He knew more or less what he had to do. So why was he suddenly paralyzed with abject fear? Frozen in the kitchen, with Debbie's iron skillet sitting within arm's reach in the sink, he called for Debbie, as if calling for his executioner.

Nothing.

He called again.

Still nothing.

As he was about to call a third time, he heard a scream.

The scream was followed by a shriek.

The shriek he could not place since the smashed windows had created swirling breezes inside the house. The scream came from upstairs—that was undeniable, for he recognized its source. The sound of it, elongated and desperate, hurt Howard. The shriek must have come from Debbie who was still outside— right? *Did I lock the front door?* Virginia's scream triggered an itchy rush of endorphins into Howard's jumpy nervous system. The shriek summoned the lump back into his throat. It seemed bent on slowly strangling him from the inside.

Oblivious to his last opportunity to grab a useful weapon, one that was both powerful and ironic, Howard, renewed by a need to protect his screaming daughter, ran back through the kitchen and toward the stairs. The scream from upstairs had stopped for a few seconds, just long enough for the Gingerbug to draw another breath and then start all over again. The shriek, however, went on without pause. A slow, high-pitch ululation, like Tarzan swinging from a bad acid trip. It gave Howard goose flesh to go along with the giant goose bump stuck in his throat. He had no idea that the shriek was Debbie's insane reaction to hearing not just her daughter's scream, but also her daughter's voice—something Debbie had not heard in over two years. He wished again that he had his inhaler with him. Man alive (or dead), a couple cool whiffs sure would be nice.

As Howard reached the stairs, he was hit upside the head with another surprise in this long morning of surprises. Debbie had thrown at him the tool she had used to smash the windows. It hit Howard on the left temple just as he had turned to go upstairs. Little more than a glancing blow, it stunned more than hurt. He looked down at what had hit him and then stopped in his tracks. *Could it be? Was it real? Was that human?* The depth of Howard's predicament revealed itself as he discovered that the tool Debbie had used to smash the windows, and what she had just now thrown at his head, was a bone, unmistakably human.

Howard Feck, meet Clyde Eel. Or at least part of him.

Upstairs, the screams persisted. Howard looked out the window from where the femur had come flying in. Debbie stood outside that window shrieking words of furious inquiry.

"WHERE IS SHE, HOWARD? WHY IS MY BABY CRYING, YOU DEAD FUCK? SHE WANTS HER MOMMY! MY BABY VIRGINIA IS CRYING WHAT HAVE YOU DONE WITH HER WHAT ARE YOU DOING TO HER YOU SICK FUCKING BASTARD WHAT ARE YOU DOING TO MY LITTLE BABY GIRL?!"

Looking at Debbie, listening to her rage, Howard just stood there. A thin line of blood had appeared on his temple courtesy of Clyde's femur. Suddenly but unequivocally, he felt defeated. The battle lost before it had begun—an experience Howard knew all too well and one he subconsciously expected, or at least used to expect prior to becoming a father.

Debbie went on and on without pause, standing there as if stuck in cement, blowing her top like an angry Tasmanian devil dressed in pink Gabardine.

"WHAT DID YOU DO TO HER HOWARD WHAT HAVE YOU TOLD HER ABOUT ME? YOU CAN'T EVEN TAKE CARE OF YOUR GODDAM ECZEMA LET ALONE A CHILD YOU STUPID DEAD DUCK FUCK! I SWEAR YOU WILL PAY FOR EVERY SINGLE THING YOU HAVE DONE TO HER—EVERY NEGLECT, EVERY ACCIDENT, EVERY MISTAKE THAT MAKES UP YOUR STUPID FUCKING LIFE—YOU WILL PAY! YOU TOOK HER FROM ME! YOU MADE THEM LOCK ME UP—WHY? WHY DID YOU TAKE *MY* BABY AND TELL THE NURSES TO LOCK ME UP, HOWARD? WHY? SHE IS MINE! YOU KNOW IT AND YOU TOOK HER! YOU LIED TO ME WHEN SHE WAS INSIDE ME! YOU FUCKING LIED HOWARD AND NOW YOU WILL PAY! I WILL SHOW MY BABY HOW TO DEAL WITH ASSHOLES LIKE YOU WHO LIE! I WILL TEACH HER NOT TO TAKE IT! I WILL SHOW HER HOW TO STOP MEN LIKE YOU HOWARD! TELL ME HOWARD! BEFORE I GO IN THERE AND TAKE BACK THE LIFE YOU STOLE. THE BABY YOU TOOK FROM ME. TELL ME WHY YOU DID IT. WHY DID YOU LIE ABOUT MY PREGNANCY— WHY DID YOU PUT A MONSTER IN ME—BECAUSE YOU WANTED MY BABY TO DIE? WHY DID YOU TELL THEM TO LOCK ME UP? WHY DID YOU HURT ME? BECAUSE I HIT YOU WHEN YOU HAD IT COMING? BECAUSE I LOCKED YOU UP? BECAUSE...BECAUSE...because of me? Did you finally figure out what I am? Are you that smart?"

Debbie's high-velocity monologue sputtered to silence. She slowly lowered her head toward the ground, closing her eyes in sync with her movements like an automaton winding down. Howard saw her take an enormous breath. He tensed up. Then Debbie looked at him and exhaled another petition:

"I want my baby daughter—NOW! I want my future back. I want my life—I WANT MY LIFE—I WANT MY BABY—I WANT MY VIRGINIA AND SHE WANTS HER MOTHER—THAT'S WHY SHE IS SCREAMING—YOU CAN'T HAVE HER BECAUSE YOU HURT HER—YOU TOLD THEM TO LOCK ME UP AND YOU LIED HOWARD—YOU LIED—MY BABY WANTS HER MOMMY AND YOU ARE GOING TO DIE!"

Howard's jaw dropped so low it hurt, thanks in part to some residual pain left over from Debbie's left and right hooks back at the hospital. But his reaction was not from Debbie's maniacal tirade. It was from Virginia's jarring wail. He had stopped listening to Debbie, though she was impossible not to hear, and had instead focused on his distressed daughter. Shifting focus in this way helped supplant fear and surrender with the need for action—a need to help his daughter. Howard couldn't remember Gingerbug ever making such a desperate sound before. He could make out "Da-Doh" in the sobbing slobbery screams he heard with his heart as much as his ears. Debbie would have to wait. Howard bolted up the stairs, further enraging his shrieking, freaking foe—his uncommon-law wife.

Before reaching the second-floor landing, Howard could hear Virginia's mommy belligerently trying the front door. She pounded on it and kicked it for good measure. *I knew I locked the front door.* As he entered Virginia's playroom, Debbie had moved to the closest broken window. Its bottom sill was nearly shoulder-high and full of glass shards like jagged monster teeth. Debbie was too big, and having spent most of the last couple years immobilized, too out of shape to hoist herself over. She tried anyway, slicing up her hands and wrists in the process.

She saw the blood but did not feel the pain. She knew she would find a way in long before Howard would decide to come out. Focused on entering her home, Debbie's shrieks and shouts had been replaced by a vocal panting. She walked around to the back of the house with the gait and determination of a slasher film psychopath, blood dripping from the tips of her fingers. Out back, she found a couple of old crates. They snapped like dried twigs when she tested standing on them. This time Howard did not hear the thuddy bang of the rotted cellar door being flung open as Debbie continued her search for a proper booster.

"Me again, Clyde," Debbie said to the white-and-ochre colored skeleton missing a thighbone. "Hi—sorry, I don't remember your name," she said to the other skeleton whose name she truly did not remember. It was BigDave88, and his skeleton was still partially hidden by decomposing clothes and dead flesh turned to stretched leather.

The cellar was dark and dank. Rooting around was not easy. Debbie used her hands as much as her eyes, and as fate would twist it, she hit the jackpot. BigDave88 had been resting on an overturned wooden wheelbarrow propped against a wall. She grabbed him by the ribs and chucked him out of the way. Then she wrapped her bloodied hands around the wheelbarrow's long wooden handles. As she righted it, a rat as big as her brain squealed and ran from its nest under the barrow. She let go of the handles and then stomped on the rat with one navy-blue deck shoe. It squealed loudly then sunk its teeth into her exposed ankle. Debbie felt the bite but not as much as she should have. She reacted by kicking her foot wildly until the rat let go. It flew up into a lone shaft of light and then back down into darkness where it crawled off to die. Again, Debbie reached for the barrow's handles. She grabbed hold and then backed up the cellar steps into the late morning light.

Once outside, she took a good look at the wheelbarrow. Delwin had made it, probably before she was even born. As she gripped its slivery handles and wheeled it on its rotting and crumbling solid rubber tire, Debbie's rotting and crumbling mind issued a faded memory: A little girl in ribbons and a Holly Hobby dress squealing with delight as her playful father pushed her in a more solid version of the very barrow Debbie now gripped. The memory ended with the father dumping the little girl out onto a soft summer lawn where he joined in the tumbling and laughter. The aural memory of father and daughter laughing in concert ricocheted around Debbie's mind, gaining velocity with every rebound, until it burst through Debbie's mouth. It was not unlike her frenzied laughter on the bus ride from St. Lucy's, only this time it was accompanied by tears streaming down Debbie's blotchy cheeks.

Debbie said aloud to her father, "I'm going to give her a ride, Daddy. Wouldn't that make you happy? Wouldn't that be grand?"

Across the horizon separating the living from the dead, Delwin wept.

By the time Debbie pushed the wheelbarrow to the front, her ankle had started to swell from the rodent bite. This caused her to limp slightly, not that she noticed. Slick with blood, the wheelbarrow kept slipping from Debbie's lacerated hands and banging into her knees as she trudged forward. She would stop, wipe her bloody hands on her dress, and then continue onward, confident in her mission. She bled profusely, but her wounds were not life threatening. During her attempt to climb through the window, her sleeves had protected vital arteries from the glass shards stuck in the window frame. No doubt this misadventure would positively ruin the one outfit Debbie had worn over the past two years that did not have Rancho Lucerne State Hospital stenciled on it.

Debbie upended the wheelbarrow beneath the window closest to the front door—the same one she had cut herself on.

Grabbing the windowpane for balance, she stood on the barrow and hoisted herself into the house. Had she taken a few seconds to take one more swipe at the remaining glass shards jutting from the frame, she could have saved herself from more lacerations and bloodletting. But it didn't seem to matter—Debbie was currently immune from physical pain. She hit the living room floor with a heavy thud that Howard and Virginia heard plainly upstairs. She stood up. Suddenly absorbed in her surroundings, Debbie failed to notice that her daughter had stopped screaming.

She could not stop herself from pausing to take in the living room where she had once played and cuddled with her daddy. The same living room where she had mourned over his passing. Where the kind, gentle coroner had spent a night on the couch before abandoning her to a cruel fate. The room where she had learned the bitter taste of iniquity from her daddy's bartender. Where she had killed her first evil man, a wicked man whose thighbone she had just used to destroy every downstairs window of her father's home, and which now lay before her on the carpet. The room where she was probably going to kill Howard, another evil man who had it coming. She reached down, grabbed Clyde's femur, and came up dizzy from the combination of walking all night, not eating, the meds, and, finally, the blood loss. She held the bone in her right hand. Blood on her palm made her grip slick and sticky at the same time. She swung the bone up and let it fall on her right shoulder. Then Debbie limped up the stairs.

3

She climbed the stairs slowly, and by the time she had reached the last step, her head ached and her throat was dry, two conditions she had grown accustomed to at St. Lucy's. She was now aware of a thickness in one ankle that made her gait uneven, and of a sharp itch from pieces of glass embedded deep in her bloody palms. But these things did not bother her in any meaningful way. She stopped, turned her back to Virginia's bedroom door, and looked down upon the living room. Her home now seemed utterly alien. All the furniture was the same since she was a child. Some of it she had refinished at extra expense in order to look exactly like it did when Delwin was alive. Everything was in the same place. But the things in between had made it all seem foreign. Debbie could not reconcile these things, for they told a story of which she was not a part. They were things meant for a child. Not many, but enough—a small blanket, a little board book, two stacking rings (one blue, one orange), and a video cassette box with a picture of someone wearing a purple dinosaur costume.

Debbie sighed.

The scene revealed a bitter truth hidden in her heart all along: the future promised her by her loudly tick-tocking bio-clock had slipped from her grasp, which was never more than tenuous at best. Who was she kidding?

Standing at the top of the stairs, not bleeding fast enough to save Howard from one last violent encounter with his wife, Debbie thought about jumping off right there, right then. It seemed like a good idea. Quite good, actually. But first, she had to make sure all the signs and symbols of her promised future died with her. That future was supposed to be hers. And if she could not have it, then whose future would it become? Certainly not Howard's. He was the one who had tried to take it from Debbie in the first place. If Debbie didn't make it, and she decided right then that she would not, then Howard would not either. And that meant baby Virginia had to come with them to this tragic end. She knew from her own experiences that she could not leave her alone. That would be far more cruel than a peaceful, cleansing death, together as the family (future) that almost was.

Debbie turned around, laid down her weapon, and rested her head on Virginia's bedroom door.

"Howard," she said quietly.

Her voice startled him. Howard had heard Debbie flop into the house. He had heard her walk unevenly up the stairs. Then it got real quiet. Howard expected that soon it would get real loud.

And he didn't know if he could stop it.

And he was afraid of how it would end.

"Howard," she said again, a little above a whisper. She sounded as sane as rain in spring. And that did not soothe Howard at all.

"Howard? Let's talk, okay?"

Howard hid in the hillock of stuffed animals atop the little bed that Virginia had never slept in. He hid there, holding his daughter tight in his arms, whispering for her to go night-night.

"What are you doing?" Howard asked.

Silence.

"You could have just, you know, come back regular and we could have gone right back to how things used to be, only with a baby," he said ruefully. "Wasn't that what you wanted? Wasn't that what was supposed to happen?"

Debbie contemplated this as her hands and wrists and rat bite bled, and as her ankle continued to swell.

"What happened? Why are you doing this?" Howard asked, fighting back tears. He had picked up on Debbie's feelings. Maybe things had gone too far in the wrong direction, like the pendulum of a clock being pulled forward instead of swinging from side-to-side. Once you let go, it was going to slap back and pop springs and gears like a cheap mechanical toy smashed with a hammer. Then time would end.

Debbie snarled, "You had it coming, Howard!" Returning to her disturbingly calm tone, she added, "Look at all that had happened. You should not have gone on without me. You know better."

"Go away. Can you please go away—just for now?"

"Why should I? My house. My baby. My future—not yours. Why should I?"

"Because—"

"Because why, Howard?"

"Because there is something wrong with Virginia. I need to take her to the doctor, and I'm afraid to open the door."

"No more doctors, Howard." Debbie's voice rose slightly but was still restrained. "Doctors don't help. No more doctors."

"She's sick Debbie. I can take her by myself, and you can stay here, and when I get back, we can pretend this never ever happened. I will clean everything up as soon as I get back, I promise. Then you can be the mom and I can be the dad and Virginia can be—"

As if on cue, Virginia coughed a small cough.

"What's wrong with her?"

"She got bit by a spider. She's having a bad reaction and she needs a doc—"

"You never could listen, could you," Debbie said wistfully. "I said no doctors."

"Then what?" Howard sounded exasperated. "She's getting worse, Debbie."

Then after a short pause, "Debbie, are you going to... you know?"

"Am I what, Howard?" Anger crept back into Debbie's voice.

"Never mind. If no doctors, then what? The baby needs help. I ain't lying."

"No doctors."

"What about paramedics? They're more like firemen. They're not doctors."

Debbie sighed. "It's over Howard. No more hiding. You can come out now."

"I'm afraid. What about the Gin—what about Virginia?"

"Ain't going to leave my own baby alone, Howard. Her too. All of us. We didn't make it. It's all wrong." There was silence on both sides of the door. "Don't be so afraid, Howard, you know I hate that," Debbie added.

"I am. I am afraid. What are you going to do? Please tell me."

"I'm going to start a fire. And then I will lay us down in it.

Through the door, Debbie heard Howard hiss like a cigar burn. She tried the door. It confirmed her intuition that it was locked. Sometimes Howard wasn't so dumb.

"Debbie, you can't."

"Oh, yes I can. I have to. There's no other way. I could start it with you in there if I have to. But that's not fair, and you owe me. We will do this together, Howard, like a family. I will hold the baby. You can hold my hand if you still want to—like old times."

Howard started to cry. "Please, Debbie. We can make it better. I can fix it. You, too. Let's just forget the whole thing happened and start over, okay? Please, Debbie. Please? Virginia needs a doctor." Then, in a raised voice choked with tears, "SHE'S YOUR BABY TOO!" Howard's loud voice startled his drowsy daughter who lay in his arms. She looked up at him, gently touched his face with her hand, then returned to chewing on the ear of a stuffed bunny held loosely in her arms.

"I know, Howard," Debbie said, too calmly. "But you took her, didn't you? You stole my baby. You stole my *future*." Debbie started to cry now, softly. "I just wanted a future that wasn't so ugly and painful, Howard. Just once, I wanted love, to give it and to accept it. My baby was supposed to give me that future, that love. And you took my baby away. You took your sweet time, but you hurt me just as bad as all the others—maybe worse. I LIKED YOU! I knew I never should have trusted you. You cannot do what you did and still be a daddy. I'll see to that. It's time, Howard."

"No, Debbie, no! I didn't take her, they gave—"

"Shut up, Howard! I'm making this easy for you, so don't be an idiot," she barked. "I could make it hard and slow, just like my death has been all these years. Hard and slow, Howard. That's what you deserve."

"I'm not going to come out unless you go away, Debbie, I mean it."

"You got any food in there Howard? How about water? Want me to make this hard and slow? Don't think I don't know what's best. There are other ways if you want."

Debbie sighed. She could break the door down, but she was tired. She figured it would be best if Howard came quietly, like he normally did. She did not want to reunite with her daughter by breaking down her door and charging into her room. Nor did she want to scare Virginia. She just wanted to lie down with her. Mother and daughter taking hold of one another. Feeling one another as they shared their last breaths—together as if one. Debbie didn't care if Howard joined them, as long as he was dead. She looked over to the long bone and thought it would work as well as a frying pan if Howard remained uncommonly stubborn. "Are you coming out so we can do this together, like a family? Short and sweet, I promise. Dignified even. What do you say?"

Howard didn't say anything. He kissed his Gingerbug softly on her sweaty forehead. Oh, how he would miss that simple act of grace. At least he never took a single kiss or hug for granted. "I love you, baby," he whispered.

She smiled and touched his cheek in response.

Then Howard quietly rose from the plush menagerie like a toy phoenix whose stuffing had all fallen out. He wrapped the baby in a small, yellow blanket—Virginia's favorite. Pulling the bundle to his chest, one corner of the blanket fell over half-closed eyes. He walked the few feet to the door. Howard stopped, closed his eyes, squishing tears out as he did. He hastily prayed under his breath, then wished for his asthma inhaler one last time. He wanted to see how effective it was against the lump in his throat and the tight pain in his chest. He figured in a moment or two it probably wouldn't matter.

He unlocked and opened the door as quickly as he could. He could tell by the look on Debbie's face that he had surprised her. She was a mess—bloodied, mussed, with a look in her eyes that he had never seen before. A look that did not suggest violence so much as loss. A look that suggested all hope lost forever. Debbie tried to speak, but Howard didn't give her the chance.

"Here, you want her?" he said excitedly. "Take her, she's yours." As she accepted the bundle, Howard lunged and pushed Debbie back the few feet toward the stairs. With adrenalin over muscle, he succeeded in pushing her off balance. He now had her teetering backward, the baby clutched to her chest. Howard meant to push Debbie down those stairs. He'd fall with her if that's what it took.

Despite her filicidal designs, Debbie's maternal instincts kept her clutching her prize, making her unable to defend or steady herself. Howard pushed and wheezed and jumped onto Debbie, knocking their heads together. He suddenly seemed to have forgotten about keeping the Gingerbug safe. It was that jump onto Debbie while she was off balance that did the trick. Debbie fell straight back off the landing and onto the stairs head first, with Howard atop her and the blanketed bundle in between. He appeared to be riding Debbie down the stairs like a kid on a big, pink, inflatable pool toy. As they fell, Debbie gained momentum, so that by the time all three were close to the bottom of the stairs, she began to flip, her legs and hips suddenly airborne, the back of her head raking against the last few stairs. Howard flew off Debbie, who now flailed in midair with her feet nearly directly over her head. Her center of gravity prevented her from flipping completely over, so she landed on her head at the bottom of the stairs, her large frame temporarily balanced above her. Howard came down chest-first onto Debbie's tipping feet and legs, knocking the wind out of him. He might have heard a bright "crick" before landing head first on the living room floor, tumbling to rest a few feet from his wife. His eyes were closed. He listened to see if Debbie would make it to Virginia before he himself could recover and get moving. Instantly, it seemed, Debbie now stood over him, straddling his legs and staring down in a way that that made her look exceptionally monstrous. The front of her outfit was covered in blood. He saw embedded in the stains the round outline of a baby's face. It even appeared to have the impression of lips and a nose—a pediatric Shroud of Turin. He tried to move, tried to scream, but remained paralyzed beneath Debbie as she bent down toward him, her arms outstretched, reaching for his throat, her face contorted with madness and wreathed by falling, wild hair. He was still trying to get that first lifesaving breath that comes after getting the wind knocked out of you when Debbie knelt on his chest, making it doubtful that the breath would ever come. He felt her fingers around his neck, her face inches above his own as he franticly tried to suck oxygen back into his lungs. Debbie whispered, "Do you still love me?"

Howard heard a loud thud, opened his eyes, and she was no longer on top of him. Debbie strangling him had only been a vivid nightmare suffered while lying unconscious on the floor for mere seconds. The thud that woke him was one of Debbie's legs succumbing to gravity after balancing above her. He sat up just as Debbie's dying breath left her body.

He noticed that her head was at an unnaturally sharp angle relative to the rest of her body. She had come to rest on her back with her posterior propped up by the bottom step and one leg splayed over her and to the side. Her eyes were open and unblinking. The soft hiss coming from Debbie's open mouth ended in a stuttered moan as her final breath seeped out into the living room of her father's house.

The blue flame had gone out. The cellar door crumbled into the earth. The open wound of memory closed. And every corridor in Debbie's mind fell into the darkness of eternity.

The pain was finally gone.

Howard heard his daughter whimper. He looked at the bundle. It was stained with blood and lay motionless on the floor right next to Debbie. The plump, toy babydoll wrapped inside had worked better than Howard could have hoped, for Debbie truly believed she was holding her daughter—once again. Howard had never saved a life before. He had never successfully lied let alone committed such a stupendous bamboozle. *What a day.* And it was not quite noon. He spotted his inhaler on the couch. Choosing not to take it, he bounded up the stairs to his whimpering Gingerbug.

He reached the playroom where amid the confines of a mountain of stuffed animals, his daughter cried for her daddy, merely because she wanted him.

Such music, Howard thought, as he went to answer her cries. *Such music,* he thought, as he picked her up and kissed her forehead exactly where he had before leaving her. He had been afraid that kiss might have been their last. He kissed his daughter all over her head and face, smelling her, hugging her, and listening with rapt attention as her crying segued into coos and cheery giggles. *Such fine, fine music.*

Epilogue

D EBBIE HAD BEEN AWKWARDLY laid to rest in the cellar, where to Howard's immense surprise she was not the first but surely the last. After cleaning up the downstairs and arranging for new windows to be put in, Howard and Virginia took a bath together. They played in the tub and blew suds at one another, enjoying each other's place in their world along with their own. Howard dried off his daughter's glowing little body as she reveled in the freedom of innocent nakedness. They put on their jam-jams and crawled into the big bed that had once been Delwin's. Howard looked across the room to a mirror above a low dresser and saw Virginia and himself in its reflection. This was one of Howard's favorite things of all time, witnessing and reflecting upon the two of them together from an out-of-body point of view. How kind fate had been in taking him to such a magnificent and wonderful place as fatherhood. He looked into the mirror, saw his tribe, and was proud, honored, and grateful. Tears ran in tribute. He did not think of Debbie, for he had made peace with her over the long strenuous ritual of her disposal. He instinctually knew that had he called the police, his way of life (courtesy of his late wife) and his plans for raising their daughter would be in serious jeopardy.

Howard looked into the mirror at the perfect image it reflected. What he could not see were the two soft silhouettes alongside them. Virginia saw them. She had not yet grown the filters to block them out. The ghost of her mother stroked her hair, causing a tickle. Delwin watched, every bit as proud as Howard, and grateful too, being reunited with his daughter. Debbie bent to the child she had known ever so briefly, the child that had forgotten all about her mother, though could still recollect her essence. She was content but sad, having learned that regret is the one thing you take with you to the other side. She put her lips to her daughter's little ear where her whispers contained the words, *love*, *hope*, and *forgiveness*. The words became feelings that fluttered inside Virginia as she drifted off to sleep in her daddy's arms, again.

The End

Acknowledgments

The following talented people contributed selflessly to this book and this writer:

Jan Leininger and her writing group, Kellie Monahan, Linda Haas, Cheri O'Neil, and midwife Leora Fromm. I also wish to extend my gratitude to my dogged agent, Lee Sobel, the wonderful team at Rare Bird, and Tina and Davey Mobley, who kept me up and kept me going whenever falling down and stopping seemed so damned appealing.